Oct 22nd 2022

David P O'Coinn grew up at Balderton, Nottinghamshire then a sleepy village close to Newark and went to a local grammar school. After several jobs including working on British Rail he won a scholarship to the Royal Manchester College of Music. After graduation he worked mainly as a teacher. He has lived in Lincolnshire for many years and this county has provided much of his inspiration. He is married with three children and enjoys writing, railway travel and cricket in his spare time.

David P O'Coinn

STRETTO

A Story of Two Bostons

AUSTIN MACAULEY PUBLISHERS™

LONDON • CAMBRIDGE • NEW YORK • SHARJAH

A CIP catalogue record for this title is available from the British Library.

This is a work of fiction. Names, characters, businesses, places, events, locales, and incidents are either the products of the author's imagination or used in a fictitious manner. Any resemblance to actual persons, living or dead, or actual events is purely coincidental.

ISBN 9781528901321 (Paperback)
ISBN 9781528905978 (ePub e-book)

www.austinmacauley.com

First Published 2022
Austin Macauley Publishers Ltd®
1 Canada Square
Canary Wharf
London
E14 5AA

Synopsis

The story begins in 1645 during the English Civil War and follows the fortunes and misfortunes of two families, the Robinsons and Willistones. Before she is about to be drowned as a witch, Elizabeth Robinson puts a curse on her late husband's brother, who has been responsible for her arrest and torture. The curse will only cease when the male line of the Robinsons dies out. She is swept out to sea and her body is never found.

There is a gap of two hundred years by which time the Robinson family have prospered and are living in Northwest Boston, USA. The Willistones, at the end of the nineteenth century, emigrate to Boston and become servants to the Robinsons and later discover there is a link between their two families.

The development of aviation in the early years of the 20th century is a key feature in the story. Also, central to it is an important musical theme running all the way through. The story shifts from USA to the ill-fated *Lusitania*, to Southern Ireland and the battlefields of WWI. The climax of the story occurs back in Massachusetts, when tyranny is defeated and the curse is laid to rest.

1.Boston, Lincolnshire, UK 1645

The Civil War began its second year with increasing brutality and yet more loss of life within the opposing armies and the civilian population alike. Intermittent battles raged in many parts of the country and many of the citizens of England were living in perpetual fear and deprivation. The chaos and resulting death toll in England and Ireland was unprecedented; people woke up each morning wondering if this day was to be their last or at least have their livestock plundered and thus their living confiscated.

There appeared to be no clear winner although at one point, the armies of King Charles I had some cause for feeling that they were gaining the initiative. Charles' nephew, Prince Rupert, had recently been released from prison in Linz, having been captured during the Thirty Years' War. He then lost no time in joining his uncle and was immediately promoted to General of Horse, a coveted commission in those days.

His somewhat reckless but very effective measures often led him into hot disputes and disagreement with the King who understood little about the strategy of waging war. Against Prince Rupert's advice, Charles hesitated and thus gave his Parliamentary opponents the opportunity to reform and regroup. After the last quarrel at the *King's Head* in Southwell, the Prince was banished. From then onwards, the King's fortunes began to slide irrevocably leading to his arrest, imprisonment, trial and execution.

The opposing sides of Roundheads and Cavaliers each had areas of sympathy with the former enjoying much support and manpower in East Anglia, that is the counties of Essex, Cambridgeshire, Suffolk, Norfolk and even South Lincolnshire. As the tide began to turn, the Parliamentary forces gained a decisive victory at *Marston Moor* in June 1644 just as the second year of the conflict was ending. From that point onwards, King Charles abandoned much of the North and concentrated his resources elsewhere. Thus, the Midlands and

South of England then bore the brunt of *this unhappy war*, as Cromwell described it.

It is a distressing fact that times of unrest, upheaval and breakdown in social order always seem to spawn the most undesirable, fanatical and inhumane individuals who for their own egotistical ends and material gain cause abject misery and suffering to their fellow human beings. At this time and with religious dissension rife, it was a fact that in nearly every case, the perpetrators of these sort of crimes claimed to be carrying out the will of God.

Two people in this category were, in the late spring of 1645, seen approaching the Norfolk and Lincolnshire border at the little village of Sutton Bridge. They were dressed smartly in Puritan attire and exuded an air of confidence and authority to which, incidentally, they had absolutely no right whatsoever. There was a third person with them and who was smartly dressed but rode behind the others being merely a valet and bodyguard. One man had a nasty cough that at one point forced him to halt; the others paused as he produced a handkerchief. A small amount of blood resulted from his spasm and the ornate cloth was closed quickly so that the others would not notice.

'Are you unwell, Matthew?' said one of the trio whose name was Jack Stearne.

'It is nothing of any consequence,' was the reply.

The second speaker was Matthew Hopkins, self-styled *Witchfinder General*, who, during his relatively short tenure of a bogus office, had already been responsible for the deaths of dozens of innocent men and women during his reign of terror in the Eastern Counties. He had been given no official sanction or status but had taken it on himself to root out anybody, male or female, who had been dubbed witches usually by superstition, vindictive opportunists or jealous opponents.

Men who merely saw an opportunity of terrible and painful revenge for, perhaps, a personal feud or merely a difference of opinion sought the services of Matthew Hopkins. The people of East Anglia lived on the edge; some had recently suffered land enclosures and thus appropriation of their property whilst others lost young men to Cromwell's model army who otherwise would have been providing vital contributions to the family income and welfare. Meanwhile the deeds of the infamous Hopkins were widening and proving to be very lucrative for him.

Whilst Hopkins was recovering from his bout, Luke Whythorne, the servant, took the opportunity to dismount and relieve himself. He was well educated, accomplished and his excellent talent lay in his artwork. Although he did some painting and occasional portraits, his formidable skill lay in drawing likenesses of people, which was a secondary source of income until an indiscretion had lost him his teaching position. Thus, hard times and the war had forced him to take almost the first employment offered to avoid starvation.

This was with Hopkins whose activities were virtually unknown to him. It was not long before he began to despise his two companions but at the moment, he was trapped. He looked around as if there might be some respite in the surroundings but the bleak landscape known as Holland served only to compound his troubled inner feelings. His conscience was nagging at him more and more each day he was with Hopkins.

He had taken the position on because he needed money but each evening as he recounted the day's events, he found his situation to be more and more distasteful. There was never a moment of respite. He finished his task and looked down and decided to have a bit of amusement.

'Great God in heaven,' he exclaimed.

'What is it?' said Stearne.

'I can't believe it possible,' said Whythorne.

'Of what do you refer?'

Luke Whythorne kept them in suspense as long as possible then looked up with an air of triumph.

'My want of nature this morning has brought about a miracle.' He paused theatrically. 'I believe it has uncovered something of immense importance. Wait.' He rummaged around. 'Yes. Yes. It must be and after all this time. Alleluia.' He pretended to bend down and pick up something.

'Gentlemen, we are rich. It says on it, Johannus Rex and the date 1215. Fret not. I'm not a greedy man. We'll say nothing to anyone and divide the treasure three ways.'

Stearne saw the joke and smiled weakly but Hopkins, who had been slow to grasp the humour and thus not a little embarrassed, turned on Whythorne and vented his wrath. The fact that he felt unwell caused his irritation and anger to be out of all proportion.

'I am tired of your frivolity, Master Whythorne. Get on your horse and let us be gone. Nothing must stop us getting to Boston by tomorrow. Our meeting with Mr Jacob Robinson is vital and must not be delayed. We do God's work and He waits for no one.'

Without any further ado, he pulled sharply on the reins, causing the horse much discomfort, and forged ahead. Stearne looked at Whythorne and shrugged his shoulders. The latter could not resist a mischievous grin; however, the incident reinforced his hope that this, his first employment with Hopkins, would be his last.

The men pressed on and shortly found the *Olde Ship* inn at Long Sutton where they lodged for the night. They ate in silence over their meal and then immediately Hopkins and Stearne retired. Whythorne, to his chagrin, had to spend the night in one of the outhouses. He wondered whether Hopkins had arranged this deliberately because of his humour and levity earlier that day.

He sat for a while sketching the Inn and then called a halt as darkness encroached. The landlord, lamp in hand, came to the barn with some extra blankets and ale then stayed for a chat. He expressed much admiration for the drawing but on this occasion was more interested in putting his question.

'Is that really the man himself?' he said.

'Matthew Hopkins in the flesh,' said Whythorne. 'So you know his name.'

'We have heard of him even here as we hear much from travellers. By now half of England must know of him but nobody expected him to come up to our county as 'tis so far to travel. Moreover he looks unwell.'

'This is the first time he has ventured so far north,' said Whythorne.

'In confidence, sir, I have to tell you that he disturbs me greatly. His manner and bearing and his reputation. I would not like to risk offending him. My customers said much the same. Some left early,' he said ruefully.

'Your perception is accurate, landlord, though 'tis an easy conclusion of which to arrive.'

'Indeed, sir. I believe I am a good judge of character and if I might say so, you do not seem to be fully in accord with the man. May I enquire as to whether you are married?'

'In confidence I tell you I am not in any way in sympathy with Hopkins and took this position as a last resort. I am not married. I was hounded out of my job as a teacher in Essex because of speaking out about our loathsome and callous

King. As a result, I have no home. The only possessions I have you see on me, in front of you, and my horse over there.'

The landlord paused and considered this last statement.

'I tell you, sir, that there would be a place for you here if you were of a mind. We need a man of letters as there are few here who read or write. This is a prosperous place but it will fall behind in this new age unless there is learning and somebody to lead the way.'

'First, we go to Boston where we are to meet a merchant named Robinson. Perchance you may know of him.'

The landlord stiffened. He whispered, 'Jacob Robinson.'

Whythorne nodded. 'But with no great love in your heart?'

The landlord merely nodded his head but said no more. He turned and spoke as he left.

'We are somewhat remote here, sir, except for the boats and ships that come and go. But there is always enough to eat and help is always at hand. There could easily be a place for you here. There is something else. The girl that served you is my daughter of 18 years who no man has taken. I would be happy for her to have a man such as you. Good night to you, sir.'

'Goodnight,' said Luke Whythorne. He pondered for a few moments.

Goodness, he thought. *An offer of a position and a woman thrown in all in the space of a few minutes. Matters might be looking up. I wonder if she is pretty...* He dismissed that idea. The landlord was desperate to get her off his hands. He dreamt of jewels and Fenland mists. A servant girl was stretching out her hands to greet him. Was this his escape and salvation?

In the morning, Hopkins arose early and asked the landlord to hire a guide. The next part of the journey was only possible at low water as the area, known as the Cross Keys Wash, was treacherous and dangerous for anybody unfamiliar with these surroundings. Somewhere in the vicinity lay the baggage and crown jewels of the infamous King John that had been lost over 400 years previously and about which yesterday Whythorne had joked then been rebuked. A guide was readily found and a fee agreed upon after which the three men then partook of a hearty breakfast. The landlord's daughter was called to wait on the men and ordered to smile sweetly on Luke, an action that both found very agreeable.

'I believe you are the one to whom the wench has taken a fancy,' said Stearne.

'Well, that is to be expected,' said Luke Whythorne. 'Even country town girls have good taste.'

Stearne smiled. He admired Whythorne as he recognised the latter was not going to be dominated by the figure at his side. That man, the morose Matthew Hopkins, was impassive as ever and remained silent while he finished the rest of his meal. Shortly afterwards, they took their leave and disappeared into the Fenland mists and endured a monotonous journey through a nondescript landscape. The sea was close as the land at this time had yet to be drained. Several hours later they were making steady progress when they were unexpectedly met by a horseman five miles south of Boston and who halted sharply in front of them. At first, they thought he was a highwayman and there was a moment of alarm.

'Good day to you, sir,' said Stearne, his hand reaching towards his knife.

'Good day to you, gentlemen. Mr Matthew Hopkins, I presume. Jacob Robinson at your service; I have ridden out this far to meet you as these parts are dangerous for newcomers.'

'We are most grateful, sir.' Hopkins turned and after a few words paid his guide in full even though he had been contracted to take them all the way to Boston. The man touched his hat and turned to begin his homeward journey. Hopkins continued: 'We received your note some six weeks ago and are come to rid you of this pestilence and any other you care to bring to our attention. I pray you, sir, what is the name of this person of whom you accuse?'

'Alas, my late brother's wife, Elizabeth Robinson. She refuses to confess, hence the need for your services. And there are several others for you to question.'

'We shall do the Lord's work, sir, of that you can be assured.'

'Amen to that, sir. And now, if you will kindly follow me.'

The four men rode northwards. Soon, the Boston Stump that dominates the skyline appeared in its majesty. Luke's heart soared but only for a moment as he knew what was to happen when they reached the town. They made tracks for the Inn.

After eating well, Hopkins gave orders to set up court. Witnesses had to be called and notified, which caused a delay of one day. There was also the necessity of bribing the local magistrate who accepted the terms offered instantly. Early the following morning, Hopkins and Stearne proceeded to take evidence from a group of women, all of whom had been paid handsomely by Jacob Robinson to commit perjury.

'She did speak to the devil on one night in the churchyard. I 'eerd 'er talkin'.'

'She did stroke 'er black cat whilst speakin'.'

'I have never had a black cat,' retorted Elizabeth Robinson. 'You are a liar, Eliza Atkinson, and belong in hell.'

Hopkins bashed his gavel furiously. 'The prisoner will remain silent and will speak only when given leave to do so,' he said.

The unfortunate woman, who realised that the deck was already stacked against her, pointed her finger at her brother-in-law.

'He only wants to get his hands on what money I have left. He had his brother killed, my honourable and dutiful husband.'

'Silence or I will have you whipped.'

However, Elizabeth Robinson refused to be quiet and was subjected to the most barbarous treatment first by ducking and then by whipping. She was then gagged but somehow managed to wriggle off her bond. Before it was replaced, she had enough time to denounce her brother-in-law in very forthright terms. When the magistrate was replacing the gag, she bit his hand forcibly causing him to cry out in pain.

Hopkins could see that she was getting the better of them and jumped to his feet, ordering some helpers to restrain her whilst the cloth was restored tighter and thus more painful. She received some tacit sympathy from the crowd but for the most of the ordeal the onlookers, although squirming inwardly, stayed silent, not wishing to risk incurring the same treatment from Hopkins and his helpers.

They felt terrified and helpless. Stearne then went to one of the local taverns to enlist the help of a few men who were not from the town and could be bought easily. He found the names of those likely to speak in favour of Elizabeth Robinson and had them all taken to the rectory. They and the rector and his family were then kept under guard until the trial was over.

Whilst all this was happening, Luke Whythorne was an anonymous member of the crowd. However, he saw some interesting faces and thus began to sketch them unobserved as all eyes were on the trial. He was quite prolific until the trial ended but then put away his drawing materials and with others awaited the verdict. The outcome was never in doubt and Elizabeth Robinson was found guilty. Hopkins stood up.

'Elizabeth Robinson of Skirbeck in the town of Boston, today you have been found guilty of witchcraft.'

The unfortunate woman's hands were tied to a chair before she was condemned to be thrown into the Haven. As a witch, she had renounced her baptism so water would reject her. To comply with the rules of immersion, the gag had been removed. She used what little time she had left to deliver a denunciation of the people responsible for her ordeal as they carried her to the water's edge.

A curse on you, Matthew Hopkins. You will be dead before this war is over. A curse on you, my wicked and scheming brother-in-law. Your seed will suffer greatly and die out. It will end when the birdman falls from above into the mire. Last night I prayed earnestly and made my peace with my Saviour and was given a vision from above. His message tells me so. St Botolph, hear me. Send me the "devil wind" and carry me away from these workers of iniquity. Men who believe they are from God but are really the sons of Satan himself.

Unfortunately for Hopkins and Stearne, nobody had bothered to tell them of local conditions, least of all of the "devil wind", something Hopkins, when he heard Elizabeth speak of it, had merely passed it off as a local superstition. Already, the tide had begun to turn and the Haven had become volatile as these were the days before the building of the Grand Sluice. It was only a matter of seconds and to everyone's amazement and fright, the wind began to whip up and gradually increase in intensity. *The Devil Wind of Boston.*

Women had brought their babies and infants with them and one after the other, the little ones began instinctively to sense something was terribly wrong and started to howl. Gradually, the crowd began to leave as the wind swirled and became more ferocious. There was someone in the river to supervise the retrieval of the chair when the unfortunate woman would be dragged out dead but things did not go to plan.

The men who had been hired to lift the chair were finding it more and more difficult to keep their balance. They managed to get to the bottom of the bank and prepared to cast the chair in the river. They then used a rope, which had been looped around a hoop fastened to the chair, and aimed to retrieve the chair and Elizabeth Robinson when she was finally pulled out. Nobody for a moment thought she would be anything but stone dead.

This iron hoop, which was somewhat ancient and rickety, suddenly snapped and came away with the rope. Before anybody could do anything, Elizabeth Robinson was gradually being pulled into the Wash. The chair was just too far for the man in the river to catch. Nobody else lifted a finger when Hopkins shouted to them to retrieve the chair.

In any case, by now it was in water too deep in which to venture. Hopkins bellowed but to no avail as nobody wanted to risk the swirling mire. He bellowed again but this brought on a coughing fit, which brought blood onto his lips. This was enough to frighten what was left of the crowd and while he was occupied and his face buried in his handkerchief, many of them took the opportunity to disperse and disappear.

Elizabeth Robinson gradually receded into the misty Wash, all the time cursing Hopkins and her brother-in-law. Her voice gradually faded but everyone remembered her words.

My curse will end when your seed ends; when the birdman falls from above and sinks into the mire. Then love will prosper and I shall have everlasting peace.

As a result of this fiasco, Jacob Robinson was most reluctant to give Hopkins his full fee and only some arguing and hard bargaining resolved the matter. Robinson gave orders to some men after paying them a small sum to scour the coast for any corpse. He needed the body in order to claim his rights to Elizabeth's house and possessions. It would be like looking for a needle in a haystack.

They spent several days looking far and wide but it was hopeless. In the end, they all gave up and went home. The townsfolk who had witnessed the ordeal breathed a sigh of resignation and departed from the scene to get on with their lives. Elizabeth Robinson's body was never recovered and several legends appeared during the next two centuries and some verse as well.

Local people were quite adamant that as long as she remained undetected, her curse would last and be terrible in its retribution. Hopkins and Stearne went into the Inn to dine as did Luke but in a different corner with his paper and

Cumberland graphite pencils. He made a sketch of Hopkins and Robinson who were unaware of his actions as at that time, they were arguing about Hopkins' fee.

His sombre mood that had been caused by the day's proceedings were alleviated somewhat when he was approached by three people who, witnessing his prowess, were willing to pay for his services. Luke insisted that they should go outside in the light, which suited him well as he could be out of sight of the evil duo who were causing his conscience increasing pain.

The next day, Hopkins and Stearne left Boston never to return; Luke Whythorne was with them. They retraced their steps, and in due course reached Ely where they lodged for the night at the *Lamb Inn*. Hopkins, meticulous as ever, was fully aware of the fact that they had been appreciably longer than expected.

'Master Whythorne, we have kept you over a whiles. Allow me to settle with you now and say that you do not have to escort us back to Manningtree if you do not wish to do so.'

Of course, this seemingly generous action was actually an advantage to Hopkins as he would not have to pay Luke for a few more days of service. Luke felt elated about this unexpected and bountiful dismissal.

'I thank thee, sir, both for this purse and for your release as it would be of benefit for me to stay in Ely and then visit Cambridge as I might find old friends and some work with my likenesses,' said Whythorne. He added, 'When are you likely to be needing me again?'

He said this deliberately to allay any suspicion by Hopkins that he might not want to be employed again. Inwardly, he had no intention of further association with the sadistic and cruel men at his side unless he was on the point of starvation.

'In about two or three weeks,' said Hopkins. 'Where will you be when I wish to send you word?'

'You may contact me through my cousin Jane Whythorne at Kattawade who works on the estate.'

'Good. So be it. It is settled then.'

Hopkins rose and without shaking hands drifted out of the room, oblivious to the stares and disquiet of some of the onlookers. Stearne did shake hands and also left. Luke lingered a while and spoke to a few guests at the Inn, some of whom, realising they had seen the feared Hopkins himself in their midst, fired more questions than he, Luke, wished to answer.

When he reached the stables, he was informed that Hopkins had paid for stabling and had left almost an hour before, a fact that Luke was very glad to hear. He checked his purse. Hopkins had indeed been generous but then again, he could afford to be as his business had become very lucrative. Luke was about to set off when a prosperous couple called out to him and asked for a portrait, which he duly completed in about twenty minutes.

As a result, he was tempted to stay even longer but after drinking too much with them, he eventually set out northwards rather than return to his roots. There was little or nothing for him back in Essex and no prospects of employment. More important was the fact that up in Lincolnshire, he could be completely out of Hopkins' clutches and disappear almost without trace. Although an educated and very refined man, this was a day when he let his high standards slip. Filled with a sense of emancipation, miles from anywhere and fuelled with the strong drink imbibed in Ely and the bottles brought with him, he started singing a version of the *Old King John* ditty.

I'll tell you a story, a story anon, about a man whose name was John
He was first a prince then a king of might. And he did much wrong and little
of right
Derry down, down, oh hey derry down, He did much wrong and little of right.

By the end of the 5th verse, he was mixing up his words and was far from coherent. He got down to relieve himself and then spoke to his horse who nuzzled up to him fondly.

'What about a duet, eh, Copper?' The horse nuzzled up again. Luke tried to mount again but failed. He walked unsteadily for about half a mile and began to sing again:

Old King Cole was a merry old soul and a merry old soul was he, he, he,
He called for a light in the middle of the night to go to the lav-a-tor re re re,
The clock struck four while the wind did roar and the candle took to flight
ite, ite,
Old King Cole fell down the hole into the bowl of scite, ite, ite.

Luke Whythorne was jolted back into reality when he heard slightly suppressed giggles only a few feet away. He turned around, feeling a little alarmed that he was not alone and for being taken unawares. He saw three young female field workers who had paused to take a long look at him. He was tongue-tied and felt acutely embarrassed that his behaviour had been witnessed.

'You might sing in tune and sing a finer song,' said one of the girls.

This was a challenge he could not ignore.

'Madam,' he began.

'Miss,' she corrected him.

He paused. 'If that is the case then it will be a folly and a criminal waste if that status were to last much longer,' said Luke, bowing and flourishing his hand with exaggerated politeness.

The girl looked embarrassed but was inwardly pleased about the compliment.

He continued, 'For your information, *Miss*. I ALWAYS sing in tune. In fact, recently, I sang *Spem in Alium* by Thomas Tallis with 39 other personages in St John's Cambridge.' Luke pointed his finger as he spoke but had no idea whether it was the correct direction.

'Oh goodness. I have never heard of that one. I have heard his *If ye Love me.*'

Luke marvelled. A discerning and knowledgeable lady out here in the sticks.

'I can see you are a person of taste and intelligence even in these remote parts. Do you live here?'

'Over there.' She pointed to a farmhouse. 'That's my father keeping an eye on us.'

'No need, I assure you, Miss, I am a gentleman of honour.' He bowed again. 'I beg you to forgive me for my deplorable behaviour and appearance on this, the first, and probably only occasion that we meet.'

The three girls giggled again. They rarely saw strangers and this one seemed very interesting and was certainly very handsome. They continued to scrutinise him and with ever increasing approval.

By now, the farmer, feeling his daughters might need protection, approached with suspicion written all over his face. Luke thus felt it was his duty to face him and not to bolt off like a wanted criminal. He would have found difficulty mounting anyway. He instead spoke to his horse but loud enough for the women to hear.

'Copper, my companion and only love in this world of sin. Beware. We are about to face a great inquisition. You must defend me at all costs. What do you say?'

Copper gave little heigh and tossed his head in agreement.

'Does he understand all you say?' asked a different one of the young women.

'Madam, or miss. He understands everything. All that exists in the deep recesses of my heart, mind and soul.'

All three of the young women giggled again just as their father joined them and inspected Luke thoroughly.

'May I ask who you are and what is your business in these parts?' said the farmer.

'You may, sir. Luke Whythorne is my name, a forlorn waif merely passing through.'

The farmer gave him a thorough appraisal and realised there was more to this man on just one cursory appearance.

'It is a sad fact and regretful for me to say that you appear not to be in complete command or control of yourself, sir.'

'I crave your pardon, sir, but if you had witnessed what I have recently seen, you might look kindlier on me and give me the opportunity to redeem myself.'

'Then where is it you have recently come and wherefore are you bound?'

'Last night from Ely and I am bound for Long Sutton.'

'There is very little of consequence there. Are you familiar with that place?'

'Hardly at all and that only recently. I was offered a somewhat tenuous position of employment and, having lost my living due to these volatile times and no other prospect, I feel I have no option but to test the validity of he who offered it.'

'I see you are an educated man, sir. It saddens me to see one such as yourself in this state. Do you feel no sense of shame, especially in front of these ladies?'

'Yes, I do. Again, I earnestly ask your forgiveness, sir. I have just parted company with my sadistic employer and unfortunately, due to my elation of this bountiful release, I have celebrated just a little too much. I am ashamed and sorry that you see me like this. It has occurred only once before and that was the day of my graduation.'

The farmer softened when he sensed a sincere apology and after considering the situation, invited Luke to sit a while with him. It was not long before he realised his first impressions of this man were false. After a few minutes and seeing that the man beside him was suffering mental turmoil, asked Luke about his immediate past and offered him the opportunity of a full confession.

Luke, who needed a sympathetic ear after the ordeal he had gone through of seeing innocent people perish, was quite frank about the events in Boston and expressed his profound and everlasting regret. On another occasion, he would have been more guarded with his narrative but the strong drink, heat and the desire to unburden himself of his recent history had loosed his tongue more than he realised. He emphasised that this was his first and last association with Hopkins. Farmer Maurice Parcot from that moment understood Luke's mental anguish and never for a moment doubted his sincerity and integrity.

'We have heard rumours of this man Hopkins but hoped that he would not set foot in these parts.'

'He is long gone and by tomorrow, will be back in Essex. It is doubtful he will ever come here again.'

They arose from under the tree and walked to re-join the path. The girls were working close by. Luke said, 'May I have some water for my horse and I before taking my leave of you, please?'

After a short period of consideration, the farmer lowered his guard and said, 'Come up to the house. Meet my wife and have something to eat. You will feel better and will recover much quicker that way. That is a mighty fine horse you have.'

'I accept your very generous offer, sir. You are kind and you offer me more than I deserve. Yes; as to my horse he is a wonderful and special animal. He answers to the name of Copper and is very devoted, loyal and even protective. He understands English in depth but alas, cannot speak it. At least not yet.'

Luke returned the farmer's smile whilst the young women, in a delightful soprano pitch, laughed spontaneously in an uncontrollable yet harmonious trio.

The two men went to the house and, after drinking the well water and putting his head under the pump, Luke lay down under a bed of straw in the barn. He was too exhausted even to eat. Somebody must have visited him whilst he was asleep as he awoke to find a cushion under his head and a blanket over him. He slept long, soundly and when awaking was somewhat disorientated until his mind settled. He suddenly realised it was morning and he was very hungry. On reaching the house, he found the others up and about and a place laid for him at the table. Farmer Maurice Parcot greeted him:

'Good morning. Come and sit with us. We worship the Lord Jesus here and dedicate our lives to him,' he said looking at Luke intently and awaiting his reaction to that statement. The reply he got was exactly the one for which he had hoped.

'As do I, sir, with my heart and soul. I have already craved His pardon for yesterday and those days preceding it although I had no part in the actual proceedings. It is my earnest wish that Parliament is made fully aware of this man Hopkins and deals with him and his like. You have my word, sir, that I had no hand in the fate of those unfortunate people. I was merely his guard and was quite unprepared for the events which followed.'

Farmer Maurice Parcot was beginning to like Luke more and more. The girls kept looking at him and vying for his attention before bowing their heads for grace. Luke was told that he was close to Wisbech and he therefore calculated that he could be at Long Sutton without any problem to Copper by late evening. However, he still had a blinding headache and was easily persuaded to stay a while longer.

He chatted with them in the evening and then retired. He slept again until mid-morning and about midday felt more like his old self. As there was nobody about, he took out his pencil and paper and within a few minutes had drawn the farmhouse. Soon after, the others returned for their midday meal and came over to see what he was doing. They were fascinated with what he had created and were very appreciative of his exceptional talent.

When the meal was over, he took hold of his writing materials and began to draw again. The sun was shining through the kitchen window on three exquisite and beautiful young females. Luke had never seen such girls of beauty and was determined to capture the moment. The elder ones were twins and already 22, the youngest was almost 21.

Maurice had raised no objection to the sketch so Luke went ahead slowly and with extra care. It was not plain sailing as all three found it difficult to keep still and refrain from giggling. Eventually, his finished work was put on the table to be scrutinised by the others. An eagle and artistic eye would have discerned that he had favoured the youngest, Colette, but the others, unaware of technical details, viewed the sketch from a different perspective. Both parents stood respectfully at a distance and then drew closer to examine and then admire the finished article.

'That is my humble parting gift to you,' he said.

The family looked around at each other in an awed silence but their faces revealed great delight and admiration.

When he arose to take his leave, he offered something for his keep but Maurice would have none of it. He therefore gave the girls, who by this time were getting increasingly despondent because of his impending departure, a shilling each. Their names, they said, were Aimee, Martine and Colette Parcot. They whooped with delight, curtsied and kissed him although there was somewhat a look of disapproval on the faces of their strict parents.

'You must be of Huguenot descent,' said Luke as he and Maurice walked out.

'Indeed we are, sir. I came here with my mother and father as a baby in 1598 when the traitor King Henry changed his faith and thus we feared for our future and also our lives. We arrived with five other families who live here in these parts. We brought many different fruit tree plants as well as seeds and gave thanks to God when they found the soil here to their liking. You can see the results all around.'

'Just so,' said Luke looking around at the orchards. 'At this time of year, they must look their best.'

'As I once remarked, you are obviously a man of learning. But where did that take place, may I ask?'

'For a time at Cambridge until the advent of this terrible war. I then made a clumsy indiscretion that caused me to be in the status you see me.'

'You do not have to say more unless you wish to do so,' said Maurice.

'All it was,' said Luke, 'was a rather unflattering illustration of our present tyrant of a King and my Royalist landlord threw me out without a thought and a care.'

'Please feel free to call and see us again if you are ever this way. If possible, make that soon. Thank you for the gift to my daughters and also for the portrait, which my wife would have framed.'

'A very great pleasure, I assure you.' Luke mounted Copper and with a wave was away whilst all three girls suppressed a tear. They were exceedingly loathe to see him go.

'Hm,' Luke spoke out aloud when they were out of earshot. 'Will I remember the names of all these women that have made it their business to invade my life, Copper? Never mind; for the moment, it's just we two. Now what was the girl's name at Long Sutton? Mary? No, Maria. That's it, Maria. Come on, Copper, let's get to it!'

With a neigh and with great joy, the unrestrained Copper bounded away but after a short while, Luke slowed him to a gentle and thus more sensible pace. It was going to be a lovely warm day.

It was not long before Jacob Robinson's career of cheating and thieving was to be first scrutinised and exposed by a new clergyman to the town of Boston who was incorruptible. For a few years, there had been a vacuum in the town since Rev John Cotton had left with a substantial number of the people to the New World.

His cousin, Rev Dr Anthony Tuckney, was away a considerable time at Cambridge and thus a lot of work fell on his recent perpetual curate, Rev Joseph Foorde. In the midst of all this strife, this honest man had come to the parish and as well as his pastoral duties had made it his task to rid the town of some of its nefarious people.

Jacob Robinson was intelligent but not clever enough to hoodwink Joseph Foorde, a truly honourable man of the cloth who, over a period of a few months, proceeded to systematically scrutinise the activities of Robinson and his minions and then at the crucial and critical moment pounce with great effect. He would be ably assisted by Elizabeth's errant relative, who was soon to come to the town.

2. Pursuit

On the late evening of 14 June 1645, Captain Thomas Willistone, Elizabeth Robinson's nephew, had been posted as missing or dead after the Battle of Naseby in Northamptonshire. He had been wounded but managed to continue fighting until a cut on his horse's flank caused the animal to bolt in blind panic. He held on for quite a while before inevitably being thrown but managed to crawl to a small wood beyond the battlefield's edge.

For a while, the conflict raged on whilst he was a distant spectator. When each side came to look for survivors and count their dead, he was missed, being somewhat apart from the theatre of war. He was in so much pain that when somebody did approach nearby, he was unable to call out. He passed in and out of consciousness many times and on the last occasion awoke to find it was nearly dark and therefore about 10.00 pm.

There was no sign of any activity, which was hardly surprising as the Parliamentary army had won a great victory; General Fairfax was chasing the King northwards to Leicester, eventually relieving the city. The King had lost all his baggage and papers that, when scrutinised, revealed the extent of his treachery and dishonesty. It did not take Thomas long to realise that his only hope was if there was a shepherd or scavengers that might come his way. At least it was warm and the morning fog had not returned.

There was a small stream nearby and he reached it with utmost difficulty. He inspected the cut just above his ribs and extracted a piece of dirty tunic. The wound in his leg from musket ball had gone straight through his flesh and was bleeding badly. At this point, he was unable to prevent himself from rolling into the stream for which he cursed vehemently.

What he did not realise was that this action, albeit involuntary, saved his life as the water washed possible infection away. He bound his leg as best he could and arrested the flow of blood then prayed that he would be found. It was not until the following evening that some women from Sibbertoft discovered him, being barely alive.

A great piece of luck was involved here as he was only discovered as a result of his loyal horse returning to the fray; he had smelt his master's scent and had returned and was standing over him. Thomas was cared for locally and those who rescued him from the jaws of death said later that all he could speak of was his dog whom he had left in the care of other folk in Welford. The dog was retrieved by his hosts and brought to her master and from that moment, they said he made the most remarkable recovery.

Thomas was unable to move freely for over three months but managed to send word to his commanding officer, Sir Edward Rossiter, that he was alive and slowly recovering from his wounds. He was sent papers of acknowledgement and immediately granted an honourable discharge. In his letter, Rossiter paid tribute to Thomas' outstanding bravery whilst confirming that the battle of Naseby had all but defeated the King and the Royalist cause. Thus, there was at least a temporary respite from further carnage and conflict.

As a result of the enclosures a few years earlier, Thomas' parents had lost their living and livelihood, an action that had shaped the views of their son on King Charles and his sycophants. It was not that long before his parents died, leaving him almost destitute apart from some horses and a very loyal dog called General. In spite of the name, the dog was a friendly bitch but a fiercely protective one. Thus, enlistment in Cromwell's Model Army was not merely done out of conviction but as a means of personal survival. He was fed regularly, had a roof over his head, albeit often a tent, and sixpence a day in pay.

The local people where he stayed had no compunction about helping a rebel officer. By now they were utterly sick and tired of the King and his followers. Earlier whilst Oxford prepared for siege, the countryside was robbed of much of its livestock and herded into that city to feed ever growing hungry citizens. The people in the area of Welford and Husband's Bosworth hid as many of their beasts as possible in order that they themselves might survive.

After thanking his hosts for being responsible for his recovery and rewarding them, he retrieved his horses and sold two of them at a very handsome profit. It was an opportune time to sell as horses were almost non-existent locally. Like sheep and cattle, many had been commandeered but many of the horses lay dead on the battlefield. Some of the more destitute villagers had to cut out horse meat to feed their children.

Thomas was undecided whether to go home to Sleaford and see if there were old friends who would help him pick up the pieces of his former life or to visit his aunt and uncle in Boston. There, he could earn his keep by working on their smallholding. His aunt and uncle were always fond of him and Thomas knew that they always welcomed an extra pair of hands. Like many others at this time, he was convinced that the King had been soundly beaten and that to keep his kingdom, Charles would have to learn to live and cooperate with Parliament. Sadly, those hopes were doomed and soon to be in tatters. He rode slowly and carefully to Rockingham castle in his full uniform, confident of hospitality as by now it was in Parliamentary hands.

Sometimes, General rode with him but often jumped down if the road was bumpy. Two days later, after changing into less conspicuous clothes, he travelled via Stamford but only stopped briefly for a meal and some ale. He was wary of the fact that the town was still divided in its loyalties so instead, decided to stay the night at the *Angel Inn*, Bourne.

After stabling the horses, he paid for his board and lodge in advance then wearily sat down to eat and give the General plenty of tit bits. Even though it was a warm autumn, he asked the landlord to light the fire as his wounds still ached. Later, as he warmed himself against the fire and drank his ale, a young girl came up to him and flaunted herself ostentatiously.

'Hello, stranger. Come far?'

'Far enough,' said Thomas, as detached as possible but without being openly rude.

'Can I get you anything? Anything at all? You look as though you could do with some company.'

'I am content with this tankard and I have got General here.'

'He can't keep you warm through the night, though, can he? I could do that if you make it worth my while.'

'There would be no room as the dog sleeps on my bed most of the time. Sometimes on the floor if the bed is small. As to your keeping me warm then I am sure you could do that admirably and have done so many times to a variety of customers. The trouble is that as a result of that sort of liaison with you, I might later receive some unwanted and very painful reminders. Anyway, he is a she. Find some lowlife like yourself.'

The girl was not used to this sort of rebuff. Her face distorted as she scowled.

'That's not very polite.' She waited but Thomas completely ignored her and continued with his meal.

Whereupon the girl tossed her head contemptuously and went over to a corner of the room where she whispered in the ear of a large burly fellow with a black beard. Thomas knew exactly what was to happen and experience had taught him to be ever on the alert and be prepared. Sometimes, he could sense trouble as soon as he walked into a place. It was obvious this was a fairly regular routine of contact followed by intimidation that would lead to a possible means of extortion. The bearded man came over to Thomas, leant over the table menacingly, pausing for a few moments in an attempt to establish his dominance.

'My girl says you have insulted her,' said the man. 'You have cast some very nasty aspersions on her. I think you had better say sorry otherwise I shall be forced to take the matter further.'

Thomas, with an air of nonchalance mixed with contempt, took a pull on his ale then looked into the man's eyes, pausing before he spoke.

'If she truly is your girl, which I doubt, then your taste in women is somewhat questionable, in fact I would go so far as to say quite atrocious, if I might say so.'

The bearded man glowered. 'You can always say so, mister high and mighty, but it will surely cost you dearly. Before I deal with you, I want to know why you think my taste in this woman so bad?'

The *Angel* had about six other patrons at the time who were discreetly following events whilst pretending to be uninterested. Thomas' reply automatically widened their eyes as at once they knew it spelt trouble.

Thomas sighed and deliberately kept the man waiting. He looked up and said carefully and distinctly.

'The woman you call your girl appears to me to be a low scavenging piece of humanity of whom probably half the men of Bourne have had as well as numerous travellers of questionable taste and morals through this town. She belongs in the gutter. You also belong there if you have permanent associations with people such as her. My advice to you is to find a steady girl who will bear your children but not imperil your health and salvation.' He looked away wearily and picked up his tankard, appearing quite unconcerned. The man winced and leant over the table. General growled.

'Outside, you. Come outside and say that. Outside of your own accord or I will drag you out. Who the devil are you anyway?' He rolled up his sleeves.

Thomas was unmoved. He paused again and then leant back in his chair.

'My name is Captain Thomas Willistone, formerly of Sleaford, veteran of General Cromwell's Model Army and lately decorated after our great victory at Naseby. Here. Here you are, if you can read. Take a look at this if you don't believe me. My papers. Quite honestly, I do not care a damn whether you do or do not.'

Thomas threw the discharge paper on the table, believing rightly that the man was somewhat illiterate and would not take more than a glance. He wished he had arrived in his uniform but it was no use regretting that fact. He hoped that this revelation would be the end of this discourse as he had done enough fighting recently and still ached.

The man winced again as he had been taken aback at this latest piece of information. He remained though in his belligerent posture with a look of reluctance to believe or leave. He then pretended to inspect Thomas' papers, which took several seconds. General growled again and the man continued to hold his posture. Thomas felt there was no other recourse but to play his ace and get some peace.

'One thing more, my friend. If you continue this idiotic behaviour and threaten violence then any aspirations you have of being a father will disappear in an instant. There is a loaded flintlock pistol underneath this table pointed directly at your pillock and its associates, either side that will cease to exist if you make one false move.

'Being an experienced soldier, I have the ability and knowledge of how to maim and incapacitate men rather than kill outright. In that way, they are more likely to give me the information I want. I am sore, tired and weary after a long series of conflicts and have seen much death at close hand. It is my earnest wish at this point in my life NOT to experience any more death, at least for the time being and, believe it or not, that includes yours. In your case, I don't want to be arrested for murder in spite of the fact that I wager many around this lovely town would rejoice at your passing.'

Without revealing the weapon, Thomas clicked the mechanism and this time the man recoiled. His demeanour suddenly changed and he looked afraid. Of course, the flintlock was not primed but Thomas was relying on the man's ignorance of weapons to bring about an end to his belligerence. The man began to sweat a little and at last, accepting defeat, turned to go.

The other people in the inn who looked at each other and marvelled. Here was a feared bully who in the past had rarely been challenged let alone been completely outflanked. The others had frozen at the sound of the trigger and had not dared to move thinking that remaining motionless was the safer option. Before the man had gone two paces, Thomas called out:

'Stop…Come back… Sit down… No, not there; opposite me. This chair here.'

The bearded man hesitated then obeyed meekly and sat down gingerly. Thomas looked at him intently and observed a strategic silence. He then called out in a manner that caused all in the inn to startle.

'Landlord! Landlord! Where in God's name are you, you incompetent idler? Move that fat arse of yours. Let's have some service here.'

Thomas' authoritative voice had had plenty of practice amongst his subordinates and the rank and file and it reverberated as he thumped the table, causing the General to put back her ears. She looked at him slightly disdainfully, wondering what he was about to do.

The landlord appeared and was very effusive in his manner.

'Yes, sss…sir. What is your pleasure?'

'A pot and some ale for my friend here. Set up those gentlemen over there who look as though they could do with some Roundhead hospitality. Be quick about it. The evening is slipping away.'

The landlord, who had heard all, was shaking with fear. He hastened away and duly returned and filled each pot from a large jug. In his fright, some was spilled but Thomas refrained from chastising him. When he had served everybody, Thomas stood up and assumed his imperious posture and boomed out yet again and loud enough to be heard in all parts of the *Angel.*

'Gentlemen of the pretty little town of Bourne in famous Lincolnshire, the county of my birth. Citizens one and all. Whether you be saint or sinner, squire or serf, the toast is General Fairfax and a NEW, FAIRER, JUST and more prosperous England.'

The toast was greeted enthusiastically, which pleased Thomas greatly although he was unsure whether the cheer was genuine or more likely through fear. They drank whilst Thomas remained standing.

'Gentlemen of England! And now a toast to General Cromwell.'

Thomas did not relax his guard but felt happier about the time he was to spend in this quaint old town. He turned to the man opposite and smiled. No point in making an enemy unnecessarily. Besides, wherever he went and whatever place he visited, Thomas always bought strangers ale to loosen their tongues and, hopefully, hear an account of the status quo in that area. That would be very difficult if there had been fisticuffs and impossible if a firearm had been discharged. The conversation began pleasantly but it was not long before Thomas was experiencing an unexpected pang of alarm followed by great anxiety.

The bearded man having been released from the threat of maiming and even death was only too ready to talk and his words tumbled out as a result of relief from his reprieve. He spoke of his travels between Bourne and Boston with other traders and made a tidy living bringing in luxuries and the like from abroad. He was not educated but was competent in his dealings with others and had made a good trade between the two towns.

'Me and my friends, we were in Boston a short time ago and there were some strange fellows who were taking court. They were wearing Puritan dress and stirring things up.'

'What do you mean by that?' said Thomas.

'One man described himself as *Witchfinder General* and during the day, he had several people tried for sorcery. One woman was swum.'

'Matthew Hopkins,' Thomas mused. 'And his partner Stearne this far north. Not good to hear.' He looked intently at the man opposite and said,

'Who was she? Do you know her name?' said Thomas.

'I 'eard that it was 'Lizabeth but that's all. She was put in a chair. Quite a fancy one wi' carvings and an owl on top.'

Thomas froze. His aunt's name was Elizabeth and had a chair like that. However, if it was her then whatever was his uncle doing at the time? Why had he not intervened and protected her? Thomas was very quiet and the only sound was that of distant subdued voices. The General sensed something was wrong as she had not been fussed or fed for some time and instinctively was aware that something was troubling her master. It was a while before anyone spoke. The bearded man broke the silence.

'I did 'ear that she got away but I don't know 'ow.'

Thomas recovered his composure. 'I am very grateful for your news, my friend. You may not understand why this is so but you have given me information that has been of great benefit. Let's finish this ale and then I shall retire and you will no doubt go home.' They duly raised their pots and drank.

'By your favour,' said the man. 'May I see your pistol? I have never seen one close.' Thomas without any compunction obliged and handed to the man. He was quite awed and fondled it carefully. He then held it in his hand.

'You took a chance giving it to me, didn't you?'

Thomas had no intention of telling the man the true state of affairs with a gun like this.

'Not really. You would not get as far as the magistrate. The General would have torn you to shreds.'

The man winced yet again and said goodbye. Thomas knew if he were to complete the 25 miles to Boston in one day then an early start was necessary and the horses would need several rests as the weather was warm. Moreover, he had to be careful as his wounds were still sore and at times his leg ached. He went to his room and tried to sleep.

Thomas was glad when daylight arrived and thus the opportunity of action. He dressed and went downstairs. Fortunately, the landlord and his wife were up and about and were glad to feed him and see the back of him! Rather than go by Spalding, he took the route by Dunsby and Billingborough, which was less populated.

All the way, he kept turning things over in his mind and was often taken by surprise when people greeted him on the road. He neared Boston when it was dark and suddenly found himself quite ravenous. His army training had made him cautious and he therefore decided to kill two birds with one stone; firstly to eat and secondly to glean information. He made for the *Old King's Head* on the outskirts of Kirton as this was on the secret list of friendly meeting places for Roundhead soldiers who might need sustenance or even means of escape.

There was a back entrance that led to a boat on the river Witham, which could be gained before any of the King's men could make an arrest. Before he had decided on his next moves and had drunk two mouthfuls of ale, a couple of former soldiers recognised him, a fact that pleased him greatly. They joined him and talked endlessly about the war and the future until one said:

'Well, captain. Good to see you. We heard a little while ago that you had miraculously survived but knew not your abode. What brings you to these parts? I thought you hailed from Sleaford.'

'I do,' said Thomas. 'I have come to visit my aunt and uncle and hope that they can find work for me.'

'Like as not we may know them. What is their name?'

'Robinson. Joshua and Elizabeth Rob—'

Before Thomas could finish his sentence, his former colleague grabbed him by the wrist and put his finger to his lips. Thomas, ever ready for danger, paused immediately realising that something was very wrong and prepared himself for the worst. His colleague whispered:

'I beg you, Captain, not to go to your aunt's house just yet. It grieves me to be the harbinger of bad tidings. Your uncle has died and your aunt Elizabeth has disappeared mysteriously. Your uncle's brother is living in the family house and there is much talk of dark deeds and evil goings on mainly by his hand.'

'When did this happen? I am assuming it was at the time that Hopkins and Stearne were here.'

'Just so. It happened only a few weeks ago. May I make a suggestion, Captain?'

'Please do as my mind is in a turmoil over this.'

'Do not venture to your aunt's house until you have met our curate who can tell you all that has befallen. He is a good and honest man who is a believer in our cause. He is ashamed of what has taken place. Believe you me, Captain, you have arrived during troubled times. It is lucky you met us. Let us be gone quickly as 'tis late.'

No second bidding was necessary. They left at once and mounted their horses for the short distance into Boston, reaching the curate's house just as the candles were being extinguished. Rev Joseph Foorde's initial annoyance at having to

31

answer the insistent knock on the door at that late hour dissolved immediately when he recognised two of his loyal parishioners. Men with a sincere faith who were fighting for others as well for themselves.

When Thomas was introduced, his former colleagues were wont to withdraw and leave the curate with the onerous task of revealing the recent events but Rev Joseph insisted they all came into the kitchen. Over a glass of wine, the whole wicked episode of the visit of Hopkins and Stearne was unfolded to Thomas who could barely contain his rage and immediately wanted to leave to confront his uncle.

It took a little dissuading but when Foorde confided in Thomas the details of his own enquiries whilst unfolding his plan of action, Thomas was becalmed. He agreed to lodge at the curate's house incognito until Joseph was ready to pounce and not to do anything precipitous as it would jeopardise his carefully laid plans. Thomas' former colleagues then took their leave and pledged their support should he need it.

'And now, Captain Willistone. Let me take you to the room where you may take your rest. Tell me; does that dog of yours have to be with you all the time?'

'It is almost certain that nobody knows of my whereabouts or wishes me harm but she is on hand at once if there is danger. And that would be impossible if she were to be confined to the kitchen or stable.'

'Quite so,' said Foorde. He took him up to a spare bedroom and quietly left him. Thomas got ready for bed but had his pistol on hand should the need arise.

In the morning, there was a somewhat humorous moment when he came downstairs early and surprised Mrs Foorde, causing her to drop a plate on the kitchen floor. As yet, the absent-minded Joseph had forgotten to inform her of Thomas' arrival in the house.

A defining moment happened a few minutes later when he was introduced to the Foorde's beautiful 21-year-old daughter who appeared to Thomas like a vision of heaven on earth. He experienced a jolt inside so formidable that at that moment, he believed he was melting inside. He also said what a wonderful feeling of solace it was coming so suddenly on such beauty after months of incessant slaughter and the loss of close friends and comrades.

Joseph Foorde, the perpetual curate, realising how much corruption was rife in the town, had compiled a resume of Robinson's activities and the deeds of his associates. Through his connections with the cathedral authorities, he had sent for some officers from Lincoln who were thoroughly honest. He took Thomas over to the Stump to talk to him in private. The latter was shocked and dismayed to see the state of the interior and glass on the floor as a result of the smashed stained glass windows, which still had gaping holes.

'In the name of our Lord Jesus, who is responsible for all of this?' he said.

'Not two years ago, prior to the Battle of Winceby, Lord Manchester was here and garrisoned the troops on the spot we are standing as well as horses in the chancel. Just before they left, some of the extremists in the army decided to embark on this wanton destruction. How can such things like stained glass and organs of beauty be blasphemous or contrary to the will of God, Master Thomas?'

'I wish I knew the answer,' said Thomas, visibly distressed by the deplorable mess. 'It troubles me greatly that, although I am committed to our great cause, we have such people in the army and our midst who would do those acts.'

'And me also,' said Foorde. 'Now I beg you, Master Thomas, to sit tight until the officers arrive from Lincoln to examine my dossier. Any action from you now would jeopardise all my hard work. Come and talk to Leah and tell her about yourself and your travels. It is rarely she has the chance of some stimulating conversation,' said the curate.

'This will be a task of great pleasure,' said Thomas.

'Please leave out the worst details of the fighting.'

3. Arrest

Only five days after Thomas Willistone's arrival, the officers from Lincoln jail presented themselves discreetly at the rectory. Travelling with them were two clergymen, ostensibly to give the bishop a report on the damage to the Stump but also to make the party look as if it were solely an ecclesiastical disposition. In this way, it was hoped that no suspicion would be aroused and no leak from any corrupt official in Lincoln.

The officers were appalled at the activities in the town and after careful inspection of the curate's dossier, Robinson, protesting and kicking, was arrested. In court, he vehemently denied all the accusations levelled against him including that which involved his sister-in-law.

He had not seen his sister's nephew for some years but even so, he had no qualms in denying the authenticity of Thomas. It took a little while for Thomas to prove who he was. The delay further assisted Robinson who naturally had taken every precaution against possible discovery of his villainy and had made elaborate and watertight contingency plans.

He had enough support from shady magistrate colleagues to allow breathing space and put into effect his next moves. The magistrate ordered that a second day was necessary and thus Robinson was sent into the care of the town's gaol.

Robinson realised that the die was cast and that he could only avoid Lincoln gaol by leaving Boston and England forever and disappearing without trace. Being the cunning fellow he was and knowing he had little time to effect his flight, he later that evening gave orders to Millsome, his minion, to sell what precious assets he had to his nefarious associates at a rate much less than their worth but enough and more for a ship's passage and a new life beyond.

He could easily afford the £5 for his fare but bundled many items of worth as well into a couple of sacks, which could be for sale when he reached his new abode. Some spare clothing was included. He stashed a small amount of gold that his brother had left at his early death and made sure it was hidden in his belt that he wore even in bed. Gold was a currency that could be exchanged anywhere and he would need some to set himself up in his new home.

A man disguised as a priest then hit the gaoler over the head, albeit lightly, and Robinson escaped. His baggage complete, he and his manservant stealthily dissolved into the gloom in the early hours and made their way to Boston docks to a rendezvous. His contact was waiting concealed in the dark recess behind some large bales and they were escorted to a place where there was a boat. Robinson realised that it was no use taking a boat from Boston. Eventually, somebody would talk and would dog his footsteps.

In the middle of the night, having been cut free by his minions, he boarded a small fishing boat and in fair weather a few hours later landed in Kings Lynn. All went smoothly and payment was made in full to his collaborators. Master and servant boarded the ship to London and were there a week later. Then they took one for the New World, never to set foot in England again. The only problem was having to wait several days for high tide before the ship's departure and having no option but to remain hidden in very dark and cramped conditions.

The fugitives need not have worried about capture because on the morning after their escape in Boston, the town authorities were on a wild goose chase thanks to Walker, one of Robinson's former minions, leading a false trail. He was sure that he saw riders going north.

In the end, Thomas, who had changed into his uniform, took General down to the house where Robinson had been shackled. People immediately respected his rank and status and made a path for him as he approached. The gaoler had been hit by Robinson's minion and was covered in blood. Thomas, who was well acquainted with pain and men's suffering, immediately realised that the gaoler, Walker's brother, was pretending to be hurt. The company watched while Thomas inspected the rope and then the blood on Walker. Some of them felt a slight revulsion when Thomas tasted it.

'Hmm. Sheep's blood,' he said. He tasted it again.

'No doubt about it. Right. Master Walker, let us have the facts and the truth or it will be the worse for you.'

Walker protested. The curate caused a long delay by asking him to make a clean breast of it and asking to talk to him alone. He only cracked when Thomas twisted his head and threatened him with torture.

'This is just a little foretaste of what you will have if you delay the information we require any longer,' said Thomas. 'Your pretty little neck is about to assume a new position on your body.'

'No, no. No more, please,' said Walker. 'I'll tell you all.'

He then revealed to the whole company all he knew. The one piece of information lacking was where the fugitives were headed.

'You don't think that he was going to tell us that, do you? He would be a fool,' said Walker, feeling his neck.

This made sense to the assembled group and so they refrained from any further interrogation. Thomas repaired to his uncle's house and found some clothing that Robinson had discarded. He then returned to the rectory and untied General. All the time, the others who were mystified with proceedings waited and speculated about his intentions.

However, Thomas knew exactly what he was doing. He returned to Walker's house and then gave General a smell of Robinson's nightshirt. The dog picked up the scent immediately and obediently sniffed out the spoor. They wound their way from the outskirts and through the old town. The onlookers marvelled but their initial optimism turned to dismay when, on reaching the dock, General came to a halt.

'What does this mean, Captain?'

'It means, my friend, that we are too late. We will most likely never know who it was who helped them escape and whoever it was is a long way away now. This has to be the result of a contingency plan formed a long time ago. It will be easy for any boatman to deny knowledge of the escape. Justice for my aunt, the missing, presumed lost Elizabeth Robinson is held in abeyance.'

There were groans of disappointment and frustration.

'Never mind,' said the saintly and always optimistic Rev Foorde. 'Let's be grateful for what we have achieved. There are people who will not wield their evil in this town any more. They have gone forever. The others we have will stand trial and I have no doubt that justice will be meted out.'

There were murmurs of approval of this and there followed a suggestion that all repair to the tavern for a drink. Naturally, this resolution was passed unanimously.

Thomas Willistone set about putting his aunt's house in order and working the land behind it to good effect. He was at once accepted into the local community and his uniform, general bearing and posture called for immediate respect and even reverence while ladies competed for his attention and did everything possible to entice him to their respective bedrooms. That respect was no more evident than at the curate's house where he and Joseph Foorde enjoyed each other's company enormously. It was after the festive period and in the early new year that the rector could contain himself no longer and was bold enough to put a personal question.

'You know, captain, that our daughter is extremely fond of you and I must add for some time has had high hopes of your affection.'

'And I am fond of her, sir. More than fond. There is nothing more lovely and delightful in the whole of Boston.'

Hearing that statement, the perpetual curate felt it would be advantageous to continue and lost no time in doing so.

'She has refused offers including lately the curate at Wyberton.'

'Has she now? Forgive me for saying so bluntly but I can readily understand that.'

'Yes, quite so, but mainly in the hope that you yourself might favour her.'

'Dear sir and friend. I have been a soldier and a rebel against the lawful King, albeit a tyrant King, a cheat, a liar and an abomination to the good people of our great country. Our cause was just and long overdue. In nowhere more so is this more evident in our lovely town where people have been fleeing to the colonies just to be able to live in peace. Just so that they can arise with happiness in the morning and go about their daily duty without fear of molestation or even death.

'In a sense, I feel tainted as I have had to kill or be killed for justice to triumph. My parents starved and for years, I have had no home but the army. This is the first time I have had a home plus the feeling of being settled, which was totally unexpected.

'Somehow, I do not expect to see my aunt again and if this is so, the house, land and all things in it are mine. If that is the case, I will be extremely content to remain here. As to the army, I wonder if there will be further conflict and whether I shall have to ride again, although I am somewhat restricted. If others decide so I would have to leave Leah and as such I could not bear to see her alone and unhappy.'

'Dear boy, I do not mean to press you but she wakes each day knowing that you care for her and thus hoping to gain your favour and goes to bed feeling alone and unhappy because you seem unwilling or unable to bestow it.'

There was a long pause. 'I am not blind. I just tried to put the thought out from my mind and for the reasons of which we have just spoken,' said Thomas. 'I wonder whether I am worthy of her.'

'Is it possible you could give the matter further thought?'

There was an even longer pause. 'I will. In fact I have.' Thomas paused once more. 'Very well then. Without further delay and with your permission, perhaps you should seek her out and request her to come to me.'

Joseph Foorde was completely taken by surprise. 'Now? This very minute?'

'Yes. At once, if you please, sir. That is my wish.'

'It pleases me to hear this but why so sudden?' said Joseph.

'A soldier is taught never to hesitate. Otherwise, he might easily perish. I wish to live.'

The curate, although initially taken off guard, regained his equilibrium and immediately swung into action.

'I will organise some tea and ask her to bring it in to you.'

He got up and went to the lounge where the ladies were on their own and engaged in some intricate sewing. He went over to speak to his daughter.

'Leah. Would you make the captain and I some tea, please? We are in the library.'

'Of course, father. Shall I take in some of those biscuits we made?'

Mrs Foorde then put a spanner in the works. 'You finish what you are doing, dear. I will get the captain some tea. I have finished my row and it would be a shame to spoil yours.'

'No! No. I want Leah to do it.' His voice accidentally sounded sharp, which surprised both ladies. For a while, there was a short and difficult silence.

'Is all well with you, husband?' said his wife. 'It is most unlike you to speak to me so.'

'Yes, yes, my love. I need a word with just the two of us. That is why I wish Leah to make the tea. Please excuse me if I sounded somewhat curt and abrupt.' He turned to Leah.

'Off you go, dear. Don't dilly dally. I need to talk with your mother,' said Joseph as he sought to regain control of the situation.

'Yes, father.'

Leah obediently left for the kitchen whilst Mrs Foorde who, still unconvinced by Joseph's behaviour, awaited an explanation from her usually very mild-mannered and phlegmatic husband.

'You have never snapped at me like that before, Mr Foorde,' said his slightly bewildered spouse.

'I am sorry, dear, but you were inadvertently on the point of ruining everything.'

'Ruining what?' she said, not without a little more indignation in her voice.

'Dearest. dearest. Please be calm. Allow me to explain... He is about to ask her.'

Mrs Foorde looked blank. 'Going to what...going to...' and all at once she understood. She put her hands to her face in a moment of utmost joy. She jumped up and rushed at him and flung her arms around her husband.

'Oh, please forgive me. Oh Mr Foorde. How lovely. How have you managed to contrive a thing like this?'

'It was easy. We spoke of it for a little while and then he suddenly announced his intention whilst we were talking.'

Husband and wife talked for a few minutes more and were still hugging when Leah came in to announce that the tea was ready. She was puzzled to see them in such an intimate position but was too polite to stare. Joseph jumped in with both feet.

'Leah. Please take the captain his tea. Your mother and I will be with you in just a couple of minutes. We are very nearly complete with what we wanted to discuss.'

'Very good, father,' said the young girl, polite and dutiful as always. She went to the kitchen for the tea. She opened the library door and then went back for the tray. Thomas was ready for her and shut the door rather firmly, which caused her to be surprised and just a tiny bit disconcerted.

'Mother and Father will be coming in shortly,' was all that she could think to say. There was a pause and she looked up at him wondering what was next.

'Will that be all, sir?'

'No, Leah, it will not be all. If you please, I wish you to stay and talk to me and hear what I have to say.'

She looked concerned but before she could say anything, he spoke again.

'Leah. It would please me if you did not ever call me sir again.' He held her hand. 'I want you…' he hesitated.

'What would you like me to call you? I can't call you—'

He interrupted her, 'You can call me Thomas but better still and if you wish, you can take steps to call me like your mother does to your father. Dear husband.'

Her eyes widened. She opened her mouth but nothing emerged. He held her hands.

'Leah, my dear, forgive me for taking so long to speak to you but this ugly war and the loss of my aunt and uncle affected me greatly. I feel much better and will be happy to stay here and make this my home but only if you would agree to become Mrs Thomas Willistone. What is your answer to that?'

Leah's joy was instantaneous. She forgot all convention and threw her arms around him tightly.

'Oh yes! Oh yes. Oh yes. Of course, I will. With all my heart. It has been my greatest wish for some time; in fact, as early as the second day after you arrived.'

'Did it take as long as the second day? I am mortified it took such a length of time.' They both laughed, which helped release a lot of pent-up tension. He leaned forward and he kissed her. Not content with that and wishing to make up for lost time, Leah kissed him until they parted whilst continuing to look at each other intently.

After exchanging a few small kisses, Thomas suggested that they call in her parents. They were waiting and at the same time trying to be patient. After a few female tears, which are always inexplicable to menfolk in such a situation, they fetched two more cups and drank the tea while chatting happily.

There was little to arrange as everyone that mattered was on the spot and, of course, Thomas had no family that he knew about except a sister who had long disappeared and was believed to be in one of the Deepings villages. It was agreed that the rector on his return would take the service and that Joseph would give Leah away.

Just over two months later, the couple were married in Boston Stump church to the great rejoicing of the townsfolk who were eager for a happy occasion after a long period of war and conflict. It spurred many of the townsfolk to spend some of their spare time clearing up a lot of the mess and filth that had been left and to make the church fit for a wedding. It was still an uncertain time to live and all the inhabitants had been wary and on their guard. Joseph Foorde organised a little shrine in memory of the innocent and tragic Elizabeth Robinson as a reminder to his flock that elderly women with or without black cats were not necessarily witches. Moreover, torture was a sin and they must repudiate it.

4. A Few Miles South

Coincidentally, on the same day Thomas and Leah were arranging their marriage, a young and displaced man decided that it was a time for a decision. Luke Whythorne did return to Long Sutton and was made welcome by those he had met on his previous brief visit. He earned some money in the town doing sketches for a few weeks until patronage waned. Many of the would-be customers were too poor to indulge in such luxuries. Inwardly, he was troubled because he found he could not easily get rid of the memory of the Parcot family.

As such, he decided to lodge somewhere else other than the *Olde Ship* for a short while. When he did decide to visit the Inn and converse with the locals, he found that the landlord's claim that his daughter had *never been taken by a man* was somewhat inaccurate. Luke did stay there at the *Olde Ship* for a few days and it was assumed he had returned there to woo Maria.

He began to be pressed as to his intentions. When he could not defer the disclosure of his non-interest any longer as well as the fact that funds were beginning to dwindle, he made a decision that required the utmost secrecy. The moment for action was opportune when all were asleep in the early minutes of a dawn, which heralded a dry and sunny day. Luke saddled up Copper and was away before anyone was the wiser.

Later that day, the pair trotted into the Parcot farm where the first members of the family he encountered were all three daughters working in the orchard. They squealed with delight and rushed to meet him. He kissed their hands in turn while they curtsied. He enquired as to the whereabouts of their parents and was escorted to them arm in arm. Maurice excused their forwardness but frowned slightly for a moment.

'Well, well,' he said, changing to a radiant beam. 'You have come back to us. Is this a fleeting visit or of a more permanent nature?'

'I am here in the hope you and your dear wife will grant me a lasting employment, that is, if there is a vacant position.'

Maurice looked at his wife. 'What do you think, my dearest?'

'Indeed there is a vacancy, Master Luke. Come and have something to eat and drink.'

That evening when the meal was over, three young women looked at him longingly and affectionately at every possible opportunity. They were quite unable to hide their feelings for him. Luke, however, drawing on the experience of his first encounter with this family was somewhat formal with them, believing this to be the most prudent course of action, one that would meet the approval of their parents.

He was anxious to gain their total trust and expunge any possible memories of his first ever arrival at the farm. If he was a little over formal sometimes, it was because he was conscious of the fact that he had nowhere else in the world to live and little in the way of prospects. It was difficult sometimes to contain his feelings as all three girls were so beautiful and desirable. However, it was only a matter of two or three months later that he and Maurice were sitting outside and enjoying the last rays of a beautiful evening when Maurice suddenly said:

'Are you happy to stay a while longer here with us, Master Luke?'

'I am, sir. In fact I am happy as never before and wish to be nowhere else on God's earth. That goes for Copper too.'

'Am I correct in thinking that one of my daughters has taken your fancy?'

'You are, sir, although I hope and pray I've not in any way taken a liberty by doing so.'

'Not in the least. I would be happy for you to take to wife any one of them,' said Maurice. Glad as a result of this discourse, he sat back feeling contented and drew on an evil-smelling pipe.

5. In the North Atlantic

Whilst Thomas and Leah were in their first few weeks of marriage, Jacob Robinson and his servant Millsome were still on their way to the New World in spite of the fact that the weather had been mostly kind. However, they were becalmed for a long time in the Canaries. Many people talked of possible hurricanes but as yet there was no sign of one. Each of the men carried two sharp knives that were never more than a few inches away from them. Jacob also carried with him several copies of Hopkins' book, *The Discovery of Witches.*

For the most part of the journey, the two men stayed in their cabin and had their food brought to them. Robinson would have like to have stretched his legs more and find if any women were available but a problem lay with his servant, Millsome. This man was loyal but was unable to keep a secret, especially after he had been drinking. They did not immediately go ashore when the ship docked at the Canaries. They had prearranged knocks on the door when by force of circumstance, they had to be apart.

Jacob had bribed one of the seamen to keep an ear out for any adverse news. They need not have worried because no word had reached London by the time they had left the city. By the time they were off the coast of Newfoundland, the two fugitives were feeling a lot safer and happier and walked about the ship more freely. However, one evening Robinson found out from one of the sailors that Millsome had been opening his mouth too much as a result of a surfeit of alcohol. He had instructed Millsome to tell anyone who asked about their origins that they hailed from Newark but he had revealed that it was Boston. This, with some earlier minor indiscretions, had set alarm bells ringing.

When questioned, Millsome lied. Robinson sighed inwardly and realised he had run out of patience. He then strangled Millsome and laid him out on the cabin floor. He was not going to take chances before he got to his new home, wherever that would be. He then called one of the seamen to say that his servant had suffered a heart attack and died within minutes.

'Sorry, old chum. But you are no more use to me. At some point, you will blab and give us both away. You always talked too much after drink so I can't risk it. In any case, if there are people looking for us, I will look less conspicuous on my own.'

A few days later and just before docking, the captain appeared.

'How are things with you, sir?'

'Very good, thank you, captain. Quite a smooth passage since the Canaries, I believe.'

'Indeed sir. Now, when you are feeling up to it, we will complete the details of our little bit of disposal business.'

'Absolutely. I am forever in your debt.'

'Just what we agreed on will be enough, sir. Be assured, you need have no fears; I am a man of my word.'

This proved to be completely the case and so a proven and unencumbered villain entered the colonies without hindrance and with the capacity to do huge damage there on unsuspecting and totally innocent people. Just as he was leaving, the captain turned.

'As a matter of interest, sir, where are you headed? Have you anywhere in mind?'

'To Salem, captain,' was the reply.

6. Wisbech, Cambridgeshire

When Maurice asked Luke whether one of his daughters had taken his fancy and Luke had demurred, it was only a matter of hours before everyone else's suspicions began to gather momentum. This was because there was no reason for further secrecy or restraint and thus Luke was completely unable to hide his feelings. It seemed that the probability of a declaration was now almost a certainty. After the admission by Luke and the fact that Maurice had made a possible union so easy to materialise, there was no need for any hesitance. Only two days later, when Luke found his beloved by the well away from the others and alone, he decided to seize the moment.

'Hello, sweet princess, do you need any assistance.'

'No, handsome prince. Your presence and company will suffice, but thank you.'

'What would your response be to the offer of my permanent presence and company with you every day and all night for that matter?'

Colette's heart leapt and she was almost overcome but recovered quickly and turned to face him. With great deliberation, she said: 'I would have to accept, sir, without a moment's delay.'

'In that case, will you do me the honour of becoming Mrs Luke Whythorne, please?'

'Gladly, sir. Now will you with the utmost haste give me the kiss for which I have craved and waited for so long?'

Without further ado, Luke performed this action several times to be returned by similar ones from his intended. The others were working elsewhere except for Colette's mother who witnessed events from the farmhouse window. In her delight, she immediately danced a *Branle* that her mother had taught her years ago around the kitchen floor, much to the great amazement of Aimee and Martine who entered the room whilst their mother was in full flow.

Then they understood. The sisters were glad for Colette but naturally somewhat disappointed for themselves. Little did they all realise then that the marriage was to be greatly to their advantage and to have far reaching ripples on the water. The following day, invitations were sent out to their friends for a small party at the following weekend. There was a mixture of two cultures but all went well except that one of the fiddlers almost collapsed with fatigue at the end of the proceedings.

The effect of the "ripples on the water" began thus: Luke worked on the farm but Maurice was careful not to employ him on heavy duties. He recognised Luke's gift and felt it was his duty to allow it to flourish and offer any assistance. The menial work was done by two local brutish fellows, one of which had proposed to both of the twins and had twice been refused. Maurice was keen for Luke to exploit his God-given talent and thus Luke often went into the neighbouring towns showing his work and obtaining pupils, mainly from rich families.

When one family had sketches made of them and another heard, others were keen to emulate. When invited into some of the affluent homes, he took the opportunity to take Colette and her sisters with him. As a result of gaining contacts and connections, Aimee got a post as a governess and flourished in the port of Wisbech because of her knowledge of French and workable German. Martine met a handsome lawyer and within a few months, she too was happily wed. They soon moved to Boston where they had two children and it was there that Martine began a close friendship with Leah Willistone.

During her pregnancy, Luke and Colette received an invitation from Martine to spend a few days with them in Boston. She asked Luke to be sure to bring his drawing materials and also his previous work, especially anything connected with his last visit to the town as she had been particularly asked to do so.

In this, Luke duly obliged and they arrived a day later in Boston to be greeted warmly by his sister-in-law and her husband. Naturally, the sisters were very happy to be reunited after an inordinate time apart. A party had been organised for the next day and local dignitaries came and were introduced individually or as a couple. This included the curate and Mrs Foorde. The curate was keen to speak to Luke.

'I understand, sir, from your wife that you were here once before, not so long before I came to this living.'

'Indeed I was, sir, but under much less happy circumstances.'

47

When questioned on this, Luke was content to elaborate.

'Actually, I kept myself busy and away from most of the unseemly events by drawing.'

'Yes. So Martine said. It was I that asked her to entreat you to bring all the work you did of that time. Do you have them with you, perchance?'

'Yes, at my sister-in-law's request. I never throw anything away.'

'May I see them, perhaps tomorrow when all is quieter and we can avoid interruption.'

'By all means, sir.'

'You see the couple over there by the statue. That is my daughter Leah and her husband, Captain Whythorne. They are most anxious to meet you but at a time when all is quiet. They will explain to you the reasons for this request at that time.'

'I shall look forward to that occasion, sir,' said Luke.

Thus in the morning, Joseph Foorde came to Martine's house with Thomas Whythorne and Leah to be reintroduced.

'As promised, I have brought my son-in-law and daughter with me. By your favour, sir, Thomas would like to see your work. He is most interested in seeing the drawings you drew on your previous and unhappy visit.'

Luke took an instant liking to Thomas who shook his hand firmly and warmly. When asked he revealed all his work of previous years, which was so lifelike that the curate and Thomas recognised some of the locals instantly.

'You have a rare gift, Master Whythorne. You would prosper in London,' said Thomas.

'I am content enough as it is,' said Luke. 'You are looking through these as if there was something you wish to find. Can you tell me who or what it is? It might save a lot of time.'

'Nay. I thank thee but I wish to see if I can recognise someone without your help. You say these are the ones you drew when you were last here? Ah! There we are.' He held up the sketch of Jacob Robinson triumphantly. 'My aunt's brother-in-law. I beg you to tell me where you drew this. It is so very, very lifelike.'

'In the tavern after your aunt's misbegotten trial. Robinson was not aware of what I was doing as there were others concealing me.'

48

'I see he has a rare dimple on his chin you have captured. What is this shaded part on his neck?'

'He has a port wine stain there. It is in a place impossible to hide,' said Luke.

'Has he? Has he indeed?' Thomas emphasised the words the second time and the others were slightly puzzled at this remark. Even more so when he blurted out,

'Master Whythorne. Will you name your price for these drawings. I never thought I would have something so useful as this in my quest for justice for my aunt and uncle. If not, would you make copies and I will pay you handsomely? And what is this mark?'

Luke was bamboozled over by this barrage of questions.

'It is a scar. Perhaps the result of a fight.'

Thomas was beside himself with glee. 'Oh I hoped and prayed for a day such as this. What do you say, sir?'

'Well, I can surely leave them in your care until we next meet.'

'Nay, not at all. I must reimburse you.' Thomas left the room and brought down a sum of money about six times that he, Luke, normally would have received. He was insistent and Luke felt obliged to take it and they shook hands whilst Colette beamed with pleasure and pride in her husband.

Soon after the proceedings ended, it was not long before Joseph and his wife left followed by Thomas and Leah. A couple of days later, Luke and Colette prepared to go home. On the way, Colette spoke to Luke and quizzed him about what had happened. He told her the facts and of the sum of money. She was pleased yet both of them could not interpret the mind of Thomas who at that moment was with a very bewildered curate.

'I do not understand, my boy. What do you hope to gain by possession of these?'

'Justice, dear father. By the knowledge of these, I can smoke Robinson out and bring him to account.'

'But he has been gone these three years and nobody in England has any news of his whereabouts.'

'He has gone to the colonies, of that I am sure, and will be called by some other title. Over the years, I have made enquiries and offered a reward for information and have received some interesting leads.'

'Have you received any further news from the port here?'

'Nay, father. He would not risk leaving from here in Boston as it would be a matter of time before one of the sailors would divulge events. He will have gone from London and it was there a year ago that I set enquiries in motion. Firstly, I realised he must have gone across to King's Lynn before going south. It was there I put posters and received definite information that Robinson and Millsome had travelled that way. I received many letters but discounted many and even when I got to King's Lynn and questioned people, it was easy to find some leads. Don't forget, dear father, I was in the army and know how to get information.'

'Yes indeed,' said the rector grimly.

'Two sailors described them intimately as they were on board with them. They were in the Canaries for a considerable time and Millsome had been drinking and said too much. I might add that Millsome did not live to see the New World. You can draw your own conclusions to that.'

'Yes, truly,' said Joseph. 'But if you know all this, how come you have not informed authority of your suspicions.'

'Dear father, Robinson will have changed his name and altered his appearance by now. But with today's revelations I can locate him, especially as he has a port wine mark and a terrible scar. I shall have him.'

'But surely you will not go there yourself. You will go to the authorities.'

'Neither. I shall send two men of my own choosing who will do this for us.'

'Who will want to do such a thing? In any case, the cost will be enormous.'

'Now that the King is dead and his promiscuous and godless son has been banished, we may at last have a new England and we can hope there will be peace for a time. I shall ride to my former commanding officer and ask for two men who can be released. Perhaps two men who have had slight wounds and can use the voyage to recover. I shall ask Master Luke to produce many copies of these drawings and have them posted in every major town and settlement.'

'The men you send might not wish to return and you will be back to your beginning.'

'We shall pick men of honour who would have no such thought entering their heads. There are several who owe me much including their lives and would be willing to undertake the task. They could earn their living whilst they were there and ask for information in their free time. In that way, it will not be a costly venture.'

'Then if that is the case, you have planned matters well, dear son.'

7. Boston, Massachusetts
200 years later 1854

A ten-year-old boy full of life walked, or rather danced, into his father's library and gazed around at the multitude of books surrounding him. For a youngster of that age, it was like looking at the sky on a cold and frosty clear night when millions if not billions of twinkling stars looked down somewhat benevolently yet aloof and with an air of untouchable independence. His father was about to go up a ladder to replace an old book on the top shelf. It was obviously a singular item as it had been individually bound.

'What's in that book, pa? It looks very old.'

'Almost exactly 200 years, my son.'

'That's very old. Is that the oldest book we have?'

'By a long way, my son.'

'What is it about, father?'

'An autobiography. An account by someone in our family who lived all that time ago. And others of our ancestors after him.'

'I'd like to read about that. May I see it before you put it away?'

'No, you may not. You can see it in a few years, when I think you are ready.'

'When is that likely to be, father?'

'Perhaps about the time you are 21. I think it best then. Certainly not now.'

The boy was disappointed and puzzled but said nothing more out of politeness.

'What did you come in here for, anyway?'

'Mother would like to speak to you when you have a minute.'

The father descended the ladder. 'Another time, instead of asking questions, you should deliver the message immediately in case it is important. Then if it is not, THEN and only THEN should you ask any questions.'

'Yes, father. Sorry father.'

The father pulled the boy's hair rather roughly. 'No matter on this occasion. Just a word of advice. Off you go and do something useful,' he said sternly.

The boy obeyed and like all youngsters soon forgot about the old book. It was shelved into the subconscious for several years until one day at the age of 14, he went into see his father about his school report and as he waited and his eyes wandered, he saw the old book on the top shelf. Again, his father refused access to it. He was somewhat miffed and wondered why his request was refused.

There was no chance of finding out why as his father always locked the library after each visit. Even his mother had to ask for the key on the rare occasions she needed to go in on her own. The young boy's natural inquisitiveness was aroused to such an extent that it became an obsession and a somewhat unhealthy one at that. He could not resist a challenge and his father, by his blunt refusal, had automatically issued one.

He wondered how he could get into the library without being discovered and thus force the book to reveal its secrets. The best and safest time would be when his parents were away. That, however, was not often. Some thinking had to be done and a plan hatched. There was also the problem of being able to get to the top shelf. The ladder steps were not always in the library as on occasions they were employed elsewhere.

The opportunity came several months later when some repairs were needed to the rectory, especially the library ceiling and the floor. Knowing that the house would be noisy and dusty, the boy's father and mother took the opportunity to take a four-day break to New York on church business, beginning on a Thursday and returning on the following Monday. That left only he, his sister and the servants in the house.

His plan was simple; whilst the workmen were having a break and not looking, he would unobtrusively release the latch on the window and make sure it looked as though it was closed. Then, when all were asleep, he would creep down, enter by the window and capture his prey. Simple. The library was on the ground floor anyway. The only remaining problem was not to get too impatient while waiting for the others to retire.

On the Thursday evening, he returned from school and went into the kitchen to ask for a cool drink. As luck would have it, cook was about to take a tray into the library for the workmen. The boy asked if he could take it to them as he wanted to speak to one of the workmen.

Cook was mildly surprised but did not want to kick a gift horse in the mouth. Thus, the boy took in the tray and chatted to the affable workmen. Whilst they were drinking the lemonade and had their heads turned, he deftly unlatched the window whilst pretending to look at the view outside. He then took his leave of the workmen who were totally unaware of what had taken place.

Later that evening, he lay on his bed and waited and waited. His heart began to race a little. At last, the hall clock struck midnight and the chimes gradually faded. Then, to avoid the well-known creaks, he descended the stairs stealthily and made his way to the back door. The old dog wagged her tail when she saw him but made no sound. He stroked her head and she immediately curled up again. He knew where the spare key resided for this was kept handily so he was out of doors and around to the library in no time at all.

He adjusted the bag around his neck and tried to open the window. It resisted and he immediately thought that somebody had noticed the latch and replaced it. His heart beat faster as he delved into his bag and extricated the chisel he had brought. He eased it under the window and it opened effortlessly. Within ten seconds, he had climbed in. So far so good.

He took a candle out of the bag and lit it carefully and then wedged it in its base. There must be no evidence of his presence. Once his eyes got accustomed to the light, he was ready for action. His heart sank when he thought the workmen's ladder was missing but soon his eyes adjusted to the change of light and he was able to pick it out. It was rather heavy but he dragged it across the floor, placed it in position and ascended gingerly.

Carefully, he inched out the 200-year-old book and slowly descended. As he was an intelligent boy, he realised that perusal of the book there and then was completely out of the question. There were too many risks. Firstly, the longer he was in the library, there was a greater risk of being discovered and secondly, leaving a trail of candle wax would possibly give the game away.

Thirdly, the book was the size of a volume and would be impossible for him to assimilate its contents in one dark candlelit night. He crept to the window and blew out the flame. It was an agonising wait while the wax cooled and solidified but once done, he wrapped it in the paper bag he had brought and put it in a separate pocket of the shopping bag.

Carefully, he lowered the bag on to the grass outside the window and then climbed out. Although he was itching to see what was in the book, he hid it in the corner of his bedroom, put out the lamp and got back into bed. One of the servants had to awaken him in the morning and he was only just in time for school. He had a cursory look at the book on Friday evening but had to attend a church function and thus it was Saturday before he could start reading in earnest. He locked his door and nervously opened it. The first words made him sit bolt upright.

This account is written in the year of our Lord 1652:

My colleagues, friends and enemies alike call me Jack Robson but that is not the name given to me at my baptism. My real name is Jacob Robinson and I was born not far from Boston in the county of Lincoln, England, about 1593, which means I have been on this earth for 59 years. I have had a long and varied career during which it can be said on occasions that I have been kind and useful to others. I can be generous, tender and sympathetic but the vast amount of my life has been spent thinking only of myself and the exploitation of others. That includes my family and friends in England.

I am a cheat, a liar and a thief and worst of all, a murderer. I was responsible for the death of my brother and most likely my sister-in-law. It was she who cursed me before she was swept away into the Wash on the occasion of her illegal and unjust trial. I have written the words she spoke at the end of this confession. I only escaped capture in England by my own ingenuity and the help of paid minions in Boston, England.

When I came to the New World, I sought privacy and solitude and thus made my way to Salem. My worst sins were committed there in that I distributed the infamous, cruel and utterly deplorable Matthew Hopkins' literature, which must have caused the deaths of many unfortunate and innocent people whilst making money for myself. I murdered my servant on the voyage here to ensure his silence and covered my sin with the help of the ship's captain.

I did not expect to marry but did so in the late afternoon of my days to a sweet, charming and God-fearing lady, younger than me by some 25 years, whose love and conjugal affection I did not deserve. She reformed me but lately has not been spared the details of my sordid and ignominious past and will forever be aware of those terrible deeds whilst she lives. By the time that I am writing this confession, my son is nearly 3 years old and who, I hope, will not be in any shape or form like me.

His life will be turned upside down as a result of these revelations. Soon he will be shocked and dismayed and endure agony beyond normal limits of pain on learning the facts of his father's disreputable existence. I have given my wife my estate and she intends to seek refuge in Boston where she can shake off the results of my life and start afresh. I have not asked my priest for forgiveness as my sin is too great. I expect he would have refused to grant me this anyway. I am ailing rapidly and at some point, I soon expect to experience the flames of hell fire, which is exactly what I deserve.

My discovery has been brought about by two soldiers from England and who have been sponsored by my sister-in-law's nephew. An acquaintance of his who is a master artist had drawn a likeness of me and this had been printed and distributed far and wide. Alas for me, it was only a short while before I was discovered and thus I languish here awaiting my end, which will surely be soon.

The boy read on and on reading a particularly lurid passage and heard himself gasp as he sat bolt upright. He remained so deep in thought that he missed the gong for lunch. He only came out of his stupor when he became aware someone was knocking determinedly on his door. He concealed the book and went to see who it was. It was the head servant who asked him if he was ill but he denied this and declared that he would be down forthwith.

Even so, he ate very little and soon returned to his den. He was sweating profusely by the time he got to the end of the dossier and realised two things. Firstly, he realised the writer was his ancestor and secondly, there was no way that he could remember so many facts and dates. He therefore put pen to paper and was working when the gong went for dinner. The others were surprised that he had not appeared to play outside during a sunny afternoon.

Moreover, he was unusually quiet and answered in monosyllables. He ate more this time, which pleased cook as the thought of possible blame for the young man's lethargy and listlessness might be foisted on her. His reading and copying went on until after midnight and at that point, exhausted, he sat on the bed and put his head back on the propped up pillow.

The next thing he knew was the loud knocking on the door and the head servant demanding to know where he was. He opened up and relief showed on the servant's face when he saw the boy was dressed and ready to face the day. He had some breakfast and then asked to be excused church. He looked so ashen that there was no objection at all to this request. Whilst all were at church, he found he had completed all the salient matter he wanted to copy and decided to stretch his legs. It was then that he had a real slice of luck. He went down to the library and tried the door, which opened immediately. The workmen had somehow forgotten to lock it when they left on Saturday lunchtime.

His heart leapt for joy and he made the decision to replace the dossier at once rather than wait for nightfall and creep through the window again. The replacement was done in the nick of time as the staff and his sister returned. He turned to the head servant and whispered to him about the unlocked door who in return thanked him profusely. Cook breathed a sigh of relief when the boy demolished his Sunday lunch with effortless ease.

That relief bore no comparison to that of the boy when, instead of returning the next day, Monday, his parents arrived home nearly twelve hours early. If he had left it later, his exploit would have been discovered and he would have earned a savage beating. No mention was made of anything out of the ordinary, especially missing church.

Over the next few months, he read and reread all he had copied. He marvelled at all the information and each time gleaned and understood the contents more and more. It was chilling to read about the family curse and to realise he was included in that. Even more sobering was the fact that a male member of the family in every other generation had come to grief in one way or another. That was a heavy burden to bear.

Two years later, he had an altercation with his exceedingly competitive younger sister who was ever anxious to be superior to her friends and brother in every respect. Unable to restrain himself and in order to impress and put one over on his sister who, for the last ten minutes had been bragging and humiliating him, he made a great mistake in that he told her about his escapade of entering the library undetected.

At first she was impressed but afterwards extremely jealous in that he had managed to achieve a major triumph that would have been beyond her. In spite of a solemn promise not to divulge any of the details of his escapade, she did so on the occasion when the two of them had another big difference of opinion and massive argument, which included a fight. He caused her to cry and of course, she went weeping to her daddy and spilled the beans.

Inevitably, the boy had to admit to his subterfuge and after doing so awaited his fate. In spite of his father being a man of the cloth, he was beaten unmercifully whilst his sister looked on with a triumphant look on her face and his mother watched with horror at her husband's horrific cruelty that was out of all proportion to the crime. One thing the boy did not mention was that whilst the book was in his brief possession, he had taken copious notes.

Nobody knew about these as they were safely stored away. He never revealed secrets to anyone again including business associates and even the closest friends, let alone his sister. A result of his injuries, he was hospitalised and some searching questions were put to his father, the rector. A few months after the beating, it so happened that brother and sister were alone and he confronted her.

'Well, my once beloved sister. Are you happy now you have had your revenge? Do you have a deep feeling of satisfaction that my buttocks, back and spine are scarred for life? I have been told I will never be able to run properly.'

'It serves you right for being unkind to me,' said his sister, pouting her lips in defiance.

'I see. It seems as though you have no regrets that my punishment was so severe.'

'None whatsoever.'

'Then remember that from now onwards, I do not consider I have a sister anymore.'

'I can tell you I'll lose no sleep over that. I've never loved you in any shape or form.'

When he became successful in business, his impecunious and wayward sister fell from grace in a spectacular downward spiral and was deserted by all of her fleeting and fickle friends. She repeatedly asked for his help but was always politely refused. When asking his reasons, he simply pointed out that he felt there were more deserving causes.

'Even more than your own sister?'

'I have had no sister for many years and told you this long ago,' he said. 'Our family has a history of violence that can be read in the book I borrowed. I have renounced violence but you have not. You condoned our father's actions, which have left me scarred for life. You beat your own children sometimes mercilessly. For all I know, you may be tainted by the curse in our ancestor's diary. Over the years we have spoken of your betrayal of me but there has been no regret from you or any remorse.'

'What was I supposed to do? Go on my knees and beg for forgiveness? What do you want me to do? Crawl?'

'Not at all. Except you could go on your knees and ask forgiveness from the God that you once gave allegiance and whom you abandoned a long time ago.'

8. Boston, Massachusetts
Some Years Later

George C. Robinson as a young child had come to live in Boston in the 1870s. In 1892, he inherited several small bakeries from his father who, at the age of 48, had been forced to retire through illness. The businesses were in central Boston and flourished and grew in no time, enabling them to expand further into the city and beyond whilst becoming a household name. George's father, Frank, had opened a huge bakery in the northwest end of Boston in the area known as Lexbridge next to his house, which became the focal point of the conglomerate he called *Frankfare*.

It was situated in the grounds and beyond of a former rectory set back from his neighbours and was somewhat cut off but the grounds and lake were landscaped and developed with the utmost refinement and taste. Within ten years, their business spread as far as Waltham and Somerville and could be classed as an empire, although both father and son did not like to be wearing the label of business tycoons.

George was frugal in many ways, which extended to his wife and later his children. His wife had to conceal her own assets and income wherever possible to prevent them from being appropriated by her husband. Although careful in monetary matters, George was an avid poker player who, placid most of the time, had an uncontrollable temper on occasions, which left people utterly bewildered but he himself unashamed.

"Gambling George" as he was known in some quarters won much more than he lost; he was very careful as to the joints he frequented and those who ran them were very discreet in protecting the names of their patrons. He was strong but somewhat squat and rotund in appearance, which enabled him to be a figure of ridicule to his enemies. On each occasion this happened, he would make a careful note of the date and time in his little black book.

Martha, George's wife, came from a family whose rise was quite remarkable. She did not have to push herself to any academic heights at all and was only really good at one thing; the thing that she enjoyed most of all. Music. She was a very good accompanist and was often in demand in the locality. Initially, she had several admirers and was very undecided which offer to take.

She started walking out with George but stopped after he had the first of many a violent argument with her. Enter the tall, lean Mark Williston who had come from a village near Boston, Lincolnshire, a few years before and had done quite well for himself.

Martha's parents were adamant that she could do better and made it difficult for Mark to make progress and press his suit. When Frank fell ill, George was very much preoccupied and there was a vacuum Mark did his best to fill. There was further opposition from parents so after some tearful scenes, the two eloped but were brought back kicking and screaming. A few months later, George regained the initiative and proposed to Martha who somewhat reluctantly accepted.

Martha had been brought up a Protestant and their wedding was in Trinity church in uptown Boston. George's parents were Quakers or members of the Society of Friends as they prefer to be called but they approved of the match and allowed it to develop whilst keeping a watchful eye. When George restarted walking out with Martha, it was not long before she encouraged him to attend her church.

This turned out to be a revelation because, being musical, he naturally enjoyed the hymns, the choir and the non-liturgical activities, something of which he had hitherto been denied. His violin practice that had been somewhat sporadic took on new meaning as his wife encouraged a high standard when she accompanied him on the pianoforte. Marriage made them both settle down and gradually, albeit painfully, gain maturity.

With the business in full swing, at the age of twenty, George had a lot of responsibility thrust upon him. He found himself in the management as a matter of course. His family expected no less of him and he had never had any inkling of what really existed beyond their immediate surroundings, the factory, the estate and his gambling joints. They had been married four years when George appeared in the drawing room after a tiring day. Martha was playing some new music. She stopped when he entered and awaited his embrace.

'Fancy something to eat?' she said. 'Shall I ring for Cook?'

'In a minute. Play me something.' He helped himself to a brandy and sat down.

'Anything in particular?'

'Something soothing and tender.'

Martha obliged. At the end, George said, 'What's that? That's rather nice. Who is it by?'

'By one of ours. In fact, he lives here in Boston. Name of Edward MacDowell. Mr Gossage, the church organist, gave it to me to try before publication. He's a friend of his.'

'How come I have not heard of him before?'

'Don't know. It's called *To a Wild Rose* and it's in a set called *Woodland Sketches*.'

'Play me another one.' She went to the piano and played for him *To a Water Lily*.

'Nice. Another one, please. Have you anything else of his?'

She did not answer the question but said, 'Before I do, there is some news. Dvorak is going home.'

The Czech composer Antonin Dvorak had been engaged to teach at the National Conservatory of Music and to compose and conduct as well. He had been in the city for nearly three years with his family alongside him but there had been rumours that he was feeling very homesick.

'Really?' said George. He paused. 'What a pity. I was hoping that we could to go to New York and hear and see him again. Everyone seems to have heard *From the New World*, except us. Why is he going now? What about his contract?'

'As I understand it, his sponsors, that is Jeanette Thurber and that crowd, have had some severe financial problems after the economic crisis of eighteen months ago. His salary was not always paid. We've been lucky in our sort of business, George.'

That was something George did not like to hear and was like a red rag to a bull.

'There is no luck about it, Martha,' he said with a touch of venom. 'It is all about planning and good housekeeping plus a lot of damned hard work. And, let's face it. People have got to eat. And that comes first. Music comes after you have had enough to eat.'

'Yes dear. I did not mean to touch a raw nerve,' said Martha, doing her best to look contrite but not feeling the least bit of remorse. George continued by saying:

'I also understood that Dvorak had to be fetched from Central station on occasions when he should have been teaching as he is obsessed with trains and locomotives. Somebody told me that a student came for a lesson and the first thing Dvorak wanted to know was what locomotive had brought them in. Poor girl had not a clue. Dvorak was quite peeved and that upset her. Not surprised he did not get all his salary.'

George paused for thought for a moment. 'Find out what's on in New York and let us see if we can get down there for a few days. I need a break from my routine and so do you, I guess.'

Martha beamed with delight. 'Oh George, that sounds really wonderful. I shall have to go into town and get a new hat.'

George prickled. 'No, you damn well don't. You have got loads of goddamn hats. If you wore one a week on Sunday mornings from now on it would take about eighteen months to get through the goddamn lot of them.'

'O George, really—'

He interrupted her, 'Do you think I am made of money? Isn't it enough that I am taking you away for a week? You do not need another goddamn hat.'

'Yes dear, but you are made of money. You are rolling in it.'

'Don't be rude. Come on. I'll have that bite to eat and then we will make some plans,' he said congenially.

Thus in early February, they duly caught the train to New York and thoroughly enjoyed their stay, which included the music, the hotel and the excursions. There had been gossip and speculation amongst family, friends and staff as to why after all this time Martha had not produced an heir; both sets of parents had kept their thoughts under wraps knowing if George heard them even whisper on that subject, he would explode into an apoplectic fury.

Any conjecture of George's possible impotence came to a sudden halt in May of that year, 1895, when Martha came back from the doctor's with a look of contentment on her face. She did not know how to tell him of her condition and she thought long and hard as to when the most auspicious occasion might be. An opportunity presented itself almost a week later when George came home from the bakery. He shook his raincoat in the hall and felt thankful that, unlike many, he did not have to go far to his place of employment. The cook was having a rare day off and had gone to visit some of her friends in the city. Martha enjoyed the relatively few occasions when she could display her limited culinary skills. Since they had become rich and had servants to do many tasks, she felt sometimes as if part of her life had been commandeered.

'Something smells really good. What have you got in the oven?' said George. Martha paused; then said, 'A bunny.'

'A bunny? Smells more like lamb. When have we ever eaten rabbit? Come on, what is it? Are you going to keep me in perpetual suspense?'

'Like I said, a bunny. In any case, to which oven are you referring?'

He paused. 'I don't get it. Have we got two ovens? Why are you being evasive? Is it guessing game night?'

'I am not really being evasive. There is a bunny in my oven and you put it there,' said a smiling Martha.

He waited. 'Say that again.' Martha did so.

He looked at her incredulously and then the light dawned.

'You don't mean…'

'Yes, I do,' she said.

He jumped up and seized her, gave out a loud whoop. He then whirled her and overbalanced but luckily, they both ended up on the sofa. This was a temporal location for George as he let go of her and finished up on the beautiful and expensive Persian carpet.

'You little beauty, you little beauty.'

'Steady, steady. Behave yourself,' said his somewhat flustered wife.

'I am, I mean I will, I will, O this is wonderful!' His kissed her again and again. 'Wonder why it happened now,' he said. 'How long have you known? Perhaps it was that visit to New York that did it. What a good idea of mine that was. All because of Dvorak leaving, bless him. We will put that to the test again if need be.'

'Steady on, George. One thing at a time; one at a time.'

'You mean one baby at a time, dear.'

The pregnancy was in no way difficult and there was the birth in early November 1895 of a healthy baby girl with blue eyes and a lovely smile who was duly baptised as Emma Georgia. All the house staff received a small present and a bonus, which led the gardener to express the hope that a further addition would follow soon. There was little celebration in the bakery where the hard-pressed staff viewed the birth with indifference.

9. Repeat Performance

It was in February 1897 that George suddenly found he had to go to New York on business to check on a bakery they had opened there. Martha asked if he would be away any length of time.

'Four, five days at the most,' he said.

'In that case, may I come too? We have not been away together for some time.'

'Of course,' he said. 'I've been thinking about that. We ought to buy a place a few miles somewhere up north where we can be a family; somewhere remote and quiet and by a lake where we can get to easily and quickly. I fancy learning how to fish. I love my violin but you can't relax when you are playing, particularly this latest Amy Beach *Gaelic symphony* that we are learning. She should write a New England symphony.'

'New York sounds truly wonderful. Never mind that now. When do we go?'

'The day after tomorrow. Send the new man, Marcus, in and he can book the trains. And don't you dare say you want a new goddamn hat or I shall go on my own.'

Martha laughed and went to fetch his meal.

Early the following week, they left for New York and enjoyed the journey as it was a sunny day. It took about half an hour to get to the hotel so chaotic was the traffic. They were shown to their rooms and had a short nap and then got changed. After dinner, they had time to get down to the concert hall and hear a delightful programme.

The following morning George went off to his meeting, which he said was going to be a long but he would be back early afternoon. At 5.30 pm, he had not returned and Martha was feeling miffed. By 7.00 pm, he had still not made an appearance and Martha was by then feeling utterly alone and unwanted. George telephoned the hotel to ask them pass on a message to say that the meeting was still in progress. George was lying.

At 3.00 am, Martha awoke to find he had still not returned and his share of the bed empty. The fact was that in the conference hotel basement tucked away from prying eyes a poker game was being played and George was winning and winning hand over fist. He had, for the time being, expunged all thoughts of Martha from his head. It was typical of his ruthless single-mindedness.

The opponents opposite were rich and reckless and George, who had remained sober and alert, had fleeced them one by one. The second fact was that he just could not stop. He knew that he should really be somewhere else but he could not tear himself away. The money just kept rolling in as the smoke in the basement got thicker and thicker.

At 4.30 am, the others called it a day and George collected all his winnings. He had difficulty in stuffing all the notes in his pocket. He went up to the foyer and waited for the lift back to his hotel but his friend forgot about him. George then fell asleep in a corner and nobody had the temerity to wake him. It was 10.00 am before he surfaced and in the clear light of day realised what a fool he had been.

He hailed a taxi but it took nearly half an hour to get to his out of town hotel. At that same time, a furious and inconsolable Martha was on her way in the opposite direction to the station to catch the morning train back to Boston. She had not booked out of the hotel so George wasted time looking for her. He spent time in the restaurant, on the sun lounge and in the swimming pool before he went back to their room and looked in the wardrobe. It was, of course, empty.

He dashed downstairs to the foyer entrance and asked questions that seemed to indicate his wife had gone off somewhere in a cab and with a case. By the time he got to the station, the mid-morning train to Boston had just left. He went dejectedly back to his hotel and prepared to go to his next meeting at 4.00 pm.

It was only supposed to last two hours and then he and Martha were going out for dinner. However, it went on until 10.00 pm and George returned to his hotel absolutely shattered and feeling more the effects of the previous night. He collapsed into bed and prepared to take the flak the next day, at the same time realising he did not dare telephone home.

When Martha got on the train in the first-class coach, she was alone. She started weeping quietly until someone entered to share the compartment. They did not recognise each other for a few moments. Then a voice with an English accent said: 'Why, by all that's holy, it's the incomparable Martha,' said the voice.

She looked up to see Mark Williston, her servant Marcus's cousin, the man on whom she had once set her heart. He was smiling but soon stopped when he saw the state of distress she was in.

'Lord above, Martha, whatever is the matter? Here. Sit with me a moment… Now then let's have it. Spill it all to Mark.'

It did not take long for Martha to pour out her heart and tell him everything. He put his arm around her protectively. She wept a little more even after more people joined the compartment but by the time they reached Boston, she had recovered somewhat. The other passengers were very discreet and pretended not to notice. They left the compartment first and then Mark said: 'I'll take you home.'

'Please not yet, Mark. There will be so many questions at home. I would sooner creep in after dark when everyone is asleep.'

'If that's what you want then we'll go to my place for a little while. Forward to my bachelor pad.'

They hailed a cab and reached Mark's flat in Lexbridge about forty minutes later. He made some coffee while Martha put her head back and tried to make sense of it all.

'Poached eggs any good?'

'Just fine,' said Martha beginning to feel a little bit more like herself.

They ate and talked endlessly. After a pause Martha then asked the obvious question and one she had been burning to ask from the moment she walked in the flat.

'Why have you not yet married? I am sure you had plenty of chances.'

'The girl I loved married somebody else and you know full well who that is.'

Martha dropped her head, feeling a little guilty.

'Nobody on the go? Nobody to walk in at any moment?'

'Nobody.'

Martha looked glum and kicked off her shoes and sat on the sofa. As a result of her ordeal, half an hour later she was fast asleep. He covered her over gently with a blanket and took to his own bed and read for a while. At 11.00 pm, when she was still asleep, he got ready for bed, got in the sheets and was soon asleep.

He had no intention of sleeping on the sofa and being tired next day thus ruining his well-earned holiday.

At 2.00 am, he was completely taken by surprise when she got into his bed completely naked. She pulled him to her. He was unable to resist her and spent the next hour in the blissful state that he had once hoped would be a regular event in his life. For an all too short period, it was as the time when they had eloped. She held him so tightly that he felt he might burst.

He woke early and was loathe to disturb her and all the while he waited for her to surface, he was unable to curb a real anger and contempt for his rival who had not won her fairly in his eyes; he and Martha had both been the victim of other forces who should have minded their own business and let them make decisions for themselves. When Mark made no attempt to get up, she opened bleary but blissful eyes.

'What time is it?'

'Eight o'clock.'

'Why have you not gone to work?'

'I am on holiday or vacation as you call it and that's why I was in New York.'

'Not on business, then?'

'Not at all. I just felt like a change. I am working for the Pope manufacturing company testing cars but they owed me some time off.'

'I see,' she said then added, 'I just do not know how this has happened,' she said. 'I had better waste no time in getting home.'

She dressed, gathered her things together then kissed him hurriedly as she left.

'Forgive me. I am so sorry,' she said.

'I'm not,' was the reply. 'It was the thing I once wanted more than anything. Still do for that matter.'

Martha did not make any attempt to answer that but asked him to call a cab rather than he take her home in the car he was testing. They said goodbye briefly and she left hurriedly and untidily. She got back home at lunch time just before the workers had their break. Sarah the new cook was first to greet her and her face dropped.

'Why, Mrs Robinson, you're back. What has happened? Where is Mr Robinson?'

'Still in New York. I have had to come back alone.'

'Are you unwell, ma'am? You look very pale. Shall I call the doctor?'

'I am unwell but no need to call the doctor. Just the usual female problem.'

With that, Sarah decided that further questions were inappropriate apart from asking whether Martha wanted feeding.

'Try me about 5 o'clock. I will have a couple of hot water bottles.'

'Very good, ma'am.'

Martha, thinking it best to remain in her room as she was performing a faking act, put on her nightie and awaited George's arrival. She was fearful and started to shake. He had managed to cut short his final meeting and had caught the last train arriving at about 11.00 pm.

He was home in half an hour and was told of his wife's condition. He rushed upstairs trying look innocent but all the while harbouring a real dread. As they were both guilty in one way or another, all possible belligerence or recriminations resulted in being cancelled out but, of course, they each respectively were unaware why this was so. Both parties adopted a policy of feigned innocence coupled with propitiation and desire for equanimity and reconciliation.

'Martha, what has happened? I have been out of my mind.'

'I don't know, darling; I have been feeling so ill. When you were still in your meeting, I felt I just had to get home and see the doctor.'

'Of course, dear,' said George, suddenly seeing an escape route in the offing.

'But why did you not leave me a note?'

'I told them at the desk,' Martha lied.

'They said you just walked out.'

'I don't know precisely what I did, George. I did not know what I was doing. Please don't crowd me.'

'What did doc Jones say?'

Martha then had to think quickly. 'I did not call him.'

'Why the hell not?'

'The pain almost went as soon as I got home. It must have been the air in New York. I am on the mend. George, do we still have to go on with this?'

'O darling, I am sorry, so sorry. Look, get some rest and we will talk in the morning.' He soothed her for a while and stroked her hair whilst she closed her eyes. At the moment, he felt it was the right moment to play his ace. He had one card that could not fail and so he took out his winnings and threw them on the bed. The pile of notes was prodigious.

'Look dear. Whilst I was waiting for the meeting to begin, I had a little flutter in the casino last night and was very lucky. There should be enough money for the retreat that you wanted. It's yours. All yours. See the real estate people and get something nice. Something by a lake. Take your time about it.'

Martha experienced a mixture of relief and elation. He had not ever given her anything like this before. It was a huge sum with large value notes.

'Oh George. How wonderful. I will look for a place as soon as I feel better.'

Martha stayed in her room for almost two days, wishing to see Emma but deciding to continue the act a little longer so that it looked genuine. All the while she was hating herself for her brief liaison with Mark and wondering how it had all happened and yet at the same time she knew that she enjoyed his love and tenderness. She decided to say nothing and hope that she could forget the incident and regain the status of being a good mother and wife.

She gradually shed the charade of illness and began to appear quite normal. However, there was one nagging thought in her mind. Would Mark reveal anything about their night of passion? He was not the kind of person to resort to blackmail or threats but even so she had to see him to make sure of his feelings and more important his intentions.

A few days later, there was a New England Women's Club meeting in Huntington Avenue and with George away for two nights, it was the ideal time to confront him on the issue. Martha ordered a cab and was duly taken to Park Street headquarters. She made sure of bumping into a few acquaintances and stayed for the first half of the evening's talk. While everyone was milling around drinking tea and coffee at the interval, she slipped out unnoticed and hailed a cab. About 200 yards before Mark's flat, she stopped the cab and paid the driver who made an about turn to retrace his steps.

Martha hoped that Mark was at home. It was dark and fortunately nobody was about. Gingerly she tapped on his door. To her relief she heard the sound of footsteps. She suddenly thought she might have made a big mistake as he could have easily been entertaining. The door opened to reveal an untidily dressed Mark was too flabbergasted to say a word so she pushed past him.

'Well, I must say you are a lady of surprises,' was all he said as he shut the door.

'I am sorry, I just had to see you.'

'What for? I thought it was all over between us.'

'It is and it isn't. I'm so worried that George might find out about what happened.'

'Well, he easily might if you keep coming here.'

'I just had to make sure you will not say anything.'

At this point, Mark suddenly turned angry, which was a rare event for him.

'Listen to me, Martha. I loved you once and still do. It was only your parents who came between us. George had money and I had little and they forced matters their way. It wasn't your fault; I don't attach any blame to you. The thought of revenge is repugnant to me. How you could entertain the idea of my betraying your trust beggars belief.'

'I am so sorry. I should not have come.'

'That is the understatement of the month.'

'I still love you, you know.'

'Do you now? You have a strange way of showing it.' His voice softened as he spoke. They looked at each other for a full two minutes.

'Is there anything I can get you?' he said. 'Anything? I have some wine opened.'

'Fine.'

They drank the wine and the heat of the room relaxed them. They sat on the settee and before long were kissing. They were incapable of any resistance and were soon entwined. She took off his shirt and then her own blouse. She led him to the bedroom where they gratified each other yet again. An hour later, he spoke.

'Will we be able to sneak you back without anybody knowing? I have the car handy. I am testing it for the company.'

'If you drop me at or near the gate, I will ring through. The gate-man will probably be tucked away in his hut. He won't say anything as there is nothing for him to say.'

'Good. Let's do that then.'

And so a chapter in Martha's life came to a close. She hoped that she could forget the incidents with Mark and regain the status of being a good mother and wife, later realising that is was at that moment she had at last begun to cast off the last vestiges of youth and embrace adulthood and responsibility. She busied herself around the house and spent a lot of time with her daughter who was now learning to walk. George returned to find a smiling Martha and they began conjugal relations soon afterwards.

The business was widening and prospering so when Martha found a place of retreat for them all George was able to add the small difference of his winnings to that of the required price without the slightest undulation on his bank account. He tempered his gambling for a while and was careful not to broach any subject with his wife that might be contentious. It was in the summer of that year that history repeated itself and Martha announced she was pregnant.

George was overjoyed and his mood was infectious for a while on all those with whom he dealt. The summer turned to autumn and on November 6th Martha gave birth to a healthy blue-eyed boy of seven and a half pounds. Stephen George Robinson grew up in wealthy surroundings but strictness, discipline and an unusual amount of frugality were the order of the day for both children and often Martha for that matter.

True, the grand piano in the drawing room cost several thousand dollars. Later, the instruments he bought for his children were not much inferior in quality and expense from those players in the Boston Symphony orchestra. On those sort of things, George was not averse to extravagance but in most people's eyes George was a Jekyll and Hyde personality, a tag he fully deserved.

Sarah Williston, the cook, Marcus's wife, had produced a beautiful baby girl about a year before the birth of Stephen and soon after, following a disastrous fire in their home, they and the two elder twin boys, Robert and Charles, had left England for the New World. Rachael and Stephen grew up and played together irrespective of the fact one was the son of the boss and the other a servant's daughter.

The massive bakery was adjacent to the house with only a minute's walking time away but the children were not allowed to go anywhere near there except by special permission. On the far side were some terrace houses that were the homes for some of the staff. They were well built and had running water as well as flushing toilets. On the other side was countryside and a lake marking the boundary of *Frankfare* territory. All the children were taught to swim at an early age but were only allowed in boats with an adult and a life jacket.

Emma and Stephen went to the same local school in Lexbridge as all the children of the staff. Martha did not want them to go to boarding school and

George certainly did not want to pay what he considered exorbitant fees. More important was the fact that he wanted the *Frankfare* business to be instilled in his children and for them to be out of range of any liberal and revolutionary ideas that might baulk his designs for his offspring.

He hoped for some more sons but Martha bore him no more. At school there were times when Stephen was singled out by jealous children who lacked his material blessings and inflicted physical violence. Enter Sarah's son, Bobby Williston, twin brother of Charles who, of course, was somewhat older than Stephen and whose physical superiority was used to good effect. From that point onwards, nobody dared lay a finger on Stephen. As the two got older their age gap was barely noticeable and got to a point where the pair became inseparable and their relationship akin to that of Jonathan and David.

The years passed and *Frankfare* prospered and expanded. Staff were carefully vetted and had to produce evidence of good background and repute. A condition was that all office staff could read and write but in some places this was a problem. George's response to this was to set up evening classes for those who had difficulties. He had read well and modelled the set up in England. Oxford University had introduced their evening extension classes and He did not want to be outdone and see his country fall behind.

A more important factor was that he could keep tabs on those who deserved promotion and could be sent to a satellite bakery. Naturally everyone had to contribute towards the costs and there were fines for those who failed to attain a 90% attendance. When these extension lectures, as they were called, were extended to women, there were a few eyebrows raised especially in the affluent district of Boston's elite.

However, up to now, George never mixed with them a great deal socially if he could help it and was considered to be a maverick. He did not care; he was amongst the most successful men in a very wide area and the fact that people criticised him for not being over gregarious was like water off a duck's back. All that was to change a few years later.

George became a regular and a generous patron of his local church and the fact that the bands and orchestra flourished in the district was due entirely to him and two other business leaders. He rarely missed orchestra practice on Tuesday evenings and would be picked up by one of his friends at the front door. People said they could check their timepieces to this event. The practice hall was only a mile away from home and not in the city centre.

When the rent in downtown Boston caused the orchestra finances to wobble, George and friends merely bought the abandoned Methodist community hall and had it refurbished and smartened. The acoustics were superb and this was why not just practices were held there but most of the concerts as well. All proceeds were initially ploughed back into the hall maintenance and development. In the beginning it could accommodate about 400 people but later George and his fellow tycoons had an upstairs renovated increasing the capacity to 775.

In this way, George and his friends shrewdly turned their capital outlay into profit for themselves. When the children had grown up enough to be left in the care of nanny then Martha re-joined him at orchestra practice. On Sundays, they made every effort to be at church then have the rest of the day together as a family with work being side-lined.

10. Ten Years Later

The years rolled pleasantly by and with only minor family problems. As far as the business was concerned, there were only three things to report. Profit, profit and profit. The Robinson empire grew and grew mainly because there was little or no serious competition. When work got on top of him and he needed a rest, George would suddenly announce to Martha that they would go for a weekend at the Retreat. The children initially went with them but after a few years, the parents invariably went alone and left them in the care of Marcus and Sarah.

Stephen did not mind in the least as it meant time with Bobby Williston, which he enjoyed enormously. Occasionally, Charlie was with them but very often it would be just the two of them. The age gap between them soon became hardly noticeable. A new era that was to affect them all, however, was about to begin.

In the spring of 1908, George arrived home holding a periodical from England. He sat down without hardly a word and even forgot about having his favourite evening drink. In fact, he was so absorbed in it for such a long time that Martha was wont to ask him why he was in this self-spun cocoon that was resulting in the rest of the family's exclusion.

'Tell you later when I have got to grips with it.'

'How long will that be?'

'Not long,' he said irritably.

Not long, however, took three days and even the children noticed something different in their father as there was no pillow fighting in the evening, no paper darts or playing cards. Finally, Martha plucked up courage.

'Are you going to say what's taken you away from us or will the suspense continue?'

George grunted a poor apology.

'Is it good or bad news?'

75

'Well, it all depends.'

'Depends on what?'

'Depends on whether you are coming or not.'

'For goodness sake, George will—'

'The news is,' interrupted George, 'the news IS that we are going to England.'

Martha gasped slightly. 'What…what has brought this on?'

George ignored the question. 'We leave next month, if possible, and if there's a sailing.'

'When you say we, do you mean you and one or two of the staff or what?'

'I mean the four of us.'

'The four of us? You, me and the kids? What about their schooling? Is it for pleasure?'

'Some. Just a bit of business first. Not more than a couple of days of business, which will be at the beginning of the holiday. You see, my dear, I have been reading about a firm in England that makes chocolate products and the like. Run by a family called *Cadbury*. They are well regarded and seem to keep their staff happy and moreover have a relatively small staff turnover compared to other industries producing food. I want to know how they do it as well as their sources of chocolate and so on. I've sent a wire to the firm explaining who we are and what we do and have asked for an invitation to visit. Should get a reply by the end of this week. Never mind the kids' schooling. They will learn more on the trip than they can in books. Well. Are you game?'

Martha was lost for words. George jumped in before she could speak.

'One condition, dear.'

'Which is?'

'Don't say you've got to get a new goddamn hat. I'll give you an extra allowance to set yourself up; I want you to look the queen you are but I don't want to hear you say that you need a goddamn hat or I'll scream.'

Six weeks later, the four Robinsons were driven into Boston to catch the train for New York. They had been lucky to book a passage but had done so because of a cancellation. It was not just the children who were excited as their parents felt a sense of adventure. They stayed overnight in a hotel and in the morning were taken to the Cunard pier 54, which looked like an impressive railway station shed.

The children stood in awe whilst all around there was bustling activity. The porters that were assigned to them took their luggage and they walked to the gangplank where there embarkation tickets were checked. There was a minimum amount of fuss and bother; whilst the children looked at their cabin and its luxurious surroundings, George tipped the baggage men and then poured himself a stiff drink. He then announced that he was going to rest but told them there would be trouble if they failed to wake him before departure in the event of his falling asleep.

A few hours later, they set sail from New York bound for Liverpool. They could have gone from Boston but George wanted to do some quick business in New York before their departure and also wanted to be one of the first to sail on the new ship *Lusitania*, which was the ultimate in luxury. The children were so excited about the trip that it was difficult to contain them. They had not been told about it immediately but after a while, concealment was impossible. An added bonus for them was that they were missing school, or so they thought.

Their faces dropped when they were informed that they would be having tuition aboard ship and that whilst their parents were busy at Bournville, they would be doing several hours of English and Math every day.

This information did not dampen their spirits for long as they soon realised that there would be many compensations and attractions. As there were few children aboard, they were soon the centre of attention particularly from some of the more aged travellers and thus the five-day journey passed pleasantly and without any trace of boredom.

They were on deck when the mighty *Lusitania* docked. There was the usual hustle and bustle with people jockeying for position. George and Martha hung back in order to protect the children but it was not too long before they were escorted to the dock for reclamation of their baggage. This was loaded on to the cab for the relatively short distance to Lime Street Station. The children looked at the poorly dressed youngsters begging in the streets and felt sorry for them.

They asked their parents how this could happen but neither came up with a satisfactory answer. It was not long to wait for their train to Birmingham and thence on to Bournville. The train puffed out of Lime Street station, through grimy terraces either side but beyond Runcorn the countryside was a pretty and in stark contrast to the smoky and smelly city. They were all very impressed with all aspects of the railway, although as 1st class passengers, they saw little or nothing of the 2nd and 3rd facilities. When they visited the refreshment rooms at

Crewe, George and Stephen took time to inspect the magnificent locomotives barking and whistling as they were going about their work.

At Bournville, the Robinsons were treated very courteously and made to feel welcome. Moreover, some further business contacts and contracts came George's way, an unexpected bonus. He learned more on those two days than he had done for many a long year but to see the way the employees were treated was a shock. Although there was Union presence, there was little indication of unrest underneath the surface; staff smiled and most seemed to be actually enjoying their work.

Most labour problems were dealt with efficiently and quickly. The health of the employees was vital to the company too and they had access to doctors and dentists at a very cheap rate. The personnel officer that escorted them declared that it made no sense to employ people who were too often at home in bed and who would be at work if they had affordable healthcare at hand.

George briefly acknowledged the sense of this but could not sustain any radical aspirations in his narrow and blinkered mind for very long. Although slavery had been abolished here and at home there still was a thing that was almost its equivalent and that was industrial slave labour. It was rife in the mills, mines and in the fields; long hours with little reward. George did not understand as his mind was open only to profit and prejudiced against any radical reform.

Stephen turned to Emma and said,

'Look at those workers, big sis. They look a lot better off than those in our bakery.'

'Right on, little brother. Does that bother you?'

'Yes. I don't like it. It feels unnatural and unfair. Even degrading. We should do more for our workers.'

'Be careful. Don't let father hear you say that. Don't forget, you will be expected to follow in his footsteps without question.'

'If so then my life is not going to be my own. I will just be a high-class overseer of the equivalent of cotton workers.'

'That is quite a thing to say coming from someone not quite yet eleven years old.'

'It'll be my problem, not yours. He will keep you as long as he can but you will have a husband one day and he will rescue you and take you away.'

'Knowing Father, I expect I will have a fight on my hands,' said Emma.

'We will stick together, big sis, that's for sure.' He squeezed Emma's arm very gently.

Although it was somewhat of a wrench to leave the lovely surroundings of Bournville, they all were looking forward to their visit to the capital city and the many things it had to offer. Both the Tower of London and Madame Tussaud's were rather spooky for the children but they loved St Paul's and the Whispering Gallery.

Every journey on the underground railway was an adventure and at the end of each day, Martha made them keep their diaries up to date. In that way, they would learn to be lucid and effective when their many friends and teachers quizzed them on their return. There was one potentially dangerous and frightening moment. They had all visited Westminster Abbey and George decided to take them around to Downing Street the home of the British Prime Minister.

'What is a Prime Minister?' said Emma.

'It is the British equivalent to our President.'

'That is Mr Roosevelt, isn't it, daddy?'

'Quite right,' butted in Martha. 'Although the way things are going, he might not be by the time we get back. Is it true about him planning to start a new party? What is it called?'

'Progressive party,' said George. 'But I think that he…'

George's words were drowned in a very loud explosion, which hurt their ears especially the children. Thick smoke appeared and there followed a lot of shouting, screaming and activity. Suddenly, the whole area was swarming with London policemen all equipped with truncheons and handcuffs. Their target seemed to be a group of women, some of whom were holding placards. After cowering in the corner and no subsequent explosions, they were all curious and slowly ventured out to see what was happening. Martha had a tight grip on Emma's collar.

'What does it say on the placards?' said Stephen.

'Votes for women,' said his mother.

'I've seen that at home the day we all went to Back Bay. That's right, isn't it, daddy?'

'Quite right.'

'Does mummy get to vote?'

'She relies on daddy to do it for her,' said George.

The children looked at each other both with slightly bewildered faces. But further conversation ceased as four women were unceremoniously bundled into a black van kicking and screaming and swearing. The children were a little frightened.

'Let's blow, Martha.'

They retreated and went to their hotel after this excitement and reported it to some of their fellow guests.

'Let's forget about it and enjoy the rest of our holiday,' said Martha. 'The day after tomorrow, we go back home and we want to make the best of what we have left.'

There was a lot of talk about the incident at the hotel. They all went down to evening meal and the restaurant was quite crowded. Normally, it was reasonably quiet in there but not on this occasion as the subject being discussed refused to go away. Some of the speakers had diametrically opposing opinions and conversations began to get quite heated with voices increasingly raised.

In that rich environment, most proclaimed that women ought to feel grateful and that their place was firmly in the home. One young lady got quite angry at this suggestion. When tempers had subsided, there were a few of them believed that women's suffrage would come but not in their lifetime so there was no need to worry. A young man put in his pennyworth.

'Besides, Mr Asquith has only just become Prime minister after Sir Henry Campbell Bannerman's recent death. Mr Asquith has got more important things to worry about,' said the young man.

'Such as?' said an older man. 'What do you know that we don't?'

'He has to try and stop us drifting towards war.' This statement was greeted with derision and was followed by many voices talking all at once. When the situation became chaotic, the manager stepped in.

'Gentlemen, gentlemen, if you please. Please stop this at once. It appears that it has escaped your notice that there are young children here this evening and you are upsetting them as well as the ladies. By all means have your debate but after dinner and in the conference room, I beg you.' He looked at them imploringly.

This plea was enough. From then on the loudest noise to be heard was by an obese gentleman slurping on his soup.

They enjoyed the next day at Windsor castle in spite of a heavy shower and then returned to the hotel. They then did their packing. The children were a little sad about the prospect of returning but even so were looking forward to the train journey to catch the boat.

This time, they went to Paddington station and took the train to Fishguard. The beautiful Welsh countryside impressed George but not Cardiff or Port Talbot, which was just as bad as Boston docks. Ugly acrid black grey smoke belched out of the gaunt giant chimneys and spread its toxic waste on innocent inhabitants nearly all of whom were unaware of the havoc and damage being done to their health. The slag heaps were also an unwelcome sight but soon they were at Tenby in the area of Pembrokeshire that was to be known as "Little England beyond Wales".

They drew into Fishguard where their bags were unloaded. They boarded the mighty liner and, after putting their belongings in their cabins, went on deck to wave a last goodbye. This time the journey was not so interesting for the children and they were somewhat restive but there followed an experience that was to change the lives and the destiny of all at *Frankfare*.

The *Lusitania* was doing a steady 10 knots in the approach to her berth and the four of them were on the top deck enjoying an uninhibited view. They were passing Bridgeport in fine weather and there was just a semblance of a pleasant breeze.

Suddenly, an excited Stephen shouted and said,

'Look, father! Look over there. There is something in the sky. Somebody is actually flying. Look.'

'Where, son? Show me,' said a disbelieving George.

'At two o'clock. There he is. What is it, father, whatever is it?'

George was equally puzzled. 'I don't know, son, I have never seen anything like this.'

By now just about all the passengers had their attention focussed on the strange and spellbinding scene. Someone was actually flying. One of the crew heard them talking.

'It is a glider, sir. There is a guy who has been experimenting in Bridgeport for some years now and has had some success. Someone who came from Germany but calls himself Whitehead. You know all about the Wright brothers, sir?'

'Only what we have read. My wife thinks it all a hoax and a stunt.'

'I understand that the Wright brothers are or have been in France, sir. Apparently, there was a lot of disbelief in that country but not now. While we were on leave in Liverpool, we were talking to some reporters. They said the Daily Mail newspaper was intending to offer five hundred pounds for the first person to fly the channel.'

'How about that, Martha? Things are happening that we should know about.'

He thanked the crew member. There was no further sign of the glider but both George and Stephen independently vowed to find information about aviation on their return home. They docked and waited while the crush resolved itself. It was then easier to espy the cab that had come to fetch them. They spent a pleasant two days in New York again but this time George was not with them sightseeing.

He employed a guide cum bodyguard to look after them whilst he concluded his business. On the second evening, he was already at the hotel when the other three returned. That evening the children were looked after by a hotel nanny whilst George and Martha went to hear the New York Philharmonic. George said that he enjoyed the concert but later could not remember what they had heard, his mind being quite occupied elsewhere. He was still thinking about the brave man who was responsible for the glider.

Two days later, they were back in Boston having to relate their adventures over and over again to all and sundry. Sarah's daughter, Rachael, was the most inquisitive as she was English by birth but only one year old when the family were forced to seek their fortune elsewhere. On one occasion, Stephen had gone into Marcus and Sarah's quarters and was sitting at the table enjoying a currant bun.

'Well, Stevie. It sounds absolutely super. All those places and people. I would have been pretty scared if I had heard that bomb go off.'

'We hightailed it pretty quickly,' said Stephen.

As she was in her own part of the house, Rachael decided to have a bit of gentle fun.

'What were the English girls like, Stevie? Are they prettier than American ones?'

'Without a doubt.'

'Have you one in mind and have you proposed to one yet? What about the problem of distance between you?'

'Yes, I have one in mind. I haven't proposed but there's no problem as regards distance. The English girl in question is sitting right opposite me at this table.'

This brought about a wave of laughter from the rest of the family who were present. Rachael smiled and did not mind in the least that Stephen had played her at her own game. Rachael was now already at high school and pointed out that he, Stephen, would be joining Emma and herself at the same school in just a few weeks.

Many people were mystified why George sent his children to the local school in Lexbridge instead of some fancy establishment in downtown Boston. George was like his father, "frugal Frank" who did not believe is paying out money twice for the same thing. He had designs for his children, particularly Stephen, and knew he could not indoctrinate him if most of the year he was listening to radical and loony ideas at a distant academy. Besides that, Martha did not like the idea of boarding school; she wanted them to exist as a family and in this respect, she and George were as one.

During the next few days, George made enquiries as to whether there were any organisations developing aircraft in the vicinity. There was one only just over 11 miles north west of the city near *Hillington*. He and Stephen took a trip up there in the fall after having contacted the owners who were very pleased to be able to welcome one of Boston's most affluent and influential businessmen. Before they left for England, George had ordered one of the latest Ford Model T cars and this was delivered in October 1908.

At $850, the expense to him was just like parting with pocket money. As soon as the vehicle arrived and test-run, George and Stephen went up to the airfield at *Hillington* and made themselves known to the natives. They had an enormously interesting day and were shown all around the hangers and workshops and in the offices the development plans. The director, Mr Fred Ellis, hoped that some financial help might be on the table by the time that father and son left.

The director had known *Frugal Frank Robinson* and hoped that his son might turn out to be *Generous George*. It did not happen on that day but George asked to be informed of all progress at least once a month. Realising that the company were somewhat strapped for cash, he contacted the telephone exchange and had a line put in at *Hillington* at his, George's, expense.

This made a huge difference especially by the fact some extensions were installed thus making the whole outfit more efficient whilst aiding development. Stephen was given back copies of periodicals which he enjoyed to the full. Of course there was a lot of technical information that was beyond him but there were drawings and exploded diagrams that his eager and quick mind assimilated. Some of the magazines included a page for youngsters and this increased his knowledge rapidly. When he had finished with them he passed them on to Bobby and Charlie. They made monthly visits to the airfield on the last Sunday of each month leaving smartly after morning service. On 25 July 1909, they were just about to leave as the sun was setting behind the hills when someone emerged from the office frantically waving a flag.

'Now what?' said George rather grumpily. He was hungry but they waited whilst the breathless telegraph operator ran towards them.

'Mr Robinson, Mr Robinson, sir. What do you think?' He paused for breath.

'Nothing at all until you tell us something. Get on with it.'

'Louis Bleriot has just crossed the English Channel and won the *Daily Mail* one thousand English pounds.'

'Has he now? Well, good for him… If that is the case we must double our efforts. Can't have those Frogs and Limeys overtaking us. That won't do at all.'

He kicked the car into gear and sped off to tell Martha and Emma the news. The servants were eager to hear the news and Stephen went down and revealed all. Later on that year, George made his first trip in the air and came back home full of the whole thing. Martha was pleased but a bit fearful. 'I am glad I did not know about it before you went as otherwise I would have been worrying all afternoon,' was all she said.

11. Accident

Life went on at *Frankfare* smoothly and predictably for the next few years with no sign of any retrenchment in the bakery business. Only occasionally, where baking was done on site and where supplies from *Frankfare* were too far away to be practicable then George had to make several trips to his outposts but was rarely away for more than one day. Most of these were run efficiently by loyal and dedicated staff but if George felt certain places were performing under par then he would be swiftly away to take people to account.

His imperious bearing when he walked in caused no little consternation and often he would come unannounced and catch unsuspecting managers off guard. As yet he had managed to keep union membership at more than arm's length but there were people who were watching him closely. The fact that the very large part of his staff was dissipated over a wide area and only existed in small groups prevented any militant trouble makers from having much effect.

There were workers councils and George made sure that the democratic process was in operation and publicly known. He was admired by many businessmen in a wide area and the only ones who disliked him were those who, out of envy could not emulate him. In order to be fresh and imposing before his staff George would rarely drive himself. When he was old enough, Bobby would take him to the uttermost parts of the Robinson Empire and at various points on the route people would recognise them and wave.

George would respond with the minimum amount of effort to his left hand. These visits were usually taken place at the beginning of the week which suited Bobby whose musical social life tended to occupy Thursdays and weekends. On one occasion in late 1913, they were away an extra couple of days. They had arrived at the shop in Salem, part of which was a very old building close to where the infamous Jacob Robinson alias "Jack Robson" had lived two hundred and fifty years previously. The floor was slippery and George, who always strode in authoritatively, fell and hit his head.

When he had been treated and had regained his composure, he proceeded to invoke hell on earth. What made it worse was that there was blood all over his clothes caused by a nasty gash from his head wound. Two of the staff who had gone for a break before drying the floor were sacked and the manager was warned about the state of the place although the shop itself matched many of those in George's empire for efficiency.

At one point there was the beginnings of an altercation with the manager and Bobby had to separate them. George faltered in his diatribe and Bobby led him away to a place of recovery and thence to a hotel. George's reaction to the little fisticuffs was to tell Bobby that he and his brother were to be sent on a self-defence course in case there was ever a repeat of the same and George found himself in danger. Later Bobby, on George's instructions, telephoned Martha to say that they would be delayed. On their return, an anxious Martha greeted her husband and then reeled with shock and horror at the bandages covering him. She insisted that he take time off work and for once, he meekly obeyed.

When he had seemingly fully recovered a few weeks later, he was quite jolly, gregarious and full of life. After all he was not yet fifty. However, initially the change in him was imperceptible but in less than a year his behaviour began to be erratic. Thankfully, these occasions were reasonably well spread apart and were not anywhere near as damaging to the family as they might have been. Within a few years, that was to change dramatically.

Later in the week Stephen bumped into Bobby and said,

'Amazing it happened in the very place where our cursed ancestor lived.'

'Just coincidence. A freak. Don't you start believing in that sort of stuff.'

'Emma and I have only heard snippets of the tale and when we asked about the details, we were told to shut up. What I do know is not nice at all. Why did father's accident have to happen there? I think it is uncanny,' said Stephen.

The injury did not affect the arrangements that were already in progress for the great event of early the following year. It was the occasion of the 50th wedding anniversary of Grandfather Frank and his wife, Margaret.

Now, Emma and Stephen did not see their grandparents very often due to a legacy of disputes and disagreements with George. Twenty years previously, Frank had an illness which was not only serious but necessitated isolation and constant care. George was thrust into the job of managing director, a position he relished greatly. He had long and fruitless arguments with his father about a multitude of matters who rejected all attempts to change and modernise. As soon as it was evident that Frank was to be confined for a long period, George lost no time in putting into operation all that he felt was necessary.

To be fair to him, there were a number of things that were long overdue. George visited the sanatorium regularly, which involved a long journey and whilst there received Frank's written orders and took notes himself. On returning to *Frankfare* all of these went unceremoniously into the waste-paper basket. George on his next visit would assure Frank that all was going to plan but omitted to say that it was his, George's plan.

Although the journey was inconvenient, it was necessary because the patients were not allowed to use the telephone except in the most exceptional circumstances. Frank made an almost complete recovery but was devastated on his return when he saw new buildings, new work practices, new staff and just about new everything. Although he took up the reins again, before two years were out he realised he was beaten and the stuffing taken out of him. He retired and saw his family only sporadically, much to the chagrin of he and his wife who adored their grandchildren.

It was Martha who suggested that Frank and Margaret should spend Christmas 1913 with them and after the main festivities organise the big 50th there and then. She was pleasantly surprised when George agreed. He thought that everyone would be on their best behaviour at that time and there would be less likelihood of any skeletons emerging from the closet. The grandparents duly arrived on Christmas Eve and shook the snow from their overcoats. There were kisses all around and indeed everyone behaved impeccably.

Christmas day carols at church lifted their spirits greatly. It was on the next day after a hearty lunch that Frank let himself into the *Frankfare* library. He had made sure when he vacated his home and went to live in retirement that he retained a set of spare keys in case he wanted to get in anywhere and retrieve something that he had forgotten. The occasion had never arisen until now.

There was nobody going to challenge him as just about everyone was asleep. Bobby and Stephen were outside in the snow and spied Frank looking thoughtfully around the room. The boys, after changing, came into the library to speak to him but he seemed oblivious to their presence. Bobby had never been in the library before and looked around somewhat in awe. There were a few gaps in the shelves.

Suddenly, Frank spoke as if he knew what they were thinking. 'We took some books with us when we moved; that is why there are spaces.'

'Is there anything that you still want, grandfather?'

'No. No. I was thinking of something that happened here over 60 years ago. This was the rectory library and here was where I grew up. You see that window over there. I crawled through there once in the middle of the night and almost got away with it. Well, I did for a few years, anyway.'

The two boys, who were puzzled before, were even more so after this remark. Stephen broke the silence. 'Tell us what happened, grandfather.' The old man gathered himself together and decided to oblige them.

'Up there on the very top shelf,' Frank pointed, 'was a book. A very old book which contained all our family history. It was started in the mid-seventeenth century as the writer awaited hanging. There were additions during the next 150 years but nothing to match the content of the early days. I saw my father, the rector, replacing it and asked him if I could see it but he refused point blank. He said I could see it at a later date but that didn't satisfy me; I laid my plans and crept in and read it whilst my parents were away and the servants sleeping. Our ancestor was a terrible man and was the ultimate villain. He was responsible for several deaths and swindling lots of people. He came from Boston in England.'

'We know little about the curse,' said Stephen. 'When we ask father, he just clams up.'

'You said you almost got away with it. Were you discovered?' said Bobby.

'Not immediately. Later I bragged to my sister and in spite of promising not to tell, she double-crossed me.'

Frank Robinson then told them the whole story including details of the curse, leaving out nothing. He told them that for eight generations, there was always a male in the family but curiously only one in each that had survived or produced boys. His father took up holy orders, was ordained and lived in the house that they were in. Of course, there were many alterations and additions. The boys were intrigued and full of admiration. At the end, both of them plied Frank with several questions.

'What happened to the book,' said Stephen.

'I have it at home. I took it when we left here. It is willed to you on my passing.'

'But why not to my father?'

'I have my reasons and will tell you someday but for the moment I prefer not to say or for you to speak of it.'

At that moment Bobby felt uncomfortable and out of place. 'Would you like me to leave, sir? It seems we are in a private family situation.'

'No. Not at all. Please, I wish you to stay.'

Stephen was still puzzled. 'You decided not to go into the priesthood. Why was this?'

'My father beat me unmercifully when my sister betrayed me. I still suffer from those injuries; they caused me to retire at 48. His violence led me into the Society of Friends to which I still belong. A consequence of that was that he was very angry and threatened to disown me but he did not and anyway, my mother outlived him.'

'You served in the American civil war. How on earth did you survive and reconcile this with your beliefs?'

'I went in for catering and became responsible in my area for the army's bread and supplies. I did no killing and except for some drills never held a rifle. At the end of the war, I bought some of the redundant ovens, brought them here and began in a modest way. The church authorities wanted a rectory in new and growing northwest Lexbridge so I bought this place for a pittance. Your great-grandmother lived out her time here; your father was born here.'

There was a silence. Bobby then spoke up:

'We have a family tree book at home, sir. We come from Boston, England. Charlie and I were about four or five when we moved here. Would you like to see it? I can be back in a few minutes.'

'No. We will come over to your part of the house. Let us shut up shop before my son comes and starts asking awkward questions.' He produced the key and gently ushered the boys out.

Bobby was a while obtaining the family tree so Stephen enjoyed the company of his grandfather. It was the first time ever they had been alone. Eventually, Bobby reappeared. There was no sign of life in the Williston quarters and they spread the paper of the family tree on the kitchen table. After a short while, Frank peered through his spectacles.

'This is most interesting, young Robert. Tell me why you came here from England.'

'Our house caught fire and we lost much of what we owned. There was no close family at hand to help and no prospects. Father has a cousin here and he arranged our passage after we appealed to him for help.'

'That was bad luck.' He pored over the paper and was silent for a time. Suddenly, he came to life.

'Hello, hello. What have we here? … Well…well… This is quite amazing… Well, would you believe it? Would you credit it?' he exclaimed. 'This is most intriguing, young Bobby.'

'What is it, grandfather? What have you found?' said Stephen.

'Well, I am blessed… Something very significant… Something that, if I am not mistaken, affects both our families.'

'Will you tell us what you have found?' said Stephen.

'I am not sure as yet. I will have to do some research but I promise to reveal my findings in private at a convenient moment after the anniversary celebrations are over.' He paused and the wait and silence seemed interminable to the youngsters. 'Keep that safe, young man; keep that really safe until I come next year. Under lock and key, please!'

'I will, sir,' said Bobby who, like Stephen, was puzzled at the old man's behaviour.

Frank had studied the Williston tree and had drawn some conclusions but not all were hard and fast. He waited until he and Margaret had gotten home and then lost no time in checking out his theories. It was not long before he gave out a whoop of delight, which was heard all over the house.

'Are you all right, dear?' said Margaret. 'Are you having a brainstorm?'

'No, no,' was his reply. 'I'm fine. I've discovered a bit of historical treasure and will explain in due course.'

'It must be worth something for you to make a noise like that.'

Back at *Frankfare* whilst this was happening, the triumvirate of Charlie, Bobby and Stephen were reflecting on events of the afternoon. Rachael joined them and it was not long before she insisted being brought into the whole saga. They explained it to her as best as they could and emphasised their lack of data.

'We have no idea what excited him and it is no good speculating,' said Charlie. 'We will know soon enough as the anniversary is only a couple of months away. Let's leave it until then.' All of them nodded in agreement.

'Right, Bobby,' said Charlie. 'We have work to do. Let's get at it.' The two young men left leaving Rachael and Stephen alone.

'What a wonderful achievement. Fifty years together and still devoted to each other.'

'Oh that's nothing. You and I will make at least 60 years. Maybe even 70.'

'Really? Of course, by that remark, you mean respectively.'

'Not at all. I mean you and I together.'

'Mr Robinson. In case you have forgotten, that is the second time you have made a comment like that. You should not speak with such frivolity.'

'I'm not being frivolous and have not forgotten what I said all those years ago. At some point when I tell you for the third time of my hopes and intentions for thee and me, I expect you to believe me and give me an answer. Anyway, time for me to go.'

He stood up, went around the table, gently lifted her chin and then bent down to give her a little peck on her lips. She was so surprised that it was a couple of minutes before she could rouse herself to get on with her own chores. It was a nice moment for her but she believed that the day would come when she herself would be a distant memory and drew in her mind a vision of his wife dressed in finery and sporting an expensive hat.

After a week, they all forgot about the incident with grandfather Robinson as each of them was busy in their own particular field. A few days before the great event, they began to discuss it again and were eager to hear what, if anything, grandfather Frank had unearthed. The anniversary began on the Friday evening and included a band concert. Saturday was spent in receiving people from all over the area.

There were so many to invite that the times had to be staggered but nearly everybody that mattered was there for the fireworks in the evening. Fortunately for the family and servants, it was cold and this meant that people did not stay too long and outstay their welcome. Nevertheless, it was difficult for some guests who had stayed overnight to be in church for 10.30 am for the service of thanksgiving and blessing.

Frank was surprised to see his estranged sister there. It was obvious to everyone that there was no love lost between them as they spoke only briefly. When it was all over, there were cocktails at the hall and then back home for a lunch which was for close family only. Lunch over quite a number of young and old alike fell asleep with the exception of those who had been invited to Marcus and Sarah's parlour at 3.00 pm.

Frank had to wash his face in cold water in order to be fully awake and alert. History then repeated itself when he duly appeared at the appointed time and found everyone waiting for him. He held the ancient book in his hand and, somewhat theatrically, put it on the kitchen table. They crowded around and Rachael complained she could not see. Being dainty, she remedied this by squeezing in between her brothers.

Frank then explained what he knew and what he had discovered. The family name really was Robinson and Jacob had changed it to avoid possible detection and arrest. His son had later changed it back again. Following the trial and his flight from England, Jacob had grown a beard and altered his appearance. For a long period of time, Robinson believed he would be forever safe. Frank read out Jacob's written confession and then showed each generation had produced a male heir and the line was unbroken.

All were staunch members of the church and some males in each generation had joined the priesthood, including Frank's father. Not so Frank himself. He pointed out that he had been beaten savagely on occasions by his father as were two of his fellow choir boys. Of course, the worst occasion for Frank being when he revealed he had dared to find what was in the book. Not long after this event, he left home and returned over year later to find his mother had been assaulted and his father defrocked.

The Anglican church had begun to experience declining numbers and the diocese decided a new building in the heart of Lexbridge would be a wise move. Nobody was interested in the house and its somewhat isolated position so soon fell into decay. He borrowed some money from a friend and set up the business which went from strength to strength. He saw his father once more only and that was on the latter's deathbed. Frank then showed some ancient drawings, maps and sketches.

'Mr and Mrs Williston. Do you recognise anything here?' They all leant over the map on the table.

'Why,' said Sarah. 'Bless me. That is our old house at home in Lincolnshire. Look, Marcus. I recognised it at once. How come this is in your book, Mr Robinson?'

'Your ancestor lived there with his wife who was the curate's daughter.'

'Was his name Robinson?' said Marcus, feeling somewhat alarmed.

'No, it was Willistone with an E and he was a much respected army hero. His aunt was Jacob Robinson's sister-in-law, the so-called witch who Jacob cheated out of her home. He did not reckon on the arrival of the new perpetual curate at the Stump or Captain Thomas Willistone. After seeing the chart of your family tree, I put it all together. So the families are united again after more than two centuries. And you all came to Boston.'

'Yes. We had a fire and lost much of our possessions,' said Marcus. 'The house was late Tudor and much of it was thatched. Within half an hour, we had lost most of what we owned. I saved the family silver we possessed and with a few other things sold them to pay for our passage. We arrived here with not very much more than just that we stood in. It was my cousin Mark who was already here that encouraged us to come and live here also. We had no other prospect so we accepted his offer.'

'Goodness me. How awful for you,' said Frank.

Stephen grinned. 'Who would have believed it. Sounds pretty amazing apart from that horrible curse. Was no trace of Elizabeth Robinson never found?'

'None at all. In the chronicle Jacob Robinson says she was whisked away by what locals call the *devil wind of St Botolph*, all the while denouncing him and others, including Hopkins and Stearne.'

'Makes me shiver', said Rachael. 'Has she got any hold over any of us?'

'Hope not,' said Stephen. 'If it is then it is on our side of the family, not yours.'

Rachael piped up. 'What happened to that brute Matthew Hopkins? Did he continue sending innocent people to an early death?'

'I read something about him once in a magazine at home,' said Marcus. 'Seems as though he only lived a couple more years and died, possibly through tuberculosis.'

'Serves the brute right,' said Sarah. 'A good thing that it was no more than two years.'

'That is one thing Elizabeth was right about. Her prediction I mean,' said Rachael.

'Look at all this line of Robinson men. Every other generation seems to have a villain of some sort in it. One hanged as a highwayman. Another gaoled for debt. Another for theft. Anybody here got a skeleton in the cupboard? If so I can write it down now to save the trouble later,' said Stephen.

There was laughter at this but deep down everyone held a slight unease about the curse. They gathered up the papers neatly and put them where they belonged. The last item to be folded was the Williston family tree. Stephen was just about to hand the old book to Frank when without warning, George walked into the room with a scowl on his face.

'What's all this then?' he said icily. Everyone froze. There was an embarrassing wait.

Frank took the mettle. 'We have been looking at Marcus and Sarah's family tree,' he said. 'Most interesting.'

'Why was I not invited?'

It was clear to just about everyone that at that particular moment George required his vassals and family to recognise his status and bow and scrape before his authority.

'I came for you, George, but you were asleep,' Frank lied.

'Would you like to see it now, Mr Robinson?' said Rachael jumping in so as to negate George's peevishness. 'It is very interesting.' She unfolded it. 'One of our ancestors was a hero in the English Civil War, a captain no less.' She spread the paper out. 'Come and have a look at this.' She guided him gently.

'Would you like a cup of tea, Mr Robinson?' said Sarah. 'I am just about to make one for all of us.'

'I would,' said George without any semblance of gratitude.

As there was no logical reason to continue to be petulant, he began to thaw. After all he was now the central figure and he could at any one given moment remind them who was boss. If he felt in the mood, they would have to grovel. At that moment, the paper looked interesting. Stephen kept the book behind his back and out of sight. Whilst George was scrutinising the faded paper, Frank made a motion with his head for Stephen to disappear. Stephen went out noiselessly to his room and hid the old book under his bed. When they were drinking tea, George looked around for his son who was nowhere to be seen.

'Where is Stephen? He was here a minute ago.'

'He is OK but I think he had more of those chocolates that were sent from Bournville than he should have done,' said Bobby, thinking quickly.

George actually laughed. 'Serve him right. Everything in moderation, especially after your goose, Sarah.'

Everyone laughed politely and nothing more was said. Stephen appeared a couple of minutes later. The only person whose laugh was forced was grandfather Frank. He drank his tea and peered over his spectacles at the assembled group one by one. There were some lovely people in the room and he took great pleasure being with them, which was all too infrequent. Inside, though his heart was heavy and laden as, when his eyes settled on George, he realised that he did not like, let alone love his only son.

It is a remarkable fact that instinctively and discreetly in the years following, nobody ever revealed the slightest inkling to George of their knowledge of the book's existence let alone anything in it. Individually, everyone to a person thought this to be most unwise. And thus George went through life completely unaware of its existence. The book remained in Stephen's care as he was unable to return it to his grandfather before the latter's death two years later.

The day after festivities ended, life at the bakery returned to normal very quickly. Bobby bumped into Stephen later that same week. He held out an arm to prevent him progressing and then looked Stephen in the eye with mock seriousness.

'Do you know something, MATE?'

Stephen also looked serious and pretended to frown. He put on a menacing look and then smiled.

'Not really, BUDDY. But I think you are going to tell me anyway.'

'Somehow my family just can't seem to get shut of yours.'

Stephen tried to repress a smile. 'It seems so. Perhaps we are irrevocably entwined.'

'Hm. I will go along with that although I am not entirely sure what irrevocable means.'

'Yes, you do,' said Stephen whilst giving him a friendly light punch. 'By the way. Isn't it time you started using proper American words, buddy.'

'Absolutely, mate,' said Bobby and pretended to butt him on his nose.

12. Secret Plans

On Thursday evenings, Bobby, Charlie and Rachael would join Emma and Stephen at about 6.30 pm having had an early evening meal in their respective parts of the house. Together, they would then walk the mile down to the Lexbridge hall for band practice. When they were questioned about this they all said they enjoyed the exercise and the chance to chat. They made this a rule unless the weather was poor, in which case the elder brother Charlie would squeeze them into the Ford and return with them at 10.00 pm, unless George needed the car, which was rare.

On the occasions it did rain or snow, Stephen was somewhat peeved as he enjoyed the walk with Sarah's children who over the years had not only remained great friends but had seemed to draw ever closer. Any class barrier seemed to them to be artificial.

Rachael's elder brothers were employed on the estate and it seemed logical that somebody else should learn to drive other than George. Both Bobby and Charlie were capable fellows and were doing menial jobs far below their capabilities and level of their intelligence. They had soon learned all there was to know about driving and the inside of the vehicles *Frankfare* possessed. They avidly read car manuals, which included other manufacturers from abroad. This necessitated learning the basics of other languages.

With few cars and vehicles on the road they faced few hazards except when going into the city. There the horses easily got frightened, especially when there was a backfire and their owners would curse them in the most lurid of Anglo-Saxon language. More important, they got the Ford manual and read from cover to cover many times whilst testing each other. This treated George to two mechanics on the spot and obviated the need to go into the city for even easy maintenance.

He gave the young men *cart blanche* to buy spares including tyres, oil and a supply of petrol, which meant the Model T was out of action for the minimum amount of time. One Sunday in late July 1914, George had a particularly nasty cold and after morning service declared that he was going to bed. He stomped off and languidly conquered the stairs.

'That's our trip off to the airfield then,' said a rueful Stephen to his mother.

'No, no,' said Martha. 'Your father has had a word with Charlie and Bobby who said they would take you. Charlie is keen to know about the latest goings on up there at the airfield. Not that Sarah is too happy.'

'Good old pops,' said Stephen. 'This is most unexpected but very acceptable.'

'Now, now. Less of that. You know he does not like you calling him that.'

'Daddy sounds a bit out of date, mom.'

'He does not seem himself, darling. He sometimes gets quite irate in a way he never was before.' She sighed. 'And he is convinced there is going to be a war in Europe,' she added.

'He is worried that we might get dragged into it especially if the British are involved,' said Stephen.

'No, no dearie. That won't happen. President Wilson will see to that.'

'It may happen that we have no choice, mom. Ever since that royal couple were bumped off in Austria somewhere…'

'Sarajevo, I think I read.'

'That's the place. Anyway, things seem to be buzzing over there. I do not like the look of it and threats are getting nastier. We have been learning about it at school. Rachael is convinced that there will be war.'

'Well, at least we don't have to be part of it.' To prevent any further discussion in what was an uncomfortable subject she withdrew to the lounge.

After a fairly unhurried lunch, Charlie, Bobby and Stephen set off eagerly and within half an hour they were at the airfield. Even at a slow pace the car bounced along the uneven track despite Charlie's careful driving.

'Where's your father?' said Chuck Ellis, the chief mechanic and soon to be director.

'Spluttering and shivering in bed with a streamer,' said Stephen holding his nostrils together while he spoke.

'Too bad,' said Chuck. 'We were ready to give him another jaunt. Too bad. For a moment I thought you said he was in bed with a stripper.' The two of them laughed.

'No chance of that with my father. He has got a few vices but that is not one of them. Not yet. Anyway, never mind that. I've come especially to take his place,' said Stephen.

Chuck looked suspiciously at him.

'Hey, now wait a minute, buddy. If I am correct in thinking what you mean by that then you can't be serious. You are not going up in the air. I made a deal with your pa that you were not to fly until you are at the very least 18. If he got to know that I had taken you on a jaunt, I would be hung, drawn and quartered.'

'Who's going to know? Charlie and Bobby won't say anything and I certainly won't.'

Chuck thought and countered, 'Yes, but you will tell your pals at school and perhaps let it slip then it will get back to him and I will get shot and dismembered. You know that your father has been investing in us and we all here want that to continue. Without his money, we would be somewhat hard pressed.'

But Stephen was not going to be put off easily. He tried another tack and drew Chuck aside.

'Listen, Chuck. I know you have been trying to date my sister and with very limited success I might add.'

Chuck was completely knocked off his guard. He felt himself flushing.

'You're a cheeky young fellah if ever there was one. I ought to tan your hide for saying something like that. If it is true, what's it got to do with you flying in one of my kites?'

Stephen ignored this and continued his attack. 'I have got eyes, you know. And talking of eyes, I have seen the way you look at her. All smoochy and gooey. You have got it quite bad, that's for sure.'

For a moment Chuck was taken aback. He lost his guard for a moment. 'You cheeky young whipper snapper.' He recovered his composure and then said somewhat softly, 'Is it as obvious as all that?'

'It is to me. Sticks out a mile. Don't know about anyone else. Doesn't matter anyway.'

'How old is your sister, nineteen, is it?'

'Coming up very soon. I think pa would be quite happy for her to marry one of those dude Boston city types who have rich fathers, and there are one or two sniffing about anyway. Jason Lyon has been around a few times. Took her to town once and bought her lunch. You know, his father is in the Massachusetts State Senate and has a shipping firm. My father has quite a few shares in his company. I shouldn't have told you that so keep that under your hat. I have heard pops ask her a few times whether she likes him.'

This fact alarmed Chuck and caused his mind to race somewhat. Stephen continued:

'It does not help with my mother the fact you are an aircraft builder and mechanic. A profession she considers as dangerous.'

He paused and then continued: 'The trouble is that pa persuaded her to delay university for a year and work in the business. Personally, I think he will do all that he can to keep her permanently and get her to make a life within the firm. She is a marvel with figures and so reliable. In that way, he can keep more control rather than have in people from outside. That means he would have to pay them a living salary. He does not seem to trust anyone these days.

'We have had a series of stooges in the office recently and things have been awkward for him. That bang on the head did him a lot of harm and he gets headaches. Two months running, the wages were in a mess. As she is staying at *Frankfare* for at least a year, now is your best chance. She will be here for this year and then probably apply to go again. That is, of course, if father agrees. Next year, you will be too late.'

'My, my. You make out a good case,' said Chuck. He paused. 'If what you say is true then you are a pretty smart fellow for your age. Let me think for a couple of minutes over a cup of coffee.'

The couple of minutes turned out to be rather more than half an hour. Chuck spoke with nobody on his staff but he spent a few minutes with Charlie and Bobby. At one point, he saw the twins shake their heads and put their fingers to lips. Stephen took that as a good sign and his hopes were justified. At last Chuck reappeared and came over purposefully.

'Come on, young fellah. You win. Let's get you kitted out.' Stephen gave a whoop of joy. Chuck went to the other members of staff and swore them to secrecy. They were somewhat peeved to think that Chuck saw the need to ask them. Chuck, however, was taking no chances. It was in the interest of all of them to keep mum as their employment was somewhat dependent on George Robinson's purse having an aperture constantly pointed in their direction.

Soon, they were walking over the sandy ground towards the two seater aircraft. Stephen's excitement was at fever pitch as he was strapped in firmly by one of the ground crew. They taxied down the makeshift runway which was somewhat bumpy and then suddenly with a mighty roar the aircraft surged forward and soon they were in the air. They passed over fields but avoided villages and thus saw few people. After all, it was Sunday. Chuck later explained that there was a lot of opposition about their flying on the Sabbath and he had made an agreement locally that activity would not begin until after midday on Sundays or at all on major festivals.

All too soon the flight was over and they bumped their way over the runway. Chuck explained that they would have to lay some tarmac for the runway soon as the grass was getting churned up. They had levelled the earth as best as possible but when winter arrived they would need something much more durable or at least the services of a steamroller. He also said that in time they would get down to the flying boat as that did no damage and all learners could best start there on the nearby lake before the ice took hold. Chuck brought up the subject of Emma when they were talking in his office over a coffee.

'I wrote to your sister last month and offered to take her to the dance at the Thorns. Got no reply.'

'It's possible she never ever got it, especially if it was handwritten.'

Chuck raised his eyebrows while holding a look of extreme indignation. 'What? Why the hell ever not?'

'Listen Chuck. Let me tell you something about my PA in confidence. He is good to us in the family in so many ways and we have security but in others he keeps a very tight and sometime fanatical reign. All the mail comes to the office first and we feel there is a possibility he opens some of it, vets it and reseals it. He does not even allow his secretary to do any opening. We think he steams the envelopes sometimes.

'Everyone outside the firm thinks he is the real McCoy with his generosity and quite rightly so in many ways. But in the family and estate, he keeps us rigidly under his thumb. We do get out to band, orchestra, concerts and so on because it's something he likes and wants to encourage but at times, Emma and I feel isolated. He dictates what we do, who are our friends and every now and then realises he has gone too far. Then he makes it up with something like an expensive trip or presents to cheer us up and of course, he has the money to do it. He seems so different to what he was a few years ago.'

Stephen paused for breath. Chuck tapped his pencil annoyingly on his table. Stephen continued and as he did so pulled the pencil away from Chuck's fingers.

'Hear me, Chuck. I like you and always have done and not because I need you to teach me to fly. It would be great for Emma if she had you for a friend. Listen. Why don't you write to her now and I will see that she gets it without my father knowing anything about it? There is plenty of time before Charlie and Bobby and I have to return.' He offered Chuck back his pencil.

'Don't know what to say. Not very good with words.'

Stephen thought. 'Got an idea. Did you know there's a dance on Saturday night at the hall? Tell her you will pick her up at 7.00 pm and then appear in your best bib and tucker. I know she'll agree. It is a case of coping with father.'

Chuck thought for a while and then a great broad grin appeared across his face.

'Damn me if you aren't a real smart ass, Stephen Robinson. But how do you deal with your father?'

'I have thought about that while we have been talking. I will enlist my mother's help on this. I'll ask her to get him to take her out for the day so he'll never know until afterwards.'

'I seem to remember our French teacher saying something about that sort of situation.'

'Let me think; it was Old Wally Hardcastle. Yes. A *coup de maître.*'

'I remember,' said Chuck. 'A *coup de maître.*' His face was wreathed in smiles. 'You know, I have not a clue what to say let alone how to write it.'

'Easy. We will just draft something and then write it up nicely. How about this. You have two tickets for the dinner dance on Saturday next and would very much like the pleasure of Emma's company. If she agrees, you will pick her up in your famous Ford at whatever time you like.' Chuck was writing furiously.

'What about the tickets?'

'I'll see to them. There will be a risk posting them so I'll hand them over just as you arrive on Saturday. I will meet you at the gate. And listen, Chuck, if you ever have to telephone me, make sure that it is not Fatty Richards on the switchboard. She's in father's pocket and is his stooge. Several times things have

101

got back to him when I have not given any information to another soul. She listens in. We will have to think about a series of coded messages.'

'Christ,' said Chuck. 'Your house sounds like one of those concentration camps that I have been reading about. The types that are in South Africa that the Brits have concocted.'

'And that's another thing, Chuck. Don't let dad or even mom hear you blaspheme like that. If so, you will risk ruining everything in one moment and it will be an excuse for him to bar you. And by the way, I don't like it either. Doesn't become you.'

Chuck looked rueful. 'Yes, of course. Sorry, pal. You're right. My mother would clip my ear if she heard me say that. OK. I will get on with this letter.'

'There's one more thing, buddy. I dare not give her your letter until about Wednesday at the earliest. The reason is that she will be so excited and be unable to contain herself and give the game away. In fact, Thursday would probably be better. I will see mom tomorrow and sort that side of it and if that's OK, then get the tickets for the dance. Don't worry. She'll come. Haven't you started yet?'

'Just. But how will I know if you have been successful?'

'I will telephone you and say…that the new aircraft manual has arrived.'

'Hell's teeth, what a carry on.'

'Careful, Chuck, careful.' Chuck put his fingers up to his lips.

'Put three kisses after your name. Come on, Chuck. Do I have to do all the thinking?'

A few minutes later the twins and Stephen duly returned to *Frankland* and all three went into the servant quarters. Stephen grabbed a currant bun to eat before Sarah could rap his knuckles.

'Seen my mother?'

'Been with your dad most of the day,' said Sarah in her lovely Lincolnshire lilt.

'Is he still a bit rough?'

'Seems so. Not in too good a mood these days.'

'That worries me a little, Sarah. He's a bit different to the time when we were kids.'

'Lot of responsibility on your dad.'

'That's part of the trouble. He takes all the major decisions himself and has virtually nobody when it comes to illness. Even mother seems a bit out of it.'

'That's quite a thing for a young one to say, Master Stephen.'

'O come off it, Sarah. We have the business inflicted on us 18 hours a day, six or seven days a week and 12 months a year and we are stuck out here. Sometimes we might as well be a hundred miles from civilisation. Thank goodness we have got band and church.'

'I know what you are saying,' said Sarah. 'But it's more than my life's worth to be talking about it with you. I could be out on my ear in no time if I got caught.'

'Hey, don't fret. I would not split. You know you can trust me. Tell me. If your funds were unlimited, what would you really like to do with your life? I mean everybody says you are the best cook in Boston. This house wouldn't function if it weren't for you and Marcus.'

'Nice of you to say so.' She paused for a moment and lifted her head.

'I think Marcus and I would like to run a hotel,' she said. After a few seconds she resumed her work.

'Sounds a good idea. I'll tell Bobby and Charlie we have find to find a way to become rich. Don't worry; your secret dream is safe with me. Except Bobby, of course. We tell each other everything.'

Sarah smiled, gave him a reassuring nod and carried on with her cooking.

It was not until the following evening that Stephen got a chance to speak to Martha as there always seemed to be somebody hovering about when he wanted to grab her.

'Got a moment, mom?'

'Surely... What is it, son?' Martha was surprised as this sort of request had not happened for some time.

'Not here, mom. Somewhere just the two of us.'

They sat down in Martha's sewing room. She had brought with her a flagon of nice cold lemonade. She poured a measure in each of the two tumblers.

Martha eyed her son. Several possibilities of why he wanted to speak to her went through her mind but eventually, she chose the most obvious.

'Is it girl trouble, son? If so, you ought to ask your father about that sort of thing.'

'O come off it, mom. I have seen what the sheep do in our fields at the back. I know all about it and what goes where. You need not be embarrassed.'

Martha jolted just a little and felt uncomfortable at her son's bluntness.

'If you say so. Then what is it?'

'Well, truthfully, it is girl and boy trouble.'

At this point, Stephen revealed all the salient details that had been discussed on Sunday. Martha was then in a quandary. She tended to want Emma to mix with what she termed a higher class of young man than Chuck but then did not want to baulk her daughter's social life, particularly as chances for her were limited. Martha had come to a crossroad.

She had to admit she liked Chuck as well as his parents for that matter who were all god-fearing folk and she was well aware that Emma liked Chuck. In the end after a few hours and she had given it much thought she came back to Stephen later in the evening and agreed to put in place the necessary plans. Stephen lost no time in obtaining the tickets and telephoned Chuck to say that "his parcel had arrived".

Fatty Fanny Richards was puzzled by this remark but decided not to take the matter further as it seemed innocuous. One thing Martha did insist on was that Emma should know nothing until late Thursday evening. Thus it was about 10 o'clock when Stephen gave her the letter.

At once she was a mixture of excitement, bewilderment and anger, the last because of the delay in getting Chuck's note. Martha was swiftly on the scene to take control and pacify her extremely irate and confused daughter. Emma was becalmed and then realised why the decision of delay had been taken. She admitted that she would have been a bag of nerves all week.

'But what about daddy? He just seems to put off everyone that tries to get in touch except for that clown Jason Lyon. All Jason does is hunt and kills defenceless animals and play polo. If anyone telephones me they rarely get through because of that fat stooge on the exchange who puts the call to daddy first and he decides. I know, mommy, I am not stupid but I am getting fed up with it.'

Martha nodded regretfully. 'Tomorrow you will have the afternoon off. You will have a bad headache. I will tell your father it is the time of the month. I shall take you down town ostensibly to see the doctor. Your father will not be in any way suspicious as he will want you to be well. Instead of the doctor we will get you the best outfit in town. On Saturday your father and I will go to the concert in town and will be there before Chuck arrives. It is high time I made some decisions of my own without help from my husband. On occasions, he does not seem to be the man I married.'

'O mom, thank you. Thank you.'

'You should not thank me as much as your dear little brother. He's set this up for you. You had better say sorry for being angry with him. At some point, you should go to him.'

Martha then revealed how the situation had all come to pass and Emma realised how she had misread the situation. Later Emma spotted her sibling and cornered him.

'Come here, little brother.' He obeyed by trotting to her, head down.

'What is it, big sis?' He then succumbed to a massive bear hug.

'Thank you,' she said.

'No bother. Now it is time for my beauty sleep, big sis. Keep calm. Mom and I will pull it off.'

Emma hugged him again. Next day, she sought out her mother who perceived her look of alarm.

'What is it, dear?'

'My hair, mom.' she said, slightly hysterically. 'What can I do about my hair?'

'Don't fret. All arranged, dearie. Somebody is coming here at 3.30 pm and will fix you up good and proper. The only regret is that I won't be able to see you in all your glory. We will be long gone. And by the way, I have engaged a hairdresser from the city to see to you so that no word will get back to your father. Now run along, dear. You've work to do.'

'O mom, you think of everything,' said Emma.

On Saturday, everything went like clockwork. Although he was sporting a bit of a cold, George was enthusiastic about going to the concert and he and Martha departed early in order to eat in town. Right on time, Chuck called for Emma who looked absolutely stunning. In the hall there were many admiring stares and offers of a dance.

Luckily, most of the dancers were as clumsy as Emma who had little or no experience of the latest trends. It was all great fun and nobody cared. Jason Lyon tried to cut in at one point but Chuck told him where to get off. Emma was quite proud of how Chuck handled the situation but was a little concerned about his choice of Anglo-Saxon English. Later, they all went over to a huge table to sample the eats. The dance was a charity for poor children in Palestine. It was August 1st and it commemorated St Joseph of Arimathea who was the Episcopal church's local saint.

The whole weekend was taken up with festivities and fireworks. These had to be the second to last event due to the event being in summer. There was more food and then at 11.30 pm, there was the last waltz. Chuck took her out on the balcony and out of sight. Later when he thought about it, he was surprised how bold he had been at that moment.

'Emma. I just can't wait for a kiss any longer.'

Before she knew it she was in his arms and enjoying his embrace. Towards the end she did what every woman does when they receive a kiss of that nature for the first time and that was to stiffen and encounter a little fear of the unknown. Chuck did not jump in again as he was a mature 23-year-old but waited while she assimilated the experience. He then, metaphorically speaking, held his breath whilst awaiting her next move. He bent down slightly and looked at her. She then held him and kissed him back.

'You may as well know, Miss Robinson, that I have been hoping for that for a long, long while. Too long.'

'Have you indeed, Mr Ellis. Was it worth the wait?'

'My goodness, yes. There is an important question I must ask you.'

'Which is?'

'Are there any more of those likely in the near future?' At this point there would have been many females who would have teased and enjoyed a moment of power.

Such a stance was alien to Emma who said: 'Yes, Chuck. The only problem is my father. Can we work around that?'

'Of course, now that we have your mother's help. Don't forget Stephen as well. He has been terrific.'

'I won't. I've always loved my little brother; but to do this, well, what more can I say?'

They entered the hall for the last waltz and then all dispersed. They gave a lift back to a couple of friends in the band and then drove into the *Frankfare* complex. It was pitch black so nobody could see them kissing. They made plans to find a way to keep in regular touch without any suspicion from George. Chuck drove away with a feeling of contentment that he had never experienced before. The big question now was what would be the reaction of Emma's bully boy father if or when he found out what had taken place.

George and Martha arrived back late on Saturday evening and went straight to bed. They were so tired they overslept and missed church. George left half of his breakfast and returned to his bed as the cold was still affecting him. He was hardly seen on Monday and Emma missed him because she took his place at a meeting. They all commented that he really must be feeling poorly. Had they gotten away with it? Time would tell.

On Tuesday morning the telegraph operator burst in at 7.30 am. Emma and Stephen were both up and about and shortly afterwards so was Martha. The telegraph operator asked to see George immediately and, as it was urgent, allowed to go up to George's room. There followed several exclamations of horror including:

'I knew it. I knew it. I told them and they would not listen.'

The others were rooted to the spot and heart rates soared uncontrollably. Emma went pale, Martha fidgeted and Stephen stood awaiting any fate that might befall him. Had somebody betrayed them and told him of their subterfuge? If so what would be their punishment. George appeared in his dressing gown and slippers and glared at them one by one. He waved the paper.

'Well. That's it, now. The fat is in the fire. Nobody seems to listen to me. I knew it was going to happen.' He paused and looked at each of them again in turn. They were all silent.

'We'll be in it before long. What do you say to that, Martha. You never believed me.'

'Believed you, dear. What is it you are talking about?' Martha trembled.

'What am I talking about? Why, war, dear. The British have declared war on Germany this morning. You mark my words; we will be in it ourselves sooner or later. We will be unable to avoid it.'

Each of the other three experienced a feeling of reprieve from death row and all stifled a huge sigh of relief. It was difficult for Emma to suppress a giggle so she pretended to cough. Stephen knew the thought of war should invoke a face of abject horror but he felt such a release of tension that he had to suddenly had the need to excuse himself. He was wise enough to come back in a couple of minutes. Before George could say anything, Stephen took the initiative.

'I am sorry, father. I needed the toilet. That is terrible news, father. Lots of people have been saying it would never happen. Will it affect us?'

George looked glum. 'Not the business or at least it should not. But in time lots of young American men will go into the army and die. Men have found more and more deadly ways of killing each other.' His head drooped.

Emma had kept her hair in the same way as Saturday and the gorgeous smell of perfume lingered. She was nearest to George but to start with, his mind was preoccupied with other matters. He slowly turned away to climb the stairs and then stopped.

'You smell nice, daughter. What are you wearing?'

'Eau de Cologne,' said Emma. Then bravely she added, 'Do you like it?'

'Nice,' was all he said before he shuffled off and went upstairs, coughing all the way.

For a moment everybody else froze but immediately the danger passed. They all then made a big effort to show nothing was amiss and the best way to achieve that was to appear calm. They waited until the creak which signified his last step on the landing was heard and then their uncontrollable laughter was automatically released due to their relief and reprieve from the possibility of dreadful retribution.

A few days later when one of his business associates said how lovely Emma had looked last Saturday, George did not register as he was still preoccupied with events taking place in Europe. The rest of the family rejoiced in the fact that, for the time being at least, they were safe from any inquisition and possible repercussions.

Stephen telephoned Chuck. 'The fire of the dragon (George) was non-existent. We do not expect any storm clouds over *Vesuvius* for a little while.'

'Glad to hear it,' said Chuck. 'Keep up the good work.'

Fanny Richards was listening in and like a dutiful little lapdog lost no time in telling her paranoid boss. George briefly thought Stephen was referring to the name of an aircraft but the vision died like a dream at the opening of the day. He thanked her and did nothing as he was loath to divert his preoccupation about war to an entirely different topic, which was probably of little or no consequence.

With Martha's help, Emma and Chuck were able to meet on several clandestine occasions during the next few months although for both there was not enough of them and little privacy. A special date was Emma's 19th birthday, which preceded Stephen's by a couple of days. When George said he had to be away that weekend, Stephen asked if his party could be at the airfield with Chuck and the boys; this was granted.

Emma came along too and thus she and Chuck had the whole weekend and the longest time they had ever had together. Christmas soon followed and they had even more time to get to know each other. Chuck felt that he would have to pick the right time to propose; it was too early at the moment and he believed that he would have to be patient for at least another 10 months or so. However, he reckoned without knowledge of female intuition and was taken by surprise on the occasion when they were together three months later. This was in March 1915 during an interval of a spring concert when they had stepped out for a breather. They had just played an arrangement of Mendelssohn's *Spring Song* and were about to play Schumann's 1st symphony.

'Is it true that in Spring a man's fancy turns to love?' she said whilst taking hold of his hand. He was quite unprepared for this sudden statement and wondered why she had said it.

'I guess so,' he said, lamely. However, it took him a while to grasp the substance of her remark. He suddenly realised that she was making matters easy for him. His mouth opened like a fish before he suddenly blurted out:

'As far as you are concerned, I passed that stage months if not years ago.'

She looked a little shy but nevertheless pulled him to her and kissed him.

'Not long now, Chuck. End of the summer and we can make some plans. If father makes it awkward, I will pack up work and go to college. He will not like that because it would take months to train someone to do what I do. You know the thing that bugs me is that he could divide my work between two people and still pay them a fair salary. He has money to burn and yet Stephen, Marcus, Sarah, mother and I have to work long hours for little return. He seems to get more and more paranoid.'

'Won't he stop you if you try to leave? How will you exist? What about money?'

'Now listen and tell this to nobody. Mother has put a bit of money by and I am pretty certain if it comes to a head, she will help us. I know she was not keen on us as an item to start with but since you spend most of your time on the ground now rather than in the air, she feels a lot happier, even though you are covered in oil a lot of the time. I think it is fair to say that she has accepted the inevitable.

She likes your mom and father and actually she does quite like you although you were not part of her plans for me.'

Chuck's heart sank at those words. He suddenly thought aloud, 'But college. That would be three years.'

'No, it would not. I would take a one-year course in something. It may be we might be apart during the week but it would not be too far for us at weekends. If problems do occur, remember that next year I will be 21 anyway. However, I don't expect it to come to that. I sincerely hope not.'

They were interrupted by calls from members of the orchestra who had discreetly given them some room and had not played gooseberry. Most of them knew the situation and to the credit of all the players nobody whispered to parents of the association or anyone who might then let it slip in front of George C. Robinson. Suddenly, the sound of the first phrase of *Eine Kleine Nacht Musick* was played fortissimo by Bobby on his clarinet outside the changing rooms. That was the signal for the instrumentalists to reassemble.

'Come on, you two. Canoodle time over. Second half in two minutes. Hurry up,' said Joanne Radstock, pointing her trombone like a gun at them.

Emma retrieved her instrument and filed on to the stage feeling very happy; Chuck in an equally buoyant mood went back to his place in the stalls, his only regret being that he could not play a musical instrument.

It's not too late, he thought. *I'm still young and am no idiot.* He looked at his programme to find what was first in the second half. It was an arrangement of Scott Joplin's *Maple Leaf Rag*. He grimaced to himself and thought about the terrible condition that poor man was in. It was an open secret as why this was so but nobody spoke about those sort of subjects. He soon forgot about it and enjoyed Schumann's *Spring Symphony*.

That night Emma found it difficult to get off to sleep as, in spite of pacifying Chuck, her mind was beset with a few niggles. Although she had eased the burden of uncertainty that existed in Chuck's mind, she did not expect all would be plain sailing in the months ahead. As time went on, she realised that matters were not going to get easier and that problems would not disperse of their own accord. When oblivion did occur for Emma, not all of her dreams were of a peaceful nature. At one point she experienced her father taking the cane to her which he had done years before. Chuck on the other hand was asleep in less than a minute after his head hit the pillow.

'We're on the home run,' he had told himself as he got into his bachelor sleeping bag.

Chuck's equilibrium was disturbed greatly only a couple of weeks later. It was a Sunday afternoon when Stephen and Bobby had driven out to *Hillington* to find only a few people at the airfield. By now, the trio of young men were rapidly becoming experienced airmen. The days of being observers were over and they had quite an impressive tally of solo hours under their belts. Sarah always wondered why her twin boys never seemed to have much money to spare but if she suspected anything, she never said a word. At least she knew that the money was not being spent on women.

Quite a bit of their money was spent paying for the fuel they used and for their instruction by one of the staff. Chuck had flatly refused to teach them due to their close friendship. It was left to others to be strict and if necessary stern with them. The new two-seater was there but nobody seemed to be in attendance. Stephen checked to see whether she had been fuelled and found this to be so. Stephen who was not impulsive by nature at that moment did something completely out of character.

'Let's get kitted out.'

'Me as well?'

'You as well.'

In a moment of weakness and not really knowing what he was doing, Bobby obeyed. Stephen climbed in and did all the necessary whilst Bobby swung the propeller. She fired instantly.

'Get in.'

'Should we not wait?'

'Get in.'

Bobby meekly obeyed. They taxied out and were soon aloft. It felt good for both of them. They did not spend much more than five minutes in the air but when they landed, they found Chuck and the others had returned. There were some pretty grim faces, particularly Chuck's, whose hands were on his hips. Immediately, Stephen knew he had made a really bad error of judgement and that he had also involved his best friend in the deed.

'Get down and come to my office,' said Chuck, angrily. He wheeled around and strode off. The pair looked at each other, then duly followed. They entered the office gingerly and stood awaiting their fate.

'I am absolutely livid and dismayed to think you would do this. What have you got to say for yourselves?'

'We did not know how long you were going to be.'

Chuck bashed the table. 'You know damn well you should not have gone out on your own without permission from me or somebody with that authority. We were only down at the lake and you would not have had to wait long. What the hell possessed you both? You did not even leave any details of your flight path.'

'It's not really Bobby's fault. I more or less forced him to get in.'

'Oh I see. The boss's son rules, is that it? I am surprised at you, Bobby, for allowing this to happen.'

'I'm truly sorry, Chuck. I've no excuse and will take what punishment you give me.'

'The same applies to me, Chuck. I will jack in flying altogether if that is your wish but I beg you please do not tell my father.'

'Why? What would he do?'

'I don't know. He might beat me badly even now at my age. He would think of something in the way of sanctions. Sometimes I wish he were not my father.'

At this point Stephen hung his head and looked away. Bobby stared ahead impassively and waited for Chuck to continue. But Chuck remained silent at that remark and waited a while before he spoke again.

'Bad as that, is it?' said Chuck softening a tad.

'And sometimes worse. We are just his damn coolies. Pawns in a chess game.'

'You are not going airborne again today,' said Chuck sternly. 'There's jobs needing doing in the main hanger. Change into some overalls and get busy. Do exactly what they tell you to do in there. Get going, both of you.'

Stephen and Bobby did not waste a second leaving the office and doing exactly what Chuck had ordered. Later that afternoon, when it was time to down tools Chuck sent a message to Stephen to report to the office. Bobby looked at him with a look of great consternation and wondered why he was not included.

'Just you for the chopping block?'

'Seems so. Right. I will get it over with. There is only one trouble.'

'Which is?'

'I have not made my will.'

Bobby tried to suppress a laugh but was only partially successful. Stephen left reluctantly and realised he was scared as never before. He entered the office somewhat furtively where Chuck was already seated.

'I am really sorry, Chuck. I will try and grow up after this.' He nearly choked on the last couple of words.

'Sit your arse down and shut that gaping mouth of yours tightly and listen to what I have to say to you.'

Stephen sat and awaited his punishment. He found himself fidgeting, which was quite out of character.

'I will forgive and forget about your utterly irresponsible action this afternoon provided that you give me your solemn word that nothing and I mean nothing like this will ever happen again plus one other promise.'

'You have my promise. Does the forgiveness extend to Bobby? It wasn't really his fault. It was all my doing.'

'I'm aware of that and, yes, it does include him,' said Chuck, lightening a little.

Stephen breathed a sigh of relief and involuntarily closed his eyes for a second.

'Now as to the other promise,' said Chuck looking at him intently.

'Yes Chuck, anything. You have my word. Hope you don't want me to jump in the lake.'

Chuck ignored Stephen's poor attempt to defuse the tension. 'Don't you want to know what it is first?'

'No. Not really. I trust you and will try and make amends and do whatever you ask.'

Chuck lifted his chin in the air. 'I want you to be my best man when I marry your sister.'

A period of calm and serenity that followed at *Frankfare* was an illusion. One April Monday morning in 1915, only a month after the concert, George was heard shouting and even cursing. Everyone held their breath and awaited the outcome. The upshot of it all was that Bobby and George had been involved a fearsome spat which was unprecedented in that house. It was bound to happen at some point; it was just a question of who was bold or foolhardy enough to be first. It was amazing it had not happened sooner.

Bobby had cracked and had confronted George and was not going to back down under any circumstances. Nobody was quite sure how it all came about or what the main issue was but that did not matter. The die was cast. Bobby had at last had enough of his lot and informed George that he had decided to return to England. He told everyone that he was going to enlist. After George had calmed down, he eyeballed Bobby who at one point thought George was going to bite him.

'Do your mother and father know about this insane and utter foolishness?'

'I have merely expressed it as a wish, sir, but nothing concrete.'

'What did they say?'

'Very little, sir. Naturally, they are none too happy about it.' Here, Bobby had lied as he had applied for a post on the *Lusitania* and been accepted. He was fortunate in receiving the letter as it was on a day when George was ill in bed. Stephen was sent to take the post up to George's bedroom and seeing the letter addressed to Bobby, he merely dropped it off to him on the way. Years later, they realised what a lucky break that was.

'I can believe that readily,' said George venomously. 'Do you realise what is going on there, boy? Men are being slaughtered. We are getting more accurate information over here than the British are. The authorities are concealing the numbers of dead to prevent the public knowing. Why, women in British towns and cities are even pinning white feathers on men who have not as yet joined up and calling them cowards. Yet in some places men are drowning in mud.

'We have heard that about five days ago the Huns discharged tons of poison gas towards the French lines killing hundreds. They have already done the same on the Russian front at some goddamn place called Bolimov and its reckoned that at least a thousand men died. What kind of creatures are they that are prepared to do that? Can't you at least wait a few more months? We will be in it soon enough, you mark my words.'

'I've had enough of living in a modern day serfdom as well as working for you. If I stay here any longer on your pay and conditions then I will go stark staring mad. That's about the size of it. I have only kept quiet all these years in case you would take it out of my mother and father who you treat like slaves. I wish Mr Abraham Lincoln were here at the moment. He would be shocked to find in this day and age at a place called *Frankfare* there still exist white slaves let alone black ones.' George glowered and clenched his fists.

'For saying that, you have one hour to get your possessions together and leave my house. Don't ever come back or I will tear you in pieces. Your name is never to be spoken again in this house. If it is the speakers can join you. Get out of my sight.'

Bobby stayed at the airfield for the next few weeks and requested the Cunard office to communicate with him there. It was a good thing he did as he was as yet not fully convinced that George Robinson's tight reign went as far as censorship of the mail. A telegram arrived asking him to report to head office a fortnight before the original date. Then after tearful farewells with the family, Bobby departed with his meagre worldly possessions and headed off for New York.

Stephen was quite distraught at the loss of one who was as close as a brother but managed to keep his composure. Rachael was unable to do so. George only found out later that Bobby had lied to him and had everything planned with Cunard but by then, there was nothing he could do. This made it hard on his family who felt a deep sense of shame and who feared for their own positions.

George gathered all the staff and senior workers together.

'That boy's name is not to be mentioned in my house ever again under penalty of instant dismissal,' said an irate George in front of everyone and turned on his heel. Sarah wept and for a time was inconsolable.

13. Family Affairs

There was no time to dwell on this event as Martha received news of the death of her sister's husband in Fall River. They had been expecting the worst and it had been a comfort to Martha that George had offered to take Shelagh in. Martha had expressed her gratitude in a way that only women could do but was totally unaware that George was being practical and could see huge advantages. This was because Shelagh had brought two fine and able sons into the world who were aged 18 and 17 and who had done well at high school.

Shelagh's husband had been somewhat a wastrel and had gradually ruined his business due to a combination of drinking and gambling. Martha only found out later that George had been in on the same gambling sessions and had effectively taken money off her brother-in-law. Once Shelagh's husband had poisoned his liver, there was no chance of recovery physically or financially so the family became almost destitute.

The Robinson family attended the funeral as well as Charlie who drove the spare van in order to bring Shelagh and the boys back to *Frankfare* with their furniture and possessions. When all was over and George had settled outstanding debts they prepared to return. Shelagh was effusive with her praise of George and expressed her gratitude very vocally but what she did not realise was that George was already laying plans for them even while her husband fought for breath through alcohol-sodden lungs.

Here was a source of cheap labour and one which would be very useful in the future. The boys, William and Gordon, were eventually going to be travelling inspectors but first they would serve their apprenticeships in the bakery itself. No point in letting them get ideas above their station at the outset. There was no alternative for them and they should be very grateful for being rescued from being potential gutter material.

George's mind was forging ahead and his thoughts were only interrupted when the congregation stood up at the end of the service to sing the last hymn.

He had no remorse about missing the content of it; he viewed his brother-in-law with contempt and that was an end of it. Having to have his wife and offspring come here was a burden but he could see many great financial advantages in the long run.

They all arrived home and with the hope of unwinding and having a rest. It was the weekend anyway and one of the houses in the terrace which had been empty for some time had already been prepared for Shelagh and the boys well in advance. Martha had supervised and had done her best to find furniture and fittings that would make her sister comfortable but this was difficult owing to the stringency of George's allowance. In the end she had to raid her own savings to provide for them. When Martha went to the kitchen area Marcus, Sarah and Rachael appeared distraught and curiously silent. It was obvious they had all been weeping.

Martha informed George who immediately told Charlie to leave the bags and find the cause. The day before, 7th May, *Lusitania* had been shelled by a German U-boat and had sunk in 18 minutes. It appeared that there had been great loss of life but other than that, news was scanty. For many days they waited for news of Bobby but none came. The effect of this news spread far and wide and was disquieting to many staff, local people and above all the family. A miserable gloom settled on the Williston quarters and refused to disperse.

A few days later, George repeated his fears, 'We'll be in it soon. We'll be in it soon.' All the staff knew that George would never forgive Bobby for leaving in the manner he had. For once George had been challenged and had come off second best. Sarah never gave up hope but for Marcus, Charlie and Rachael there was nothing but a feeling of desolation.

The summer passed without any further news and Rachael's 19th birthday was rather sombre and certainly not a celebration. A month later Stephen decided to have a walk down towards the lake and enjoy the autumn sun. He wielded his stick and walked purposefully in spite of the heat and occasionally swore at the parasitic insects that seemed to have taken an unrequited liking to him. His thoughts were dispelled by the sound of sobbing.

It came from the direction of a small clump of trees near the bank and where a small boat was kept. His first reaction was not to interfere and he did not know how many people were there. Curiosity got the better of him and he discreetly went to investigate. To his surprise it turned out to be Rachael all on her own and who jumped when she heard him. On seeing Stephen, she was just a little alarmed and prepared to rise.

'No, no. Don't go. Stay a while and talk to me. It is easy to guess what the trouble is.'

'I really ought to go. Mother will be needing me.'

'No, she won't. She has just gone into town to one of the shops with my mother. In any case, it is Saturday and your day off. Please stay…I hate to see you like this,' he added.

'Is that an order from the boss's son?' said Rachael uncharacteristically and with just a hint of bitterness.

'In no way. It is a request from somebody who cares for you deeply and is going through a lot of the pain that you are experiencing. My guts don't feel as though they belong to me.'

This remark took her by surprise but it was obvious what he had said had affected her.

'That's kind,' was all she could think of to say. She dropped her head and looked away.

'Don't forget, he was like a brother to me.' There was a pause.

'Am I like a sort of sister?' she said without any malice.

'No, no, no, Rachael. Not as a sister. You are much, much more than that to me. More than you realise. I don't think you have any idea what I feel for you. That feeling grows and multiplies every day.'

She was quite shocked. 'What on earth do you mean by that, Mr Robinson?'

'It means that I can't bear the thought of anybody else touching you or even looking at you for that matter. Sometimes I have been out of my mind when others have shown you interest and have breathed a sigh of relief at band when things have fizzled out. In some ways I have been hoping that time passes quickly and I can be old enough to declare my innermost feelings for you. I did not intend it to be today or so soon as I thought you would be frightened and as such that would ruin everything.'

Rachael was at a complete loss for words. After a full minute a few tears appeared; he drew closer to her and put his arm around her shoulders. She did not resist and allowed her head to rest on his shoulder; after a while she looked up and into his eyes.

'You don't know what you are saying. You are still a boy.'

'In a few days, I will be 18. That was the age at which your parents married.'

'How on earth did you know that?'

'Your father told me.'

'I see. You are not suggesting…' her voice tailed off as he interrupted her.

'I am not suggesting anything…yet…just hoping for your affection. I am old enough to know that matters of the heart can't be rushed. Will you think about what I have just told you, please? Can we just go gently while you take it in?'

'I have no option…' Again her voice tailed off because he had leant down and kissed her. Rachael's eyes were wide for a moment yet she had no wish to stop him.

'Tell me,' he said. 'In all these years, you've not lost your English accent. How come?'

'That is easy to tell. If you think about it, mother and father speak like it with us all in the house. Most of the time we are cooped up in this place and see little outside.'

He nodded. 'Look at me. If you care for me just a little then kiss me.'

She did so gently at the same time surprising herself that she had done that. There was an interval whilst neither of them spoke but just faced each other. Stephen broke the silence.

'Do you remember I said that on the third occasion that this subject arises, I expect you to believe me?'

'Yes.'

'Let me put my arm around you, please.'

She said not a word but willingly submitted although still trying to make sense of it all. It was a tender and poignant moment for them both. They repaired to the house holding hands and then parted. She managed a smile which he accepted as au revoir and then made for the privacy of her own room. She lay on her bed thinking of the last few minutes wondering whether yet another problem had been added to her life as well as the loss of her brother.

Later that evening as the spring light faded and she got into bed she realised he had not in any way trespassed on her emotions or made unrequited advances. It became clear during the next few days to her how deep down she really did care for him. As these feelings developed, the grief of losing Bobby became less acute. She had never entertained the idea of a liaison with Stephen as he, the owner's son, was destined to be the head of the firm and who would eventually

119

move into the higher echelons of Boston society and marry a rich girl. That notion had been turned on its head.

For Stephen and Emma, it was a novelty having cousins living close by who they hardly knew. All went well although they and the boys did not have much in common with each other as the newcomers were not really musical. However, they adapted themselves to their new environment and acquitted themselves well in their respective jobs. In their recreation time, they spent some time fishing in the lake and twice a week went to the sports club on the opposite side of the town. Emma realised that the elder cousin was being groomed by George to take on some of the executive part of the business. She realised that this was possibly going to be to her advantage and thus she began to make her own plans.

By the spring of 1916, George had realised that further obstacles put in the way of her association with Chuck were having little or no effect and he deluded himself that the liaison would fizzle out. Normally, he would have been able to have exercised more power of make or break over the liaison but he needed a working relationship with Chuck over his need to be a pilot.

He was getting more and more peeved that the children were spreading their wings and ready to flee the nest and was losing the control and dominance he had erroneously thought he would have forever. He believed this was his God-given right. Martha tried in vain to get him to see reason and at times thought she had achieved a breakthrough but always the ground she had gained seemed to gradually be eroded, thus leaving her back to square one. He had never been right since his head injury.

Finally and in utter frustration, she took the couple aside one day and told them to formulate their own plans and do what they had to do. Armed with a new sense of confidence, Chuck and Emma went to their local minister to tell him of their intentions.

'Are your parents agreeable?' said Joseph Wilkes the minister.

'Father is none too happy,' said Emma.

'Any good reason for that?'

'Not really. It would not matter who it was that I chose to marry. Father would always be reluctant to give away something which he deems to be his property and to exploit,' said Emma sardonically and deciding not to hold back added,

'Of course, if it were to the son of a no-good senator or a rich business man that would be of benefit to him financially then it would be different. When we were in London a few years ago, I saw what lengths the British women were prepared to do to get what they felt was theirs. I am going to take a leaf out of their book and marry Chuck, come what may.'

The minister was somewhat taken aback at these pungent remarks and so was Chuck to a certain extent. Rev Wilkes realised he was on tremulous ground and wisely decided to shift the line of enquiry.

'Have you a date in mind?'

'Yes,' said Emma. 'Saturday 4 November 1916, which is two days after my 21st birthday.'

They chatted further on other topics including the airfield and the war in Europe that was getting more and more bloody. The business was duly completed and the minister was sworn to secrecy. He explained that reading of banns was optional and it only remained for Chuck and Emma to decide when to break the news to George. They decided on the end of July which would be only three months to endure if George proved to be either difficult or intransigent. If it were the latter then Emma would leave *Frankland* and live with Chuck's parents and work at the airfield.

There was always plenty to do there and Chuck had difficulty in recruiting and keeping staff due to its somewhat isolated location and low pay. He hit on the idea to write a letter to George asking for a formal interview and word it so that he, Chuck, was only asking permission to marry Emma out of politeness. Emma was really glad to see that there was some steel in Chuck as hitherto in their dealings with George they seemed perpetually to be on the back foot. Chuck added that he hoped that Mr Robinson would provide the necessary financial support for his daughter's great day. At least there should not be any problem with the catering!

Little did they know it but their timing was perfect. They chose the last weekend of July which was the date of the band's last engagement. Normally, it would have been the weekend before as that was when the holidays began but, on this occasion, they were performing on the Saturday and Sunday in Salem. They left on Friday evening for the 25-mile journey to be greeted cordially by their hosts. Emma trusted Stephen with Chuck's letter rather than the postal service. He was given strict instructions to put it on George's desk first thing on

Saturday morning and then drive up to join them. Stephen accepted the task with pleasure and Emma was taken aback when Stephen hugged her quite strongly.

'Careful, careful. You'll crush my wobblers before he has a chance to see them.'

It was Stephen's turn to be amazed. 'Goodness me, sister. Don't let father hear you say that. He'll find any excuse to baulk you. In any case, are you trying to tell me that even now Chuck has not seen your wobblers?'

'Not as often as I would like,' said Emma.

'You devil! My sister. You temptress!'

'I am not the only one. How is it between you and Rachael?'

This was the first time they had ever spoken of the subject and although a twinge of alarm crept into his chest at that moment he found he was glad to tell someone and more importantly confide in the sister he loved so dearly.

'Progressing slowly but surely, thanks, sis. How on earth did you know?'

'The way you look at each other. You always hold hands to and from band practice.'

'I thought we had given nothing away. ...I may need your help at some point, sis.'

'You will have it, dear brother. Any way I can and that goes for Chuck too.' This time she hugged him. He looked down at her chest mischievously.

'Are they OK? I hope I have not done permanent damage.'

'Quite OK, thank you,' she said with mock seriousness. 'Now get you gone and behave yourself.'

Thus on the Saturday morning, George entered his office and proceeded to deal with some unfinished business. He missed the letter Stephen had deposited to start with and even when he saw it by mid-morning he discounted it assuming it was from one of the staff putting in an insignificant request. When he did open it his fury knew no bounds.

It was not because he was going to be able to stop the wedding. It was not because there was any rudeness in the letter. It was the way Chuck had assumed that there would be no obstacles or objections. George wanted Chuck to beg, even to crawl. George had come to behave like a benevolent despot and just about the only person who did not realise this was George himself. He got a real thrill when anybody approached his desk to beg for a boon. He revelled in the effusive praise that emanated from his subjects when they appeared in front of him cap in hand; when their requests were granted never realising how hollow they were.

He went over to the house to vent his rage on Martha but she was on a women's group outing and did not return until late evening. By then he had calmed down somewhat and, on her return, Martha took the opportunity to put the situation into perspective, pointing out that any long-term opposition was futile. Even she did not realise the real reason for her husband's manner as it was so far in the uncontrollable deep recess of his genes. Besides, she remembered the man she had loved and married and prayed earnestly every night that he would regain his old self. She prayed in vain.

They retired late in the evening having gone round in circles about the suitability of the match and the prospect of an oily aeroplane mechanic in the family rather than a well-dressed business man of their choice who could join and add to the wealth of *Frankfare*. It was Martha who reminded her husband that if he still had ambitions with his flying, he had to treat Chuck with respect. When they had been over the subject so many times and were weary, they gave in and went to bed. George was still very peeved and exhausted and was even angrier when the telephone went at 5.30 am.

'What the hell do you want at this time of the day?' The voice at the other end sounded urgent. Martha's request for information from him was ignored.

'What? Give it to me.'

There was a pause while George listened intently.

'Great God in heaven. Yes, yes I will be there. Count on me.'

'Please tell me what is happening,' said Martha.

'A bomb. A mighty bomb. People dead.'

'Where?'

'Black Tom.'

'Where?'

'Black Tom, New York. Where munitions are stored before they get shipped to the Limeys.'

'Is it sabotage?'

'Most certainly. It's those damned Huns again. Damn them to hell.'

All thoughts of Emma and Chuck were temporarily dispelled, the incident causing George to be away for some time. Business leaders met with senators and congressmen for hours at a time all putting in their points of view and proposals. Senator Lyon had a small warehouse nearby which was severely damaged in the blast. At a meeting he expressed his everlasting hate for everything Germanic in such lurid terms that the chairman had to intervene and beg him to moderate his language.

For Stephen and Rachael, it was a boon as they had more time together unhindered than ever. On one occasion, they were down by the lake. The seclusion and heat awakened their physical desires in an intensity they had hitherto not experienced. These were only halted by the sound of a rifle shot being discharged fairly close by. The possibility of discovery alarmed them.

'Sounds like cousin Billy on a mini hunting trip,' said Stephen disparagingly.

'We're in danger of making a mess of things,' said Rachael, recovering her self-control.

'We are. We must be satisfied with what we have for a little while yet.'

Rachael agreed and suggested they return to the house in order to restore their equipoise.

George only picked up the reins of responsibility a week later. All talk was of impending war and its possible consequences. Graphic details of carnage on the Somme were published in the American newspapers without any censorship that existed in Britain and her dominions. He had asked for special showings at the Movie Theatre of the results Black Tom and with his associates studied the films that had been brought back from France and Belgium. He and his friends were appalled and frightened.

Whereas the British, French and other countries had gone into the war generally oblivious of what a mechanised conflict would entail, the US would go in with their eyes fully open and find great difficulty in concealing the certainty of wholesale carnage to the American public. He resumed work but was absolutely shattered and had completely forgotten that Chuck had offered several dates and times to see him. After receiving no reply Chuck himself chose one of the later dates when he had nobody for training flights and took the bull by the horns. He grunted in his inimitable way when to his surprise, Chuck presented himself.

'Good to see you, sir. Have not seen you at the airfield for a while,' Chuck started affably and confidently. He would have offered his hand but George deliberately kept his head down. George grunted again and deliberately said nothing in the hope of making Chuck uncomfortable. Chuck decided to break the silence.

'Can we talk about our wedding?' he said.

'By *our wedding*, I presume you mean your proposed marriage to my daughter,' George said testily. 'I thought it had been decided. What is there to talk about?' George was hoping that he could reduce Chuck to the status of a serf. It soon began to get harder for him than he thought as Chuck continued regardless.

'It has, sir,' said Chuck. 'I came to seek the blessing of you and Mrs Robinson, to decide on the date and ask what conditions and arrangements you are prepared to offer, if any.' Chuck had certainly rehearsed his lines carefully and over and over again. He put on a false smile.

'I see,' said George. He paused for some time working out how to put Chuck off his guard and regain the ascendency but Chuck was ready and he jumped in with both feet.

'Of course, if the regrettable situation occurs that for some strange reason you are unable to offer the normal benefits a daughter receives on her wedding then Emma and I will have to make alternative arrangements.'

George began to go red. This was the last thing he expected. He was losing even more ground and turned his back on Chuck to pour another sherry which he did not really want. He tried to think quickly.

'And what would those be, may I ask?'

'Oh come now, sir. Those would be the very last resort. I do not need to make contingency plans as you are aware that in November, we will both be over the age of 21.'

George realised that he was on the point of ignominious defeat. Being selfish and shallow the feelings and hopes of his daughter were secondary to the desire to dominate. He wanted the feeling of power for at least a while longer but he knew that this was a problem because if he, George wanted to continue flying then he had to keep a good relationship with Chuck who had grown in stature since he had first met Emma. The experience of having to deal with would be fliers, staff and others had taught him to keep a cool head and his large feet on the ground besides improving his vocabulary. George's money was not the overriding factor in this case and he reluctantly succumbed to the inevitable.

'I will talk to my wife and we will arrange a meeting with the four of us,' he said icily. He got up. To Chuck's surprise, he offered his hand. Chuck took it but noticed that George proffered no sherry.

'Thank you, sir. Thank you very much. Much appreciated.' He left to tell Emma the good news. When Emma heard of this, she was also surprised but her overriding feelings were of joy and relief.

Earlier in the summer, George had been pleased when Stephen had accepted his offer to delay application for university for at least a year. It saved him the task of a protracted argument and refusal. What George did not realise was that his son's chief concern was his growing relationship with Rachael. It was no good being miles away from the person you love with possible predators lurking around every corner. In any case, Stephen was not sure in which subject he wished to specialise. His ability was spread but in no way was he outstanding in any one particular field. His greatest asset was his knowledge of aircraft and his experience of flying. Unbeknown to his parents by now he had a lot of hours solo under his belt and he spent a large part his mean allowance on paying for his time in the air. That was soon to become a very crucial factor in his future.

On 4 November, the great day arrived and all was ready. The church was packed with standing room only at the back. The college choir sang beautifully as Emma on her father's arm walked up the aisle while Chuck tried in vain to loosen his collar without being seen. Stephen nudged him to stop. He wasn't seen, of course, as everyone's eyes were fixed on his bride.

The couple's request during the communion was Mozart's *Ave Verum* but neither Chuck nor Emma could recollect hearing a note afterwards. The ceremony ended with the band and organ playing a rousing arrangement of Mendelssohn's *Wedding March.* At the end of the service the band packed their instruments quickly and rushed down to the concert hall whilst the photographs were being taken.

The reception at the concert hall comfortably held everyone including the band who excelled themselves. As the couple arrived, the band played *See the Conquering Hero Comes.* The caterers were all the staff at the bakery, of course. Frugal Frank's legacy extended to his son that was for sure. It was however a huge success although when the photographs arrived a couple of weeks later everyone remarked how serious George looked. The retreat on the lake had been prepared for the couple's honeymoon, a venue suggested by George as he would be able to further keep down expenses that way. Emma and Chuck did not care. It was not far to go and they would be together as husband and wife at last. The whole proceedings were completed late in the evening with a spectacular firework show.

The month before the wedding Charlie, Rachael and friends of British origins had devised a plan. The day after the wedding, 5 November 1916, would be bonfire night in Great Britain, the day that Guy Fawkes was discovered attempting to blow up the Houses of Parliament. Charlie asked Stephen if he would order some extra fireworks, especially rockets and Catherine wheels, and save some of the leftover food. Although it would be a Sunday, nothing was to happen until after dark; churches would be shut and therefore there should be no opposition.

The local English contingent were invited as well as some notable guests in the district. The whole story was enacted for the benefit of the American members of the audience although the fact that the antagonists were Catholics was glossed over to avoid the event being invidious. It was a huge success apart from an unsavoury incident after the main bloc of guests departed.

Rachael had gone down to the lake hut to store the now empty buckets which were on hand in case of emergencies. These she put in a little tool shed and was about to lock the door. It was pitch black but she kept her footing until an unwelcome pair of arms grabbed her painfully and caused her to drop what she was carrying. The arms belonged to Senator Lyon's son, Jason, who was reeking of alcohol and obviously intent on mischief.

'Well, well. What have we here. Sweet little Rachael. How about it, little kitchen maid? Fancy a bit of fooling around?'

'No, I don't, especially with an overweight and obscene moron like you,' said a very angry Rachael.

'Ooh. That's not very nice. You know, I do love your English warble. Makes me go all funny inside.'

'Let go, you oversized reptile, or I'll shout for help,' said Rachael. Lyon was strong and held her in a vice-like grip whilst holding his hand over her mouth. His mood turned nasty.

'I don't like skivvies denying me my pleasures or talking to me in that way.'

He pulled her blouse open just at that moment and grappled with her for a few seconds.

'Let me go, you brute. You dirty-minded rat. You are a disgrace.'

'Not until you have given me what I w—'

Suddenly, something hit him on the head and he collapsed in a heap like a poleaxed buffalo. Stephen and Charlie had both appeared silently and bent down to see if Jason Lyon was still breathing.

'He will have a sore head tomorrow but I couldn't care a damn about that fact,' said Charlie.

'Charlie, will you go and fetch me a bottle of something strong. Bourbon if possible.' Without questioning Stephen's request, Charlie nodded and disappeared instantly. Rachael was angry but none the worse for her ordeal, although she was puzzled as to Stephen's immediate intentions.

'Wondered where you were,' said Stephen. 'Good job we guessed correctly. Are you hurt in any way?'

'No,' said Rachael. 'Just shaken. I feel a bit cold. Will we be going back, please?'

'In just a few minutes. There's a little job to do first. Please be patient.' He took off his jacket and put it around her shoulders as she was shivering. He took the opportunity to give her a little peck on the cheek, which brought out a semblance of a smile from her. Less than three minutes later, Charlie appeared and gave Stephen the bottle.

'Only half full, Stephen.'

'That will do nicely.' Stephen proceeded to pour some bourbon over Jason Lyon's face and his clothes. He put the almost empty bottle in the unconscious man's hand and closed his fingers around it. Rachael gasped.

'You can't leave him there on a night like this; he will freeze to death.'

'Don't worry. He won't be there for long. Just trust me. Time for us to hit the road.'

They returned to the party and appeared innocent and unconcerned. There were still quite a number of people who had not left, much to Stephen's relief. After a few seconds, he walked over to Rachael's father.

'Mr Williston, a favour, please.'

'Certainly, Mr Stephen.'

'Charlie, Rachael and I are going back to the house. I want you and a couple of helpers to get the emergency stretcher from the first aid hut then go down to the lake hut near the little bridge to locate a rather drunk and prostrate young man. Not a gentleman by any stretch of the imagination, I might add. Name of Jason Lyon; do you know him?'

'Unfortunately, yes.'

'Bring him back to the house. By now, his parents should be home. Telephone them and say he has had a bit of a nasty fall and will they fetch him. If it is Mrs Lyon who answers, ask to speak to Senator Lyon. Got all that?'

'Yes, sir.'

'I will explain tomorrow.'

'No need, Mr Stephen, I think I get the picture.'

'Talking of pictures, the reporter from the Boston Globe is still here. Take him there with you and make sure that the photographer gets some shots. Don't forget, the Globe's politics are completely the opposite of Senator Lyon's.'

Marcus nodded with approval and grinned. He disappeared purposefully into the dark and told the Globe photographer to follow him and put two fingers to his lips. The reporter nodded trustingly. Stephen followed Rachael into the kitchen to grab a much needed large hot cup of coffee. Rachael was seated and was wiping her eyes. Charlie's eyebrows raised when Stephen put his arms tenderly on Rachael's shoulders and then tenderly drew her head on to his chest and held her there. Charlie kept his own counsel.

The unfortunate Jason Lyon was brought out barely conscious. When he saw people staring at him with a mixture of disgust and amusement, he closed his eyes and pretended to be out cold after pulling the blanket over his head. Even in that short space of time, he was blue with cold and had to spend a week in bed recuperating.

George was informed of the whole episode and gave orders that nothing more was to be said of it. However, on Monday morning Stephen telephoned Chuck at the airfield and gave him the salient details of the incident. By Monday evening, the news had spread far and wide thanks to Fanny Richards who, inimitably of course, added some extra spicy bits of her own. The Globe made plenty of capital of Jason Lyon's drunkenness but was unaware of the attempted rape. It did not matter as fat Fanny, when she had left work, had left her listeners in no doubt as to what were Jason Lyon's true intentions.

When Senator Lyon learned of the incident, it was already common knowledge and talk of the town. He was beside himself with anger, especially with his son who he proceeded to berate and threaten with sanctions. He then tried everything possible to keep the matter under wraps including a few bribes, which were unfortunately fairly successful. His enemies who hoped for a gilt-edged opportunity to embarrass him were a little disappointed.

The thing that made it infinitely worse for the senator was that every so often and without warning, his wife would break out into a wail which sounded akin to a wounded hyena. The senator's abilities to soothe and assuage his spouse were low on the comforting meter. Work at Massachusetts Senate beckoned, to the senator's great relief. Jason Lyon recovered but was sore for a month during which time he spoke incessantly with his rich and irresponsible friends about his desire for revenge and his resolve to achieve this.

On 6 April 1917, George's prediction finally came good. Public opinion had swayed dramatically and there was very little opposition when the United States finally declared war on Germany. George went about like a bear with a sore head for a few days but then his demeanour softened. He had been under the impression that the bakeries might be under pressure somewhat during wartime. People had already dug up land and parks for the growing of vegetables and fruit. It did not affect daily bread, of course and George was relieved.

The bakeries did cut down on cakes and luxury items but he found that any fears of loss of trade were groundless. Before long his business was making even more profit than previously although never enough for George. He would have been a lot more in the black had he not begun to suffer severe reversals on his poker nights out. He had been extremely foolish having got involved with some heavy dudes who had come up from New York and were gradually taking over the area.

There was another expense as well. He had gone back to regular flying at the airfield and began to enjoy it once again. When he first arrived, Chuck was very wary but was surprised when George seemed very affable and quite generous. George informed Chuck that he had been fascinated by reading about the new interrupted mechanism on aircraft, the synchronised technique by which a pilot could fire through a propeller without damaging the blades. It so happened that Chuck had been studying this subject avidly with the help of Fred, his father. As well as this the pair of them had gradually received leaked information about a new British fighter, the Sopwith "Pup". Its early success impressed the men but they both felt they themselves could improve on the machine but it was a case of getting hold of one. When they were held up by red tape George opened his purse and used his influence with Senator Lyon and others to get matters moving. George looked at the bills and cursed but when the "Pup" arrived in its packing case at Hillington all that was forgotten in the excitement that ensued. After test flights the impatient George had his turn. It was difficult to get him out of it and he was quite aggrieved when it was out of action due to the modifications Fred and Chuck were introducing. Once these were complete, and incidentally very successful, George became a nuisance as he expected to be able to fly whenever he wished irrespective of how inconvenient it might be for others. Chuck did his best to accommodate his father-in-law as he realised nothing would have materialised if it had not been for George's input. However, both Chuck and Fred were very disquieted with the thought of the increasingly bizarrely behaved George flying with live ammunition for no real purpose other than to satisfy his massive ego.

14. In the Celtic Sea

The months passed and there was still no news of Bobby, yet Sarah clung to the belief that he had survived and pointed out that he was fit and strong. The others were totally unconvinced as they had read about the fiasco of the ship's lifeboats and of those trapped in the lifts. Everyone did their very best to keep off the subject and when it did rear its ugly head everyone pretended to be optimistic. Sarah on every occasion pointed out what a good swimmer Bobby had always been. Their hearts had sunk when the list of survivors was published and his name was not on it.

On the other hand, he was not on the list of known ones who had drowned or amongst the 148 who were buried in the mass grave at Queenstown. The receipt of this information gave Sarah hope and at that point, Marcus pleaded with everyone to keep off the subject and thus reduce their very deep suffering.

In the letter from Cunard that had offered him a job, Bobby had been given orders to report ten days before sailing for training purposes. Whilst staying with Chuck he had been surprised to receive the telegram requesting that to be extended to more than a fortnight and meant an almost immediate departure from *Hillington*. The telegraph boy had put the telegram personally into Bobby's hand at the airfield and waited for the reply.

Bobby made ready and prepared to leave but not before he had seen his parents secretly and revealed the latest news and his intentions. He asked that these might not be imparted but with George's interdiction on even the mention of his name this request was superfluous. He arrived in New York and immediately went to the Cunard Line shipping offices to check in. He duly reported to the duty officer and within minutes was in the interview room where three men were sitting behind a large table and already scrutinising him intently and watching him walk.

'Please sit down, Mr Williston. Good journey?' said the middle of the triumvirate for openers.

'Very pleasant, thank you, sir. My first trip on a train.'

This comment was ignored as the interviewer was keen to proceed. He opened and examined a buff-coloured file even while Bobby was replying.

'We have asked you to come here earlier as we would like you to consider an offer of a different post. Instead of being a stoker, how would you like the position of a steward? The pay is more than half as much again and there are, of course, gratuities and possibility of promotion. Much more pleasant than working down below, I might add.' He looked up.

Bobby was taken by surprise. 'I really don't know what to say, sir, except perhaps it would be foolish to refuse.'

'I will be frank with you, Mr Williston. We can get menial staff without too much trouble but stewards are a different thing. Although our country is neutral, there are plenty of people who have concerns about crossing the Atlantic, especially as the Germans have unleashed this U boat war against the British. We are not in it and hopefully will not be in it and therefore by rights should be safe. Do I make myself clear?'

'Perfectly, sir.'

'You are the type we want, Williston.' He leant back and studied Bobby for a moment or two. 'I must confess to being somewhat curious. You have had a decent education and you say you have learned to speak French and a bit of German. How come?'

'Initially, the need to understand automobile manuals, sir. They all come in the language of origin. We were somewhat isolated and cooped up where I worked. Winter evenings were the worst unless one had a project. Mine and my twin brother's interests were languages and band nights.'

'We often have French-speaking Canadians on our ships and in that instance, you could prove to be very useful. You would therefore serve on the saloon deck, that is, with the first-class passengers.'

'What instrument do you play?' piped one of the other interviewers with a somewhat soprano voice.

'Clarinet, sir.'

'Have you a favourite piece for that instrument?'

'I suppose the Mozart concerto,' said Bobby, trying to think quickly.

'How many times have you heard it?' said the third man, obviously testing his honesty.

'Only once in the concert hall but often on the gramophone.'

The man merely nodded but looked as though satisfied with the reply Bobby had given. The first gentleman resumed.

'When you leave this room, the secretary will give you details of how to get to your lodgings where you will find other stewards, most of them, like you, first timers. There is a travel ticket enclosed for the tram. Your pay will be $21 per month and paid to you on Thursdays. A small amount will be taken out of your wages for your keep during the time you are training but not after you have qualified.

'All other items including toiletries that are not normally part of the company's stock plus alcoholic beverages you will pay yourself. I must emphasise that the company does not encourage any alcohol whilst you are training and certainly not aboard ship, especially before you go on duty. Your manners and presentation before our passengers should be of the highest standard. I hope I make myself clear on those points.'

'Perfectly clear, sir. I will not let you or the company down.'

'We hope this will be a long and happy association with our company,' said the second man. He then stood up and offered his hand as the others did in turn. When Bobby left, the men conferred and nodded to each other believing they had signed a good prospect.

Bobby found his lodgings easily. There was a mess room which served as a lecture and information room. Wednesday afternoons were free as were Saturday afternoons. On Sundays all were encouraged to go to church and most did so. On the third and final week they were joined by some of the old hands, many of whom were veterans of the *Lusitania's* first voyage in 1906. Bobby expected that there might be bullying and rivalry but to his surprise and pleasure, this proved to be unfounded. The head steward on his floor warned that such behaviour would not be tolerated and would result in not just loss of wages but instant dismissal. He took a liking to Bobby and gave him plenty of good advice.

Nothing could have prepared Bobby and his fellow stewards for the awesome feeling as Lusitania steamed into harbour on 24th April. Peskett's masterpiece appeared in its full glory amidst the sound of horns and the wave of noise coming from the crowds most of whom were patiently waiting for loved ones. It was more than a day before they were allowed on board as an army of staff including technicians right down to humble cleaners set about their various duties.

The experienced stewards went their own way while the newcomers were taken for a whistle-stop tour of the ship. Even so, much of it remained unvisited by them. When the novices first came into the first-class lounge and then the restaurant, they all treated it with the reverence of a large church or cathedral. Bobby stared at the results of designer James Miller's inspiration for such a long time that he had to be brought back to earth by the head steward moving them all on.

He realised that he would be seeing more of these locations and knew he could see anything he had missed later. They were then taken to their own cabins to stow their gear and given a last minute set of instructions which again emphasised their own individual responsibilities and the demand for impeccable behaviour. There was not one of his group that had not got the message by now. The novices each shared a cabin with a more experienced steward for obvious reasons; Bobby noticed that some of them were wearing a badge that denoted a service with the company of five years or more.

Finally, on 29th April, the great day arrived when some of the first passengers trickled through. These were ones who had travelled a fair distance and were allowed on the ship rather than having to book into a hotel. The company had thought of everything. Even the third-class passengers had cabins rather than open spaces and this was where the bulk of the passengers were located. Bobby and his colleagues saw little of them as they themselves were on the boat deck, that is, the first-class deck situated between the first and fourth funnels. Then on the afternoon of 30 April, the trickle of passengers became a flood. All boarded and were shown around and given up to date instructions.

At last on May 1st at 12.20 pm, the ship set sail to the accompaniment of a lot of noise, which included horns, cheering and clapping. Passengers waved to their friends and family on the quayside who shortly faded into the distance. Bobby went down to attend to the passengers in his care and listen to the senior steward for their deck.

They were a mixed bunch but nearly all wealthy and well to do. An attractive blonde who was on her own spoke to him at length and he did some little errands for her. It was later that first evening that one of his colleagues said that the passenger in 118 wanted to speak to him. Without further ado, Bobby went to knock on the door and was bidden to enter. It was the blonde lady who smiled very sweetly. She looked very pretty and was well dressed and gave him a good looking over.

'Now then, dear boy, will you run an errand for me, please?' Without ever contemplating a refusal, she said, 'Please go to cabin 101 and speak to the gentleman there. Go fully into the cabin and say 9.00 pm. That's all. And very quietly, please. A whisper, no more.'

'Yes ma'am.'

Bobby did as requested and returned to his patch. Later that night at about 11.00 pm, he was asked to go to one of the halls and hand a note to a gentleman at the bar. He was off duty at the time but did as he was bidden. When he returned to the bar for a drink, a couple of older stewards came up to him.

'Well, who's a lucky boy, then?' Bobby was completely baffled at this remark.

'Don't worry. We can keep a secret.' They both went away laughing.

He confided with one of his fellow freshmen who was also baffled. Finally on the morning of the second full day, the blonde lady called him in.

'Hello, dear boy. Little job for you. Same drill but different number and then this afternoon at 1.30 pm. Go into the main lounge and give this to a gentleman who will be wearing a red rose. He is about 50 and has dark spectacles. Got that? I understand from your colleague that you are musical. Come and talk music to me as soon as you are free.'

Bobby obeyed but did not for a while realise what it was all about. It was only later when one of the senior stewards met him in the corridor that he began to fully understand.

'Hiya, steward Williston. Getting on well with Lady Justine?' He winked. 'You're the chosen one for this trip. Make the best of it. She'll make it worth your while. Dip your bread while you have the chance.'

Next time she called him in, it was just to talk. She eyed him pleasantly.

'May I call you Bobby?'

'Please do if there's nobody else about.'

'You know, you have such a lovely innocent face. I don't think I have ever seen such a lovely innocent face as yours.'

'Thank you, ma'am,' said Bobby, feeling somewhat confused and quite uncomfortable.

'Are you innocent, Bobby?'

'Innocent and probably ignorant as to the ways of the real world,' said Bobby frankly.

'Why is that?'

'Being cooped up for years, I suppose. Only knowing things through books.'

'Tell me about it. I want to know all about you.'

Bobby then gave her a quick resume of his rather sheltered existence. At the end, she did not comment but said to him: 'Do I shock you, Bobby?'

'Not really, ma'am,' Bobby lied and tried very hard not to look guilty.

'Do you know this is only the third or fourth time I have had anybody to talk to someone who understands music. And this is my umpteenth crossing.'

'That many?' said Bobby, beginning to be nervous about being in the cabin for so long.

'Did you know that there's a famous opera singer on board? Name of Josephine Brandell.'

'No ma'am. If you please, I don't wish to appear rude but may I go now? I will be missed.'

'Of course. Sorry. Come back and talk some more music when you are off duty.'

'Yes ma'am. I will look forward to that.'

He was just leaving when she said: 'Who is your favourite?'

'Mozart at the moment. Trouble is that there's only about three or four of his symphonies have clarinets.'

'Mozart. Ah lovely.' Lady Justine put her hands to her face. 'Off you go now and come back to me later. Don't you dare look at another woman in the meantime, do you hear?'

Bobby left, feeling more than a little apprehensive. He must have had part of that written on his face as one of the senior stewards thought he looked somewhat subdued. Bobby confided in him and said he thought it might be a good idea to speak to the chief steward. Whilst he was hesitating to arrange a chat with him, the chief steward himself sent for him. He knocked at the door feeling very nervous when asked to enter.

'Come in, come in, Williston. How are things? You soon seem to have found your sea legs,' said chief steward Foster kindly.

'Pretty good, thank you, sir.'

137

The chief wasted no time getting to the matter in hand.

'Look here, Williston. Your colleague has spoken to me and I know what your problem is and we all fully understand. What you are witnessing is the world's oldest profession. It will seem shocking to somebody like you and it is nothing that I personally condone or encourage. It is a fact of life.' He paused before continuing.

'Lady Justine, and that's a stage name, by the way, is a fixture on this ship. We turn a blind eye and let her get on with it. She is quite a cultured lady, you know.'

'Yes sir. I am aware she is well educated and knowledgeable.'

'I know that the rule book says we must not do anything to assist this sort of thing but we can't stop it even if we wanted to. It is impossible. Some men who are middle-aged, full of zest and energy and have wives whose arses look like a bashed up old tram come on the ship, especially to meet women like Lady Justine. There's another lady on C deck, I believe. She is one who caters more for those who are termed lower class.'

'I just do not want to get into trouble, sir,' said Bobby ruefully.

'You won't. All you ever would need to say is that you carried messages and I will back you up. By the way, stop calling me sir. It's chief.'

'Yes chief, sorry.'

'I have read your file and know your history. You seem to have had a pretty sheltered life up until now, Bobby. Some things come as a shock in this imperfect world of ours.'

'They certainly do, chief. Nearly forgot.' He laughed through the feeling of relief.

'You'll be fine. Keep your nose clean and you will have a friend in me. You can count on that. Go on. Off you go. Finish your turn and then relax. It's better doing this job than being down a coal mine wouldn't you say?'

'It certainly is, chief. A whole lot better than the job at home.'

'There's one other thing worth mentioning. A lot of women are forced into this way of life just to be able to exist. It is a fair bet that most of them do not do it out of choice. I don't know Lady Justine's background and am not going to ask. Even if I did there is no way, I would sit in judgement. By the way, did I see you on Sunday evening in the music room?'

'Yes. I went in the hope of hearing some music before I went on duty but it was taken over by that fat evangelistic preacher. Sounds to me as if we are all bound for hell fire.'

'Oh, that ugly reptile. Does not impress me. Big body and big mouth. Don't like those two men with him either. The US does turn out some pretty weird men.'

'And some good ones.'

'Yes, well, you seem to have a foot in both camps. Where were you born?'

'Boston, Lincolnshire.'

'I was born in Nottingham. As a boy we used to pass through it on the way to Skegness for a holiday. I remember the Stump. Very impressive. Anyway off you go and remember to smile at the customers. And if the lady wants to talk when you are off duty then the best thing is to change into your civvies and meet her on deck. That way you won't draw attention to yourself. Go on. Bugger off.'

'Thank you, chief, and good evening.'

'And to you, Bobby. You're a good lad and a good prospect. You'll go a long way.'

By the time Thursday 6th had arrived Bobby was enjoying life as never before. He felt liberated, free from the confines and shackles of *Frankfare* and very much alive. He felt as if he had been doing the job for years instead of a mere few days. Not only were his duties a delight but the tips were mounting already. One tipsy English passenger was about to fall on the dining room floor until Bobby caught him and prevented a nasty injury. Afterwards, Bobby found himself £5 better off. He tucked it away safely.

The chief had told him to keep his money and valuables on his own personage wherever and whenever possible, especially when off duty. Lady Justine remarked how happy and cheerful he looked when they met later that afternoon. She looked smart and elegant. Around her neck she wore a large wooden cross about three inches long and a little shorter on the cross beam. Bobby was surprised to see her wearing such an item but refrained from asking any leading and personal questions.

'I feel as free as a bird,' said Bobby. 'Can't believe this is happening after being somewhat of a slave.'

'In that case, what would you sing for me if you had the music.'

Bobby considered for a moment. '*O for the Wings of a Dove.*'

'Ah, Mendelssohn. How delightful. In fact, it would be quite apt if someone were to play *Fingal's Cave* at the moment with all this water.'

'Tomorrow we shall see land. I believe some poets refer to it as *The Emerald Isle.*'

'Yes indeed', said Justine. 'And then the day after we shall regain our land legs.'

'What will you do? And may I ask where will you stay? Do you have your own place?'

'I shall do some sightseeing before returning to the ship and no; I do not have a place which I can call my own. In a few years, I shall have when I feel the time is right.'

'When the bank balance hits the bell of the high striker?'

'Not really, Bobby. Some of what I have is with me or on me but ask no more.'

'I would not dream of it,' said. Bobby.

'Of course, you wouldn't,' said Justine, 'You are such a nice polite boy. I don't think I have met anyone quite like you before.' She gave him an engaging smile while Bobby felt slightly embarrassed.

There then occurred a really unsavoury moment which shook both of them to the core. They were walking around the stern of the ship when they encountered the preacher and his small entourage. Justine and Bobby deviated from their path to accommodate them but as they did so the preacher altered his course also to confront them. With a flourish of his hand, the preacher stopped and said to his companions:

'My people. Behold those who deal in iniquity. Children of the devil who dwell in the arms of Satan himself.'

Bobby and the duchess were taken completely by surprise and dumbstruck. The preacher's company watched with a pious and supercilious posture and waited to see if there was to be any response to the preacher whose imperious manner, size and oratory were used to good effect.

Bobby recovered his composure and said: 'That, sir, is totally uncalled for and unworthy of you,' he said. He moved to bypass him without success.

The preacher took no notice and drew nearer to the duchess. 'And what is more, you are not someone who is worthy to be bedecked with the symbol of our Lord's suffering.'

The preacher lunged towards the crucifix that the duchess was wearing but she was too quick for him and sidestepped. That gave Bobby the opportunity to come between them and thus protect her.

'Out of my way you, you unholy monstrosity. You, this harlot's pimp.'

'This is untrue and outrageous, sir. I shall report you if there are any more of these unfounded insults,' said Bobby, although he knew full well he would do no such thing. He hustled Justine away and they repaired to the sun lounge where Bobby ordered her a cup of coffee. Justine was visibly agitated but she tried not to show it. She was quiet for a considerable time.

'Here, drink some of this,' said Bobby. 'Are you coming to the concert tonight?'

'What's on?'

'It is a concert in aid of the Seaman's Charities Fund. The captain will be there.'

'Old bowler Bill Turner himself. Eh?'

'Yes.'

Justine had recovered her composure but was still somewhat shaken. 'This is the first time anything like this has happened and it is worrying. I shall have to think about my future aboard this vessel. I wonder how he found cause to say that. Somebody must have spoken out of turn, that's for sure.'

She only took a few sips of the coffee and then, after looking at her watch got up.

'I have an appointment. If I don't get to the concert bring me a gin and tonic at 10.00 pm,' she said tersely and left without further ado. Bobby finished off her coffee and went back to his cabin and contemplated the incident but said nothing to a soul.

Bobby duly took the gin and tonic at the appointed time and knocked on the door. Justine answered immediately and asked him to enter. She looked surprised when there was no chit to sign and enquired as to why this was so. Bobby then did a slightly exaggerated bow and said:

'This one's on me, madam,' he said. She smiled with pleasure and thanked him. Nobody had ever done that before.

'You really are a lovely boy,' she said again. 'What are your hours of duty tomorrow?'

'Busy,' said Bobby. 'Officially 6 until 2 and then 6 in the evening until we dock depending on weather conditions. I say officially as my room-mate is relieving me early, about 1.30 pm so that I am able to see the Old Head of Kinsale. By the time you are up, we shall be in sight of land. I find that rather exciting.'

'What time do we expect to be in Liverpool?'

'They are talking about 2.30 am or maybe just a little later. There will be a lot of partying so I will be occupied. Tomorrow's walk around the ship will be our last together.'

'Oh don't talk like that. It will not be long before the return journey,' she said.

Bobby was silent and took a furtive glance at her. Justine at once sensed something and looked for an answer and thus scrutinised his eyes.

'Hello, there. Hello. No reply means there is something you do not want me to know. What is it that you are not telling me?'

Bobby was unable to say anything but the truth. 'I had thoughts of joining up.'

Justine was first appalled then somewhat scornful.

'Pah. Not for you. You do not have to risk getting killed.' She softened. 'Besides, I want you to be on hand to look after me,' she added. There was a silence while both reflected on what had just been discussed.

'I thought I ought to do my bit. My real skill is looking after aircraft. And I can fly. I have a pilot's licence.'

'For what purpose? OK, the Kaiser is off his rocker but apart from that the working class of most of Europe have been dragged into a fight against their will and which is all about colonialism, territory and gain. We are not wholly innocent in Great Britain, you know. Did you hear what happened that first Christmas Day in the trenches?'

'No. What happened?'

'There was the sound from the trenches of voices singing *Stille Nacht*. Something that most people know by now. The Tommies met the German soldiers in no man's land and EXCHANGED CHRISTMAS PRESENTS! How about that? This war is absurd. I forbid you to have anything to do with it.'

Bobby was silent but Justine had not finished.

'What is that famous phrase? *War's a game that were their subjects wise, Kings would not play at.* That is pretty apt at the moment. I have forgotten who said that.'

'William Cowper,' said Bobby. 'And that was said something like 150 years ago. I too really don't understand why we are in this war. You know much more about the world and people than me. Heavens above, this is the first real trip I have been on outside my own locality. Salem is about the furthest north I have been which is about 25 miles from our house. I never have been more than a few miles south until a month or so ago.'

'That's probably why you are such a lovely boy.'

'Bed for me, duchess. Up at 5 o'clock.'

'Pity it is not the same as mine,' she said.

Bobby hid his slight embarrassment as he turned and left for his cabin. He slept well and was refreshed when the call came for he and his room-mate for breakfast and then duty. He managed to get a bite to eat during his break time and the rest of his turn went quickly as there was much to do. When he replied in the affirmative that he was going on deck at 1.30 pm, his colleague advised him to wrap up warm as there had been heavy fog. The captain had ordered the *Lusitania* to reduce speed to 18 knots. He put on his smart black overcoat which was standard issue and which he had not yet worn. It was warmer on deck than he imagined and he was just about to go below and change it when Justine called out to him. She was already on deck.

'We will go to the bow today and pretend that we are driving the ship,' she said smiling radiantly.

'Let's hope that we do not get accosted today by that nasty preacher,' said Bobby somewhat grimly.

They walked up to the bow slowly. Justine smiled at one or two elderly men some of whom smiled back. Bobby wondered if they had been clients. There was no way, though, that he was going to ask. Without any warning, she produced an envelope.

'This is for you,' she said. 'No. Don't open it now. Do so when you are in port and feel like having a small celebration. My way of saying thank you. And,' she put two fingers over his lips as he was about to protest, 'not a word, do you hear, Bobby? Not a word.' He nodded obediently.

'You really are a lovely boy,' she said yet again.

They walked towards the bow of the boat still chatting and which they did for another half hour. They were on the port side along with others in order to see the coast of Ireland. It looked impressive and beautiful at the same time.

'*The Emerald Isle*,' said Bobby. 'What an apt description.'

'Who called it that.'

'I looked it up as I did not know until yesterday. Somebody called William Drennan, I believe and a great man so it appears. Founded the *Society for United Irishmen* and did great work. Somebody had to stand up to the British Upper class and the wealthy landowners even in those days. I think a United Ireland is only just and fair. Pity Mr Gladstone's reforms and proposals were defeated over 20 years ago. Some of the British MPs a few years ago should have been arrested for treason. What Bonar Law said was absolutely diabolical.'

'My, my. Who is a clever boy then? You impress me more and more. You obviously believe in justice but may I enquire as to whether you believe there is a God?'

'Yes,' said Bobby emphatically. 'Although it's not easy to do sometimes. Like in wartime. What about you?'

'Sometimes. On a beautiful day like this who could fail to—'

Justine's words were cut short by the most violent explosion. They had reached the bow of the boat and were suddenly jerked off their feet. Justine fell on top of Bobby who cracked his head against the safety rail. For a few seconds, he was unconscious. Justine recovered and tried to revive him.

'Bobby. Bobby. Wake up. What's happened? What was that terrible noise? Are you alive? Speak to me.'

Bobby stirred but it was nearly a couple of minutes before he could speak coherently. Justine took out her handkerchief and soaked it in some water that had splashed on deck. She dabbed it on his forehead carefully.

'Talk to me, Bobby. What is going on. There are people screaming over there. What's happening?'

Before Bobby could think about speaking there was another almighty explosion. It was not long before they felt the sensation of dipping of the deck. At last Bobby spoke.

'We have been hit, Justine. We have been torpedoed, probably by a German submarine. I have no idea what the second explosion was. Justine, I can't get up. I am hurt. Hold on to me and we will see if we can get into one of the lifeboats.'

'Oh merciful God, Bobby. It's surely not as bad as that, is it?'

'It is and worse. We will be lucky to get out of this. I must think about my training.'

Bobby, however, found it difficult to move. He was unsure as to whether he had broken anything but it did not seem so. Every time he tried to get up his head began to swim and he sank down again. By now a few yards away there was screaming followed by panic. Lifeboats were being lowered but it did not appear that the operation was going in any way successfully. Bobby and Justine looked in horror while some lifeboats overturned and bodies were tossed about indiscriminately like toys in the nursery of a petulant spoilt child; screaming intensified and suddenly chairs and tables that were on the deck began to slither into the sea. One lifeboat fell on top of another as it was launched, which caused even more screaming and panic.

'Justine, the ship is going down. In a minute we shall have to jump or we will get sucked down with it.'

'Oh Bobby. No. Surely not. Is there nothing else we can do?'

'Pray to that God we were talking about only a few minutes ago.'

The bow was gradually being immersed. 'See those chairs in the water? We will make for them and then hope we can get picked up. Are you ready?'

'I haven't asked whether you can swim.'

'Bit late for that, isn't it'? But yes. Not too bad.'

'Here we go.'

They jumped over the last bit of safety rail that was still visible and into the Celtic Sea. The shock of the cold water was like being stabbed but they gradually got used to the pain. They swam to the chairs and for a few minutes hung on grimly. They looked all around and hoped they had been seen. Luckily, they had been spotted.

'Look,' said Bobby, 'there is a lifeboat coming towards us. They've seen us. There are only two other people in it. Hang on, dear lady. It looks as though we are in luck.'

Helping hands reached out. Bobby was in so much pain that he remembered little of the next few minutes except for the bitter cold. When he did regain consciousness, there were several others in the lifeboat. Justine's head was in his lap and for what seemed an age they remained in this position. The fog had long gone and there was bright sunshine. He looked at his watch which, by some miracle was still functioning. It said 5.40 pm. When he next looked, it was 6.20 pm and the movement of his arm caused Justine to speak.

'Where are we and what chance have we got?'

'Not far from the coast of Ireland and hopefully, we shall be safe. Can you sit up? You are quite a weight. I think we both will be more comfortable if you do that.'

Bobby was then quite unprepared for what happened next when a familiar voice boomed out, shattering the unearthly silence.

'O ye that work iniquity. Be gone from us. It is you two that have caused this evil.' It was the preacher of whom he had been quite unaware was in the same lifeboat with only one person in between.

'Not you again. Haven't you said enough for one journey, you pious pompous prat?' said Justine.

'How dare you insult me. You insult the most high and mighty with your words and deeds. I tell you, you have no right to wear that symbol of our Saviour's death. Give it to me at once or I will take it.'

There were murmurs of disapproval from some of the others in the boat who were huddled together and hitherto had been silent. They were too frightened and cold to do or say anything that might be effective. The preacher nudged his minion.

'Take it, Arnold. Take it from this worker of Satan.'

Arnold tried to do as he was bidden but Bobby, even though he felt weak, put himself in between him and Justine, causing the boat to wobble. Arnold grabbed Bobby and as a result of the melee within a few seconds pushed him overboard. Justine screamed as did one or two others. She tried to grab him but as she did so the man called Arnold just lifted her legs and pushed over the side. The preacher was rather irate.

'You did not retrieve the cross. You have failed me, Arnold.'

'I humbly beg your pardon, master,' said the hefty bodyguard.

'No matter. They are bound for hell fire and will be there very shortly. Get us to safety, rowers. Put your backs into it,' he said in a venomous voice. The only sound as they rowed away was from two women whimpering.

15. Bunmaskiddy

Within a minute of frantic effort to keep afloat, Bobby and Justine heard the sound of Irish voices.

'There they are. Get them quickly or we will lose them. Ah, begorrah, that was a wicked thing to do.'

The unfortunate pair were hauled in. Bobby said later that he could just remember that before passing out. His next fleeting memory was the boat they were in landing by a small jetty and willing hands reaching for him and carrying him away. His next feeling was that of his back being rubbed whilst he intermittently went in and out of consciousness. He also later remembered leaning over the place where he was sleeping and retching into something like a bucket. Then without warning he suddenly was aware that he was alive. His head hurt and his stomach ached. It was dark and his eyes fastened on somebody sitting in an easy chair not more than a few feet away and who seemed to be dozing.

'What time is it?' he said. And then he suddenly realised the absurdity of that comment as his brain came back into function.

'Where am I?'

This time the body in the armchair stirred. 'Glory be but you've come back to us.'

'Back to us?'

'Yes. Are you remembering anything yet?'

'Just about. What happened in the boat we were in? I remember now; somebody pushed us overboard.'

'Ah, that was a cruel and wicked thing to do.'

'Justine.' He suddenly thought of her. 'Justine. Where is she? Pray God she is alive.'

'Ah, do not fret yourself now. She is in another room. And I might say that she was in better shape than you when they pulled you out.'

'I remember hitting my head on the ship deck.' He paused trying to piece the events together. 'I remember being in the water. Who pulled us out?'

'My sons and their friend who were doing a bit of fishing as they always do on a Thursday and Friday evening. Friday is fish day in these parts. Recently, we have been living off just fish.' She sighed but did not elaborate on this remark.

'How long have I been like this?'

'Two days and two nights.'

'My goodness. That long. So it is. Sunday morning. Please excuse me but I have not asked your name.'

'Aoifa Conlon. And what will we be calling you?'

'Robert Williston is my name. Everyone calls me Bobby.'

'And the lady. Might she be your sister or an aunt? She would most likely be too old to be your wife.'

'Neither. A passenger. Just somebody I was talking to on deck. It was lucky we happened to be at the bow of the ship when the explosion took place and I fell and hit my head; then when there was only one option we just jumped into the water. We could do nothing else. I never saw much of the ship because I was half knocked out.'

'Ah, a terrible sight they say it was. She went down in less than 20 minutes. A lot of people drowned. Most of the lifeboats that they managed to launch reached Cobh. Queenstown, the English call it.'

'It is gradually coming back to me. I'm beginning to piece some of it together.'

'Now why don't you put your head back for a while longer and then see how you feel in the morning.'

'When will I be able to see Justine?'

'When one of you is fit enough to travel to see the other.'

'Why? Is she that far away?'

'It is a big farmhouse and we have had to do a bit of rearranging of the rooms.'

'I see. We are very grateful. Who else lives here?'

'My son, Declan, his wife, Eilish and my younger son, Ryan. It was my boys who pulled you out.'

'Praise be to God for that. I will be able to thank them personally soon. That's when I don't ache so much and I can get up. May I have some water, please?'

'To be sure.' She handed him a pot to which he just managed to hold on without spilling the contents.

Bobby put his head back and only opened his eyes again when he felt hands on him and heard voices. It was still daylight. A kindly middle-aged gentleman was looking at him and smiling good naturedly.

'Ah yes. He's awake and he's going to live and make a few hearts go flutter, there is nothing more certain than that.'

'We fetched the doctor to see you but he has to come a fair way,' said Aoifa to Bobby.

'You've had a real ordeal my son but you and your friend are much luckier than most.'

'How many went down with the ship?'

'Well over a thousand they say. It appears the power went off after just a few minutes.'

'That means the elevators would have stopped working. I bet a lot of people were trapped. Whereabouts are we doctor? All I know is that we must be in Southern Ireland somewhere.'

'Not too far from Cork and Queenstown if you can visualise that. Was there anyone I could contact for you when I next go there. Were you travelling alone?'

'I was a steward, doctor. And thank you for the offer but hopefully I will be up and about soon enough to do things myself without having to trouble you.'

'Fine my boy. Now you take it steady for a few days. You are young and strong and you will recover in a very short while. No more talking, just rest. And then a bit more rest. And now if you excuse me I'll take me leave of you all.'

That afternoon and one by one the other members of the family entered his room and introduced themselves. To their surprise it was Bobby who recovered first. There seemed nobody about the following morning and he got up feeling stiff and awkward. As he walked he realised that somebody had kitted him out with a pair of pyjamas and top but he could not for the life of him remember putting them on. He thought they were Declan's spares and this proved to be correct.

His second choice of room was right when it came to search for Justine's bedroom, which was slightly ajar. She was awake and sitting up looking much like a queen let alone a bogus duchess. The light from the small window shone on her golden hair, which looked lovely. Bobby paused for a moment so as to take it all in. She had heard him so there was no need to knock. Her face broke out into a spontaneous smile of pleasure.

'So, Mr Bobby Williston. You have come back to me at last.'

'I was never that far away,' he said. 'But yes, I'm here but unable to fetch your orders, I'm afraid.'

'Your orders are to come here at once and help me up just a little.' She put her hands on his shoulders and instead of his helping her up she drew his face next to hers. The kiss that she gave him was full of tenderness and lasted several seconds. Inwardly, Bobby was completely taken off his guard but at that moment his body was not his to command. All he could do was to submit willingly.

'Ah. That's better. It seems a long while that I have been waiting for that,' she said. 'Now then. Come and sit beside me on the bed.'

'What if the others come back?'

'What if they do?' When he had obeyed she asked him to put his arm around her back.

'It is Monday morning and they are all at work. Close your eyes and give me your left hand… That's right.'

She gently drew his hand inside whatever she was wearing at the same time opening his palm. She then placed it carefully over her right breast and held it there. Bobby at that moment felt like jelly. After a few moments, Justine spoke.

'Do you know, Bobby, and this is the truth; that is the first time I have really wanted somebody to hold me like that.'

'It is the first time ever for me anyway.'

'Nobody at home?'

'Not like that. Hardly came into contact with girls after I left school. We were somewhat isolated as I think I have already told you.'

'My, my. The world is a strange place, that's for sure.'

'I have not experienced much of it.'

'We'll talk about that another time. Now listen. I have learned some facts about this family who have taken us in. Aoifa has been confiding in me whilst you have been recovering. These people who have saved us are in deep trouble and are in danger of being evicted. Aoifa's husband died about four months ago in some rather sad and horrible circumstances. When you have the opportunity talk to Declan and Eilish and get the details. Some of them concerns the creamery and the machinery in there which is too technical for me but not for you because

150

you understand mechanical things and there may be a way in which we can both help.'

'Now that I can walk more than a few feet at a time I will see him tonight and find what it is all about.'

'Good boy.' She paused. 'My goodness I am hungry. Will you go and find if there is anything for us, please?'

'If you let me have my hand back I will. The trouble is that you are holding there and in any case it doesn't want to go,' said Bobby.

As he released himself he bent down and took her completely by surprise when, this time, he kissed her.

'My, my. Who is a bold boy then?' she said, pretending to reproach him for his liberty.

'Me,' he said feeling more confident. 'There might be a few more of those later.'

Three days later, they were both able to come to the table that was prepared for them at lunch. Hitherto, they had been given bread and milk and very little else. On the table were some vegetables to go with the chicken that had recently been prepared. Everyone sat in silence. Bobby and Justine looked up whilst Aoifa was serving and observed that she had been weeping. She had obviously been missing her husband. There was still a lot to learn about the Conlon family. At the end of lunch, Bobby was bold enough to open the topic of the family's fortunes and find out about the trouble of which Justine had hinted.

'Declan, my friend. I understand you have had a tragedy and that all is not well for your family. Would you be willing to tell me all about it? I do not mean to pry but would like to try and understand your problems and, if possible, offer help.'

'We will take our leave from the others and talk outside.' As they left, Justine gave Bobby an approving look.

Declan explained that they had been relatively well off and the business of the farm had been going well. The fields they possessed were fertile, their only drawback being that they were somewhat isolated from the rest of the village, which was a tiresome half-mile climb away. They were an important centre where milk was brought to the creamery from other smaller farms and made into a variety of dairy products. His father who was reasonably literate and business like had decided to invest in some of the latest equipment that would be more efficient and provide more work locally.

'What form did the machinery take?' said Bobby.

'They are called centrifugal separators. The idea is that it separates the milk and cream and does so efficiently and saves a huge number of man hours. All was well for a few days but after a short while the new equipment leaked and ceased to work. Father came indoors one morning in a rage I had never seen before. He mouthed something about being cheated; took his stick and galloped off on his horse. We never saw him alive again. He was found on the road to Cork by some passers by late that evening. We knew something was amiss because his horse found its way home.'

'Did he say anything else?'

'We could not make head nor tail of it. Something like 'the rubber has been cut. I am going to the police.'

Bobby mused. 'May I take a look?'

'Of course.'

They went to the large building that housed the machinery. It was empty and forlorn. It took no time at all for Bobby to realise what had happened. The equipment had seized up and had gradually ceased to function. This had happened to all of them, which could not have been a coincidence. There had been a deliberate act of sabotage. Whoever had been responsible had been very astute and cunning as there had been leakage, first imperceptible, and then it had gradually caused the machines to malfunction and grind to a halt.

'What did the police say?' said Bobby.

'Frankly, they seemed out of their depth. They wrung their hands and then went off to deal with some fighting in Cork. There is a lot of unrest in Ireland at the moment, Bobby.'

'In your father's papers is there an exploded diagram of the separators?'

'What is that? I am not good at all when it comes to reading and writing, Bobby.'

'Whoever caused this was depending on your being like that, including your father.'

'So it wasn't the fault of the manufacturers. Do you mean somebody actually did this on purpose?'

'Yes, without a doubt. Who stands to gain if you go bust?'

'It might be somebody who wants the farm, I just do not know. It might be the people who run the co-operative. We did not join because there were no advantages to us all, being remote here. It wasn't as though we were against them. Father said the terms were not right. They were very upset. They will buy us out soon because we have little money left and still owe a lot on the separators. We are living on what we have plus the fish we catch. It is hard on those who we employed as they are in a worse position in some cases.'

'I'd like to see the diagram, please,' said Bobby. 'And any other relevant information.'

The exploded diagram did not require any searching as it was on the top of the pile of papers in Tom Conlon's study. It must have been the last of his papers on his desk that he had handled before his untimely demise. Bobby examined it and then went to work. There was a host of tools including adjustable spanners and wrenches all handy. Slowly, Bobby undid the first of the separators. He knew exactly what he was looking for as Tom Conlon's last words had given it away. He exhaled a triumphant sigh when he found where the root of the trouble lay. It had taken less than half an hour for him to pinpoint the problem. He went into the house and looked for Justine who beamed with pleasure to see him.

'Well now. I hear you have been up to something. Tell me what you have found but not too technical, please.'

Bobby revealed his latest findings and Justine remained silent until he had finished.

'Is there anything you can do to remedy the situation?'

'Three problems. One, replacements. If I can get some spares, I could easily refit them and get them working again. Two, the whole apparatus needs taking apart to be washed and scrubbed before it is reassembled. That part is going to need many hands. Whoever was responsible for this was no fool. He or she knew exactly what they were doing.'

'I see. That is not something good to hear. What's the third trouble?'

'They are in debt. The payments for the equipment have fallen behind. Although none of the family have said much, it looks as though you and I have arrived at their eleventh hour and a bit more. They are either hoping for a miracle or resigned to their fate. It will be soon that they expect a final demand notice.'

'Maybe we can supply a miracle,' mused Justine. 'Do you know how much they owe?'

'No. That will be your job to ask Aoifa and Declan tonight. More to the point, how are you, anyway?'

'Can't seem to walk far without feeling a little dizzy. Good thing the toilet is near. Does anybody know yet that we have survived?'

'Not yet. Not unless the good Doctor has said anything. We have seen nobody else.'

'Might be a good idea to keep it that way if there are naughty people about. What I can't understand is why they did not set fire to the creamery and take their revenge, if that's what it is all about.'

'Just think. Firstly, there would be questions asked and there would be police involved even in these parts. Plus the fact that whoever is responsible for this I am sure wants to take over the place intact. They don't want to have to start building again and replacing expensive equipment from scratch.'

'Silly me,' said Justine. 'You really have a head on your shoulders. Tell me what is our next move.'

'If there is a place that does spare parts in Cork then I will take the horse and go and get them. Cost will be small. That's why they chose the rubber washers. They weren't taken out. They were cut. That way it would not cause permanent damage, easy to fit and soon be working again. They banked on Declan and his father being unable to find the trouble or do anything about it. They did not foresee you and I turning up.'

'Not sure I can do anything.'

'I am formulating some plans for you.'

'Are you indeed?' said Justine, pretending to be indignant. 'And what might they be?'

'Tell you when I have finished work and Declan's back home.'

'In that case, come here.' He obeyed willingly and she kissed him tenderly.

'I have been formulating some plans,' she said. 'When they are all communicating with "the big fellah" next at Sunday morning…'

'Who?'

Justine looked slightly peeved at his lack of understanding.

'When they are all at Mass next Sunday morning, I want you to come to me. To my bed. To be with me.'

Bobby, completely inexperienced as he was, had known in his heart that this request was going to come at some point. As such, he was ready with his reply.

'Justine, I will come to your bed. But not in it. Not until you say you will never go on ship or boat ever again unless we share the same cabin and share the same house and bed when we are on land.'

Justine was completely taken by surprise and utterly astounded at his reply. It was a first time for her that a man had laid any conditions to her. She was not angry and only momentarily a little displeased. She was just astonished that this thoroughly decent, honest and loveable young man had declared himself her equal and that she, who had for years had total mastery of her movements and decisions especially with men, would have to take a different approach in her dealings with him.

As he waved his hand as he left, she could not help feeling total admiration for someone, albeit nearly ten years her junior, that she was day by day beginning to love and respect more and more. At the same time, she was worried about the future of a relationship with him.

The only person missing from the discussion that evening was Ryan who they thought it best to leave out particularly as there was reference to his father's premature death. The others were shocked when they learned that there was the possibility of a murder having taken place. Aoifa remained impassive and her head slightly heavy and bowed but Eilish was almost overcome and shed tears.

'Aoifa, normally Justine and I would be soon on our way now that we have recovered sufficiently and relieve you of a burden and try and restart our lives afresh but having learned of your plight we would like to see if we can get you out of this mess. We would do it anyway if we had just been merely neighbours but Justine and I are alive thanks to you all and we are eager to see if we can help.'

'You're no burden, Master Bobby. Tell us what you have in mind.'

16. A Plan of Action

Bobby outlined his plan. His belief that he felt he could mend the separators was met with a feeling of reticent scepticism. None of them felt they could indulge in minute optimism at that time as too many bad things had befallen them. Although they had begun to respect and like Bobby, they were in the dark as to his competence in the world of machinery and mechanics. As he unfolded his plan their spirits rose a little but it was only a little as pessimism had taken a firm foothold in all the family. He proposed to go into Cork and attempt to get spare parts and then fit them. Nobody would know him and probably no awkward questions asked. He explained what would be needed to get the system separators up and running.

'That's wonderful to hear but there's another problem. We owe the bank money and they are ready to foreclose on us. We have been gradually sinking into quicksand since father died.' Even the powerfully built Declan gulped as he said the last few words.

'This is where I can help,' said Justine. 'When we go into Cork, we will make plans to pay off the debt and thus we will get you back to near normality.'

'But I can't take your money like that,' said Declan, 'it would not be right.'

After several minutes of arguing, Justine told Declan could pay her back once he was solvent. In the end he saw the sense in that and agreed. In this way he felt his pride and honour seemed to be intact. Bobby again took up the reins.

'I am undecided as to whether to go to the firm that sold the separators or to buy some rubber and cut the washers to size myself. It would only be a few more hours' work. Where are the best chandler's shops for that sort of thing in Cork?'

'John Perry's in Academy Street,' said Eilish, piping up unexpectedly. 'They have everything.'

It was only when Justine told him that she was going with him that he stopped in his tracks and looked at her intently.

'Why do you want to come? Any special reason.'

'Yes. Firstly to stretch my legs and to kill two or three birds with one stone. Come with me. Declan! May I have the bill for what is still owed for the equipment please? Are there any others?'

'The money we borrowed from the bank. Just some for chicken feed and a few bits and bobs. We are getting very low on everything, especially flour. Only a week's supply left.'

'Just tell us what you need. Give me all the bills.' He specified a few other things they could do with and Justine made a list.

'If you are coming then we will have to take the pony and trap. Are you up to it?'

'Of course. Come to my room. I want a word.' They excused themselves and left.

'Now I know what you are thinking,' said Justine when they had reached her room. 'Where's the money coming from?' She took out of her bag a roll of £5 notes. 'I told you that I kept some of my assets with me.'

'How has it managed to keep dry? I see there is a pocket by the side. Did you keep the roll in there?'

'Yes. And there are some US dollars there. Now Bobby, all my life I have wanted to do some good for somebody and now is my chance. You want to help them out of this mess I know so tomorrow we will hit the trail together, pard'ner,' she said making an indifferent job of imitating a Texan accent.

'OK, pard'ner. And there is something else. It's time I went to the post office and let them know that we are alive. I would like to send a cable home.'

'Why not go to the Cunard office and get it done for free?' said Justine.

'Because I do not want pressure on me to go back to work on another ship. I have no idea what was in the small print in my contract. I can't face going back to being a steward yet in the face of this U boat menace, much as I enjoyed the work. In any case, like you I want to see this through with the Conlons first before I embark on the next phase of my life. Now then. Tell me about your proposals, partner.'

Justine outlined her plan. They would take the pony and trap and Declan's horse in tow. They all would first go to the Bank of Ireland to obtain a form for Declan to open an account. During the last few days Justine had made Declan practise his writing and had been pleasantly surprise by her pupil's progress. Ryan had later joined in but had to be taught the fundamentals. He had been reluctant at first, mainly through fear of the unknown but had gradually warmed to his task.

Justine looked at Bobby and awaited his response. He was silent so she weighed in.

'Well, partner.'

'Sounds good. Right. I'll talk to Declan.' He turned to go.

'Just a minute. Haven't you forgotten something?'

Bobby looked surprised for a minute and then the penny dropped. He went over to her and their kiss was long and full of passion.

They set off the next day well wrapped up as it was a mite windy and there was the occasional squall of rain. Just over three hours later they were in Cork where the streets were in marked contrast to the bumpy road they had endured. Justine declared that she was black and blue. At the bank they had been welcomed and Justine had deposited £100 into Declan's new account. A cheque book in his name duly arrived, which Justine immediately confiscated; she was taking no chances until she felt Declan was fully competent.

That done, they trundled around to Academy Street to see what equipment John Perry's shop could offer so that Bobby could explain what he needed. On entering the shop Bobby found that, inadvertently, he was saying a prayer. He realised that the future of a few dozen people hinged on the outcome of the next few minutes. The assistant was unsure as to the washers and thus went to enlist the aid of an older man who looked optimistic at the paper with Bobby's dimensions.

'I do not want to go to the firm that supplied the separators as information of our intentions might get back to our opponents,' he said out of earshot of the assistant. 'We may end up there but I hope not. Did you not ask them to send somebody to take a look at the damage and make suggestions, Declan?'

'Yes. The first man was puzzled and said he would send someone else. Nobody arrived. It was then that father decided to take one apart. He was not mechanically minded. He spent hours looking at the plan and then said he had found the trouble. He was in the most terrible rage and rode off. Of course, he never came back.'

'Tell me about the first man that came.'

'He looked more like a solicitor than a craftsman. He didn't stay more than an hour.'

Bobby and Justine looked at each other.

'Are you thinking what I am thinking?' said Justine,

'Without a doubt. The man was a phoney. The real man was bought, perhaps threatened, or even worse.'

The assistant returned so for the present the subject was closed.

'I think we have got what you need, sir. Follow me.'

Bobby looked at the goods and could hardly contain his delight. He bought the washers and as a safety precaution several spares as well as some galvanized rubber sheet together with a Stanley knife. Some scouring and cleaning powder was also produced and paid for as well as writing paper, envelopes, pens and ink. The assistant was curious as to know where they all came from but gave up when he was given a series of non-committal answers.

'In case plan A fails then I will cut some to size myself,' said Bobby.

They began to feel more confident and decided to have something to eat. Afterwards, Declan took his leave of them and went back to Bunmaskiddy. There was work to do and plenty of hours left in the day. He would have liked to have seen Cork again but there were other priorities.

'Where to now, pard'ner?'

'Patrick Street. Ask the way, please.'

A few minutes later they stopped outside T.W. Murray's shop. Bobby had not told Justine the reason for this visit and her eyes widened a little through alarm when she saw all the firearms in the window.

'Hey, Bobby. I do not like the look of this. Is this really necessary? I am worried. I have never liked guns.'

'Believe it or not, neither do I but it is a precaution. Whoever is against the Conlons and their group is going to get a shock if today is successful and we get them all back on their feet again. That means they will have to step up a notch. Declan's father was bumped off. Murdered in cold blood, I am sure.'

'Well, if you say so. You know better than me on this subject. It chills me to the marrow, though.'

'Will you still be willing to pay? Gladly I mean. I would not do this unless I thought it absolutely necessary.'

'Yes. I have the utmost faith in you but I can't help feeling really scared.'

The gunsmith showed them a variety of shotguns and handguns. They bought one of each and plenty of ammunition. The whole visit took only an hour. The guns were wrapped up and placed in the trap.

'The others need not know about these,' said Bobby. 'This is between you and me.'

'If you say so,' was all Justine said, still somewhat unconvinced as to the need of them.

As Justine was leaving, Bobby put a question to the shopkeeper who wrote an address for them. They left and picked up the chicken feed and other items Declan had specified. By now Bobby was itching to get back to the farm but first the horses needed a feed and watering. When this was done they went to a large house on the outskirts of the city and saw the proprietor on his own. Justine lay in the shade of the wagon with her head propped up on the wheel.

'What's here?' said Justine on his return an hour later. 'You've been a long time.'

'Furry canine friends,' was all Bobby said.

Justine was mystified but asked nothing as she was beginning to feel very tired having still painful reminders of the *Lusitania*. Although they had put some cushions in the back, the road was so bumpy that she asked Bobby to stop and took her place again beside him. At last they reached the farm and, after drinking a copious amount of water, collapsed into their respective beds.

Bobby was up in an hour and eager to start work. There was some daylight left and he was going to make use of it. He had already cleaned and oiled two of the separators himself a few days previously with Ryan's help and was bursting to get started. To his absolute joy and delight, the washers fitted perfectly and he whooped triumphantly. He returned to the house and told Declan the results of his labours. Declan looked pleased but obviously awaited proof of the pudding. They each retired and vowed to make an early start.

It was dark when they ate their breakfast in almost total silence. As dawn appeared the two men entered the cowshed holding the Tilley lights. Eilish, Ryan, Aoifa and two of the farm workers who had been retained were already milking. Declan took enough for their purpose and went into the creamery. They poured in the milk and began to turn the handle. Nothing happened for several seconds which felt like an eternity. After about a minute Bobby paused. His heart was beating fast. He had only experienced this sort of tension once before on the occasion of his bust up with George. He wound and paused again. He took a deep breath and began winding. Slowly but surely, the cream appeared. It had worked. They were ecstatic.

Both men clasped each other and danced around whilst they sang the tune of the *Irish Washerwoman*. The others heard them and appeared first with incredulity on their faces and then the reality dawned; the miracle they had prayed for had happened. They were saved and barring an unforeseen disaster would soon be back in business. Justine appeared in her dressing gown when she heard the news. They joined in the celebrations, which ended with tears of relief. They could now begin to hope again.

'Right,' said Bobby. 'We now have to clean up all the others. Declan! We need help from the neighbours. Be sure not to tell them what it is all about. I don't want any word getting back to individuals unknown and who are definitely *personae non gratae.*'

That morning, the farm was a hive of activity as neighbours cleaned and polished and polished and scrubbed again. The oiling Bobby did himself as he trusted nobody but himself. By mid-afternoon, all machines were working bar one which was being very stubborn. Bobby spent several days getting it right but even this maverick had to submit to the new order and join the others in functioning properly.

'Now then,' said Bobby to Declan. 'You can send word to everyone that employment is back to normal and it will be business as usual from tomorrow onwards. No more milk thrown away. No more waste.'

Declan issued a series of orders to some of the girls that had arrived and who whooped with delight.

'Don't get ideas with any of these young women, Mr Williston,' said Justine. There was quite an edge in her voice. Bobby just smiled and went on his way, whistling a melody from the Mozart clarinet concerto.

'One thing puzzled me,' said Declan. 'We could have paid the money into the National Bank whilst we were in Cork. Why didn't we?'

'Simple,' said Justine. 'If there is an enemy, and surely there is, he will hear at some point that you are back in business but hope you have not enough money to pay your debt at the National Bank. That's why we went to another bank so that hopefully, they will know nothing of your assets or plans. This means they will wait until near the deadline time before thinking about doing any possible dirty work. You haven't as yet told me the date.'

'That is sometime in September or October.'

'Good. No point in paying off the debt until then. Hopefully, we should be safe until that time. And there is an enemy. No doubt about it.'

'Time for a break,' said Declan, allowing himself a huge stretch of his legs and arms.

The following day the farm at Bunmaskiddy was getting back to its old self. Workers laughed and joked, something they had not done for some considerable time. Later in the morning a car appeared which the onlookers viewed with interest and a little suspicion. All except Bobby that is. The driver got out and waved to them with a beaming face and then beckoned Bobby to join him.

'Top of the morning to you. Good to see you again, Mr Wilson.'

'And to you, Mr O'Hanlon,' said Bobby, not bothering to correct him.

'Here they are then. They are raring to go.'

He opened the door and out jumped two large German Shepherd dogs who immediately relished their freedom and rushed about with no particular direction in mind. O'Hanlon barked an order and instantly the two-year-old dogs obeyed and came back to heel. They looked up expectantly.

'You will have to be very strong and severe with them to start with, Mr Wilson. Use the stick and carrot technique. The next few days will be vital. I will help you for two days and then it is up to you.'

'Understood,' said Bobby. Now that everything was working properly he only needed to pop into the barn now and then to issue orders or supervise when he felt like it. He was glad of a fresh challenge. He put his foot down firmly with the dogs and began as he meant to go on. It was getting towards dusk when O'Hanlon declared his intention to leave.

'Must get away before dark on these roads. They are so bad down here that when I get home I'll have to check some vital lower parts of me body.'

'Let me settle with you. We must unload the dog food that is in your car,' said Bobby.

These tasks completed, O'Hanlon drove off while Bobby went to resume his early apprenticeship with the dogs. As he walked to where they were tethered he wondered how and when those who were planning the ruination of the Conlons would show their face. The dogs looked up and assessed the man who was now their master.

Bobby later went into the house which contained radiant and adoring faces. There were tears of joy on both the menfolk. It had been a similar sight on the faces of the workers who had little concept of the dark events of the past but believed their future might now be assured and they could have a simple plan in their lives. Only Justine and Bobby tempered their feelings and later expressed them to each other. By the time they had finished talking, it was getting on for midnight and they were both over tired and aching.

'I had to explain to Declan why we deferred settling the debt and it was not easy. He wanted everything resolved. I told him that the big weakness of our enemy or enemies is that they believe they are dealing with people of low ability and intellect if not imbeciles. If I am not mistaken somebody will contact Declan from the Land Bank and offer him a low price for his farm, land and equipment with it, believing that the re-establishment of normal service here will not be sufficient to pay off the debt. I have read the small print and they can foreclose by October 1st. That means we must go to Cork a few days before that date.'

Justine nodded and then yawned.

'Time for bed. Let's resume tomorrow. I am so proud of you.' She rolled over and was asleep almost before he reached the door.

17. Legal Matters

In mid-September, a letter duly arrived with a cream-coloured type-written envelope. Before he opened it Declan asked Bobby and Justine to come into the kitchen and join he and his mother. He read it out carefully while stumbling over a few long words and thus having to be gently helped without making him look a moron. It asked for a meeting with Mr Declan Conlon on 21st September to discuss the sum due to the bank on the 1st October. The letter boy was asked to wait whilst Declan composed a reply. Justine wrote it and Declan signed it carefully. The letter boy was paid and departed whistling happily mainly because of the generous tip he had received.

The balmy September days gradually fell away. The day drew nearer for the visit to Cork and everyone individually felt a little apprehensive to say the least. Justine asked Aoifa for some old clothes and a hat and when she presented herself to the others, they were amazed at the transformation and not a little amused.

'What's to do?' said Declan.

'You are going to take me to terminus and I'll get the tram. Meet you at the coffee house at whatever time you arrive. Do what you have to do and don't worry if you have to keep me waiting. We shouldn't all be seen together as when you pay off the debt, someone isn't going to rush out and be lighting a thanksgiving candle.'

Declan and Bobby saw the sense in that and agreed. Justine then departed on her way.

'Quite a lady that, Bobby,' said Declan. 'Is she too old for you to marry?'

'Don't know about that. She hasn't asked me yet.' After a pause while his somewhat slow brain took in the remark, he looked at Bobby and laughed.

The 21st day of September arrived and the plan they had formed was put into action. Instead of taking horses or the pony and trap Aoifa took them to the tram. They all sat separately and enjoyed the journey into Cork. They had several minutes to wait but decided not to go into the Bank early. When they did go in they were not kept waiting and were shown into the office of the manager who looked up in surprise when he saw two men.

'Good morning, Declan. How are you? Good to see you and in happier circumstances than last time. I was at the funeral. I am so, so sorry about your father. He was a good man. You do remember me, then?'

'It's Mr Harris, isn't it?'

'That's correct. Now introduce me to your companion.'

Bobby jumped in before Declan could answer.

'Robin Wilson; Mr Conlon's friend and advisor.'

'I see. It's good to know you have someone helping you, Declan. Tell me what the state of affairs are like at the farm before we continue.'

Declan was about to speak but underneath the table Bobby put his hand on Declan's knee to check his reply.

'We're recovering slowly, sir. We're not out of the woods yet but are getting there. We feel there's a good future for the farm and the smallholdings who rely on its good health.'

'That's good to hear but I've a problem at this end with the debt. I've been issued with instructions that the loan period cannot be extended, a fact of which it grieves me to say.'

'We understand your position, sir,' said Bobby, stopping short of playing his ace.

'Before we continue down that road may I ask if you have received any offer for your land and property?'

'Not as yet,' said Declan.

'Perhaps I should not say this but I've heard a rumour that you were about to get one in a few days. You understand that it is easy for word to get around in a small city like this. I think there is only one place where there is more rumour and gossip and that is the city of London square mile.' He laughed at his own joke. Then his face darkened.

'The scavengers are after you, Declan, and there is nothing I can do to help.'

'Yes, there is,' said Declan. 'Please look at the contents of this envelope.'

Harris looked surprised but did as he was bidden and his eyed widened with delight.

'This is excellent. Excellent. Almost unbelievable. Congratulations, dear boy. Do I take it that you had help from this gentleman here?'

Again Bobby jumped in before there was any chance of an indiscretion by Declan.

'Just a little, sir.'

'Well, well. That is the best news for a long time. Your father would be proud. So sad to lose him. And a good horseman too. Can't think how it could have happened.'

'We have our own ideas on that, Mr Harris. We think he may—'

Again, Bobby checked Declan but this time with his foot.

'Yes,' said Harris. 'Now is not the correct time for that subject. This calls for a small celebration. This is most unexpected but good news.'

'Thank you, sir,' said Bobby. 'Would you let us have the deeds and then after the kind libation you have offered we will be on our way as we have much to do.'

'Of course. Let me organise that first.' He went to the telephone and awaited a reply.

'Ah. Is that you, Naysmith. I want the deeds of the Conlon farm sent up, please. Ask Miss Quinlan to bring them up as I need a word with her.' He paused whilst the voice at the other end spoke.

'Mr Naysmith. I have made a simple request. I am aware of the deadline of the farm. I do not expect to have my orders or requests questioned by my subordinates. Just get out the Conlon farm deeds and get Lucy to bring them. Is that clear?'

He put the telephone down somewhat exasperatedly and then went over to get the decanter. He was over at the far end of the room pouring out three sherries when a knock came on the door and a man in his late forties entered with a sheaf of papers. He handed them to Harris.

'I thought I told you to send them up with Miss Quinlan, Naysmith.'

'She's indisposed at the moment, sir, and I thought you wanted them urgently.'

All the time he had been talking the man was trying to get a look at the two men at the opposite end of the room and whose faces were hidden. Declan and Bobby could see a reflection of the man in the outside window. Bobby whispered to Declan not to turn around.

'Get back below and send up Lucy and make sure your feet do not touch the ground.'

'Yes, sir. At once. Sorry, sir.'

Harris brought the drinks and they knocked them back quickly.

'Well, gentlemen. This really has been a pleasure,' said Harris. 'Now if you will excuse me.' They shook hands and left just as a young woman was about to knock on the door.

'Come in, Miss Quinlan,' said Harris and closed the door as the men left.

As they walked out of Harris' office, Bobby was about to make for the outside door when he was suddenly guided by Declan to one of the writing desks and put his hand on it.

'What's up,' said Bobby.

'Don't look around now, Bobby, but when I pretend to write I want you to take a look at the man talking to the lady by the marble statue.' Bobby waited a few seconds then did as was bidden and awaited for Declan's explanation.

'Who is he and what's the big deal?'

'He is the man who came to inspect the separators when they broke down, I am absolutely sure of it. I seldom forget faces.'

'Wonder what he is doing here. This looks decidedly fishy.'

Bobby was trying to think rapidly. He made his decision and waited to pounce. As soon as Lucy Quinlan came out of Harris' office, he went over to speak to her and pulled Declan, somewhat roughly along. The girl stopped suddenly in her tracks.

'Hello. It's Lucy, isn't it? Lucy Quinlan.'

'Yes sir but do I?....'

'I met your father once or twice. My, my, you have grown. Tell me how are you getting on with Mr Harris?'

'Not all that well, sir, but—'

'Don't worry, his bark is worse than his bite. Now listen, Lucy. We need your help. I have a £1 bet on with my friend here that the gentleman in the corner by the statue is Tommy Arkesden who years ago played for Manchester United, or City I forget which. Am I correct? Steady. Take your time looking around and don't stare. Slowly now, slowly.'

The girl slowly looked across to where Bobby had indicated.

'No, sir. That is Mr Walter Naysmith. He's a businessman, I believe. His brother is our department head. They are planning on buying up a farm; nothing to do with football.'

'Cha,' said Bobby in insincere exasperation. 'You win, brother,' he said giving Declan the pound note.

'Tell me, does he live locally?'

'Wexford I believe, but I think he goes everywhere on bank business. Will that be all, sir?' said Lucy, still somewhat puzzled.

'Not quite, Lucy. If this should get out amongst my friends I would die from embarrassment. Can you keep a secret? That includes Mr Naysmith. If he asks you what we were talking about just say, I was asking about your father's health. He is well, isn't he.?'

'Oh he was fine when I left home this morning.'

Whilst she was saying this, he took her hand and put a golden guinea in it. The girl gasped with pleasure.

'Your secret is safe with me.' With that she smiled and walked off.

Bobby turned to Declan and said: 'As we leave make sure you resist the temptation to have a look at Naysmith as it will give the game away.'

'Just as you say,' said Declan.

There were plenty of people in the bank milling about so they followed a group of people to the door. Out of the corner of his eye Bobby could see Naysmith was eyeing them intently. Outside, they walked around the corner and continued for at least a couple of minutes whereupon Declan tapped him on the shoulder.

'That was clever with the girl. How did you think that one up? Here's your pound.'

'I can't take any credit for that. It goes to Sir Arthur Conan Doyle.'

'Who?'

'Conan Doyle. Creator of Sherlock Holmes. The Blue Carbuncle. Now do you get it?'

'Well, I have heard of Sherlock Holmes but what in the name of the Apostles is a blue carbuncle?'

'It's one of the Sherlock Holmes stories and he uses that trick to extract the information that he needed. I thought we'd use it today to good effect and it worked. Keep on walking. Don't slow down.'

'It did. Whether your original idea or not it was good one to use it now. Bobby, why in the name of all the saints are we walking so fast?'

'Because we are being followed.'

'Are you sure?'

'Quite sure and the person concerned has either not done it before or is very poor at it. Now when we get to that alley down there, we turn left. Got it?'

Declan nodded and followed, still mystified. They turned into one of the side streets and then into the alley. Bobby was counting on the fact that there would be nobody about. Immediately he pulled Declan into the niche and waited. The figure was just about to pass by when Bobby grabbed him. His self-defence training all those years ago suddenly became very handy.

'Right, young man. Let's have a look at you. In here where nobody can see us having a friendly little talk. Now then what's afoot? You seem to have a somewhat unhealthy interest in my friend and I.'

'Nothing, Mister, nothing. Honest. I was just going to get my lunch,' said a youth of about seventeen.

Bobby slapped him around his face and cut his lip. Declan frowned disapprovingly but did not intervene.

'If you insult my intelligence any more, I am going to tear you from limb to limb so that they will not recognise you at home tonight. That's if you are still alive.'

'Please, sir. I was only doing what I was told. I didn't mean any harm,' said the terrified young man.

'My friend and I will be the judge of that. Who sent you to follow us and why?'

'Mr Naysmith from the bank. I was told to follow you and report back where you had gone to,' said the boy, nursing his lip and shaking with fright.

'Here. Let me see if I can fix that,' said Bobby. 'You should not stalk people like that as they might take exception. Now what are you going to tell him when you get back?'

'Nothing, sir, nothing. Honest. Please don't hit me again.'

'Yes, you are. Tell him we went to the *Imperial Hotel.*'

'The Imperial? Yes sir. I promise I will.'

'Now there is no need to tell him about this part of today's events. We just walked into the *Imperial*. Right?'

'Yes, sir.'

'If I find out later you have not kept your word, I will use my training and personally come and make sure that your death is a long and extremely painful one. Do you hear?'

'Yes, sir. I promise. Please let me go, you are hurting my arm terribly.'

'Now here is a little token of our goodwill.' He pressed half a crown in the boy's hand.

'Thank you, sir.'

'Right. Get going quickly before I change my mind.' The boy rushed off still terrified.

Declan, whose life seemed to have been turned upside down at that moment, looked inquiringly at Bobby.

'Where to now?' said his bemused companion.

'Why, the *Imperial Hotel*, of course,' said Bobby with a smile.

18. Enter Joe Cassidy

They reached the *Imperial Hotel* and immediately Bobby made for the bar and ordered a Guinness for both he and Declan. Bobby offered the youthful barman a drink to which he readily accepted. The three of them chatted a while about nothing in particular. Bobby, who had been constantly assessing the man who was serving them, then thought it time to start the ball rolling.

'Are you a local man, bartender?'

'Born and bred, sir. What about you?'

'Boston.'

'Which one?'

'Both.'

'That's interesting. You must have had pretty wide feet when you were born.'

'Born in one; bred in the other,' said Bobby, taking an instant liking to the Irishman.

'I won't ask which way round.'

Bobby smiled. The bartender then diverted his gaze to Declan.

'You've been here before, sir. I remember; it was a wedding. You were best man.'

'Begorrah, you have a good memory.'

'That's easy. We all remember the fight that occurred after the meal. You were hurt pretty badly. Where did they take you?'

Declan was about to reply but Bobby interrupted as his mind was working quickly and he wanted to get things moving. He looked at the bartender and blurted out: 'How would you like to earn a little something extra to put in your pocket?'

'As long as it's legal or at least almost so and mother wouldn't mind then Joe Cassidy is your man. What is it that you will be wanting?'

'A private room with a telephone and nobody to be near about or likely to come in. If £5 would be to your satisfaction, then we would like to start immediately.'

'Sir, you have a deal.' A delighted Joe lead them away behind a curtain and spoke to the girl on the switchboard.

'These gentlemen need a private line for a few minutes, Annie.'

'Fine,' said Annie. 'Through that door there, sirs. No one will disturb you.'

Bobby took out his little book and gave the first number to Annie. They went into the room and after a delay were connected. All this time Declan was still very puzzled but he continued to have absolute faith in his friend. He looked out of the window whilst the conversations were in progress and waited patiently. After a very lengthy wait, Bobby turned around triumphantly and faced Declan.

'As I thought,' he said. 'Exactly what I expected.'

'Are you going to fill me in? I haven't a clue what you are up to.'

'Of course. Can we get to Justine as quick as you like?'

'Are we about finished here?'

'Almost. One more little job. Wait here. I am afraid this is the moment we have to take a really big leap in the dark.'

Bobby went out and spoke with the barkeeper.

'Can you get somebody to fill in for you, Joe?'

'Yes, but no more than five minutes.' He spoke to his colleague who took over. 'What is it that I can do for you gentlemen?'

'There's some men following us, Joe. They've got somebody watching us now. They will be coming to ask you a few questions about us. By all means tell them we came to borrow the telephone. If they ask you if you heard any of our conversation tell them whilst we were drinking, we were talking about this gentleman selling his farm to me next week. Casually now. Don't rush. Doesn't matter that you do not know which farm. That's all you picked up. Have you got all of that? Say it back to me.'

Joe repeated it, the second time with more accuracy. He made some notes and put the paper in his breast pocket.

'You see this gentleman and I have made a deal but they will stop at nothing to get what they want. You did not hear anything else. Got that?'

'Right on the line, sir.'

'Now here is £5 for the phone and £5 for doing the job. We will go now and come back here at 5 o'clock to see whether you have had a visit. You promise to keep everything else under wraps and there will be some more in it for you. Plenty. We must tell you we have not done any crime. Have we got a deal? There will be more in it for you later.'

'We have a deal, sir, and that's mighty generous of you. You both have honest faces. I won't let you down. Must get back or I will be in a lot of bother.'

They left the office and on the way out, gave Annie the very pretty girl on the switchboard a half crown piece.

'Come back anytime,' she said to Bobby. 'Never mind if you run out of half crowns.'

'I may take you up on that,' said Bobby. They shook hands with Joe who was feeling very flushed at his good fortune then went to meet Justine at the coffee shop. They went into one of the corner seats and waited to see if anyone was following. They had dodged about on the way and if there had been anybody following, they had given them the slip. At the coffee shop, Bobby then gave Justine and Declan an account of the events and actions of their morning.

'Right. I phoned the firm who supplied the separators and they said they had spares of every sort. I'm relieved about that because the ones from Perry's were makeshift ones. I've ordered the correct types and they promised them in the next two to three weeks. We might not need them for a while but I am not taking any chances.

'They also said that the repair specialists were located in Dublin and they had regional operators. They looked in their records and the name of the man who visited you was Lambert and certainly not Naysmith. When your father contacted them again to say the trouble persisted, they were surprised as Lambert had returned to say all was working well.

'They couldn't speak to him about the matter as he'd left the firm a week later without a leaving a forwarding address. One of the girls in the office said she thought he had gotten a job in the National Land Bank in Belfast. He's probably there now sporting a different name. Either that or our enemies have bumped him off. Your father in his frustration opened up a separator and diagnosed correctly where the fault lay. They were neatly tampered with. Just a nick so that it was a gradual seizure. Clever, but not too clever for your father, Declan. He knew what it was all about.'

'But it doesn't explain how they were waiting for him on the day he rode in; that is, if he was murdered as you say.'

'Correct. Let's assume that your father telephoned the repairs department. You said he did use a phone on that day.'

'He went to Father O'Leary's who said he repeated the same jumbled statements.'

'Right. That is the missing piece. The repair shop had been primed to let them know anything. Somebody there has been bought. Why is there no telephone in the village yet except for Father O'Leary?'

'Too expensive to come down just for us. We are a way out, you know. They tried once but it is windy on the hill and in a gale, the posts and wire finished up in the sea.'

Declan and Justine were all silent for a while yet inwardly they held a tremendous respect for Bobby and found it difficult to express their appreciation. Declan, ever the pacifist, looked at Bobby.

'Do you not think that they might believe enough is enough and leave it at that?'

'Not likely. They have spent a lot of money and murdered for it. Your farm is a potential goldmine and they want it badly.'

'Haven't we taken a chance relying on that barman to keep his mouth shut?'

'I'm afraid so. It is a gamble we have to take,' said Bobby. 'I had no other option. Let's hope he's loyal to us. There was no other way and I had to trust him.'

Their meal arrived and they suddenly found they were hungry. Afterwards Bobby continued with his thoughts but they were interrupted when Justine intervened.

'I can't help thinking that this is more than just running you out of business, Declan. There has got to be something more, a deeper reason, and we must get to the bottom of it.'

Bobby agreed although he realised that it might be difficult to pinpoint. He said: 'What's more important is that we must try and stay at least one step ahead of them.' He paused for a moment. 'Anyone for coffee?'

They idled the time away for the next few hours. Justine was left on her own so as not to be seen with the other two. She said she would catch the first tram after 5.00 pm and wait for them at the terminus. The men walked a while around the city and Declan pointed out some of the sights. They made a few strategic stops and waited but this time it did not appear as if anyone was following them. Just before 5 o'clock, they walked back into the *Imperial Hotel*. There was a delay this time as Joe had several people to serve. He passed responsibility to another man.

'Just two minutes, gents. Round the back here.' He took them through the curtain.

'They came in and I gave them all the information casually like you asked. There were four of them.'

'Four of them?'

'Yes. I know one of them. Name of Peter Doyle. Was at school with him. Real nasty piece of work. Bullied me a few times. Took my dinner money off me once and I have never forgotten or forgiven him. So it's now become a pleasure to help you gentlemen.'

'That name sounds familiar,' said Declan.

Both Declan and Bobby from that moment felt a whole lot easier in their minds. As they bid goodbye, Joe caught Declan's arm. He put two half-crowns into his palm.

'What's this for,' said Declan.

'They gave me this for the information.'

'So? Why are you giving it me?'

'It wouldn't be right to take it, sir. It rightly belongs to you. No man can serve two masters. And I could never serve Peter Doyle. He's a bad one, that fellow. Keep your distance, sir if you are able.'

The two men smiled and took their leave. Joe's honesty and the fact that he had thrown his lot in with them had taken a huge weight off their shoulders. The tram was extremely crowded but numbers thinned out with only a dozen on it when they alighted.

After taking precautions to make sure they were not being followed, they walked on from the terminus to find Justine sitting on a large boulder waiting patiently. As they had no idea what time they were going to return they had not asked Aoifa to meet them. The remainder of the journey was more than two

175

hours' walk but they were in luck for part of the way as they were given lifts, one on the back of a buckboard and the other by a stranger in a motorcar.

19. Aoifa's Secret

When evening meal was being served, there was only one topic of conversation. Consequently, the meal itself took a lot longer than usual. All three who had been to Cork expounded their theories. When Bobby informed them of the names of the people they had seen, all the others shook their heads except Aoifa who went into the kitchen ostensibly to fetch the coffee. When the others heard the sound of a plate breaking, Justine and Eilish immediately went to investigate. Aoifa looked white and unsteady on her legs.

'What is it, mother?' said Eilish. 'You look ill. Come here and sit yourself down.'

'Oh nothing. It's all been a lot to take in. I think it is the result of the last few weeks and months. I am now beginning to miss Martin badly and it has suddenly caught up with me. Would you mind finishing off in here for me, Eilish? I think it would be a good idea for me to rest my head for a while. I'll go to my room.'

Eilish did as she was bidden and told the others that their mother had felt faint. Their concerns assuaged, they carried on talking. It was Justine with her acute feminine instinct who knew something was amiss and who resolved to investigate. Saying nothing to the others, she crept out quietly and went to Aoifa's room to see what state she was in. Aoifa looked rather preoccupied but warmed when Justine appeared and managed a weak and somewhat distorted smile. She still looked very pale and was far from being her usual self.

'Good of you to come and see me,' said Aoifa.

Justine merely smiled. As often when tension is released, a person talks rapidly and somewhat incoherently and this was no exception. The wise, experienced and sensitive Justine deliberately let Aoifa ramble on about trivialities until without warning Aoifa suddenly burst into tears. Justine held her closely and waited for the deluge to abate before speaking. A period of several minutes thus elapsed.

'There's something very wrong, isn't there?' said Justine.

'Oh I'll be up and about tomorrow to be sure,' said Aoifa without conviction.

'Of course you will but there is still something wrong in your mind. Deeply wrong.'

'How do you know?'

'Because I have experience of the evil of the world and the others have not. Anyway, they are men. Is it a terrible thing?'

There was a pause.

'A damnable one.'

'Is it connected with a person of whom we have been discussing.'

'Yes. I never expected to hear his name again. I prayed to God that I would not.'

'Then you owe it to Bobby and me to tell us in case it has a bearing on what happens next. If you don't, we might lose everything we have worked so hard for.'

'I believe you but it is very hard for me. None of the family knows a thing about it.'

'Will you tell me?'

'Give me an hour to think. Promise that Eilish and the boys will never know and certainly Father O'Leary.'

'The clouds are beginning to disperse. I am beginning to get the picture,' said Justine.

It was midnight before Aoifa had finished her narrative. She had been born in Wexford to a poor family that somehow had managed to get through hungry and lean times. She had gotten involved with a man in the town who had improved her life but at a cost. He had proposed and been accepted but soon after found herself pregnant.

For several months, she managed to keep it secret due to being slim. When her parents threw her out with nothing, she had nowhere to go. Her fiancé was in the army at the time and was away. She wandered aimlessly along the highway until she collapsed. A friendly crofter and his wife took her in and nursed her. She was at death's door for a week and as a result of her condition, the baby only lived for a few days.

'Did you reveal the name of the father to the farmer and his wife.'

'Yes, and they told me what a bad lot he was and named two of the other girls locally that he had jilted.'

'You were well rid of him then.'

'He did some awful things to people. Fighting regularly and stealing yet he went to Mass every Sunday, confession every other Thursday. Then back to what he was before to start his crimes all over again.'

'There's more than a few people in this world who act like that,' said Justine grimly.

'Just one thing, Aoifa. If you are ever worried about my silence let me tell you this; I have just about the same amount as you to sweep underneath the carpet. There is no need to tell you the gory details just that I have lived by my wits and my clients have been men with too much money and too little standards in the way of morals.'

'Does Bobby know? He seems to be very fond of you. More than fond in spite of you being older.'

'He knows although he has never pressed me on my history. He is the only man I have ever loved and do you know, I can't understand why. At some point I think I have got to let him go because he deserves somebody a lot better than me.'

At the end of this statement, Justine choked and it was Aoifa's turn to put an arm around her shoulder. When Justine recovered, Aoifa then continued with her narrative.

When her former fiancé came home and eventually managed to trace her, he accused her of killing the baby or having an abortion. He was beside himself with rage. He attacked Aoifa and was eventually thrown out by the farmer not before he had threatened some terrible things. He had said that Aoifa would burn in hell if he did not burn her first.

The only thing Aoifa could do was to leave and see if she could find work in a city where she could be anonymous. The farmer and his wife gave her money for the train to Cork and fortunately, she found a job in a laundry. She changed her surname but not her Christian name, which was to prove fateful. Not many years later she met Martin, a prosperous farmer, and eventually they married and were happy.

'Did you tell him?'

'I didn't dare,' said Aoifa. 'He kept asking me to marry him. I felt tainted but I wanted him and in the end gave in.'

'And I assume that when you heard one of the names mentioned this evening, it brought back some memories. Some very unpleasant and grievous ones, that's for sure.'

'Very much so. One awful name I had hoped would never surface again.'

'But somehow he must have found out that you were here. How could that have happened?'

'We bumped into each other at the Christmas dance in Cork last year. After all those years and yet there he was. When he saw me and heard someone call my name, he came over when I was on my own. He said that nothing had changed and that I had killed the son he always wanted. He had not forgotten and that he would do everything possible to see that I would burn on earth before I burnt in hell.'

'I see,' said Justine. 'Right. That's enough for tonight. Sleep now and tomorrow we will decide what to do for the best. Here. Drink this. A little milk for you. By the way, I notice you have a shotgun in the corner. Is it a case of just in case?'

'Yes. And it is loaded. Not a word to the others. Not a word about anything we have spoken. Promise me.' Her voice rose again in her anguish.

'Not a word except to Bobby. He won't say anything but he has to know. I hope you understand the reason for this.'

Aoifa could only nod her head. Justine then left and almost collapsed on her own bed.

In the morning Justine, who was already dressed, woke Bobby early. She shook him.

'What's to do?' he said. 'Where's the fire?'

'Only in my heart for you.' She kissed him. 'Listen to what I have to tell you.'

'Go ahead. I know what you are going to say. You are going to give me a gold mine.'

'More than that, Bobby. Just bide your time.'

Justine did not elaborate on the last comment but sat down on the side of the bed. She then revealed the conversation with Aoifa a few hours before. When she had finished, Bobby sat up and scratched his head as if the action would induce some inspiration.

'Well, we now have the motive and the people but there is one thing that puzzles me. The Naysmith brothers, Walter and Saul, are in the banking business, not the dairy farming trade. How come they hit upon the idea of sabotaging the separators? There is a missing link and I have to find it. I am going to get dressed.'

He got out of bed somewhat absent-mindedly, forgetting she was still there. He was wearing a pyjama bottom only and before he realised what was happening, she grabbed him and drew him closer, neatly pulling the pyjama cord whilst holding him in a firm grip. He was helpless to do anything and allowed her to kiss him tenderly. For an all too brief three or four seconds, she fondled him then turned to go.

'Pity I got dressed first,' she said as she left. Bobby was rooted to the spot for several seconds as part of his mass felt like jelly. He suddenly pulled up his pyjama bottom and tied it as he felt somewhat taken off his guard. He washed, dressed and joined the others.

He was quiet at the breakfast table. So quiet that Eilish remarked on it.
'Are you feeling well, Bobby? You are still with us?'
'Yes, fine, thank you and still with you in dear old Ireland.'
'You are very quiet as never before in the morning,' she added.
'I am trying to think. Trying to think like Sherlock Holmes.'
'How so?'
'Because there is a missing link. The Naysmiths are bankers not dairy farmers. How come they knew what to do and what damage to cause?' He was silent again and the others looked at each other quite mystified. After a few minutes, Bobby spoke his thoughts aloud.

'There has to be at least one other person involved in this saga... A long shot. Tell me, Eilish, did Martin dismiss anyone these last few months or more for any reason?'
'I don't know. I don't really have much to do with that...wait a minute... Yes. Of course, there was an instance. I remember. One about a year ago.'
'Yes', said Ryan. 'Peter Doyle. Father had a real row with him. He accused him of pilfering but Peter denied it. He told him to quit.'

181

'I recall that,' said Declan. 'I remember father saying a man Doyle had left but that's all. He wasn't with us that long; I hardly knew him. I can't even put a face to the name.'

'It was when you were in Cork when you were best man for your friend's wedding. That was when you got hit and arrested,' said Ryan.

'My, my. Who was a naughty boy then?' said Justine sporting a wry smile.

'Some drunks came into the bar. Soldiers. I asked them not to spoil the party and one of them hit me. Broke my nose amongst other things. I was in the hospital for two weeks then the police came in and mistook me for somebody else. They took me to Dublin and held me for a month until they realised they had made a mistake. I had to hitch-hike back which took a long time. My best suit looked a mess. Peter Doyle must have gone by then.'

'Father was sure he'd been stealing.'

'Father just said to me he had left and no more. He left it at that and so did I.'

Bobby put his hand in the air to stop anyone from talking.

'Just a minute. Doyle was the name Joe Cassidy mentioned yesterday at the *Imperial.*'

'Yes, it was,' said Declan. 'And even my poor brain can now begin to work things out. His brother worked for us for about two months; just before and just after father's death. I had forgotten about this.'

'What were their respective jobs?'

'Well, Patrick worked in the main barn. Peter did a lot of the menial odd job work. Patrick lived in the village. When things got bad he had to go. He was very angry but there was no money coming in to pay people.'

'So Patrick worked in the main barn, the one that houses the separators?'

'Yes,' said Declan.

Bobby bashed the table, whooped with joy and stood up to do a little jig. The others looked a mixture of amusement and bewilderment. He composed himself and then sat down with a more serious disposition.

'There we have it. At last. That is probably the missing part of the jigsaw. Your father dismisses Peter Doyle who goes away disgruntled. Never mind whether he was guilty or not. My guess is that Peter is friendly with Naysmith and tells him wants to get even with Martin. By a freak coincidence Naysmith works in the very place where all Martin's details are kept. Namely, the bank. He is a greedy man and realises that he might be able to make some money.'

At this point Justine looked anxiously at Bobby hoping that he was not going to slip up and reveal anything about Aoifa's secret. Bobby continued.

'Meanwhile, your father orders the separators and whilst they are in the warehouse or somewhere, they are tampered with. Or it could have been done here, of course, as it is a simple job. The Naysmiths know everything that is happening because they have an inside man in the form of Patrick. He is probably the one who does the damage to the equipment. It is easily done; a child could do it. The farm then grinds to a halt.

'After your father dies, Patrick is made redundant along with the other workers which is no problem to the Naysmith's as all they have to do is to wait and watch whilst the farm goes bust. They know that the money for the separators and other things can't be paid. Simple. The four of them will be in on it, you can bet your bottom dollar because it needs four people on a plan like this. Right. The only thing missing is when and how. Come on, Smasher. You too, Grabber. Let's find Aoifa and tell her what we have discovered and put together.'

The dogs jumped up as they seemed to sense his buoyant mood and were very eager to take advantage of it. They bounded over the yard frolicking with each other and drawing on a reservoir of boundless energy. That evening all the household collected around the table after the evening meal was eaten and the dishes washed. Bobby sat at the head of the table and everyone noticed that he looked very worried.

'Let me spell it out for you if you haven't worked it out already. We now have a very good idea of who and how many are working against us. They laid their plans on how to steal this farm but have come unstuck so they will have to formulate another stratagem. There may be more than of them I don't know, none of us does. Even with all this information they have the upper hand because they have the element of surprise. We can only wait.

'There is no doubt they will case the joint and see where we are most vulnerable. They know that the rest of the staff go home every night and that there are only a few of us on site. We can't have people on patrol all night as it is just not practicable. There is not enough of us and we don't want to hire people. Word would get about and get back to them anyway and we don't want that.

'It's true we have the dogs who can warn us and would cause a few injuries but if there are enough of the opposition, they can cause all the damage they want by the time we get up. They will probably have firearms.'

'Are you so sure they are set on ruining us? The debt is paid. Surely there's no point in their prolonging this.'

Bobby was sworn to keep Aoifa's secret so he had to find words to convince Declan. This was difficult as they all were simple and gentle folk who had been shielded from most of the evil in the world. Moreover, they little realised that Naysmith would somehow have to dispose of them without trace if he were to capture and own the farm thus gaining his revenge. Bobby and Justine were well aware this but knew it would be a mistake to point this out to the family, with the exception of Aoifa. Bobby carefully couched his reply.

'They will not give in having got this far. They have no scruples. Just think what they did to your father. They couldn't squeeze you out so now they will try and burn you out in some way and then dispose of any evidence.'

'I can hardly believe this is happening,' said a slightly tearful Eilish.

Bobby continued his thoughts out loud,

'I wish I could work out what they were planning. Hopefully, they think we do not suspect them and they most likely do not know of the existence of Justine and me.' He paused:

'I've ordered some of the latest firefighting equipment and we all must learn how to use it but it still isn't enough. We need to know more. We need to know when they are coming and I haven't a clue as to how we find that out. I'm glad we fed that information to Joe the barman as the Naysmiths know that if you are going to sell the farm in the next fortnight they will have to make their move soon. I suppose you have never had anything like insurance out here, Declan?'

'Almost unknown in these parts.'

20. Justine Takes Control

Bobby said he felt tired and went to bed early. Justine was the last to retire and she waited a while until there was no sound anywhere in the house. She then got undressed and crept into Bobby's room with just a spare gown around her. Deep down she was a caring and gentle person who, if she had not been an orphan and had to live by her wits, would have done well in whatever sphere of life she chose. She was clever and well-read yet had been denied one important thing in life. Opportunity.

She possessed all the female cunning and guile that was necessary at that moment and realised her actions that morning would be sufficient to pave the way for the desideratum she badly required at this late hour. She crept in by Bobby's side and when he was about to speak, she put her hand over his mouth and then kissed it tenderly. He was powerless to do anything else but submit having been reduced to a form of human putty.

The next few hours were blissful for them both but for Bobby a completely new chapter had begun in his life. As dawn was breaking, Justine crept out and into her own bed. This action was to occur a few more times in the succeeding days. On the last occasion, Justine pulled the sheet over her head and began to weep.

When Bobby asserted that they now had the missing part of the jigsaw, Justine realised that he had been somewhat premature and there was still information that was needed if the farm and its occupants were to survive. They had to know if they were going to be subject to an attack or all their mammoth efforts, not forgetting a considerable amount of effort and expense would be lost. There were the livelihoods of the people nearby who had, at one point, given up all hope of ever being employed locally again.

She waited three days and then put her plans into action. On the evening of the third day, she took Aoifa into her confidence over her scheming but nobody else. Aoifa at the end of this discourse looked sombre but nodded in agreement whilst all the time feeling very worried.

The following morning when everyone was still asleep, Aoifa and Justine got up and got dressed. They had spent the night together in the same room. Carefully, they went into the kitchen and ate a sparse meal before going around to the stable and saddling the horses. It was just getting light when they mounted and went down the track which lead to the farm's entrance. It had been dry, which helped their progress.

It was not long after the sun came up above the horizon and being behind them enabled them to trot along at a fair pace. After about an hour and a half, they reached the tram terminus where Justine dismounted and unhooked her bags. Without any further ado, she said *slan* to Aoifa and went up to the tram stop. Aoifa held the reins of Justine's horse and began the return journey, this time in a more leisurely manner. She reached home to find the others all at work with the exception of Bobby.

She peeped into his room to find him still asleep and wondered what it was that Justine had put in his evening drink that had put him out for so long. Bobby woke up just before 9.00 am with a bit of a headache and a lot of curiosity as to why he had slept for so long. He set to work doing a few menial jobs until just before midday when he returned to the kitchen for a bite to eat.

'Where is Justine?' he said.

None of the others had any idea. Aoifa had made herself scarce knowing that Bobby would be asking this question but could not delay any longer at about 1.00 pm when he came in to get a drink. He asked her for information.

'I do not know rightly where she is, Bobby, but she left this note for you,' said Aoifa.

Bobby immediately felt alarm bells ringing. He tore the envelope open almost savagely. It read thus:

Dearest sweet Bobby.

By the time you read this I shall be in Cork. I did not tell you my plan beforehand as I am quite certain you would have said no and stopped me from going. You were not quite right when you said the jigsaw was complete. True, we have identified those who would do us mischief but we have not found the missing piece; that is, when will they be coming to do their dirty work?

We have no choice but to find that out or all our efforts will be in vain. I am going to see if I can establish contact with Naysmith and see if he will reveal anything. Please do not follow me as it might give the game away. As soon as anything is revealed, I will return or send word by a letter boy.

Love from your Justine. xxx

Bobby was angry but deep in his heart he accepted, albeit reluctantly that her diagnosis of the status quo was correct. It was her manner of dealing with it that made his flesh crawl. He tried not to think about it but by and by, he knew it was eating at him. The thought of her being with another man and in his arms was an anathema. In fact, it hurt like hell.

Later that evening, in a modified form he told the others what was happening. They had to be on their guard. One of them would stay awake until 12.00 midnight then they would have to rely on the dogs to sound a warning. It was absolutely no use enlisting any help from the village as there would be nobody who could keep a secret for long and there was always the chance of betrayal. How long could they keep this up? The tension was mounting by the hour.

Justine made her way to the *Imperial* and when Joe Cassidy came on for his turn of duty, she lost no time in making herself known. It took Joe over a day to find information with regard to Saul Naysmith and where he took lunch. Justine patiently waited while the chair opposite him was vacant and then swept in before anyone else could claim the seat. She gave him one of her engaging smiles and asked if the chair opposite him in the cafe was available, to which Naysmith said it was.

Conversation ensued and when he asked her business in town, she replied that she was a journalist employed by a New York periodical who was gleaning information about the Irish question and possible independence. Naysmith was surprised that a woman was doing this on her own but Justine was ready in case that comment was made. She said that her partner had been taken ill and she was waiting for his replacement, a statement that satisfied him.

On the second day, Justine invited him to dinner at the *Imperial*, which he accepted. It was not long after that she worked her magic and induced the man to reveal some of his past; she made out to be so sorry and comforted him by holding his hand and calming him. The following lunchtime, they went for a walk by the river and Justine pressed him gently for further information about himself. She got it easily but knew exactly where to draw the line of her enquiries.

The information itself was not that important; she was well aware that whilst he was with her, there should be little danger of anything happening to the farm. She was confident that Naysmith, his brother and the Doyle brothers would have to do their dirty work themselves as involving others in mere arson would be a costly business and one later that could be open to exposure and even blackmail. She just needed a snippet of information to be able to ascertain when they were going to act.

Whilst they were having dinner on the second evening, Walter Naysmith appeared. He was first introduced to Justine but appeared quite agitated. He apologised to her for the interruption but quickly guided his brother over to the bar. They spoke for a few minutes and then Saul returned full of profuse apologies. Justine remarked on his brother's state and asked if he was deeply worried.

When the answer was in the negative Justine asked if there was anything she could do to help. This forced Naysmith to reveal a snippet of information. He said that they had a job to do and that it needed organising quickly. She said that it sounded exciting but Naysmith said that it was nothing special, just a fishing trip.

It was at this point that Naysmith made an odd statement, which brought out the goose pimples in Justine.

'I really like you,' he said.

'Thank you. You are an interesting fellow yourself,' she said, smiling engagingly.

'You know, there is something about you.'

Justine waited for a compliment, which never came. In fact what followed cast a cloud over her plans and was more than disconcerting.

'There's something about you that does not add up. Something fishy. Something very exciting but deeply intriguing.'

'And there was I thinking that we were going to have fun together.'

'Oh there is no reason why that should not still happen. But you are a lady of mystery and I believe I shall have to be on my guard with you.'

'If you say so,' said Justine and smiled rather weakly. 'I can't think why you should feel that way.'

'Purely instinct. Nothing more. I set great store on instinct.'

This jolted Justine as she knew that she would not be able to return to the farm in person as it would most likely give the game away. First thing in the morning, she would have to gain the services of a letter boy. She strolled over to the bar and spoke to Joe and asked him if he had heard anything.

'They were whispering,' said Joe. 'The only thing I heard them say was about the moon. The elder one said it was a full moon tomorrow night. Does that make sense?'

'It might,' said Justine.

She spent some time talking to Joe when he was less busy and thought long and hard. Finally, she went over and whispered to him.

'Joe. Can you get me a gun and some ammunition?'

Joe paled visibly.

'It has come to that, has it?'

'I think so.'

'I am not keen on the idea. There's too many guns and too much talk of guns in my country at the moment.'

'Neither am I keen on guns but he said something that chilled me to the bone. Can you buy one for me from Murray's tomorrow?'

'I dare not, miss. I am too well known. These are troublesome times. I am glad to be helping you and you are paying me well but this is something I did not bargain for.'

'I understand. Say no more. I will deal with the matter myself.'

Justine went to bed where she experienced some troubled dreams. In the morning she penned a note and had it taken by messenger to Bunmaskiddy. They at the farm would get it well before noon. All she said in it that they *should expect a visit from the heathen tomorrow night or night after. Will be back as soon as possible.*

After breakfast, she changed into her casual kit and put on the wig that she had bought. She went out the back way as if a servant and then paused at the corner of the next street to see if anybody was following. As soon as Murray's opened, she slid into the shop and asked to see the manager privately. He appeared with a serious and questioning face and looked at her intently.

'Yes madam.'

'Could I have a word in private, please?'

He paused for a couple of seconds.

'Certainly. Come to my office.'

When they were in the office and seated, the manager looked at Justine intently.

'I would like a Webley and some ammunition, please. Cash purchase and no questions. I will pay any price you ask and some more for your silence.'

'Are you in trouble, madam?'

'Not with the police. Just with a rather nasty Englishman set on causing me mischief and a few others besides. The gun is primarily for deterrent purposes.'

'I see.' He mused. 'You are sure you are not involved with the police. Can anybody vouch for you?'

'Yes, but I would rather keep them out of it, if you please.'

There was a very long pause before his reply.

'Very well but if there are any repercussions, we will deny ever selling you this item, you understand. There is no serial number on it.'

'Of course.'

Five minutes later and after paying a huge price, Justine had the Webley in her bag with ample ammunition when she left by the back door. She went into the toilets and changed into a maid's smock and then returned to the *Imperial*. When she went into the rear entrance, nobody took the slightest notice of her. She went up to the first floor and to her room and waited to see if there was anyone in the corridor.

Satisfied that there wasn't, she let herself in. She was tired and lay on the bed for a while to take stock of things and try to crystallise the dozens of questions and demons that were invading her mind. She had a little doze and on awakening, washed and put on smart outfit, loaded the gun and put it under her pillow. She then read until evening time and at the appointed hour went down to the restaurant to await Naysmith.

He was a little late and apologised but Justine merely smiled. They ate and talked. He asked lots of questions which Justine felt she had answered well. Whenever possible, she spoke of New York and London which seemed to arouse interest in him. She hoped it would allay any fears that still troubled him about her. At the point that it seemed right, Justine began to weave her spider's web. She looked at him over the table and said: 'It seems strange after only a short while but I am getting quite smitten with you. I was wondering whether we could step our relationship up a gear, say tomorrow. What would you say to that?'

'Sounds rather wonderful. Tonight no good?'

'No. There is a different man in the foyer by the stairs tonight. It is his job to see any outsiders don't go up to the rooms. People he does not know have to show their key to him. Tomorrow, I can sort out any problem with the boy on duty. For a small price, of course.'

'If it is to be tomorrow then it would have to be early as I am busy later on and won't be back until perhaps the early hours.'

'Six o'clock for an early meal and then whatever takes your fancy.'

'Both of those sound marvellous. See you then.' He winked at her as he left.

Justine went to bed feeling somewhat apprehensive but nevertheless after an hour slept soundly. In the morning she got up, washed, dressed and went down for a somewhat late breakfast where she ate a hearty meal. She had barely finished when to her amazement and anger, Bobby walked in.

'What the bloody hell are you doing here?' she rasped. 'You might give the game away. What's the matter, don't you trust me?'

'Of course but—'

'But nothing. I was going to send you a note. Tonight I was going to follow them down and when they were at the farm, they would be surrounded. It is not as if we did not know where they are going.'

'How the hell were you going to take them on? Swing your handbag at them?'

'I've bought a gun although I hate firearms. Go pour yourself a cup of tea.'

Bobby was shocked and said: 'I keep underestimating you. Suppose something went wrong. How were you going to follow them if they are in a lorry?'

'Very simple. Joe Cassidy has got a half day off having swapped with his mate. He is watching the Doyle house to see when they leave, which will be when it gets dark. They have planned it well because there is an almost full moon tonight—'

'But how the hell were you going to keep up with them—'

'Will you shut up and listen? We have got two of the hotel's bicycles on hand complete with those new carbide lamps. We are going to follow them and dowse them half a mile before the farm just in case. Anyway, you will be ready and waiting and between us we will nab the bastards in the act. I've got a gun and some ammo. Joe could not understand why we don't bring the police in but I have told him we have nothing to go on. No evidence that was cast iron. Our enemies could and would deny everything. I have brought him around to our way of thinking. Now I have got the same to do with you.'

Bobby was dumbfounded and he had to admit that all she had said made sense. He felt a little blue realising that he was not at this moment supreme commander of the farm's defence. Rather, it was the determined and very astute lady in front of him who had promoted herself from lieutenant to general in one fell swoop.

'Time I went and left you to it,' he said. 'For the love of our Lord Jesus, be careful.'

'That must be the most sensible thing you have said all day. I know you will keep calm but try and get the others to do the same, particularly Eilish. The less she knows, the better.'

'Will do. Bye for now.' He got up and was about to kiss her but she got up and out of his way before he had the chance. It turned out to be very fortunate that she did so.

21. The Tables are Turned

Justine spent the day going to various places including the bank. She wore her usual outfit but when she returned to the *Imperial,* she changed into her disguise and left by the servant's entrance. At midday she had a prearranged meeting with Joe in a backstreet café and who was there already drinking a cup of tea. Justine ordered one and told the waiter they would eat shortly.

She outlined her strategy. She would eat early with Saul Naysmith and then go up to her room. Joe frowned at the thought but made no comment. When Naysmith left her, Justine would change and they would follow them down at a distance. They would park the bicycles, douse the lights and creep up behind them as they entered the farm. The others would be ready and waiting and would nab them as they prepared to do damage whatever form that would take. With luck, it would all be over without a shot being fired.

Hopefully, there would be enough evidence for the police when they were called. Nothing would happen at the farm before 6.00 pm as the day staff would be there until then. Whatever it was would be later and after dark. Joe said he would watch the Doyle house from that time onwards. They agreed that Joe would come to the hotel as soon as the enemy foursome made their way down the road to Bunmaskiddy. They both then parted company and Justine retraced her steps.

The waiting seemed interminable and she could feel the tension in her mounting. After a while she took a walk but later could not remember where she had been. She lay on her bed and dozed for a while and occasionally looked at the clock. At six o'clock precisely, she went down to the bar, ordered an aperitif and waited. Naysmith came at 6.30 pm and beamed at her.

She said,

'You look very pleased with yourself. What have you done today that has put you in such high spirits?'

'It's not what I've done today but it's what I'm going to do today that's the cause of it.'

'May I ask what it is?' she said with a convincing air. 'Is it going to be exciting?'

'You may. It is the culmination of many years' waiting when I get some redress for what I suffered and endured years ago. But I have not come here to talk about that; let's eat as I am hungry.'

Justine left the subject, knowing any further enquiry might be fatal. They ate, talked and joked then he said: 'It's time for a bit of fun and frolic. The dessert can take place in you room, I think.'

Justine knew that she had reached the point of no return. The thought of Naysmith pawing her all over was nauseating but a necessary evil. They mounted the stairs with no challenge and Justine put her key in the door. As soon as they were inside, rough hands grabbed her and pulled her hands behind her back. She was taken to the bed and pushed face down and her hands and legs tied. As soon as they turned her over, a handkerchief was stuffed into her mouth. She looked up to see three masked figures who scrutinised her through evil-looking slits. Naysmith allowed one of the others to do the talking.

'Now then, little lady, we want a few answers from you and quickly. Tell the truth and we might let you live. Just nod if you understand.' Justine nodded fearfully.

'My friends and I have been having some doubts about you. Some things seemed just a little strange so I asked my boy at the bank to keep an eye on you. This morning you had a cup of tea in the restaurant with a gentleman who interests us very much. We want to know your dealings with him. I am taking the cloth out of your mouth. Just a quiet honest reply, if you please. Don't make me ruin your pretty little face.'

Justine knew that she could not think fast enough so she had to tell the truth.

'I met him only a few weeks ago aboard the *Lusitania*. We were rescued and brought here. He must have recognised me and came over to speak.'

This put the man off for a minute; he looked at the others before resuming.

'What else do you know about him? What else did he say?'

'He was a steward aboard the ship. He served me several times, that's all. He said he had been picked up by a family who were fishing at the time. I think he said the name was Conlon or something like that. That's all. I had not seen him for some time and only recognised him when he said who he was.'

'What is his name?'

'Wilson.'

The man looked around at the other masked men as if for reassurance. They went into a huddle as if to decide what to do with her. They then searched the room carefully and after a while found the gun.

'Well, well. What is this for, I wonder? Never mind; time is getting on. We can't do anything with her now.' He turned to Justine.

'I would like to say sorry about this but I am not. That gun means you are not who you say you are.' He tied her to the chair, which hurt and burnt her skin. Then he put some tape over her mouth.

'Let's go. She'll keep. We will deal with her later when it's dark and nobody about.'

Justine knew exactly what that meant and a sudden chill went right through her body. She cursed herself for being stupid enough to have bought that gun. Now they had very good reason to doubt her and she had played into their hands.

Whilst this was happening, Joe Cassidy's mind was one of total confusion. He stalked Peter Doyle carefully and was most surprised when he realised he was making for the *Imperial*. His brother and another man were waiting for him and they went inside. It was some time before they came out. He followed them at a discreet distance and then was baffled when they did not take the south road out of town. Instead, they took the opposite direction which was to the docks and marina. He was careful not to let them see him and when they went down to the jetty and boarded a neat little boat with a searchlight on it, Joe gasped.

So that was how they were going to do it.

Bobby and Declan had not thought of that possibility. They were going to go in by boat. By boat! He cursed himself for his lack of brain power. He waited for a while and suddenly the boat sprang into life. He lost no time and turned and ran full pelt to the *Imperial* but when he got there, there was no sign of Justine. He waited in the lobby but still she did not appear.

One of his colleagues who was a vindictive busybody came over and asked what he was doing there being not on duty. Joe answered that he was waiting for a lady to which the other man scoffed and said he did not believe him. He did not dare ascend to the rooms under penalty of losing his job so he waited and waited. Another colleague watched him hoping that he would commit some misdemeanour and therefore have the opportunity of informing on him and thus enhancing his own prospects.

He began to sweat. Suddenly, the lobby man was called away by the assistant manager and Joe realised it was a case of now or never. He rushed upstairs to level three and knocked on Justine's door. There was no answer. He peered through the keyhole and thought he saw something moving, which made him panic more. He looked around in frustration hoping for a miracle or a sign from above. None came and Joe knew that he could not get down to where the spare keys were housed and back without being discovered. And then a couple of minutes later, a divine agency seemed to get involved. One of the maids appeared with some towels.

'Ellen. Come here.'

'What's up, Joey? What are you doing up here at this time of evening? You're up to no good, I can tell. You'll get into trouble.'

'Never mind. How would you like to earn a pound, no questions asked.'

'I would sooner you take me to the autumn fair next week.'

'I will do that as well. Now do you still love me?'

Ellen side-stepped the second question.

'You will?'

'Yes. Promise. Cross my heart and hope to die.'

'Where's the catch?'

'There isn't one.'

'What do I have to do?'

'Open up the door of room 314.'

'Hey, come on now, Joey; that is going a bit too far. We could be caught if anyone comes up here and it will be the chop for both of us.'

'Look Ellen, I think there might be a problem for the lady in 314. She was due to meet me hours ago and it is not like her to be late. She may be ill. There's nobody about. All right, two pounds and the fair.'

'You swear?'

'I swear. Now for the love of God, open the bloody door.'

Ellen did so and it was as he feared. Justine was trussed up like a chicken. He rushed to take off the plaster over her mouth. Once released, Justine called out: 'Shut the door girl. Shut the damn door,' said Justine. 'No. Stay on the inside, please, and help me get out of these. Have you got a knife in your kit?'

Ellen, her face still shocked, did as she was bidden and helped release Justine. She still looked very scared. Justine examined her.

'Listen…what's your name?'

'Ellen.'

'Listen carefully, Ellen. Nobody and I mean nobody must know about this. I know it looks bad but I am working undercover and Joe is one of my special agents. Did you promise her something, Joe?'

'Two pounds and—'

'Here's five for your trouble. And if Joe and I make it back alive, there will be some more for you in a day or two. Joe and I are after some nasty men. Now check the corridor and carry on as if nothing had happened. Nothing has happened, do you hear?' Justine almost shouted the last few words.

Ellen nodded but with fear and sweat etched all over her face. She left quietly and went to deliver the towels.

'Right, Joe. I am just going to get out of this and into some more comfortable kit. Where are the bicycles?'

'Out back. They are all ready.'

Justine was taking off her clothes without a care. Joe turned his head politely but reluctantly, and waited. At one point, he could not resist a quick peep.

'Have you got a key?'

'No. They took it with them. I suppose they were going to use it later when they returned.'

A few minutes later, she was ready and they descended not before she had remembered the gun under the pillow. The lobby man looked at Joe and made a mental note to shop him the next day but said nothing in front of a guest. Joe would have to face his betrayer tomorrow. Out back of the hotel were the bicycles ready in the shed.

'Do you ride?'

'I can manage,' said Justine.

'There's something you don't know. They are going in by boat.'

'What! Sh**. Are you sure? How come you know this?'

'I followed them down to the marina. They will use the motor until they get close and then row in.'

'And nobody at the farm will be ready for them. Oh bloody hell fire! Come on. There's not a moment to lose. Let's get there.'

It was fairly quiet with little traffic about. The only time Joe's heart was in his mouth was when she overtook the tram as it was preparing to stop and there was a lorry coming the other way. Joe held his breath but the driver saw her and swore as he swerved. It was getting dark and they knew that it would be soon that they would have to light the lamps. When they did so, Joe's proved difficult and they nearly gave up. Even so they only managed a modest rate and ten miles took just under two hours. About half a mile from the farm and as far as they dared, they extinguished the lights and walked with the bicycles for a short distance.

'I am sweating like a pig,' said Joe.

'You are not the only one,' said Justine. 'And I smell like a cess pit.'

'Don't worry. It has not reached me yet,' said Joe with a false levity.

Justine ignored the remark and said: 'We must look for somewhere to store these for the night. No point in wheeling them any further. They make too much of a noise and we must be silent as the cemetery.'

They reached the village and decided to leave the bicycles in Father O'Leary's back garden.

'Let's make haste,' said Justine.

There was still a distance to cover but eventually, they reached the farm gate. The moon was up and they crept behind the bushes. There was a light in one of the triple store rooms on the other side of the creamery. Suddenly, there was the sound of voices and then laughter.

Justine whispered: 'You know what that laughter stands for, Joe? They have beaten us to it. They must have all been captured. Let us inch our way to the back of the storerooms and then see if we can do anything.'

They dodged through the undergrowth but not before encountering some nasty stinging nettles. Joe cursed under his breath. At last they managed to reach the storerooms and carefully Joe looked through the window. His eyes took a while to adjust but when they did so, he saw to his horror that Declan and Ryan were tied up. Ryan had been gagged. Joe crouched down and informed Justine of the situation.

'There is a back entrance. Let's see if we can sneak in unnoticed. There are no locks in this part of the world, fortunately.'

They carefully used the bushes to conceal themselves and opened the back door. There were two more doors to open. Justine gave orders to Joe to leave them open in case of quick retreat. They peered in very carefully and heard the sound of hissing. The gas cylinders had been switched on.

'Declan,' whispered Justine. His head turned.

'Justine. Thank God. Quickly.' He coughed involuntarily. 'They have planted a bomb. There are knives in the drawer. For God's sake be quick as it's due to go off at any second.'

Justine and Joe worked feverishly and they cut the ropes on their feet. It was not easy as the knives were none too sharp.

'Hurry, hurry.'

'We're going as fast as we can.'

'Quick. Out the back way. Quick. For God's sake, be quick.'

But they were not quick enough. Justine and Declan were at the door as there was a sudden roar. Most of the force of the blast thankfully went into the wide world the doors being open. They were both thrown clear as the old building collapsed. There was a silence followed by several piercing screams as part of the roof fell on Ryan and Joe. It then went very quiet. There was a lot of smoke and dust, which gradually dispersed.

When the day staff had left in the early evening, Declan had told the other members of his family what they must do and they rehearsed their plans carefully. Eilish was very nervous but she was told she and her mother would be in the house, out of harm's way and in the cellar. The cellar entrance was a concealed trapdoor with a carpet over it and was once used as a priest's hiding place.

As soon as it was dark, Declan, Ryan and Bobby took up their positions at the end of the track near to the entrance of the farm and waited. The aim was not to confront the enemy there and them but to follow them until their act of mischief had been put into action. Eilish, with a Tilley lamp in hand, descended the steps to the cellar and at the bottom looked around to see Aoifa behind her. Aoifa was still at the top of the stairs and said: 'You will be safe down there. I'm not coming with you.'

'No, no mother. Don't leave me all on my own, please don't leave me.' There was panic in Eilish's voice.

'Now don't you be making a fuss, child. I may be more use to them upstairs and I know how to use a weapon. You have the light, which will be good for a few hours. This has to be settled one way or the other before the night's out and you know that. Don't you be making a sound until we bring you out. For the love of God, don't call out.'

'Let me come with you, please, please.'

'Oh goodness, child, you would only scream and give the game away. Surely you can see the sense in your being down here. Nobody will know. Anyway, my mind's made up so quit your blubbin.'

Aoifa replaced the trapdoor and carpet, which extinguished Eilish's protests and went to fetch her loaded shotgun. For a time she waited in the farmhouse and put out the lamp. The only light in the room was the glow from the fire and that of the moon shining through the window. After a while her spirit was restive and she decided to venture outside. She went in search of the dogs who were tied up as Bobby had thought they might make a noise and reveal their location. They were pleased to see her and she kept them on the lead for the time being. For a moment she thought she could hear distant voices on the breeze but these soon disappeared.

She went around the outskirts of the farm's land not really knowing why she was doing this. After half an hour she finally reached the jetty where their boat was moored. To her surprise, there was another boat there tied up alongside. A few moments later she heard voices and instinctively hid. The dogs were uptight and straining but Aoifa spoke to them reassuringly but sternly and they obeyed instantly.

Ryan had been entrusted with one of the rifles and was hidden halfway between the farmhouse and the creamery. It was cold but dry and they had wrapped up warm. They had also taken something to eat and drink. Bobby and Declan were some distance way covering the other two entrances. The plan was to allow them in and pounce just as they were about to do any dirty work.

They waited and waited but nothing happened. Even five minutes felt like an hour. The night was clear and when the moon climbed everything seemed to stand out clearly. The silence was shattered when, just after midnight a voice called out: 'Put down your weapons. We have the boy here and we have a gun on him. If you want him to live, drop your guns and put your hands in the air.'

Declan and Bobby did just that and stood up. Their hearts sank, knowing that they had been outdone.

'Turn around.' They did so and made out four masked men in the moonlight who were armed with shotguns.

'Looks as though you were expecting company. You were right except for the correct entrance. Tell me, Conlon, how did you know when to expect us?' Declan hesitated.

'Come now. Haven't lost your tongue, have you?'

'We guessed,' said Declan.

The masked man laughed.

'Of course. No matter. Now we have little time, Pete. Light the lamps. It is safe now.' One of the other men prodded Declan with his shotgun.

'Where are the women?'

'In the house,' said Declan. He knew it was futile to lie.

'Of course,' said the man. 'Go get 'em. We need to do this in one go. Right, you three. Down to the outbarn.'

Bobby, Declan and Ryan duly obeyed. They had their hands tied and were made to sit on the floor. Then their feet were tied. One of the men looked at Bobby.

'Now then, Yank. A question for you. If you don't answer or lie, I will cause you a lot of pain. Understand?'

'You are going to cause us pain anyway,' said Bobby.

'Oh no. It will all be over in a flash. You won't know a thing. See that man over there. He is preparing a nice little boom boom bang and will be ready in a few minutes. I take it that you are the person who has been putting this place back on its feet.'

'You are correct in assuming that.'

'Was it your idea to install these gas cylinders? These are right up to date; no doubt about that.'

'Yes. I had them installed at our airfield in the states.'

'My, my, who's a clever brain box, eh? You have made things very awkward for us to start with but now it will be to our advantage. Someone told Pete of the cylinders and we worked out our plan using these instead of starting a fire. It will look like a tragic accident.'

'It is a pity some of my finest work will end up in the hands of scum like you.'

The man gave Bobby a nasty blow in the chest with the butt end of his rifle.

'Listen to me, American cousin. You have had your last sleep. Now what is your relationship with a certain blonde lady in the *Imperial*?'

'Not much. She was a passenger on board ship. The *Lusitania*. We were rescued.'

'Where were you bound for?'

'I was a steward. I recognised her and went over to speak to her and say I was glad she survived.'

The masked man paused and looked at his partner in crime.

'Hm. Sounds about right. Good. I can have some fun with her when we finish here.'

'What will become of my wife and mother?' said Declan.

'Easy. There is a North African ship coming into Cobh tomorrow and we have an arrangement with the captain. Your wife should fetch a good price.'

'Why not bump us all off together in here?'

'It would look too suspicious. You three were inspecting a problem and boom and that was that. Your mother. Easy. We are going to tow your boat out with a few of their odds and ends in and then overturn it. Another tragic accident. The police won't want to dwell on this for too long as the whole country is on a powder keg and they have other priorities. We have a couple of them in our pocket anyway. Sergeant Flanagan is straight but he hasn't got much of a brain as he drinks too much.'

He paused and then continued: 'Are there any last requests?'

This was said to confirm his total command and not through any magnanimity.

'Yes,' said Declan. 'I am curious to know why you are blowing us up here and not in the farmhouse.'

'Why? Simple. After the dust has settled and the place is up for auction, this gentleman will buy it. You see, he works in the bank and has his hands on plenty of money. We'll then run the place which you have kindly got going again for us. Don't want to ruin our future assets. We can easily build this outbarn again. Unfortunately, we can't reward you for your hard work. There won't be much left of you; we can't dump you all at sea, just your mother and this man as there would be a long wait for an auction of this place if there are no bodies.

'Hopefully, they might think this man shot them. We have set rumours going with the help of someone at the Herald that you, Conlon, were finding life too hard. The coroner will say at the inquest about your mind being disturbed. We've already paid out a sum for setting up that. There's another reason but we will wait until we find your slut of a mother. Now where the f*****g hell is she?'

'She was told to stay in the farmhouse and keep the light on and stay out of sight.'

The man looked around for the one who had gone to the house. He appeared a couple of minutes later.

'There is no sign of either of them in any of the rooms. I have looked in the cupboards and under the beds.'

One of the others piped up.

'We either all go looking or we blow it up and hope it brings them running.'

'That's a last resort. They must be somewhere. Search again.' He pointed to Bobby. 'Untie him and bring him with us.'

'Why?'

'I've changed my mind about it being quick because he has caused me a lot of trouble so he can have another swim when we are on the way back.'

'Why don't we get on with it? We might be an age finding them and time is getting on. Shall I set the fuse?' There was a pause.

'On second thoughts, yes. How long is it?'

'At least thirty seconds for me. Get further away and with your hands over your ears.'

'Right. Let's do it and let's hope it brings them to us. You're sure there will be no trace of the ropes holding them?'

'It'll be an inferno in there and there will be only ashes I can assure you. No trace of them except a few bones.'

They took the lanterns with them. Bobby was pushed roughly along the long path which lead to the jetty. When they felt they had gone far enough, they turned to witness the blast. Behind them and a few seconds later, a soft Irish voice came out of the gloom yet its owner was concealed.

'Drop your gun, Saul. You too, Walter. Careful now. I have a shotgun which is loaded. Don't think about doing anything silly; you know I am a good shot. That's right, nice and slow and easy. Pick their weapons up, Bobby. Careful now. Don't come between them and me.'

'Aoifa. There's two of them laying a fuse for a bomb in the outhouses. Declan and Ryan are in there.'

'Is that so? You had better quickly get up there.' Her next words were drowned as there was a loud explosion and their ears sang. The pain was excruciating. A few seconds later two men appeared but were too late to notice Bobby and his next move. Even though his hands were tied, Bobby quickly released the dogs.

'Get them, Smasher. Get him, Grabber.'

The dogs were away at once and before the men could do anything they were seized. The dogs bit into the men who screamed and screamed but Bobby in his rage let them continue the carnage.

'Call them off. For God's sake, call them off,' screamed one of the men next to him.

'Why should I, Mr Naysmith, or should I say Mr Lambert? Which are you tonight? You have been rumbled good and proper. You were only going to kill us, that's all. You have just blown up innocent men.'

Aoifa joined in.

'Don't you think you ought to take off those silly masks? It must be you, Saul, and you, Walter.'

The other two men did as they were bidden. Bobby held out his hands for Aoifa to cut his bonds all the while the stricken men were still screaming.

'I am glad I did not have to use it,' she said. 'The dogs do a better job.'

'Heel, boys, heel.'

The dogs obeyed, even though a little reluctantly. Bobby walked up to where the men lay still. He stood over the bodies who were so bloodstained that it looked like a mini battlefield. One of them whimpered:

'No more, please no more.'

'I presume I am addressing Mr Peter Doyle or is it Patrick.'

'Peter.' He just managed to gasp the words; his face was contorted with agony and he rolled over.

'One alive, Aoifa. Not sure about the other one.'

'Get them down here,' ordered Aoifa.

'Get up,' said Bobby. 'Help me drag this one down. One false move and I'll plug you.'

Peter Doyle had no intention of doing anything but obey. His right arm hung loosely and blood was evident even in the moonlight. His trousers and jacket were ripped in such a manner that even shocked Bobby. Smasher and Grabber had really done their work well. Bobby thanked the day that he decided to get them in spite of Declan's and Aoifa's scepticism. When they reached the other group, the lantern shone on a truly grisly scene.

'Jesus,' said Saul Naysmith. 'You'll pay for this, Aoifa. You won't get away with it.'

'As you got away with murdering my husband, Saul? As you have got away with murdering my two sons?'

'Like as you got away with murdering my son?'

'I murdered no one, Saul. Your mind has festered all these years and all for nothing.'

'That was your fault. You let him die to hide your shame.'

'How little you understand, Saul. He died because you had deserted me. I had not eaten for three days and only little before that. He died because I could not make any milk for him, you stupid imbecile.'

Walter intervened. 'You'll never get away with this. I have got friends in high places.'

Aoifa ignored this fatuous remark,

'Bobby. Get Patrick into their boat. You help him, Walter. Peter, you get into your boat. Stay nice and still, Saul, or it will be your last move on this earth.'

'What are you going to do?'

'You are going for a little cruise. I am letting you go.'

'Letting us go?' he said incredulously. Even Bobby was surprised at this remark.

'Yes. Now turn slowly and walk down after them.'

Bobby could not resist a last dig.

'Come along, Mr Naysmith. Or is it Mr Lambert? Chop chop!' He could see the man grimace even in the dark.

It took a couple of minutes to get them all in the boat. Once they were all in, Aoifa said: 'One of you take the oars. Bobby, push them off when you are ready. Then fetch me a lantern. Quickly now.'

Bobby did as he was bidden and Aoifa held the Tilley light as they pulled away. He was still unsure as to Aoifa's intentions but gradually began to understand. He thought it prudent to remain silent and await the outcome as she was the one who had by her actions assumed command.

'Right Bobby. Into our boat and after them. Row and keep close to them. It should be easy as there are four in their boat to our two. Wait until we get to deep water and then get me close without touching them.' She held the Tilley light as high as she could so as to see the other boat. The moonlight only enhanced the scene. This action took quite some time so Bobby had to keep turning his head but did just as she had ordered and then at Aoifa's command drew adjacent.

'What's this then, Aoifa? An escort to Cork? Or are you going to shoot us?' said Saul Naysmith sarcastically.

'No, no. That's your style, Saul. You never did learn to swim, did you?'

Saul was silent. Then Aoifa, with great deliberation, took careful aim and shot two holes in the boat a fraction below the water line. The men cried out, knowing immediately what was to be their impending fate.

'No, Aoifa. You can't. You wouldn't.'

'I just have, Saul. It's my intention that you will never cause any more suffering on this earth to anyone again. And that includes me.'

The water filled the boat quickly. Walter Naysmith tried to swim over to them and grab the side of the boat. Aoifa hit him on the head with the oar. He was the first to go under followed quickly by Patrick Doyle. Peter made some terrible gurgle noises, which made Bobby feel sick but Aoifa was cold, determined and impassive. Finally and aptly, Saul Naysmith went down thrashing and cursing.

They waited and waited.

They waited for what seemed an interminable age and finally, Aoifa broke the silence.

'Let's go back.' She threw the shotgun into the water. Bobby asked why such a waste.

'There are four new ones on the jetty,' she simply said.

When they reached the jetty a few minutes later, their only concern was to see the result of the outhouses. Their hearts leapt when they heard voices. To their astonishment they saw Declan and Justine pulling at rubble. They turned around and saw each other. Their joy was unbounded when they saw each other alive.

'What miracle is this, my son? You're alive and I believed you dead. Hold me tight.'

'No time, ma. Ryan and Joe are trapped under that rubble and we must get them out.'

'Who on earth is Joe?' said Aoifa.

'A saviour, mother. Now everything else later. No more talking. Let's get them out.'

It took nearly an hour to free them. Joe was shocked more than anything although his leg was cut badly and chest hurt. It turned out he had two broken ribs. Ryan had some nasty cuts. His ankle was broken and his arm fractured but he had avoided the worst because the hay had fallen from above and cushioned the impact of the rafters and slates. They carried him up to the farmhouse and on to a bed where he immediately passed out.

'Don't worry. I have got something for both of them for the pain,' said Justine.

'What's that, doctor?' said Bobby.

'Laudanum,' said Justine. 'A very effective painkiller. We won't be able to get them to hospital until late tomorrow morning so this will prevent them from suffering badly.'

'I see,' said Bobby although at that moment he had no idea what the properties of the substance really were. There was a moment of light relief when somebody suddenly thought it about time to see how Eilish was faring in the cellar. She was brought out blinking and bleary-eyed and, thankfully, quite unaware as to what had gone on.

'I thought I heard a bang and the earth trembled for a second,' she said.

'It did,' said Aoifa. 'But it's over and soon we can get some sleep.' Eilish was quite confused to say the least but gradually all was explained to her. She did not know whether to feel angry about being shut in the cellar or glad that she had not befallen to being taken at gunpoint to a Middle Eastern harem. It was left to Bobby to be the one to bring up the subject that they were putting off and were loath to face.

'When it is light one of us will have to go to a telephone and inform the police. We can't cover this up indefinitely. We could cover it up for a time but it would not be long before the day staff would say something and word would get about. Ryan and Joe are reasonably comfortable at the moment thanks to Justine's potion but soon they will need the hospital to deal with their breakages.

'What we must all do is to make sure we are singing from the same song sheet when they come. That means we have just a few hours to decide how much we are going to tell the law. AND we must not at all appear guilty in any way.

'Another thing. There will be blood all the way down to the jetty. Nobody must make any attempt to wash it down or cover it up. If we do, the police will know we have something to hide. We have, of course, but all that has happened is not of our making.

'We will tell them we were broken into, tied up in the barn and the gas turned on. We managed to escape but the guard dogs must have gone for the intruders. The men were masked so we have no idea who they were. Though they must have been bitten, they obviously got away in their boat. They got more than they bargained for.'

Everyone agreed but even if they had not, they would have all been too exhausted and traumatised to argue. A sombre and weary atmosphere then permeated the farmhouse and everyone longed for sleep and rehabilitation through oblivion. Eilish started to shake and was led away by her husband to be comforted. One by one the others drifted to their rooms and got into bed. Bobby did not bother to change but just threw the eiderdown over him. Everyone slept fitfully and awaited the first comforting rays of dawn.

22. Enquiries

It was just light when Declan walked up to Father O'Leary's house. It took a while before the priest's housekeeper opened the upper window and looked at him with an air of abject disdain.

'Well now, it must be something greatly amiss that gets you out at this time in the morning, Declan Conlon, and it certainly won't be your confession.'

'Quite right, Miss O'Neill. No confession just a statement. We've had some unwelcome visitors in the night with guns and explosives and they were not particular who got in their way. We are lucky to be alive. The gas cylinders exploded in the barn.'

'Glory be,' said Miss O'Neill. 'So that was the big noise I heard.'

'It surely was and if you'll let me use the telephone, I'll tell the same to Sergeant Flanagan in Cork, that is if he's sober.'

'Give me a moment and I'll be down.'

Although in her 70s, Mavis O'Neill was soon downstairs and drew back the bolts; she opened the door and looked at him somewhat disdainfully.

'Just look at the state of you. I hope you have a good explanation for this.'

'I hope so too, Mavis.'

'And it's Miss O' Neill to you. Don't be thinking you can take any liberties at this time of day.' Declan was giving the details to the night duty officer at Cork main police station when the good Father appeared having dressed hastily. Declan was told that Sergeant Flanagan would have to be fetched and would return his call.

'And what will you be wanting at this time of the morning, Declan Conlon. Disturbing a man's beauty sleep.' Father O'Leary hastily managed to put the back of his shirt down his trousers. Declan, who was by this time feeling a bit lightheaded, took the bait.

'Father O'Leary. If you were to have three sleeps a day each lasting eight hours, you would never catch me up for beauty. Not if you lived to be a hundred.'

'Declan Conlon. I've never heard you be so rude since you were a wee boy. The trouble is that what you say is true.' He paused and assumed a more serious comportment. 'Do ye think ye had better tell me all about it. Mavis, dear. Make us a cup of tea.'

When Declan Conlon had finished his narrative, the good Father drew himself up and looked grim-faced. It was a while before he was able to reply. He said: 'For the love of Jesus, Declan, it is what you might expect in Chicago but not in these parts. It chills me Galway bones. Now then I think ye'll be wanting to get back to the farm as they will be wondering what is keeping you. If you don't mind, I would like to be with you when the police and I daresay the newspaper men arrive in force.'

'Yes, please, Father. We need you there. And another favour; there are two bicycles belonging the *Imperial* hotel in your yard. Will you get someone to take them back and I will pay them on return.'

'Leave it to me, boy. When Flanagan telephones, I'll give him the gist. You get back to the others as they might be needing ye.'

Mavis O'Neill interjected: 'Not before I've seen to that cut on your neck, Declan. Up you get and off to the bathroom.'

'Yes Mav—I mean, Miss O'Neill. I've only just really noticed it.'

After Declan had departed, Father O'Leary and Mavis indulged in a second cup of tea. For a while neither of them spoke. Then suddenly Mavis blurted out, 'If you ask me, there is more in this than meets the eye, Father. What would anyone be wanting to blow up a farm, for the love of our Lord Jesus.'

'You are right. And to think such a thing could happen in my parish.' He paused. 'We had better have a quick breakfast and then I'll be getting down there to see them all.'

Sergeant Flanagan arrived an hour and a half later and was indeed quite sober. He had not experienced anything as exciting as this in all his years of service. It is true that he would not wish this to happen to anybody but since it had happened he was relishing the situation and the challenge that now ensued.

It made a change from keeping an uneasy peace in the city of Cork where there was further talk of an uprising. Everyone at the farm was interviewed and all told the same story barring a few details. Justine was very anxious for her not to claim any credit for the four of them being saved from the storage barn so she heaped all the heroic feats on Joe. It was this part of the events that worried Bobby and Justine most as they had to invent a yarn that was credible.

Joe was in no fit state to answer any questions and with the collusion of the good doctor all requests to speak to him were refused and he was only allowed him to be interviewed a few days later. This gave Bobby an opportunity to rehearse the yarn they had concocted about events in the hotel. Joe said he had heard the men talking and came down to the farm to warn them. He said he did not recognise them although he thought one of them was familiar.

Surprisingly, this was not followed up and the subject dropped. The police had no idea of the events at the Imperial and they merely thought that Justine was at the farm when the intruders struck. In that way Justine was able to keep a low profile and away from the limelight.

It was quite bewildering for Joe when he came out of the effect of the laudanum to find he was a hero and celebrity. As soon as the police had given a statement to the press, they descended on the farm like vultures. Joe was asked if he wanted anything. He asked if a bunch of flowers could be sent to Ellen at the hotel as he would not be able to take her to the fair. He asked if somebody could bring her to see him and this was duly arranged.

Naturally, Ellen enjoyed being in the limelight immensely and smiled sweetly. She kept very quiet about her part in the events that took place in Justine's room at the Imperial. That episode was neatly swept under the *Imperial* carpet.

Whilst this was taking place, there were several uniformed officers probing in the grass and looking in every possible and impossible places for clues. When they got in a huddle there was many a time when they shook their heads. Bobby noticed this but it did not make him feel any more or less tight inside. Sergeant Flanagan came back to the farm, looking somewhat disturbed. He looked at them intently and said:

'There's a lot of blood just above and on the jetty. Can you account for that?'

Bobby was ready for this question.

'I think it must have been the dogs, Sergeant. They are very calm most of the time but they don't like intruders and they can sense when something wrong is happening. They are allowed to roam free at night. They are very friendly to all the people they know but I am sure they must have known something was badly wrong.'

'Ah. That might explain it. Do you all possess firearms?'

'Not all of us. Eilish doesn't have one.'

'Would you fetch the ones you have, please. Do you have a shotgun, Mrs Conlon?'

'Yes. It was my husband's. You went shooting with him a time or two.'

'That's what I was thinking.'

The guns were brought out and laid on the kitchen table. The sergeant sniffed the barrel of all the firearms several times.

'None of them appear to have been discharged recently.'

'That's it, Sergeant. We were taken by surprise and led out. We would have been bits and pieces now if Joe had not appeared. What is a mystery is who it was and why we were their target. And where they have run to.'

'It is a funny business, to be sure,' said the sergeant. 'Well, I'll be leaving you and will return tomorrow just to take a few statements. You'll be needing a bit of peace and quiet so we'll do all of that later. Thank you for the tea and cakes. I must get the recipe off you, Mrs Conlon, for me wife to have a go at them. I'll bid you all good day.'

Good day was said in chorus by the others who all exhaled in varying numbers and strength of sighs.

Sergeant Flanagan did come down for a short time the next day but most of the statements were taken down by his uniformed juniors as well as a detective. He went everywhere but shook his head when he saw the result of the explosion. Two days later he appeared with the chief constable who expressed his regret at the whole episode.

He stayed quite a while talking to each and every one in turn. It was obvious that he was most unhappy about the whole affair and even more so by the fact there was little to go on and no real clear motive unless it was for robbery. He went into see Joe and interrupted he and Ellen kissing. He apologised profusely.

'Is this your intended, Mr Cassidy?'

'Oh I've been intending lots of times, chief inspector, but I have not had the courage to ask her.'

Ellen looked at him with wide eyes. The chief inspector smiled weakly and shook hands with them both. He stayed talking with them and made a few comments about Joe's bravery. After he had gone, Ellen turned on him and said: 'What did you say that for? Do you like embarrassing me?'

'Lord no. It's true. I have always been too scared thinking you would say no.'

'Well, I would not have.'

'Well, how about it then?'

'About time too.'

A few days later, when Sergeant Flanagan appeared a third time, he sat down thoughtfully whilst taking an occasional sip out of his cup of tea.

'Are we any nearer solving who did this, sergeant? Are there any suspects?' Bobby led the way to see how the officer would react to his question.

'Well, it is strange. You said there were four men. It just so happens that four men seem to be missing from inside town. And a boat is missing too. Very singular. I am wondering if you knew any of them.'

'What are their names?' said Declan.

'Two sets of brothers. Peter and Patrick Doyle and brothers Naysmith. Do they mean anything to you?'

'Certainly the Doyle brothers. They worked here. One was dismissed and the other left at a later date. Not a very nice or trustworthy pair at times, sergeant. Some of the girls were afraid of them from time to time,' said Aoifa.

'Ah yes,' said the canny sergeant, 'I can understand that.'

Bobby jumped in before anybody had the chance to say anything and began his pretence.

'I remember the name Naysmith, sergeant. I am trying to think where it was…I remember…it was in the bank. That's it. A man called Naysmith brought the deeds of the farm into the manager's office. I am sure that was where it was. As I recall we were at the other end of the room so I did not get a look at him. Is there a connection, sergeant?'

'Yes, that's the same man. Curious. He would have had privy information about your affairs Mr Conlon. He may have been involved but how and why is the question. If it was they that came by boat then they did not complete their return journey and may well be at the bottom of the estuary. If that is where they are then they will never be found except by fish. I am wondering if they were just leaving after their dirty work and were attacked by the dogs. It does not explain why they wanted to blow you up or why they never got back to the marina. Why the barn and not the farmhouse?'

'Is it possible they may have had a grudge against Mr Conlon senior, sergeant and wanted revenge? Not being a local I wouldn't know but it is all I can come up with.'

'You know, something like that did cross me mind, Mr Williston, but I have a feeling in me bones that we will never get to the bottom of this. It is a strange case, to be sure.'

'Can you tell us whether any of them had a record, sergeant, or is that confidential?' said Justine.

'Well, it is really but I can say that there were a few things on their files and not all of them trifles.'

'All four of them?'

'Well, perhaps you should be satisfied with that for now. In any case there is nothing for you to worry about. Put it all behind you and get on with your lives. Be on your guard but I think you'll have no more trouble.'

And so it proved to be. Joe returned to Cork a hero and was feted, much to the chagrin of his vindictive colleagues at the hotel but to the absolute delight of his mother. It was not that long after that he got married except it was not to Ellen but to Annie on the telephone switchboard at the *Imperial*. The manager made a real fuss of them both, including a step up to management for Joe Cassidy who for a time became a real local celebrity. He received a bravery medal from the city's mayor.

After a week had elapsed, Declan decided to have an open day for the village and the following Saturday, this took place. The crowds rolled in including a few from elsewhere who managed to tag on with some of the locals. It was a huge success. Some games were organised followed by music and dancing in the evening. The fiddlers were on top form with reels, jigs and a fair bit of folk singing thrown in.

Being autumn, it had to end sooner than all would have liked. The clearing up had to take place before it got dark. The only incident which was somewhat out of order was when two of the young villagers were found in the undamaged hayloft with no clothes on. The girl's giggles had been heard when Eilish had gone to fetch a lamp.

Justine said good night to Bobby and said she would sleep late the following morning. It was all quiet when Bobby went to bed just after midnight except for a few moments, he thought he heard somebody weeping. He hesitated for a few moments but there was no further sound causing him to put the incident out of his mind.

In the morning, Bobby, along with the others, awoke late. As it was a Sunday there were no signs or sounds of the day staff. As to the family they had all agreed that they would have an extra hour in bed to help recover from the past few days and the festivities. At the appointed hour they all arose and breakfasted together before going to mass. This time Bobby was persuaded to go with them.

Afterwards there were lots of people to talk to and this prevented them from being home until after 11.00 am When they were in the kitchen and seated there was still no sign of Justine. Aoifa went to her room. It was several minutes before she returned with a handful of envelopes addressed to each of them. Aoifa had opened hers and was looking pale and remote. Bobby picked up his. It read as follows:

My Darling Bobby,

When you get this, I shall be a long way from you all. I will not tell you my destination as you might do something foolish and try to follow me. It is time for me to leave as I have fulfilled my purpose at the farm. To hang on too much longer would be a bad mistake. That, I think, applies to you, dear Bobby.

You know that I always wanted to do something really good in my life and together, you and I have done just that. Aoifa and family can look forward to a new and settled era with perhaps some prosperity which includes a fair amount of the local people. It is very sad and a tragedy that she will not have her husband with her. It is in the light of all of this that makes me feel it is time that I should move on and I am fairly sure that you too in time must seek fresh pastures, Bobby.

I have had to tear myself away from you even though I have come to love you, the first and only man I have completely surrendered my heart. Because of my past, I feel unworthy of you and feel that you should have somebody better, purer, stable and more home loving. The fact that I am older than you did not really matter but I am not the one for you. The right girl is waiting for you somewhere. One day I shall have to come back here; there is a simple contentment to be found here which many people, particularly ones from the city cannot understand. Any return, however, might not be for some time.

As for you, I would not be able to tell you what is best for you, dear Bobby. Only you know that but whatever you do please make sure it is for the good of as many people as possible for as long as possible. The world needs honest men like you. Most of the time I have seen nothing but bad things; greed and selfishness but somehow because of surviving the ship and then all that has happened at the farm I want to believe there is good in this world. I am weeping as I write this.

Goodbye, my lovely boy, Bobby. Remember me and know that you will always have my love and admiration.

Your Justine.

Bobby felt as though he had been shot in the chest. After a while he found himself shaking uncontrollably. He sat in his room for a long time until Aoifa came to find him. Neither of them spoke but after a short while Aoifa drew his head into her midriff. He stayed there for a long time until she silently withdrew. Upon that, he kicked off his shoes and lay on the bed.

The others understood and left him alone as they had no idea what to say and no means of comforting him. After putting the farm back on its feet and tasting victory over evil forces he believed he was on the crest of a wave and there were only good things that could follow. Miraculously, they had all survived and they had only sustained injuries. Now the woman of his life might just as well as died. He was now plunged into utter despair just as he had been months earlier on the *Lusitania*. He had been in a wonderful new job with a secure future that had only lasted about six days and now history had repeated itself. At about 6.00 pm he came out into the kitchen and ate what had been left for him and then went out to find the dogs.

They walked for a few miles on the cliffs before returning home. After he had fed them, he went back to his room and remained there looking vacantly at the ceiling. He wanted to weep but could not. At some point he must have dozed off because it was dark and he felt cold. He undressed and got into bed. His mind was in a total and unrelenting turmoil so it was only after complete exhaustion that he was able to sleep. He awoke to find his shaking had ceased but then lapsed into a series of nightmares, the worst of which was being shipwrecked yet again.

216

23. Back at Frankfare

While Bobby was supervising the resurrection of the Conlon farm, there was a period of relative calm at *Frankfare*. The year ended and there was optimism in the United States that the war in Europe would not affect them. However, trade worldwide began to dwindle and people everywhere started to feel the pinch. There were no wage rises for the staff at *Frankfare* and as dollars began to buy less grumbling and tension increased. George was ruthless with anybody who made objections and stepped out of his narrow line.

The beginning of July 1916 witnessed the commencement of battle of the Somme and film which had been censored in Britain reached a horrified and deeply concerned America. For well over four months the battle raged and casualties mounted. A million men were killed or wounded and the pictures which reached the News Cinemas were graphic and disturbing. Many people were chilled to the marrow when film of tanks appeared and some religious orders were convinced that the Day of God's Wrath was imminent and would happen as prophesied in Revelation at Armageddon.

A month after hostilities ceased for a while in France, Christmas 1916 for most was in no way a celebration. The New Year came and then the spring arrived on time to everybody's delight and relief. One evening Sarah was knitting in their snug living room when Marcus arrived home. He kissed her and then warmed himself against the coal fire. His still pretty and still quite slim wife looked up and smiled.

'Soon we must start thinking about something special for our daughter's twenty-first birthday, dear husband.'

'Indeed we must, darling wife. Have you anything in mind?'

'Not as yet. I don't seem to be able to broach the subject somehow. No problem when it was you and I, dear, we were already wed.'

'Quite so,' said Marcus.

'I often wonder what will happen to her in that respect. There have been boys recently from the band who have tried to make friends with her and take her out but she never seems that interested. We are so cut off here and it is like living in a fortress.'

'Come now, Sarah, we both know why that is so but we are unable to speak of it. In fact we are afraid to speak of it which is a constant burden to me.' He sighed and continued: 'You know we are settled here and have cause to be grateful but deep down, there is always an element of fear with us and in all of us every day of the week. Normally, we would have no cause for worry about our children's liaisons but the situation is different here. There is no doubt that something happening between the two of them.'

'You mean, Rachael and Mr Stephen.'

'Yes, of course I mean them. We don't speak of it because, although we are fairly certain they have been close for some time now we don't know how far it has gone and we dare not ask. We can be certain what Mr George would say. I think it is quite a miracle that he knows nothing.'

Sarah sighed. 'That is true, my love. I do not like to confront her with the subject in case of stirring up a hornet's nest. Mr George's temper gets worse. Luckily we have, so far, not given him any cause to vent it on to us. That could change in a moment and where would that leave us? Have you heard him shout at some of the people in the bakery? It's awful and so unnecessary. I don't want a repeat of the Bobby situation.'

'It is lucky that I am outside a lot of the time and you are here in the house. Most weeks I only see him for just a few minutes and that suits me fine.'

'That still does not get us very far with Rachael. When shall we have a talk with her and see if we can find out the truth and what their intentions are?'

'What about Easter? It is only three weeks away.' Marcus's proposal was somewhat arbitrary but logical to Sarah as there would be some holiday time at which all four of them could be brought together. It would be quiet and there would be little chance of eyebrows being raised or of being disturbed.

'Where is she tonight?'

'Band night.'

'Of course. That is about the only regular time they get together, I suppose.'

'One or two people have said some pretty cruel things about her not having boyfriends and the like. The worst one is that woman Fanny Richards, you know the telephone operator,' said Sarah. 'Sits in the front row at church.'

'Oh her! Good thing she was not in Salem 300 years ago. She would have been burned at the stake.'

They laughed together.

'Easter it is then,' said Marcus. 'I do not know how to start the subject off or whether I should do. It is so difficult to know what to do for the best. Perhaps we should leave it for a while.' He paused.

'No. We must strike while our iron is hot. We can justify no more delay as it would be a mistake.'

Each of them marvelled of how well Rachael and Stephen had managed to keep their friendship from wagging tongues but as yet both parents were, like many others, quite unaware as to the depths that it had already reached.

Easter arrived and both Marcus and Sarah had not wavered from the belief that they could defer matters no longer. It was eating into them so much that it could soon be a health issue. Easter Monday turned out to be apt time to chat as Martha and George had sped away after church the day before to spend a couple of days at the Retreat. They were not due back until Wednesday.

When Sarah proposed a chat for the Monday evening about her birthday, Rachael suggested Stephen attend as he would be doing a lot of the arranging. Martha was suffering with back pains and the burden of running the household was being put more on Stephen now that Emma had left. This saved Sarah the trouble of asking for Stephen to attend a *tete a tete*. Arriving early and believing that Marcus and Sarah were elsewhere, they both were taking advantage of some privacy and were locked in an intimate embrace when they were suddenly aware that both parents had rounded the stone wall separating them and were waiting whilst they had finished.

Both Rachael and Stephen had flushed bright red and were very uncomfortable until Marcus, after being transfixed for a moment, recovered and politely motioned for them to sit down. After what had just happened, he believed the next few minutes might be much easier for him than they had initially thought. In this, he was quite correct.

'We are wanting to plan for Rachael's 21st, Stephen, and wondered if we would be able to hold it here.'

Stephen experienced relief at the switch of subject but he still felt uncomfortable and unprepared.

'Of course, we will have it here and the company will foot the bill. Hope you will not invite half of Boston,' he said with a feeble smile. The others politely smiled at his weak joke. The discovery of them kissing had completely thrown them all into a quandary.

'Thank you, that is very kind and we appreciate it very much. We wondered if…' His voice tailed off as Stephen interrupted him. He could wait no longer for Marcus to reveal his reaction to what he and Sarah had witnessed and was bursting with apprehension. It was time for his confession.

'Mr Williston. Marcus. Can we postpone that for a minute, please? After what you have just seen, well… We have just got to level with you. It is no longer secret from you and Sarah. I have been putting off and even dreading this moment but you know now how it is between the two of us. I was going to be brave later this year but after what you just saw that's impossible. We've had to keep matters under wraps from father and meet secretly.'

He paused for breath. 'You know I'll be 21 next year and any objections he may have will be of no consequence. Mother might appear neutral but in the end his bullying is usually effective and she often gives in so as to have a quiet life. Not always, though. I do not know what she will say or think about this. At the moment father needs me more since Emma left but that might change soon now that we have our cousins learning the ropes. We never meant to deceive you and Sarah. We earnestly hope for your blessing.'

Marcus waved his hands. 'We understand the position you have been in but how would you earn a living if you were not here?' he said carefully and respectfully.

'Easy. There is no shortage of people wanting to learn to fly and Chuck would find me work as at the moment he is turning people away. Soon he will be able to buy another couple of kites and that will bring in more income. The great worry I have is that now that war has been declared, I will have to go to Europe. There is hardly what one could call an American Air Force. We are miles behind the British and the French. The Germans are turning out some fine aircraft and are winning the propaganda war. There is one fellow called the Red Baron and another called the Black Count who are shooting down our allies in large numbers.'

'Kites?' said Sarah.

'Aeroplanes, dear,' said Marcus. Sarah laughed at her own ignorance.

'How have you managed to get to know each other when you only seem to be together on band nights,' said Sarah.

'Sundays at the airfield,' said Stephen. Both parents looked surprised.

Stephen continued, 'Every other week after church I would drive straight off towards the airfield and park at Stock Wood and wait whilst remaining hidden; Joanne Radstock would pick up Rachael supposedly for them both to go out for the afternoon and just drop her off at the prearranged venue. We would then spend the afternoon together. Then we would do the same in reverse later on in the evening. In the winter, we did not have to bother Joanne about the return journey as it was dark and Rachael just ducked down low in the back seat. It worked every time. We lived for those occasions.'

Stephen did not mention that he had taken Rachael airborne several times and that, after the initial shock had passed, it had pleased her enormously and caused her to ask for more excitement. Marcus was full of admiration. He beamed with pleasure and then hooted with laughter, which soon became infectious. His eyes were quite moist but he recovered quickly and then reverted to his penetrating gaze.

'Is this what you want, my darling daughter?'

'More than anything in the world, daddy.'

He looked at Sarah who merely nodded. 'Then you have our blessing, both of you.'

Marcus looked at his wife. Her face was one of radiant delight. She stood up.

'It's likely that I've lost a son but I am going to gain a wonderful son-in-law,' she said.

Stephen was embarrassed but got up to enjoy Sarah's first ever hug, which was full of warmth and sincerity. The rest of the evening for all of them was a joy. The revelations and acceptance which had taken place caused the burden of secrecy and furtiveness to be dispelled in a matter of minutes. The release of tension made them somewhat light headed and when drinks were partaken there was humour and laughter in abundance. It was late when Stephen reluctantly took his leave.

Stephen's prediction that he would soon be called up proved to be incorrect. He waited but nothing happened. When he was finally contacted by the Air Ministry, it was to train pilots at *Hillington* ready for possible combat. George raged when realised what that would entail. However for a time he had no choice but to let Stephen go almost full time to *Hillington* and thus find another manager for *Frankfare*.

For Stephen, it meant missing Rachael on band nights and seeing her about during odd occasions during the day especially the lunch hour. Lately when George was missing on business, he, Stephen, would have a bite to eat in the house kitchen with both Sarah and Rachael but all that had now become a thing of the past. The only compensation was that at last he was earning some real money and nothing like the pittance George gave to him and other members of the family.

Both cousins remarked on this; they were now in full swing doing office duty as well as visits and they actually confided in Stephen that if it went on like this for too much longer, they would "up and off". They considered they had paid George back and more after being pulled from the brink after their wayward father died. Stephen made a point of finishing on Saturdays at 12.00 noon and Chuck did also. He went over to the office when he saw a familiar face and gave Emma an intense and long cuddle.

'How's it going, big sis?'

'Wonderful, little brother. And a lot of it is thanks to you.'

'How's married life?'

'I can thoroughly recommend it,' she said. They reconvened the hug.

'Whoops. I had better be careful,' he said.

'What about?'

'Some time ago, if you remember, I was in danger of ruining your prize possessions.'

'You naughty boy. What do you know about that sort of thing?'

'Nothing at all, thanks to you.'

Emma pretended to be indignant. 'What do you mean, thanks to me? Was I supposed to find you a book or do a drawing of them and other things for that matter?'

'You could have saved the trouble and educated me by showing me the real thing.'

'Why you shocker, Stephen Robinson.' She pretended to swipe him and he left laughing and said:

'See you soon, Mrs Ellis.'

All the staff were surprised when no official body contacted them about putting *Hillington* airfield on a war footing. They did receive a letter saying that they would be having a visitation but this did not come until three months later, that is in July. Chuck presented the official to the staff who shook hands with everyone and in between each member of staff mopped his heavily sweating brow.

Consequently, the niceties which took place in the baking sun took far longer than was necessary. The Lieutenant was dressed in the uniform of the new Aviation Division Signal Corps which was more designed for a January day than one in July. He explained that they had not been overlooked deliberately; it was just that Chuck's outfit was one of the very few that were in the Eastern side of the country whereas most of the others were in the far west and some were engaged in the fight against Pancho Villa.

The Lieutenant was forthright in his description of US aviation and told them all it was chaotic. They listened intently to what he had to say. Furthermore the Lieutenant said that there had been far too many crashes and in particular a couple at Fort Sill. However the Curtis JN2 aircraft had been superseded by the JN3 which were much more reliable and that Chuck was to receive 3 of these machines. There was also going to be an allowance for fuel and that arrangements were to be made for a fuel store.

Chuck had to first prove that there was room for a site which would be protected and out of reach of any thieves. When the Lieutenant got up to leave they were all feeling very pleased with themselves. He told Chuck that there was no chance of he, Chuck, going to foreign climes; he was too valuable at home. Just about all civilian training would have to go; it was now up to Chuck and his team to train men for aerial warfare.

Chuck had mixed feelings; in one sense he wanted to feel adequate and worthy but in his heart he knew he was slow and that he lacked the killer touch. Naturally, on receipt of this news, Emma breathed a huge sigh of relief. Charlie was delighted when invited to work full time at the airfield and was glad to get away from George's clutches. Fortunately, there was someone waiting in the wings for his job at *Frankfare* so George's grumbles were muted. Charlie thought he would be called up at some point but at his medical somehow failed an eye test.

The following month, November 1917, was Rachael's 21st birthday and Stephen had the excuse to see her more. George was content to let Sarah and

Stephen do the work. Martha did chip in but sometimes was still in pain with her back trouble. It was a modest but happy affair which took place not at *Frankfare* but down at the concert hall. George did turn up but when finding others were the centre of attention departed early and was missed by no one. He made Martha return with him citing a nasty headache for an excuse.

There followed a warm and lasting fall so much so that the so-called "English" group decided to have another Guy Fawkes November 5th night but this time it was a low-key affair with only a small group of invited people. Official invitations were sent at the last possible minute to avoid gate crashers and any chance of a repeat of the fracas a year before. Measures were put in place should Jason Lyon and his cronies appear but there was, thankfully, no sign of them. Lyon realised he needed an occasion when there were a large number of people about to do any dirty work but the desire for revenge still festered in him.

With the onset of winter and darker nights, Stephen took on the task of teaching and lecturing deep into the evening. He despaired at the quality of candidates and he had to be very firm when showing a number of them the gate. As a result, there was a large turnover. Some additional housing in the form of pre-fab buildings had been provided by the government and would be pilots stayed there for several days on end before leaving to return home. Stephen then was able to keep Tuesday afternoons and evenings free. He would leave the car hidden and enter the grounds of *Frankland* by a back footpath and go straight to the kitchen without detection.

In the evenings, George would go out, having resumed his interest in orchestra rehearsals; Rachael and Stephen knew they were safe from discovery for the evening as he would wait for George's return and the light to go out in his bedroom before making the return journey. The only hazard of the 11 or so mile journey was the approach to the airfield campus in the dark. It was impossible to telephone the airfield as, after the bakery staff left in the evening, the switchboard was connected directly to the house entrance hall.

Charlie hit on the idea of stands and torches and this worked very well. The only problem was that Stephen's arrival had to be carefully synchronised with the torch lighters. It was not long before they got it off to a fine art. Only once was there a near disaster when there was a very strong gale blowing. The system was vital in the snow when the approach to the mess and the houses was completely obscured. As autumn merged into early winter and the war raged on, there were still no moves to conscript or contact the men of the *Hillington Airfield Company.*

Christmas came and went and there was a heavy fall of snow which lasted long into the New Year. Activity at the airfield was confined to maintenance and thus George insisted that Stephen return home to attack a mountain of paperwork. This suited the young couple as their meetings which had been curtailed were for a time as before. They accepted any drawbacks as inwardly they felt confident about the future for them as an item. That confidence was shattered when an official letter arrived in for Stephen requiring his attendance at the Boston recruiting office.

George grumbled but Stephen took no notice believing that it would not be long before he would be travelling abroad anyway. He trampled through the lingering snow and presented himself to the gatehouse reception who inspected his letter and the pass which he had received earlier. He was then directed to the main building and was shown which floor and door to find. He was not kept waiting long. The major in the office looked at him kindly. They shook hands but Stephen noticed they trembled slightly. The major had obviously been drinking but looked at the file and said:

'Hm. Robinson S.G. You know why you're here so I will cut the corners.'

'Yes, sir.'

The major eyed him and took an instant liking to this good-looking polite young man.

'We need you badly in France. From what we know, you have more flying experience than 90% of our fellows over there. Tell me a bit about yourself.'

Stephen then gave the major a detailed but concise report which was down on the desk anyway. The major inwardly marvelled how honest and accurate it was. It had been done to test him.

'How old are you?'

'Twenty, sir. Twenty-one in November.'

'You will be on training duty and reconnaissance therefore you are 21. You can rub out eleven and put the figure one. Don't ever write November; use figures and blame it on an administrative error. Don't quote this conversation to anyone; in any case, I will deny it ever took place. We can't risk your authority being undermined. Let me be frank with you. We have no real air force as such.

'I have come back from France having seen it for myself. The top brass now want me to organise things from this end. Talk about the blind leading the blind. The British and French are miles ahead of us in just about every respect. This is pretty galling as we had a great start from the Wright brothers and a few others. Then, when we were making strides they all get sent down to Mexico to the Pancho Villa show. That's nearly as far away as the war in Europe. Things have been made worse now that all those Hun troops in the east can be released to fight in Belgium and France now that the Ruskys have thrown in the towel. Millions and I mean millions dead. The Ruskys finished up throwing bricks at the Germans because they had no supplies of ammunition.

'Great God, what a mess. Did you know that the Czar has abdicated and since been arrested with his family?'

The major did not wait for an answer but carried on talking regardless.

'We have lost the initiative and need to regain it in order to stand on our own two feet. Aerial warfare is the future which I guess you realise already.' He paused. 'I have to ask you this. Do you feel capable and are you ready to go? My God, we need people like you. The Huns have launched several new fronts and look like taking the war away from us. There is evidence from some of our agents in Belgium that the Krauts have built a new gun. Even bigger than that infernal Big Bertha. Paris is about in their range.'

'Krauts, sir?'

'Oh, my fault. It's the new term for the Huns. I picked it up whilst I was over there. My God, boy, was I glad to be back home. Apart from my duties and liaising with the Limeys, I got taken to one of those field hospitals and saw the carnage. Limbs everywhere, men screaming. Most of them were out of their goddamn minds. Do you know what most of them were calling for, boy? Their mothers. Yes, that's it, their mothers. Unbelievable. Grown men. I have nightmares about it all regularly. Good job nobody else can hear me otherwise I might be arrested or at least face a court martial.' For a few moments, he buried his head in his hands.

'I am sorry, boy. I got carried away.'

'That is quite all right with me, sir, and thank you. I know now what I am letting myself in for. No illusions at this end and no blabbing to anyone else about this conversation.'

The major looked up. 'You're a decent lad. You are baker George C. Robinson's boy, aren't you?'

'Yes, sir.'

'This part of the world owes a lot to him. He is a very respected and influential man.'

'Yes, sir,' said Stephen with contorted feelings going through his body.

'Now I suggest you return home and tell them the good or bad news as you see it.'

'Yes, sir. Any idea when I will be leaving?'

'Two or three weeks. No more.' They shook hands and Stephen left to tell his father and then Rachael the sombre news. He knew exactly what his father's reaction would be but at least he knew there was no longer any reason to be afraid of him or any objections he might throw up. There existed authorities even more powerful than his father and George Robinson would have to dance to somebody else's music.

Stephen returned home and immediately went to his father's office. George stamped his feet in fury and paced up and down.

'I'll see about this,' he said, 'they have had you long enough and I need you back here.' He stormed out and immediately spent over an hour on the telephone. Stephen doubted that his father to do anything to stop his leaving but knew he would do his best to try. The draft for exemptions included the words 'licenced pilots in the pursuit of their vocation.'

Here, George could make out a case but as soon as Stephen returned to *Frankfare* to run the business, he would automatically lose this status. George was getting the situation around his neck and could not see the wood for trees. Stephen left his father and then went into the kitchen to break the news to Rachael. She had anticipated the news and already been weeping but rose to greet him.

'So it has come to this,' she said starkly and not as a question.

'Yes.' He paused. 'Let's find somewhere more private.'

They walked down to the lake holding hands. Suddenly, Rachael could contain herself no longer.

'It sounds terrible over there. It is worse than they are telling us. The death toll on both sides is…there aren't words to express it. I keep thinking that you'll never come home.'

'Listen. I can't pull the wool over your eyes because you are too intelligent. What I can tell you is this. If you believe and hope and pray and hope and pray again and concentrate hard then I will have a chance. If you falter then I have had it. If you tell me now that, come what may, you will be here and waiting for me on my return then I will pull through. Can you get that through your lovely English head?'

'Yes, yes, of course I—' Her words were drowned because he kissed her with a certain degree of force. She did not mind in the least. He took something out of his pocket.

'See this? It belonged to old granny Robinson.' He showed her a rather beautiful sapphire and diamond ring. 'She left it to me in her will. I expect it cost a lot but that's by the way. Now listen. We dare not get engaged publicly for reasons of which you are only too well aware. But we will the moment I return, father or no father. Wear this for me when nobody is about or looking or will ask questions. Wear it in bed and hold it before you pray and remember that I'll be doing something similar a few thousand miles away.' He put the ring on her.

Rachael hugged him but could not halt the flow of tears. She held him so tightly that even he thought he might burst.

'Time to go back,' he said. Rachael nodded. They walked slowly and somewhat ponderously back to the house.

24. At Bunmaskiddy

Life at Bunmaskiddy was buoyant and thriving with a new sense of purpose. All had seemed just about lost until two strangers had appeared and miraculously restored their fortunes. Of course, it was the result of divine intervention and there could be no other explanation. The ungodly had perished and fallen into the pit that they had prepared for others. Except in this case if the inquest was to be believed, it was Cork harbour and not the pit.

What also was important was that this was a time of unrest and trouble was brewing. Something had to crack soon and various factions for Irish independence schemed and plotted to rid the country of an unsympathetic regime in London who appreciated little about Ireland's culture and traditions. Many who owned parts of the land had never set foot in it and were only interested in the rent that it yielded. Still, the folk of Bunmaskiddy were cut off from all of the violence and were pretty well self-sufficient.

They were in general a simple but sincere people who left others alone and wished to be left alone themselves. That did not mean they were inhospitable to strangers; far from it but after work their simple pleasures of music, dancing, sports and other pastimes were integrated into a gentle and non-intrusive lifestyle which seemed to suit just about everybody and did not cause a scrap of harm to anyone else.

The atmosphere of optimism was not in any way short-lived except for one person. That, of course, was Bobby. He had felt a new sense of purpose whilst being a steward aboard ship. After only six days or so his life had been turned upside down. He had been lifted up to the clouds by an experienced woman nearly ten years older than himself and of whom he wished to cling in those same clouds for a long while.

She had vanished into thin air without a proper goodbye and he had plunged to earth with a feeling of loneliness and desolation. Amidst all the euphoria of his friends and associates there was a feeling of mystery as to why he was unable to share fully in their joy, particularly as he had been just about the most important person in securing their deliverance. Bobby at times went into a shell with not much of an opening for anyone to enter and this puzzled his immediate associates and friends in the village.

"Brainy Bobby", as he became known, found he was in big demand with his skills. It was not a title that was spoken disparagingly or with jealously but rather in a manner that held respect and even reverence. He could mend many things, especially the new tractors and farm machinery and it was only once that an engine defeated him. He went from farm to farm and place to place plying his trade and earning many friends, and plenty of money, and a growing and far reaching reputation.

Quite often, he went to Cork and had to stay overnight whereupon he treated himself to a night at the *Imperial* and kept up his friendship with Joe Cassidy which included free drinks or at least ones with drastically reduced price! When Joe's day off coincided with Bobby's visit, the two of them would find things to do together including trips to other towns.

There were errands to do for Declan and Aoifa but these were often interrupted when somebody would arrive by car or horse to whisk Bobby away to perform some sort of service for them. Bobby himself bought a motorbike which was an absolute boon. Having still had no reply from his parents, he decided that at some point he would go into Queenstown and report his survival. He would have to think of some excuse as to why it had taken so long.

When a request for his help was required in Queenstown, he duly completed both tasks. He was treated cordially by the staff who were extremely surprised at the delay in reporting his survival but he managed to convince them that he suffered a long period of amnesia due to a blow on the head.

The office staff at Cunard who, having no idea about any medical matters, accepted this explanation and were only too pleased to add another name to the survivor's list. They duly sent another cable and Bobby, in a moment of naivety, hoped his suspicions about George and the mail were unfounded. He could not believe George Robinson could be that heartless as not to inform his family of his rescue.

No pressure was put on him by Cunard to return to his former duties. Moreover, there was a small amount of pay. It hurt him badly when reading the list of colleagues that had perished or been unaccounted for, which included the chief steward.

There was dissension in the family the following Easter when Ryan went to Cork to join Tomas MacCurtain as both Declan and Aoifa were against his participation in a possible uprising. There was relief when he reappeared and told them that all the men had been stood down. The next few weeks were tense but most of the fighting and conflict took place elsewhere.

Aoifa made a special trip to church to give thanks; she had lost a husband and would not be able to survive losing a son who was now 19 years old and approaching his prime. It was time for her to encourage a liaison between Ryan and one or two of the girls in the village, particularly if they worked on the farm. She was delighted when, after a few months, this did happen and her hopes materialised.

Meantime, Bobby was receiving lots of attention from hungry girls in the village and indeed further afield. Invitations came thick and fast and whilst he was away he often took friends to the cinema. There were several young women and even older ones for that matter who would go to any lengths to get him. He was young, fairly mature, handsome, talented and with plenty of money and more to spare.

On one occasion when there were rivals for his attention there was a dispute about supposed encroachment on another's territory and there followed quite an unseemly bout of hair-pulling. Each time Bobby had his arm twisted to take someone out and there was no further development in the relationship the locals were totally bemused, thus giving rise to gossip and speculation. Surely there was one of all the eligible village maidens that was to his fancy? What was wrong with them?

There was, of course, nothing wrong, Bobby just could not forget the mature and worldly blonde woman and the delights and tenderness to which she had introduced to him. He could not entertain the thought of somebody else in his heart. This withdrawal on his part was beyond the understanding of the local females who felt there should be at least one girl in the village who would meet his needs, do the godly thing and produce a family and all the while could also be loved in return.

A handful then began to literally throw themselves at him and his rejection of them gave rise to some nasty and sometimes vicious aspersions behind his back. There were one or two who unbidden would gladly join him in the rebuilt hay loft for a night of passion but the price to pay for that would be to tie the knot. For somebody of Bobby's upbringing that seemed fair enough but it would then mean a lifetime in the village which, despite its draw, its charm, location and tranquillity was not a prospect that appealed to him.

The year 1916 came and went and he found his increasing income was directly proportional to the females pursuing him. These included a few older women and at least two middle-aged widows. He began to get fed up with the situation. When 1917 had shown its face, Ryan was wed and his wife pregnant. An unmarried and almost destitute cousin came to the farm looking for work and was welcomed. There was suddenly a shortage of space in the farmhouse and Bobby felt there was no option but to move into digs in the village and although the Conlons felt embarrassed, they were, on the other hand, happy to have his room back.

Thus, eighteen months of residence with the Conlon family came to a regretful end and he looked for somewhere in the village to stay. He found a nice place with a family called Mullen whose daughter worked at the farm. They made him welcome and certainly appreciated the extra income. Up until then, Aoifa would not take a penny for his keep. All was well for a time until his peace was shattered three months later when, for the first time he was alone in the house with Mullen's daughter, matters got completely out of hand.

Kate Mullen was a young and passionate 18-year-old who was forever sitting on his knee then putting her arms around him when he was unable to resist without hurting her. This often happened when he was dozing or any time she could catch him unawares. On the occasion in question when her mother was late home one evening, she changed into her rather revealing nightdress, jumped on him on the settee, grabbed him and kissed him violently then flung her arms around him.

At the earliest opportunity he withdrew to his room and locked it. The girl herself went immediately to all her friends and said that Bobby had kissed her all over whilst she was in her nightdress. She was sure that they would get married. Two days later, Bobby heard this story second-hand from Mavis O'Neill who was concerned for his reputation. Father O'Leary questioned him about the incident and readily accepted Bobby's version of events but the damage had been done and gossip was already widespread. Bobby confided in the congenial clergyman that he felt it might be best to make a break and leave altogether.

'Well now, I understand but I and others will find it hard to lose you.'

'That's kind of you, father, but if I stay then matters are in danger of becoming more than complicated. May I house my motorbike here? I am going to tell Joe Cassidy that he can have it. Would you telephone him for me and tell him to meet me at the station tomorrow? I am catching the midday train to Dublin.'

'It seems as though your mind is made up.'

'It is, father. Tell me, is there room in your house tonight for a Protestant heretic. I don't want to stay in the Mullen house ever again.'

'To be sure. I will tell Mavis you are coming.'

'Tell her I will be a good catholic just for tonight.'

Father O'Neill smiled but inwardly felt too sad to enjoy the joke.

Mavis O'Neill was delighted when she was told Bobby was staying but her face dropped when she heard of the reasons for sanctuary.

'Lord above. That family Mullen. Nothing but trouble and now we are going to lose him. He and that woman that came with him have been the best things that ever happened to this village in a hundred years if not more.'

'How right you are.'

'Mark my words, Father, there's going to be some angry people when they know the reasons why he is leaving'.

'You are right about that too.'

'No chance of him changing his mind?'

'I fear not, Mavis.'

The words in Justine's letter about seeking pastures new at some point now hit Bobby directly in the face. He always knew that she was correct and this was the time she said would inevitably arrive. Where to go was a problem but he began to sift ideas in his mind. The following morning on the eve of May he went down to the farm to say he was leaving and had come to bid everyone adieu. Declan was so shocked that his face became distorted.

'This is a bit sudden, Bobby,' he said in a very surprised and rueful tone. 'We thought we were going to hold on to you for a whole lot longer. In fact for keeps. We had got used to you as a fixture.'

'Maybe it is sudden, Declan, but I have no option. Mullen's daughter is nothing but trouble and I can see severe complications if I stay any longer.'

'I can understand that and am sorry. We can squeeze you in here for a while until you find somewhere else. You don't have to go. We don't want you to go. You are practically an Irishman now.'

'Very kind of you but I think it is time for me to pull up stakes. It has been wonderful here and it has been a great privilege to help you and get you out of the mess you were in. If Justine were here, I think she would tell me that this situation spells danger. Thanks again for saving our lives. I am sure I speak for the absent Justine as well.'

'You'll be sorely missed by all,' said Declan. 'Don't forget you saved ours as well!'

'I suppose so. Can you find some excuse to get Kate Mullen up to your office whilst I say goodbye to the others. I don't want her about when I tell them.'

'Will do,' said a very rueful Declan.

Bobby said lingering goodbyes to all of them that he knew one by one and there were copious tears in the barn when he told them of his intentions. Work came to a standstill. He passed the returning Kate Mullen on his way to the farmhouse who spoke loudly enough for the others to hear.

'See you tonight, darling Bobby, for some more fun.'

Bobby smiled but said nothing and went to seek out Aoifa and grab what few of his possessions that were still in the house quickly. Inside the main barn, Kate Mullen could not understand why people were speaking to her only in monosyllables or not at all. It was only later that afternoon she learned the truth when two of the girls turned on her and vented their wrath in no uncertain terms.

When the truth dawned and she at last understood the ramifications of her crass behaviour and forwardness, she broke down and wept bitterly. Nobody made any attempt to comfort her; not just on that day but for many months to come. In the end, she too upped stakes and left the village for good. This time, there were no fond farewells. Memories in Bunmaskiddy were long.

Aoifa understood the situation best of all. After he had kissed her and held her tight, she produced a small box.

'I am somewhat amiss in that I forgot some time ago to give you this. Before she left, Justine said you were to have this. She said to take special care and open it up only when it really mattered. Guard it with your life were her exact words.'

She produced a little box about six inches by three the top of which could be slid open after being unlocked. The key was already inside. The cross which she had been wearing to which the infamous preacher had taken great exception was also there. There was a little note inside which said:

To my dearest Bobby with all my love. You will find your treasure in the cross.

Bobby read it again and felt puzzled. He showed it to Aoifa who was equally mystified as Justine had been to the church precious few times while she was with them. He vowed to try and make sense of it at a more opportune occasion. His last act was to go and say goodbye to his beloved dogs at which point he himself shed tears. Aoifa promised to look after them and not give them away under any circumstances. Aoifa said she would take Bobby into Cork and so they left for him to pick up his worldly belongings at his digs and announce to Mrs Mullen that he was leaving. Mrs Mullen was seething.

'So we are not good enough for you,' said the normally mild-mannered woman.

'Yes, you are, Mrs Mullen. It is me, not you. I have never been the same since they pulled me out of the water.'

He thought later that this was a lame excuse but it was all he could think of on the spur of the moment as he did not wish to pour oil on troubled waters by blaming her daughter as the reason for his decampment. Mrs Mullen, however, had ideas of her own on this subject.

'And what have you been up to with my daughter, then? Is she with child?'

Bobby was about to speak but Aoifa intervened and looked at Mrs Mullen angrily.

'He's been up to nothing, Jane, in spite of your daughter throwing herself at him. In your heart you know that's the truth. Bobby is a good boy and you should not let him leave with thoughts like that. He has been good to you all. In fact, to all of us. He lost the girl he loved and now, thanks to your Kate, he feels he has to go. Shame on you!'

With that, Jane Mullen dropped her head and relented. She said: 'Off you go then…Godspeed.'

They got in the trap and the pony trotted away. At the tram stop Aoifa bade him a tearful farewell. They gave each other a final hug.

'You never got over losing Justine. I am sure, though that what she did was the right thing in the long run.'

'True about losing her and perhaps it was right her leaving like that. I don't know. I am still confused inside. Maybe I will bump into her again. Meantime be good until I see you again. I will come back some day.'

'See that you do, Bobby. See that you do,' said Aoifa, feeling increasingly desolate.

She had never contemplated ever losing him and found it difficult to comprehend why the Almighty had allowed such a situation to materialise. The inside of her stomach felt tight and alien to the rest of her body as she said goodbye to one whom she had come to love as much as a son. He was the only one who knew the truth about events at the jetty and in the boat when she had disposed of the Doyle and Naysmith brothers.

He had said nothing to the authorities or even mentioned it privately to Aoifa herself. He had saved them all from complete annihilation and yet here he was being forced to leave by people who owed him their livelihoods. Aoifa felt at that moment that not enough had been done to help him to stay and for once she felt impotent and inadequate.

Bobby was about to get his ticket at Cork station when a hand was put on his shoulder.

He looked round to see a rather sorrowful looking Joe Cassidy.

'Hell, Joe, I thought for a moment it was the law after me.'

'Well, you have committed a crime.'

'Oh yes? What was it?'

'Leaving without a proper goodbye.'

'I'm sorry, Joe. It has been murder these last few days. The Mullen girl has been a right pain in the arse and forced me into a very tight corner. It won't take long for her uncle to find an excuse for a fight; big brute that he is.'

'I understand.'

'I have written you a letter. Did Father O'Leary contact you?'

'Yes. He telephoned and told me you aimed for the midday Dublin train.'

'Of course.'

'You'll be going to England. Do you know where.'

'Not totally made up my mind. I have a few relatives in a fairly small area. I thought I would look one up and then get a job. Hopefully avoiding the war.'

'Anything I can ever do for you?'

'There is. Now that you have my bike, will you get down to the farm and exercise the dogs now and then? When I'm settled and know what I am doing, I'll come and get them.'

'I surely will. Now take this bag of goodies. It will keep you going in case you are peckish on the way. Come back one day, Bobby.'

With that, he turned without waiting for a reply. He did so to prevent Bobby seeing some moisture coming down his cheeks. Inwardly, he was livid at losing his best friend who was not leaving of his own accord but rather because of the selfish actions of others.

25. Boston, Lincolnshire

It was only on the train from Cork to Dublin that Bobby finally made up his mind where his destination was to be although he had more than 90% decided when he made the decision to up stakes. Although he had a strong wish to see his parents and siblings, he could not face being back at *Frankfare* where he was not only unwelcome but banned from the complex. There would be pressure on his parents who, when it came to a simple analysis, had no real security at all.

He would also have to endure a potentially hazardous and expensive journey whilst risking being torpedoed again. He shuddered at the thought of jumping into the cold sea again. He and Justine had been very lucky and he was not about to tempt fate for a second time. He had a strong desire to see his roots now that he was old enough and able to appreciate them properly and also the fact that they were not too far away.

He would look up his uncle and aunt in Boston, where he was sure to be a welcome and see how it was with them and find some work. Although he was not yet five when he left England there were quite a few memories, particularly the "Stump" and being taken to the market once or twice a week. He crossed the fair city of Dublin, caught the overnight boat to Liverpool and slept fitfully in the chair; on arrival he enquired how he could get to Lincolnshire and to his hometown. All the time fleeting memories surfaced but happy ones at that.

He remembered nothing of the fire in their old house and only had sporadic memories of travelling across the Atlantic. He estimated that he had enough money to live on without doing any work for about 3 years or even more if he was careful so there was no problem in that respect. It all depended on the price of things in Britain.

The reason for all his money was that he had hitherto no real opportunity to splash out when he was at the farm and nobody to buy things for. One important consideration now was that he had no ration book. It was still cold even though May had arrived. He walked from the docks to Central station, thinking vividly about the description Stephen had given him when he and his family had passed this way a few years earlier.

There was no such luxury for Bobby. He reached the station after passing a large number of beggars. He threw a few coins down to a few of them and was besieged by others. After managing to extricate himself forcibly, he reached Central station. There he was told there was an express at 10.30 am to London and that he would have to change at Nottingham for a local train to Boston.

He was hungry and as he had demolished Joe's sandwiches and cakes. he made for the station restaurant where there were lots of servicemen milling about. It was noisy, smoky and unpleasant after the pure air of the farm. He was not in a sociable frame of mind after an uncomfortable night without real sleep but he could do nothing when three soldiers brusquely clattered the empty chairs and sat at his table which seated four. After talking amongst themselves for a while, one of them took a keen notice of him and shot a quickfire question.

'Not joined up then?'

'No,' said Bobby after a pause.

'Going to?'

'Don't know. Only just got here. I've not decided on anything yet.'

'Where have you come from?'

'Ireland. Near Cork.'

'You don't sound Irish.'

'That's not surprising because I'm not Irish.'

'What are you, then?'

'Difficult to say. I sometimes wonder myself,' said Bobby, hoping the man would stop his interrogation. He was tired after the boat journey and did not feel affable. He nonchalantly drank his tea but the man was still not satisfied.

'What do you mean difficult to say? The way things are at the moment, you might get asked for identification at any time. If the police stop you, and they do if they feel like it, then it might mean they would arrest you as a probable spy.'

By now Bobby was getting irritated with this fellow and he paused before replying.

'If I keep revealing any more information about myself then you probably won't buy my autobiography when it comes out.' The other two laughed but the first man persisted and would not be put off.

'I hope it's worth it. Come to think of it, you look like a spy especially in that dark raincoat. I have never seen one like that. Very nice. Very nice indeed. Must have been expensive. Where did that come from?'

'New York. Standard company issue.'

By now the other officers were feeling a little uneasy. One of them butted in and said: 'Easy, Pete. No need to be rude to the gent. None of our business.'

'I'm interested and nosy. Come on, fellah. Out with it. Let's hear what you have to say.'

As the situation seemed to have no sign of abating Bobby decided to see if he could draw it to a close in a civilised manner.

'I'm English born but lived in Boston, USA, from an early age. Nearly a couple of years ago I took a job as a steward on the *Lusitania* and six days later almost went down with her. I got pulled out and have been recovering these last months on the south coast of Ireland. This is my first trip since the day of the sinking. I am in a state of flux at the moment and wondering what to do and that includes whether to join up.'

The man completely changed his tune after then and, together with his friends, asked for all the lurid details of the sinking. Afterwards, the first officer said: 'Listen mate, I am sorry if I sounded nosy. Don't join up unless you are forced to. It's hell out there. Carnage. Do you know that a couple of years ago women were actually pinning white feathers on fellows that did not join up. They don't do it now. Whole streets of men wiped out in a flash. Pals who joined the same regiments all blown away. Parents losing all their boys in one go. Keep out of it. Have you got a trade?'

'I've been in the aircraft business most of the time before becoming a steward. Mostly maintenance but I do fly.'

'Well, mate. Keep on the ground, keep out the trenches and you'll most likely make it through the war. Can't see that happening to us three, though. Can't see an end to it all.' He got up and the others followed.

'Sorry about being a nosey Parker. Best of luck, mate. Sit the war out.'

'Apology accepted. And all the best to you three.' The others raised their hands in a polite goodbye.

Hm, he thought. *Justine would have approved of the soldier's last remark.*

Bobby got on the train in good time and dozed before it left punctually at 10.30 am. The rattle and swaying lulled him off again until they pulled into Manchester. From there onwards, he looked at scenery that was completely new to him. The long tunnel at Woodhead was slightly disconcerting as it seemed to go on for ever and he had to shut the window because of the smoke pouring in but it was not long before the outskirts of Sheffield appeared and the train stopped at Victoria station.

He took it all in with relish and somehow felt a little excited about going to his old home. He hoped that his relations would welcome him and had enough space for him for a few nights. It was by no means certain that they would recognise who he was as they had not seen him for the best part of twenty years and he had changed somewhat since then! For a few moments some serious doubts set in.

It was true he had escaped an over amorous female and prised himself out of a rut but he began to realise what he had lost. First and foremost was Joe Cassidy and the Conlon family. Then Smasher and Grabber. There was always plenty to eat and plenty to do which took place in a gentle and beautiful environment. Before him lay the unknown and the reality of it all hit him.

It was not long before they were in Nottingham where he had to change. He sat on the seat admiring the awesome structure of Nottingham Victoria station train shed, still not yet of age, and watching the hubbub of activity all around him. He remembered the chief steward on the *Lusitania* who, being a Nottingham man, would have stood on these platforms without ever thinking that such a tragedy of his ship sinking could be possible.

Bobby wondered if the chief like him had got out alive and was somehow concealed somewhere. He searched in his mind the phrase from Joe Hill's book, *The Preacher and the Slave* that he had read a few years before when it had come out. *Pie in the sky.* That was it.

It was almost certain that the chief had gone with many others to a watery grave. He experienced a lump in his throat. His thoughts were interrupted as the locomotive and coaches rattled in and squeaked to a stop. He found his seat and settled down to enjoy the journey. The Boston train stopped everywhere and reversed at Grantham where there was a long wait. He dozed and was jolted awake at Sleaford where several people joined him in his compartment. Every time this happened people seemed to stare at him suspiciously.

Bobby was glad that it was still daylight when he alighted at his destination. There was more than a slight thrill inside him as, here he was in the town of his birth and about to surprise his relatives who he had not seen for twenty years. Would they welcome him? Was this a wild goose chase he was on? He began to have more doubts. He admired the well-kept flower beds and the ornate station roof and thanked the ticket collector as he left.

Amazing, he thought. *One side of the country to the other in six hours and twenty minutes. I wonder what Stevie would have made of it. Wonder what he is doing now.*

He strolled down towards the market place which still had plenty of people buzzing about after the day's business. Bobby realised it was Wednesday and market day, he having lost count of the days. He continued towards the Maud Foster windmill and crossed the river to where his mother's sister and family lived. As he approached the house, he now began to feel even more nervous about turning up out of the blue like this.

It was too late to have second thoughts on that as the die was cast. He knocked on the door and waited. A voice called out for him to wait a minute which turned out to be two and felt like five. It did not sound like an older person's voice. A young and very good-looking woman at last opened the door and looked at him intently. For a moment, Bobby lost his voice and was tongue-tied.

'Yes?' The woman said the word with slight impatience and looked at him intently.

Bobby recovered. 'Is the Wesley family home and are you by any chance Marion?'

'Yes, I am. Who are you?'

'In that case I am your cousin Bobby lately of northwest Boston, USA, and have come back to Boston to see you, my aunt and uncle in the hope that there is a welcome for me.'

The young woman looked incredulous. 'Bobby? Bobby Williston? But…but we heard you were dead. Drowned. Aunt Sarah wrote to say that they thought you had gone down with the ship. What was it?'

'The *Lusitania*.'

'That's it. But where have you come from and why?'

'Well, it is a long story and if you are able to believe I am who I say I am, you can either let me in for a few minutes or we can go down to the pub, have a drink and I will try and convince you there.'

'O come in, no need to do that…come in…I am sorry to have kept you waiting. In any case the pub does not open until 6 pm.'

They entered the living room which was somewhat lighter than the porch. Cousin Marion was wearing a nurse's outfit and looked either to be going on or coming off duty. She picked up a photograph that was on the sideboard and then looked at him. They looked at the photograph together.

'There's me and Charlie, sister Rachael in the front. Mum and Dad are at the back. Taken two years ago just before I left.'

'Who is the other boy?'

'That's the boss's son, Stephen Robinson.'

'How came you to be here Bobby? We heard you had left the bakery. Aunt Sarah wrote to say there was a terrible argument with the owner and you walked out. It sounded as if it almost got to fisticuffs.'

'I was the only one to stand up to the boss who is a cruel pig at times. He lost no time in kicking me out. He is a man who never questions his own actions.'

'I remember reading Aunt Sarah's letter. She said that the owner had forbade anyone to mention your name on penalty of instant dismissal. Your poor mum and dad included. Aunt Sarah said she had to smuggle out our letter.'

'That is about the size of it,' said Bobby. 'That's the sort of man he is. His children are just the opposite. What I can't understand is that I have had no reply from my parents and friends in two years including two very expensive cables.'

Any doubts about Bobby's identity were now dispelled. Marion turned around and looked at him intently.

'Welcome, Bobby, welcome. This is a miracle.' Bobby inwardly felt a great relief.

'Where are Aunt Ethel and Uncle Arthur?'

'Mum is still out shopping for some late bargains. Dad, I am sorry to say is in Ruhleben prisoner of war camp. He's been there since just after the war began. It took well over a year for us to be informed. His trawler was torpedoed as were many others. He was picked up and has been a prisoner ever since. It has been hard for us since then.'

Marion paused to reflect a moment or two while Bobby murmured how sorry he was to hear that. Marion was not prepared to let the fact of her father's incarceration spoil the happy occasion of Bobby's appearance.

'Mum will be overjoyed to see you. And so am I. This is wonderful. How about a cup of tea?' She squeezed his hand.

'Best words I have heard all day,' said Bobby.

Bobby looked around the room which was modestly furnished but with taste. There were quite a number of photographs of them all; that was one hobby Martha enjoyed doing and at her own expense. Consequently, there were more taken of the Willistons than most families would have had taken, which was a bit of luck when it came to establishing his identity. Marion put the kettle on the stove and came back to him immediately.

'What happened to you, Bobby, and where have you been all this time?'

'You realise that I shall have to repeat all this to Aunt Ethel when she returns.'

'Give me the gist, then,' said Marion with eagerness written all over her very pretty and radiant face.

Bobby began to do just that. However, soon the kettle started to sing and Marion went out to make the tea just as the front door opened and closed. She rushed to greet her mother.

'Mother. Mother. Keep calm. A miracle. There is a big surprise waiting for you. It will be a shock but a very pleasant one when you have got over it. Come and see who we have here in our very own home.'

Aunt Ethel entered and somewhat gingerly looked at the stranger. She stared and stared again until the penny dropped.

'It's Charlie. No. No…it's not, it's Bobby… It's Bobby…I can't believe it. It's true… It's nothing but a miracle. We thought you had gone forever. But you are here. Here. Come here to me, you lovely boy.'

The shock of hearing those familiar words jolted Bobby for a moment but he embraced his aunt which seemed an eternity. When she eventually withdrew he saw tears in her eyes and she feverishly searched under her blouse for her handkerchief. Marion insisted on a belated hug as well.

'Hey come now. None of that. This is a special day. We must go out and celebrate in style. And it is on me. Mother and dad always said the *White Hart* was always the best place in town.'

The women looked at each other anxiously. 'It is Bobby but it is very expensive. More so since the war started,' said Aunt Ethel. She blew her nose loudly.

'That's the least of our worries. Why don't we have the tea and a chat then you girls go and get your glad rags on so that I can swank you off when we are in the *White Hart.* No objections. Meanwhile, I will see if I can get inside my one and only suit.'

The women looked at each other with a small degree of consternation but could not or even dared not raise any objection, especially as one had seemingly returned from the dead so a few minutes later, they duly went upstairs to get ready. It had been a long, long time since they had any luxury bestowed on them. Bobby was shown to his room and he put all his belongings in the drawers or wardrobe.

Whilst he was there, he checked his pockets in his raincoat and found an envelope. He realised that it was the one Justine had given him just before they were torpedoed. He opened it and found four five pound notes. They had managed to survive the water and were still passable as legal tender. He remembered it was Justine's gift for him for looking after her so well on board ship. Little did they both realise what was to follow shortly afterwards.

After a few moments of reflection, Bobby put them in his wallet and went downstairs. What seemed an inordinate amount of time elapsed before the women appeared. They looked absolutely lovely. Aunt Ethel had kept her figure even though she was in her mid-forties. Marion was good-looking even in her nurse's outfit but within a few minutes had been transformed into a living picture; the pair of them had decided that they were going to make the best of a beautiful evening having not had one for over three years.

They walked out into the night air which had a little bite in it as a little breeze was coming in off the Wash. Bobby held the door for the ladies to enter. With the experience of being a steward, Bobby asked for a table for three at the *White Hart* and was shown to one in the corner. A few other early guests looked at them curiously for a moment but in their minds dismissed them at once as the trio did not appear to hold anyone of any particular note.

It was something of a trump card for Bobby when he ordered some wine. The waiter was apologetic about Bobby's first two requests but the third, an expensive *Sauterne*, proved to be extant. Bobby went through the ritual of smell and a little taste whilst Aunt Ethel and Marion exchanged swift glances of admiration. They were unused to this and somehow felt they were with an experienced man of the world. On the other hand, Bobby felt quite the opposite of that and was totally unaware of the feelings of his relatives.

'I shall come home tiddly,' said Marion with a premature giggle.

'Then I shall have to carry you over my shoulder. I hope your fiancé will not mind.'

'Oh, we aren't engaged just yet. Anyway, how did you know I had someone?'

'I could not imagine for one moment that a good-looking cousin of mine with a figure to match would not have a queue of admirers from here to Spalding or even Stamford.'

Marion looked slightly embarrassed as she was completely unused to compliments of this nature and certainly with words that sounded decidedly un-English and rather forward. Aunt Ethel smiled, realising that Bobby had posed the question of a fiancé to find out if such a person existed. Having had little or no alcohol for some time, it was not long before the wine took effect on the women and loosened their tongues. That is, if they needed loosening.

Bobby was bombarded with endless questions so much so that he was quite glad when the other two decided to call it a day. The effects of travelling during the last two days had caught up with him. However, the result was that they all enjoyed the evening immensely and the conversation on the homeward walk was punctuated with a more than a few feminine giggles.

Aunt Ethel said she felt quite tiddly. They did not stay up late as Marion was on duty at the Pilgrim hospital early and there were casualties coming in by ship just about every day. Some of the worst cases had to go to the hospital where Marion and others tried desperately to save their lives. Needless to say, there was a high death rate. Aunt Ethel had the opportunity of some part-time work in town which she badly needed having not had her husband's income for three years.

She told Bobby to delay arising in the morning and that she would leave something on the table to eat. They left the *White Hart* in good spirits and, arriving back home, both women hugged him and said how wonderful it was, not only to find he was alive but that he was in their midst for at least a while.

Bobby got into a somewhat Spartan bed that Aunt Ethel had prepared and thought about his very full day which had started that morning in the Irish Sea and ended here. He was cold. He thought about Justine and actually began a prayer for her but cold or not he was fast asleep before he could finish it. He awoke once in the night and took a few seconds to identify his whereabouts. A locomotive barked; shunting was taking place in the docks. It was soon that sleep took control and he dreamt he was back on the *Lusitania.*

It was quiet when he awoke and he noticed that it was daylight. He crept about even though there was no noise from downstairs. When he descended he found there were instructions on how to feed himself and what to do if he needed some hot water. He washed, shaved and put on a clean shirt and underwear. It was characteristic of him to look around and see if anything needed repairing and he made a few mental notes.

Realising he was hungry he then applied himself to the job in hand. He looked at the clock on the mantelpiece next to the photograph of Uncle Arthur. It was 8.15 am. Goodness! He must have been tired. He ate and washed his dishes and then sat in the chair and wondered what his immediate fate should be. He looked outside and saw a shed in the little garden. A few flowers were growing but there were some tomatoes and other vegetables growing as well as an apple tree. It was the shed that interested Bobby.

The door was locked but as there was a set of keys hanging up in the kitchen it was no problem to find which one opened it up. He looked around at Uncle Arthur's array of tools and knew that all that he ever would need were here. He examined a few and then returned indoors and sat in the rocking chair and took stock of the situation. It looked as though there was room for him and that he would be able to stay a while and make himself useful.

Later that morning, he went for a walk in town and there were a few glances in his direction and Bobby realised it was most likely his overcoat. He decided to ask Aunt Ethel about where to buy a less conspicuous one and one which would do for the summer. He entered the Stump and marvelled at its beauty. What made it more impressive was that someone was practising on the organ.

He realised he had not heard or taken part in any live music for a considerable time. He really was missing his clarinet which was at the bottom of the sea. He was enjoying the music so much that he stayed much longer than he intended. Perhaps that was why he became noticed and he was startled when a voice spoke behind him.

'Are you well, my son. Do you need any help? Is anything amiss?'

Bobby turned to see a kindly face staring at him. The speaker wore a dog collar.

'I am very well, thank you. and enjoying the music. The first live music I have heard for some time.'

'That's good. Are you a stranger in town?'

'Yes and no. I was baptised here something like 22 years ago.'

'Is that so? By your answer it seems that you have been away from Boston for a while.'

'Quite right. Are you the rector here?'

'Richard Hutchinson at your service.'

'Is it this coat I am wearing that is making me stand out?'

'Possibly. That plus the fact that there are not many men of your age to be seen in town at the moment for obvious reasons.'

Bobby realised the rector was not being nosey; he was trying to be helpful and see if he needed assistance. It was best to open up at once.

'I have lately been in Ireland, rector. Before then in Boston, USA, and I am staying at my aunt's who is a parishioner of yours, Ethel Wesley.'

The rector then seemed to shed a few scales. He certainly found this man's history very interesting and wished to know more.

'Ethel Wesley and Marion. I see. Listen my boy, why don't you come and have a cup of tea at the rectory and tell me all about yourself?'

'Rector, I accept readily.'

The rector was inquisitive and the chat lasted for over an hour during which Bobby gave a resume of his life. Needless to say, the worst events at the farm and the Naysmiths were omitted. The rector said: 'I hope you will come to the services at least occasionally.'

'Rector, I have a little bit of catching up to do and be assured I will be there even if it is only to hear the organ and not your sermons. Incidentally, the boss of the firm I worked for can trace his family back to Elizabeth Robinson, the so-called witch who laid a curse.'

'Goodness,' said Richard Hutchinson. 'How remarkable. Those were terrible times. You see that area down there in front of the door. It was there that one of my predecessors and his family were imprisoned for a time so that they could not speak for the unfortunate lady. The legend lives on in this town.'

'It does in Massachusetts too. The family are sensitive about the subject of the curse.'

'I can understand that. Now then, my boy. Nothing you have told me need go any further if you don't want it to do so but in any case come and see me again. Thursday, which is today of course is the best day of the week to find me.'

They shook hands and Bobby departed. He went down to inspect the impressive structure of the Grand Sluice then ate something at about 1 o'clock. He then did some more wandering around the town and for the first time he felt a thrill which helped the pain of losing Justine. Somehow he felt at home; he was somewhere where he felt as if he really belonged and that his surroundings were part of him. It was also pleasant that evening to be with Aunt Ethel and Marion and continue chatting where they left off previously.

Bobby was reading an out of date newspaper the following morning when a knock came on the door. He opened it to see the grizzled face of the local coal man who stared at the strange face in front of him.

'Will you be needing any?'

'I don't know. What do we usually have?'

'Well, Ethel doesn't have a deal of coal these days. At least not since Arthur was captured. Things been a bit tight for her. Anyway, who might you be?'

'Her nephew. Bobby Williston, and believe it or not, I'm not frim folk.'*

'Any relation to the Willistons on Tattershall Road?'

'A bit distant but I believe so, yes. And who might you be? You must be local?'

'Yellow belly, born and bred. Tim and David Whythorne coal merchants at your service, young sir.'

'Then you will be a descendant of Luke Whythorne, the artist, I'll bet.'

'Absolutely right. But how do you know that? Come to think about it, I have never seen your face around this town and I know everybody.'

'Well, rumour has it that you only have your eyes on the pretty women around this town. They say it's legs you like best. No wonder you have missed me and my face.'

Tim was convulsed with laughter. 'My, you are a saucy yucker if ever there was.'

'How much do we owe you,' said Bobby. 'Does she have just the one bag?'

'Yes, but I don't know how she manages. Good thing the weather should be improving soon. Be nice when this east wind takes off and goes somewhere else.'

249

'We'll have two. How much?' Bobby paid and they brought the bags around the side entrance to the bunker. The horse stood impassively waiting for his master.

'No lorry, Mr Whythorne?'

'Call me Tim. Yes, we have a lorry but it is laid up. My brother was responsible for that side of the business but he is somewhere in France keeping army vehicles ticking over whilst watching all the dead brought back in them,' he sighed. 'There's only one other garage in town and they couldn't cope with it. Two of their boys have joined up.'

'So there's nobody left to look at your problem. Want me to have a proggle?' Tim's eyes opened. 'If you know what you are doing. Then yes, yes, please.'

'Yes, I do know a thing or two. Where do you hang out?'

Tim told him the location of his base and Bobby said he would be there first thing on Monday morning. He also asked where to get wood for the front gate, which was hanging and rotting. The latch was still good and had not rusted so that could be reused.

Bobby walked down to the wood yard and bought a new post. He then commandeered his uncle's tools and set to work so that when Aunt Ethel and Marion came back home that evening, they found a virtually new gate; the two panels that were in the fence replaced and all was neat and tidy. Aunt Ethel was a little overawed at first when she saw the amount of coal in the bunker.

Bobby was going to give her some money for his keep but decided to save her any embarrassment and wait a day or two because this particular moment did not seem the right time. Marion said that the sash was broken on her window and it would not open properly. The next evening, she came home to find it repaired and working.

'It will be warm soon and you will need the window open or you will fry,' said Bobby.

Marion squeezed his hand. Bobby found he was enjoying the warmth of his cousin's personality, not to mention her good looks.

'When am I going to meet this doctor boyfriend of yours? I expect he is in France.'

'Yes. Everything is censored so we don't know precisely where. We are expecting him home next month but it might well be a lot longer.'

The weekend passed pleasantly and quickly due to Aunt Ethel's quickfire barrage of even more questions about Sarah and the rest of the family. On the following Monday morning at the appointed time, Bobby presented himself at Whythorne brothers, coal merchants, and immediately set to work. It was within half an hour that he had pinpointed the problems. He cleaned his hands with some Lava soap then turned to the coal man.

'The main thing is the cylinder head gasket, Tim.'

'It has packed in on us several times. Probably the excessive use and weight.'

'Then we need some *Permatex* to seal it. Anywhere in Boston or will I have to make a trip to Lincoln?'

'Probably Lincoln would be best... Would you do that?'

'It would be good to see Lincoln as I hardly remember it. I'll pay and you can reimburse me on my return.'

'You are a real good lad. What about your fee?'

'We will sort that out when it comes to the next delivery of coal.'

'You are a special fellah. What about a cup of tea?'

'Sounds a good idea to me,' said Bobby.

Bobby told his aunt about his intentions and asked if there was anything he could get for her whilst in Lincoln.

'We haven't had any Curtis sausages for weeks now let alone their plum bread. It makes you wonder where it is going to,' she said.

'Probably to the troops abroad, auntie. I'll have a proggle around the city and see what can be found.'

Next day Bobby set off on the early train and reached Lincoln within the hour. There was a lot of troop movement and for a time he was the only person in the carriage in civilian clothes. A few people looked suspiciously at him but said nothing. At Lincoln he managed a quick visit to the cathedral before getting the *Permatex.*

He got Aunt Ethel's bits and bobs then made his way back to Lincoln station. The train seemed very slow and there were lots of stops and starts. On the way back he was surprised to find they were returning a different way back to Boston. The guard informed them that there had been a derailment at Woodhall and they were going back by "the New Line". The train set off once more and came to a long wait in Tumby Woodside station.

'This is insane,' said a middle-aged man in the compartment. 'Absolutely mad.'

Another man asked him the reason for his remark. The first man was happy to oblige.

'Just before the war they build a new line to save the holiday trains coming down to Boston and having to reverse. A couple of years later they rip up one side of track because they need the iron in France. It is loaded on the ship which promptly sinks in the middle of the English Channel. What a bloody mad world we live in.'

Bobby smiled grimly and knew exactly what Justine's reaction would be if she had heard that statement. As a result of her berating him for the idea of joining up and of the conversation in Central station Liverpool with the soldiers plus this incident, he resolved to take her advice and not go anywhere near a recruiting station unless he was really forced to do so. What the stranger in the carriage said seemed to epitomise the status quo and he wondered just where he himself would end up in a world where chaos and incompetence seemed rife and where men seemed to have lost their heads and sense of reason.

Perhaps when this insane war of attrition ended, there would be a new order and more justice; after all, the Suffragette women of England were fighting for it. Perhaps it would be a better world if women ran things; men seemed to be doing a lousy job.

As a result of being late back, he could only start on the lorry on Wednesday morning but the whole job was child's play. By noon he had the Leyland ticking over sweetly just as Tim returned from his rounds. The coal merchant was beaming all over his face.

'You are a godsend, young 'un. I can now get to some of the villages again. We have lost quite a bit of trade and what's more there have been a lot of cold people about in town and around.'

'Want an assistant for a short while, Tim?'

'What, you? Do you mean that?' he said somewhat incredulously.

'Wouldn't have said it if I didn't mean it. Not sure how long I will be staying, Tim. As long as that is understood. I can tell you I am not itching to get away. Not in the least. It is really good to be here.'

'Glad to hear that. What about a cup of tea while we work something out?' said Tim with an affable beam on his face.

'Count me in,' said Bobby.

Bobby found the work quite hard. He was black as the ace of spades at times when he returned home and had to have a bath every evening. Aunt Ethel and

Marion looked on him with a mixture of amusement and sympathy but Bobby refused to give in. He rarely worked the horse as he could not control him easily so he mostly drove the Leyland.

It meant a nice wage packet and, although he did not need the money, it meant his income was exceeding his expenditure considerably. His contribution to the house finances meant improvements for the ladies who had been living near the edge in the dark months. Life for Bobby was quite hard but sweet and he made a few friends at the local pub.

From then on, there did not seem as if there could be anything to disturb his equilibrium. After all he, Bobby, had had enough excitement for the moment. It was somebody else's turn to face life's indiscriminate flak. The summer turned to autumn and during that period, life was pleasant and for him the war seemed a long way off.

On a cold day in November 1917 he had returned home about 4.00 pm because the cloud cover had caused evening to encroach early. He sat in his special easy chair with his aunt's blanket over it to catch the soot. There was a knock at the door which was a nuisance as he was looking forward to a kip before the women came home. He opened the door to reveal a man of about 30 who looked at him with an air of surprise.

'Oh dear. It appears I have got the wrong house. I beg your pardon,' said the man who immediately turned to go. Bobby called after him.

'Who are you looking for?'

'Marion Wesley and her mother.'

'Then you have the right house. I guess you must be Dr Philip Honegger.'

'And you must be, of course, the cousin recently come back from the watery depths.'

'Thankfully, I did not reach that level, although many did. Are you coming in?'

Dr Honegger did come in and accidentally sat in Bobby's chair and was very peeved to find soot all over his immaculate suit. He was aloof to begin with but soon realised in his discourse with Bobby that he was not speaking to a clodhopper as he had first thought. They were chatting when the women came home. Marion was pleased to see Honegger but Bobby noticed she was not rapturous. The four of them decided to go out for a meal at the *White Hart* at Bobby's instigation, believing a night out was apt for the occasion. The good doctor said very little and when the bill came, he paid half but with a look of gloomy resignation on his face. Bobby felt a little uneasy with the man.

For the other three at the table, it was really good to be able to have a happy occasion in amongst all the misery of war whose dark face was ever apparent. Regularly, ships came in bringing the wounded to be transferred to the railway and home. Boston station often looked like the end of a battlefield with stretchers everywhere as well as bandaged men on crutches. Bobby saw some of this while he was busy going to and fro on his rounds, which now included some of the villages.

26. An Unseemly Squabble

Philip Honegger had less than a fortnight's leave. It was leave only in name as four times he was called out to the Pilgrim hospital to help, so acute was the need for extra qualified assistance. In desperation to have some time with Marion, they made themselves unavailable by leaving the town for a few hours. In this way they had some respite and on one occasion went to Lincoln and another to Peterborough.

All too soon, his leave was nearly up and he prepared to return to France. The night before he was due to return, he and Bobby went down to the pub for a farewell drink. Aunt Ethel was at a ladies fundraising group and Marion was on a late turn of duty. She had already said goodbye to him.

They were hailed by some of the locals who by now Bobby knew pretty well. They warmed themselves by the open fire which was roaring and welcoming. This was very acceptable after their brisk walk on a frosty clear night. There were three airmen from Grantham seated around the table opposite in the pub who cast inquisitive and suspicious eyes on them. The landlord appeared and greeted the men cordially.

'Dr Honegger. Good to see you again,' he said. 'And you, Bobby. What will it be?'

'Good to see you too, Toby. The usual. Set them up and have one for yourself.'

'Thank you, Bobby. Very kind of you as always.'

Bobby looked at the airmen and said good evening but received no reply, just surly faces. Toby called out to Philip Honegger.

'When is your leave up, doctor?'

'I go back tomorrow, sad to say.'

Within a few seconds one of the airmen, who had obviously been making up lost time with his alcohol intake and was far from being in control of his actions, bashed his glass on the table. It soon became very clear that he was spoiling for a fight and wished to make a name for himself by being a nuisance.

'Honegger, eh?' He called out loudly. 'That's a German name… Hey boys, look here, we have a Hun in our midst. What are we going to do about that? We can't let that go unpunished. In for the attack. Attack, attack attack; rat a tatatatatatatatat.'

The other two grinned as the airman put his body into the cockpit position and waited for their colleague's next line of attack. The barrage came soon enough.

Bobby and Honegger remained silent during this pathetic display. When there was no response, the airman decided to have another attempt.

'What's up, lad? Lost your tongue? Afraid to speak? Tell us where in Hunland you come from then.'

Honegger sighed but thought it best to reply. 'Here. England.'

'What? With a name like that? Don't insult my intelligence.'

The barman chipped in.

'Look sir, Dr Honegger has been a surgeon at the Pilgrim but at the moment is patching up our boys in France. You ought to have a bit more gratitude and respect.'

'Patching them up, my arse. More like bumping them off. Hey lads, we have a plant in our midst. A spy.'

His friends laughed and made no attempt to curb their colleague's behaviour. Bobby intervened and said: 'For your information, Dr Honegger's grandfather was a Swiss doctor and came over here a long time ago.'

'German Swiss, no doubt. All together, boys. Ratattatatatatatatat. Shoot the bastards down. Ratattatatatatatatat.'

'As a matter of fact, his first language was French, not that it is any of your business.'

The airman stood up after this remark.

'Well, I am making it my business. I don't like drinking in the same room as Huns.'

Bobby by now had had enough and decided to put his spoke in the airman's wheel.

'Then you had better bugger off, mate. I don't like drinking in the same room as people who are a disgrace to their uniform.'

'Who the f***ing hell do you think you are talking to?' The airman lunged at Bobby who ducked the swipe and landed a punch in the middle of the solar plexus. The man staggered. Bobby should have left it there as the airman most likely would not have been able to carry on but he grabbed the man's hair and brought his head sharply down on the table and held it there. He followed this up with a blow by the elbow on the man's neck which broke his nose immediately. The others were shocked at the ferocity of it all which was over in just a few seconds.

Bobby then spoke with a touch of venom in his voice: 'Right, you low forms of life. Get out and don't taint our lovely town with your pig-like presence here again or else... We are choosy who we have here in Boston. And I have been trained in self-defence in the States. Leave right now while I'm in a benevolent mood.'

The airmen needed no second bidding and the semi-conscious and bleeding man was helped out by his colleagues. Toby, the barman, came and cleaned up the table.

'Come on, Dr Honegger. Let's drink up and go for a walk by the river. It's a lovely starry night even if it is a bit cold,' said Bobby.

Without a word, a trembling Philip Honegger did as he was bidden; he was glad to have Bobby with him as he was hopeless when it came to self-defence. They vowed not to say anything to the women and hoped there was nobody in the pub that would relate the incident to them. They returned to their respective billets and said *au revoir* while hoping to meet again. However, two days later Bobby arrived at work to be met by an anxious-looking Tim Whythorne who clutched his sleeve and led him away into the office.

'Two plainclothes police came around yesterday after you'd gone. Asked a lot of questions about you. Any reason why they should want to do that?'

Bobby considered for a moment. 'I have an idea. Sounds to me as though somebody wants to check me out. Might have been about a bit of a fracas in the pub.' Bobby then related the incident. Tim looked decidedly worried.

'They kept pumping me for facts and I told them what I knew. I couldn't do anything else. I did tell them that you were a good lad and have helped us get back on our feet.'

'Don't worry, Tim. You haven't done anything amiss.'

On the following morning, the police came around and took a statement from Bobby much to his chagrin. If that was not enough, there followed that evening a visit from the airmen's commanding officer who was extremely peeved at Bobby's method of dealing with his man.

'Instead of getting at me, you should be berating your boy for being an absolute disgrace. Saying disgusting things to an eminent and well-respected local member of the medical profession. In front of all in the pub.'

'At this moment it would not be wise to tell me what to do and what not to do,' said the flight lieutenant. 'I can see an advantage for me in this and as such, I can make life difficult for you unless you cooperate.'

'In what way?'

'We have made some enquiries about you. We do not know all there is to know but we realise you are no fool and are more than handy with the things you do, which includes aircraft and motor vehicles. It may be that we can find work more suitable for you in the air force rather than humping coal about.'

'And if I refuse? Quite frankly, I am happy as I am.'

'Then there will be case brought against you and you will find yourself in a military or state internment camp with little chance of any appeal. We can do more or less anything in wartime. There's always some loophole in the law that we can use and you effectively are stateless. Do I make myself clear. What is your response to any or all of that?'

Bobby thought. 'It seems you have me over a barrel and a pretty empty one at that.'

'That's about the size of it. Call me ruthless if you like but war is war. You are needed and I need you.'

'At Grantham?'

'Yes.'

'How far is it to Grantham? And will I have to enlist?'

'Twenty-six miles and yes, you will have to enlist.'

The officer got up and drew himself up in an authoritative stance which was the result of years of practice. He pulled his jacket into position and deftly felt his tie to see if it was in the correct position.

'Good. That's settled then and without any undue bother. You will be hearing from me shortly. Don't even think about running off somewhere as it would be pointless.'

'If I was going to do that, I would have been on my way by now.'

'That would really have been stupid. If you look out of the window, there is a military policeman on guard as well as my driver.'

'You seem to have it all buttoned up.'

'Of course I have. It's my job.'

Without another word, he gathered up his notes, whisked them smartly into his briefcase and swept out of the room.

When Aunt Ethel and Marion heard the news, they were much distressed, especially Marion who had just said goodbye to Philip as well. Aunt Ethel was genuinely sad as it was nice to have a man around the house after three years; the money factor, although extremely helpful to say the least, was much less important to her. It was a big wrench to see him go although Grantham was not far away.

In the next ten weeks, Bobby only got back to see them on leave twice, the first being Christmas 1917. After the second leave, he was called in to see his CO and told that he would be leaving for France due to the shortage of ground crew. He had not bargained for this. He was given a twenty four-hour pass and went back to Boston on the very earliest train. He had time to visit Tim and arrange for a regular supply of coal for Aunt Ethel and Marion. One indulgence in which he did allow himself was the purchase of a fine clarinet in a junk shop at a knockdown price. The shopkeeper stated that its former owner had perished on the Somme some eighteen months previously.

One important thing Bobby did do was to give instructions to Aunt Ethel about his belongings as he had no time to make a will. He told her that all his cash and worldly goods were, apart from his clothes, in a small box in his room together with the smaller one Justine had given him. Aunt Ethel was to use the cash in any shape or form that would help her and Uncle Arthur if he did not return and to buy a really special present for Marion's wedding to Philip.

Upon that statement, Aunt Ethel burst into tears. Again, her handkerchief eluded her searching. Later that evening she saw him off alone as Marion was on duty. He returned to Grantham and prepared for an early start next morning. Yet again, he slept fitfully and had a few ugly dreams of the *Lusitania* going down.

27. Departure

Bobby and his company travelled to Kings Cross and then to Waterloo for the journey to Dover. The sea crossing was rough and many were quite poorly. Bobby, was not ill as he was wise enough not to eat. He waited until they had disembarked and then attacked the sandwiches he had made before he left Grantham whilst they were waiting for the train at Calais Maritime.

'You're well prepared, mate,' said a voice out of the blue. Bobby turned to see a friendly face and with unusually blond hair above it.

'Experience, mate. Have you had anything?'

'Nothing.'

'Want one of these?'

'You're a gem... My name is Richard Squires. Friends call me Squiz.'

'Bobby Williston.'

They shook hands. They plunged further into the French countryside for over two hours. Nobody spoke until the train arrived at their destination. From when the train stopped, there was another half an hour's journey in lorries. During that time it was impossible to see out. It was still daylight when their lorry bumped over some uneven ground and came to a halt and the flap raised. It was dry but the sky was overcast.

There were quite a number of huts and prefabs and some activity all around. They were told to leave their kit and then were shown into a canteen where some hot soup had been prepared. Then they were taken to their tents and were allowed to stretch their legs in the compound for about half an hour but lights out was at ten o'clock sharp. At six in the morning, the call came from a loud bugler who was close by. After showers and inspection by doctors whilst completely naked, they dressed hastily and went to breakfast. Briefing was at 8 o'clock.

At breakfast, Squiz came over and whispered to him: 'That was unusual at the medical. It appears that nobody here has got the pox.'

'The pox?'

'Yes. V.D. is what you probably call it.'

'I see,' said Bobby but in fact he did not see it at all. That side of life was a closed book to him. Later, there were some leaflets giving facts and advice on venereal disease and other matters. It shocked him as he had no knowledge of the subject whatsoever and in the days to come, if the subject of sex came up in conversation, he managed to fake his ignorance. In some ways he felt happier when he was busy and often on his own rather than in the mess. He had no desire to disclose any of the events of the *Lusitania* and still less anything about Bunmaskiddy.

People accepted he was a quiet one and left it at that, especially as relaxation time was at a premium. As tension and uncertainty increased, all of them realised they depended on each other and a person's upbringing and background was irrelevant. Talk of their hopes and aspirations after war was over dwindled as it became clear that life was now a matter of survival.

There was no training as they had done it all in the UK and it was not to be repeated. At dawn on the second day they heard the sounds of aircraft taking off at regular intervals. All personnel were assigned to individual hangers and their respective officers. Bobby and five others met their sergeant who eyed them fiercely.

'Now then. There's a war on. If we are to win it then it is all hands to the pump. I've just lost some good men because the Jerries bombed us and killed three of them. I expect you to be as good as them, if not better. Which one of you is Wilson?'

There was no answer.

'Come on. Lost your bloody tongues? Who is it?'

'My name is Williston, sergeant. There may have been a typing error.'

The sergeant looked again at the paper.

'No, it's correct. It's my bloody awful eyesight. You others have your orders. Get to sorting out those kites. You.' He pointed at Bobby. 'You come with me.' They walked to an office where the sergeant wasted no time in speaking his mind.

'You make interesting reading, Williston. Seems as though you have something about you. Something and then a bit extra as well. Your CO at Grantham says you are pretty handy. Play the clarinet as well. Got it with you?'

'Yes, sergeant.'

'Good. Need some music now and again. Good for morale. This bloody war has lasted too long and we are all pissed off with it. Now listen; you are being promoted to corporal. Don't let it go to your head but when I am not about, you keep the rest of these buggers in shape and at it. Keep them at the grindstone and don't let up for one minute. Not for one second. Have you got that?'

'Yes, sir.'

'Good. Now get cracking. Report back at 11.00 hours sharp.' Bobby saluted and went to find his hut.

Not too bad so far, he thought. *Not too bad at all.*

Over the next few days and weeks Sergeant Bill Baker was more than happy with Bobby's work. After three weeks, he took him for a drink. It was French beer and Bobby found it different but very acceptable. They discussed ideas one of which was the protection of the field hospital that, although only a few hundred yards away, had received a hit and a near miss.

Notwithstanding the propaganda, boys had made a big issue of it and had pictures drawn of the heartless and cruel Hun. It was placed adjacent to pictures of nurse Edith Cavell who had been executed nearly three years previously.

'Some nice nurses down there in the field hospital, corporal. You should take your chance while you can.'

'I don't feel like it at the moment,' was all Bobby could think to say.

'O come now. A lusty young lad like you. You are all complete, aren't you? Everything in working order, eh?'

'Yes, I am complete. It's not that. It's…I lost my girl.'

'Oh, sorry, lad. Didn't mean to touch a sensitive spot. How come? Did she go off with somebody else?'

'Nothing like that. She was on the *Lusitania*.'

Bobby allowed the sergeant to draw a different conclusion as he wished the subject to go no further.

'Bloody hell fire. Hey, boy. I am sorry to hear that. That's bad. Was it serious?'

'She was the only one I ever loved.'

'Hey. Look. I didn't mean to land on a raw nerve. Have another drink on me. You know, I'm sure you and I are going to hit it off. We're a good team. Come on, you're young and have a lot to live for when this bloody awful war is over.'

A few weeks later, Bobby told Sergeant Baker about his early life and emigration. Bill Baker was fascinated. At the end of it, he added: 'You know, sarge, I have had no reply from my parents in two and a half years. Auntie told me that the boss had ordered my name to be banished and anyone speaking or writing it would be dismissed on the spot. I wonder whether he has kept my survival from them. Somebody said they thought he opens and vets all the mail, especially private letters. I can't rule out the possibility my parents have disowned me as a result of the boss and me. It's a fact they are always scared of him. In fact, we all were.'

'Can't believe they would disinherit you let alone disown you. From what you say, you decided to plough your own furrow and quit. You had every right to do that. Haven't you written to anybody else.'

'Yes. I put them all in one big envelope before Christmas and sent them to my parents in the hope they would get them in time.'

'Sounds both fishy and nasty to me. Maybe he is so paranoic that he threw them all in the bin. Everybody's. Is there anyone you can write to direct and tell them you are alive? What about the people at the airfield you have told me about? There is this chap Chuck and his wife.'

Bobby thought. 'Sounds a good idea. I should have thought of that; I am too trusting. In any case, I put the letters in one envelope all together to save a lot of money.'

'The next post goes the day after tomorrow. Get it written pretty smartly. Careful you don't put any place names or things; the bloody censor will scrub it out. Just tell them you are alive and well. And of course, you are being looked after by the most handsome and humane sergeant in the air corps.'

Bobby laughed and went to get some writing paper. On his walk he rued his lack of intellect and felt an idiot for not writing to Chuck and Emma direct. It seemed ever more likely that George Robinson had confiscated all his letters. He began to feel very angry.

28. Journey to War

The day they were dreading finally arrived. Months ago there had been a modicum of excitement inside Stephen about another trip across the Atlantic but all vestiges of those feelings had disappeared long since. Reality had taken a strong hold. Stephen was packed and ready and Charlie was on hand to take him to the station. Rachael was present with her parents who were trying not to look too solemn. Emma and Chuck were there as were both cousins, William and Gordon. These two were both discussing whether they would ever see cousin Stephen again but left off when their Aunt Martha came in earshot.

It was painful for both Rachael and Stephen not to have the last moments together but apart from Sarah and Marcus, the others were unaware of their relationship. George was not present but to be fair, he had gone to a meeting which meant staying overnight. On the morning of his departure, George had actually put his arm on Stephen's shoulder in a moment of rare tenderness and wished him safe journey. Stephen got into the Ford which sped off whilst some of the staff in the bakery waved and cheered.

In no time, Charlie had Stephen at Boston station. He handed him his belongings and without a scrap of ceremony shook hands and said: 'Best of luck, dear best of friends. Come back safe and sound.'

With that he disappeared immediately as he found parting with someone an ordeal. Stephen wondered if he was real at that moment let alone the world around him. He went to the check-in point and report to his commanding officer who was waiting for them all to arrive at the station. Stephen felt a huge lump in his throat as the train pulled out of the station and headed for New York.

He got up and went into the corridor for a while and watched the fields go by and wondered if he would see them ever again. This brought on another pang, this time to his chest. At that moment, the reality of it all had become apparent and he realised there was nothing glamorous in his situation. The journey seemed interminable but finally they reached their destination and were whisked off to the Aviation Concentration Centre where they were issued with their uniforms.

After briefing, they were taken down to the docks to the troop ship which was to take them across the Atlantic. It did not look anything like as appealing as the *Lusitania* that he, Stephen, and his family had all travelled in ten years or so before nor was it.

Conditions were cramped and smelly. Food was a mixture of the passable and the dire but everyone seemed unable or unwilling to pass comment. Most of those on board were going to the front and knew exactly what their chances were but Stephen did not know what to expect. There was an opportunity to stretch one's legs from time to time but this had to be done in shifts and small numbers so as not to interfere with the crew and the workings of the ship.

The crew were mostly silent and on the alert. There were lookouts everywhere with binoculars focussed around all 360 degrees of the ship. At night the tension was acute and only relaxed slightly when dawn broke. The U boat menace had not ceased even though the allies had put in counter measures with the convoy system. When one of the troops quoted the statistics of 1.4 million tons of shipping sunk during the previous year, the effect on some of the younger troops was profound and the silence which followed was more poignant than a host of words.

The feeling of dread was compounded on the third day when the sea became rough. There was a swell for a few hours which caused sea sickness in many of those aboard who huddled below and waited for this nightmare to abate. Most of them did not want to be there anyway as they were all conscripts. Neither did President Woodrow Wilson want them to be there as he had been most reluctant to accept the necessity for such a step. Stephen had listened to the warning of the swell and had not eaten anything beforehand. When the rough sea abated and he was hungry, he went below to his haversack and ate a few biscuits that he had stashed away.

On the final day, the sun reappeared and the sight of Brest harbour was a relief and joy to nearly all aboard. They disembarked and were segregated into the troops and those who were in the Aviation corps were only about two dozen. They climbed aboard the lorry, which whisked them away to the camp at *Villeneuve les Vertus* and their billets.

It was a long journey. The wooden huts and tents seemed a paradise after the troop ship. Many of them were almost dropping at the table as they ate but somehow managed to put enough away to survive. The ones who coped best were those young men who had received a rigorous or harsher upbringing than those from richer families, although this was not always the case. Stephen got into bed and fell asleep almost immediately but not before he had said a prayer for his beloved Rachael and the hope they would soon be reunited.

All too soon the call came to arise which some did with difficulty. After showering they had a breakfast that was more akin to those found in civilised society and then they were marched off to a hut for briefing by their commanding officer. He pointed out that there had been an influx of men who were just not ready for reconnaissance let alone aerial combat. The ones in front of him were there on merit although over half had not had any practice with live ammunition.

'The fact is, gentlemen, that up until recently, the Huns were looking very formidable and more than capable of winning this war, especially since the Russians threw in the towel. Thanks to the British blockading and starving them of all sorts of materials, the tide has begun to turn. That means that the Hun has got to turn his attention to other forms of attack and the one that is now most important is the war in the air.

'This is where you come in, gentlemen. Your role has assumed a greater importance and you yourselves have also a big part to play. Bigger than when you first enlisted. You will all be commissioned and be in responsible positions. Two of you will act as liaison officers with the British. Don't underestimate them for one moment. They have been in this fight a lot longer than us and know just what it is all about and can tell us a lot that we need to know. Do not be too proud to ask. They are our allies and best buddies. Never mind about the Boston Tea Party and the setting fire to the White House. That was just people being silly in a different age. They are special people to us and always will be. Do I make myself clear?'

There was a chorus of "Yes, sir".

'I shall interview you all individually. Do not be afraid to ask any questions. You'll be called in alphabetical order.' He stood up.

'Attention,' said the executive officer. All rose as the acting CO left. They then waited on hard seats to be called. Several of them fidgeted constantly and conversation was at an all-time low.

When it came to Stephen's turn, he found he was not in the least nervous or overawed. There were three officers at the table. He came in and saluted smartly.

'You make interesting reading, Sergeant Robinson. You are one of the very few from the East Coast regions. How came you into the aircraft business and why did you enlist when you could have stayed at home?'

'Very simple, sir. Firstly, I encouraged my elder sister to marry an aircraft engineer who taught me. Secondly, my father is rich and bought a kite in which I learnt. Thirdly, it was a relief to escape him and the factory that he owns.'

All three members of the panel looked at him and raised their eyebrows while they smiled.

'You don't mince words, sergeant.'

'No point, sir.'

'Quite so. We have a role for you here. After some initial training you will be in charge of some of the recruits and take them on training missions. In that way you will be able to get your hands on the new machines and test them out. I can't see that lasting too long as you will probably be needed at the front in a few weeks' time.

'We are losing too many pilots and I make no bones about that. You will have a minimum of time to get back into the swim of things. Do I make myself clear?'

'Perfectly, sir.'

'The Captain, your CO, will be back from leave shortly. Are there any questions?'

'None, sir.'

'Very good. Dismissed.' Stephen got up and saluted smartly.

It was not long before he realised he was in at the deep end. He flew several sorties and came back satisfied that, if there had been any rust on him, it had now disappeared. It was good to be amongst the clouds and to be a member of the select few. The trouble was that at no time could one relax and feel safe and contented.

On his third run, the German guns opened fire. Little puffs of smoke seemed ominously near and he obeyed instructions and never flew in a straight line for more than a few seconds. The camera clicked several times and then he prepared to return. A black plane came to intercept him but he pulled into the cloud and was obscured. When he emerged, the sky was clear of any other aircraft. On landing he went to the mess hut. One of the ground crew he had begun to get to know came over to have a chat. It was Jess Keaton from the South.

'Howdy, Mr Blue-Belly. Ready for a bite to eat?'

'Good to see you, Johnny reb,' said Stephen. 'I'm hungry but I don't feel like eating.'

'It's the same for all of us, buddy. Seems a lot different from how we felt at home. Listen. I came purposely to tell you that the CO Captain MacHeath is back from leave. He is a bastard and a sadistic one at that. If you cross him, he will give you an impossible task and when you can't do it, punish you as hard as he can. He has remained at his rank for ages now as it is common knowledge that the top brass don't want him in decision making. His vocabulary is as filthy as pig shit. His nickname is Mac the Mouth. There is nothing he hates more than fellows that come from a privileged background. Not being rude, buddy, but I am pretty certain that will include you.'

'It does in one way but not in another. We were kept almost like prisoners in some ways at home and my sister and I did not have any money to speak of.'

'I don't want to be nosey.'

'You aren't. Tell me. Is the all black plane somebody special?'

'He certainly is. His name is Count Heinrich von Herzog.' Jess Keaton pronounced the name dramatically with a poor imitation of a German accent.

'I'm pretty sure I have heard talk of him.'

'And he is one of the very best. Second only to the Red Baron. Careful of him, Stevie boy. He might have his sights on you. He has a lot of kills to his name. Boot hill over there is stuffed with his successes.'

'You bet I'll be careful. Thanks, Jessie. Join up with you for a drink a bit later.'

'I'll look forward to that, Stevie. Strewth. If at home they knew I was drinking with a Blue-Belly…' They both laughed.

It was chilling to gradually have confirmed that he, along with the others, had a life expectancy of 6-8 weeks although it was a taboo subject, especially with the senior officers. The ground crew said nothing but worked long hours to keep the aircraft not just airworthy but in tiptop condition. Stephen put negative thoughts out of his mind and went to his room. He lay on his bed and closed his eyes. Was Rachael holding the ring and praying hard?

29. Episode

Back at *Frankfare*, Rachael was indeed doing just that. The only person that did not seem to have much time for praying was George Robinson. He cursed the amount of paperwork that he had to do. His nephews, William and Gordon, seemed to be unable at times to grasp fundamentals in the time he, George, allowed and were sometimes sullen and morose when chastised. It was not like that, of course, it was a fact that George was beginning to be overtaken and new ideas of greater efficiency proposed by his nephews fell on unreceptive ears.

George let off steam by arriving at *Hillington* airfield unannounced and wanting to fly the modified Sopwith "Pup" of which he had by far the major shareholding. Chuck insisted that he pay for the ammunition he used and, of course mostly wasted, as it was getting very expensive. George was not pleased about this but had to agree.

He would enjoy himself immensely and dive towards the targets and open fire. He began to get a little more accurate but was still a pretty rotten shot, one of the reasons being that his eyesight was not all that good and he refused to wear spectacles. Chuck looked at the tattered remains of the trees either side of the targets and shook his head in despair. What an untidy, unholy mess. It didn't look good for new pupils but he felt had no option but to indulge his erratic and somewhat irresponsible father-in-law, not for Emma's sake but because of his generosity in previous years when he seemed to be altogether different; in fact in that time that he had once appeared to be a paid up member of the human race.

On a sunny day in early May 1918 on a Friday morning, Chuck received a letter which bore a British force stamp and a customs clearance. The fact that Stephen had only recently communicated caused Chuck to be intrigued. He opened the letter gingerly and let out a huge gasp involuntarily. The contents filled him with utter joy and elation as he could hardly believe what he was reading. It was from Bobby stating that he was alive and in the British air force.

269

There were requests for Chuck to inform his parents and others discreetly including Stephen who, of course, Bobby would be unaware had already left for France. The letter did inform them that letters and cables had been sent to *Frankfare* but without response. Chuck was ecstatic and did a little war dance. His alert mind put a stop to his mirth. To avoid hurting Emma, he would have to delay telling her the great news as it was now a cast iron certainty that his paranoic father-in-law had sat on the information of Bobby's survival. He would have to be very sensitive when it came to telling her the news. He went to her to ask if she would find out her parents' movements for the next few days. Chuck wanted them out of the way when he visited *Frankfare.*

'Any reason you can't do it yourself?'

'I want to speak to your father alone and not over the telephone.' Chuck left out the main reason for his request and said: 'You have a better excuse to telephone your mom.'

'What's it about?' said Emma.

Chuck contained himself and said: 'The state of the targets, for one thing.'

Chuck was grateful that Emma's inquisitiveness went no further. When she came back she told him that they were in today but out tomorrow afternoon. Chuck immediately went to Charlie to ask him to take charge of operations on the Saturday afternoon.

'Will you do that, buddy?'

'Of course. Must be quite something for you to take time off. We'll manage, though.'

'It is. Now your word of honour to keep mum the information I am going to tell for the next few hours.'

'If you wish,' said Charlie. 'I won't spill any beans. Sounds interesting!'

'It is. Great news. Get a load of this. Your brother Bobby is alive and well and in the British Air Force in France. He survived the sinking. I repeat: he is alive and well.'

Charlie was dumbstruck. After a few moments some tears appeared.

'Bobby alive. Good Lord. And well you say.'

'Yes. Now say nothing until I have seen your mother and father. If Emma were to ask where I have gone, say it is into Boston to collect a part for one of the new machines. Hopefully, that would satisfy her curiosity as to my absence. I'll break the news to her on my return. It will be hard in one way because it is now definite that her father had this information months and months ago and has concealed it.'

'That sounds pretty fair. Great God in heaven. Bobby alive. Let's get drunk and then shoot that monster who is your father-in-law.'

It was hard for Chuck to refrain from saying anything and the next few hours were very difficult for him. The following afternoon he drove like a demon possessed and reached a quiet *Frankfare* and let himself into the servant's quarters. Marcus and Sarah were having a well-earned Saturday afternoon doze. They were surprised but pleased to see him.

'Come in, Chuck. Good to have you here. Cup of tea?'

Chuck was holding a bottle of port.

'Not likely. Some of this. Are you ready for me to tell you why I have come?'

'Yes,' they both chorused.

Chuck had to pause and regain his composure. He then blurted out what he had come to say.

'Sarah! Marcus! Bobby is alive! He is alive and well and is in France. He has been staying with your sister in Boston for a time and sends all his love. He has sent several messages but they have not got through. Never mind that; he is alive! Alive!'

Sarah and Marcus could hardly contain themselves. Chuck earnestly hoped nobody would come to the door and waited interminably whilst Marcus and Sarah managed to regain their composure. He then passed over the letter for them to read. They read it and re-read it to see if it was authentic then looked at him in amazement. Surprisingly, Sarah did not shed tears. They would come in private.

'May we keep it for a while, please,' said Marcus in a croaking voice.

'Keep it and the bottle of port! At some point I will have to tell Emma and that is not going to be easy. She will know that it is almost certain Mr Robinson has concealed the various communications. You can read there that the Cunard line sent a cable so why did that not get to us?'

'We all know. We shut our eyes to things. Let's leave it at that for now,' said Marcus.

They all agreed and once Chuck departed, Marcus and Sarah held each other tightly for several minutes whilst offering prayers of thanks. For several hours they found it difficult to speak and regularly had to stop what they were doing and hug each other.

30. The Front Line

When the first day of June 1918 came, Stephen made a rough calculation. It was four months since he had departed his home shores and come to this dump in the middle of some beautiful French countryside. Admittedly he had spent time travelling, training and teaching and his action had only really begun in April. That meant he had lasted more than the eight weeks which were allotted to a pilot's survival period. He was about to go out on his scheduled run when he was called in to see the CO.

He grimaced and wondered what was coming. He knocked entered and saluted. Captain MacHeath, a Texan with his continued hatred for East Coast boys of any description, barely acknowledged him. His manner was made a lot worse as he was suffering from toothache.

'See here, Robinson, these pictures are not worth a shit. Get down lower and don't get your arse blown off. I need you back intact, unfortunately. We need more information on those batteries. Not yellow, are you?'

Stephen stiffened but kept his composure. He felt like punching the CO's nose.

'No sir. Not at all. Not one bit.' There was an edge in his last words of which MacHeath was fully aware. He barked his reply.

'Damn well get to it and don't come back if you think I'll be dissatisfied. That's all. Dismiss.'

Outside Stephen bumped into the adjutant whose name was Mason.

'Is he always as foul tempered as that?'

'Worse if he hasn't visited *27 Rue de l'ecole* for a while,' said the long-suffering adjutant.

'What goes on there?'

'It's where *les filles de joie* hang out.'

'*Filles de joie?*'

'The whore house.'

'Of course. Somebody said something about that but I had forgotten.'

Stephen did as he had been bidden. That morning the flak was intense. The pit of his stomach felt tight as never before and he began to be really frightened. He kept telling himself to keep calm but deep down he thought it only a matter of time before he was hit. He overshot the German lines and came in behind them whilst the *Bagley tri-lens* camera clicked.

Suddenly, half his tail was shot away as he tried to gain height. The time it took to get to the refuge of the clouds seemed an interminable age but when he levelled out, there was poor response from his controls. Any thoughts of fear were now dispelled as it was a matter of survival and a case of putting his emergency training into action.

He kept telling himself that he must survive at all costs. Rachael was waiting for him. He would let her down if he panicked and died. He realised that he was not going to get all the way back to the airfield and made for the allied trenches. He reached for the flare and made for the emergency landing field. The ever alert ground staff saw it and were ready for him. He coasted in against the wind and did his best to stall the engine. He achieved this but could not stop the nose tipping up because of the uneven ground. He banged his head but fortunately his helmet took a lot of the shock. Within seconds, willing hands were helping him out and on to *terra firma*. His legs were about to go but at least four sets of hands held him up.

'Well done, young fellah. Easy now. Let's get you to safety.'

'Get the camera,' gasped Stephen.

'All taken care of. Come on now, relax. We'll look after you. Take it steady now.'

Stephen was held firmly and guided to one of the first aid huts. His legs were about to go again but he was prevented from falling by strong hands. The orderly gently helped him on to the bed and put a pillow behind his head. It was not long before the British captain with a handlebar moustache came to visit him.

'A good show, sergeant. Well done. Name please. No, don't get up.'

'Sergeant Stephen Robinson, sir.'

'We'll get you back to base as soon as possible but you should take it easy for a while. Your kite will need some patching up. The tail is buggered. We saw you climb out of trouble and were impressed. That was a neat manoeuvre; where did you learn to do that?'

'Massachusetts, sir.'

'You can teach me when this damn war is over. Bloody good show, sergeant. I will report this to your CO. The adjutant is bringing you a cup of tea. I will speak to you later.'

Stephen could not appreciate the compliment as he felt sick and faint. His head swam a little but a voice made him open his eyes.

'Here you are, sir,' said the friendly adjutant bringing in the sweet tea. 'This will perk you up. Later we will see you back to base. No hurry. The captain says you must unwind a little and take it steady for at least a couple of hours.'

It was sound advice. He must have dozed a little and woke with a start when he was told there was some transport laid on to take him back to base. When he got back to base, there was no recognition of his feat from Captain MacHeath. He had no record of the flight as all the pictures had been commandeered at the front line.

He recovered enough to do three more sorties that week then suffered an attack of dysentery. He was sent to the field hospital where he was attended to by some very capable and beautiful young nurses, two of which made it perfectly clear they were available when he recovered. He hardly noticed any them because he kept daydreaming of a certain girl at home. Each time a nurse attended him and left, he would close his eyes and dream of Rachael in her parent's parlour. The first week in hospital seemed an interminable age but in the second he had a visitor who breezed in to the ward in his inimitable way.

'How do, Stevie?' It was Jess who smiled and looked as though he knew something which he was deliberately holding back.

'How do, Jessie. Good of you to come. Fancy a cuppa, as the Brits say?'

'Yes, I do. I could murder one. What about you?'

'Water, please. You go and help yourself then get your butt back here in double quick time and tell me all the latest.'

'While I do, have a look at this.' He produced a letter. 'I'll leave you for a jiffy.'

Jessie Keaton poured his tea and observed his friend whilst doing so. He was reasonably sure of the source of the letter and was hoping the news in it would be good for him. The effect of Rachael's letter on Stephen was magical. The part which contained the local news was what least interested him. When he read her words of affection and her expressions of hope for their future, there was a marked change in him from that point onwards, a fact noticed by all who attended him. The icing on the cake for him was when he read that Bobby was alive and well.

Bobby alive and well?

He was so astounded that at one point he was unaware that Jessie was speaking to him. When he came to, he had to apologise and explain to him the reason. It was simply astounding. He could not believe it after all this time. How had it taken so long for this information to be revealed? Unfortunately, the letter had been opened and Bobby's poor attempt to reveal his whereabouts, albeit in a concealed form, had been blackened out by the censor.

Stephen believed that he must have returned home to Boston in spite of George's moratorium. A couple of days later he was discharged and returned to the airfield where he did some walking with Jessie to alleviate the vestiges of stiffness. He did more sorties during the next month after which they were told that they would be soon on the move. No further details were given and an order was issued that the subject was not to be discussed. There were coloured posters everywhere. One with a fish said:

DON'T BE A SUCKER: KEEP YOUR MOUTH SHUT!

31. Amiens

A couple of days later at briefing, they were told that they would be transferred to another base in the morning but no further details were given. Security was tight. When they arrived at their destination in late July, all the pilots were informed they were at Amiens. There was the hustle and bustle of organisation but all leave had been cancelled and security was tight. A poster read:

No War Talk

The next few days were spent in looking at maps and awaiting further instructions. There were some new aircraft and huge numbers of military in the vicinity. When they were allowed time in the air for practice, it was in small groups led by the squadron leader who surprisingly flew westwards. Back in the briefing room they were all told that under penalty of court martial, they were not to fly over the German lines. Not for the next few days at least.

These sorties did not commence again until 5th August when Stephen flew west over unfamiliar ground. On returning to base he noticed the hundreds of tanks that were in position and he thought he saw a Canadian maple leaf flag fluttering in the breeze. The only comment he made was in a whisper to Jess that something big was about to happen. Jess looked very serious and merely nodded.

On the evening of August 7th they all crowded into the hut to hear what General Rawlinson himself had to say. The general began thus:

Gentlemen. You were well aware that the enemy's action in March codenamed Operation Michael caused us a setback and a lot of casualties. Following the capitulation of the Russians they were able to bring vast amounts of troops and tanks to the Western Front. However, that setback was temporary because of our resilience at Arras and the failure of the Hun to break through at Marne and Rheims. The Huns are running out of supplies and our intelligence tells us that they are exhausted. Our victory at Soissons means that we have the initiative in our grasp and we can deal out a blow that is so decisive that this terrible war will soon come to an end.

The general paused whilst there were murmurs of approval at this remark.

Tomorrow, you will go into a battle, not a raid as it has been suggested. We are going to take the enemy by surprise. You in the air will deal a devastating blow and hopefully he will be unable to recover. The outcome, gentlemen, is in your hands. You will not let anyone down; at home they will be waiting and watching.

There was great applause for this which lasted an inordinate amount of time. Hearts had been uplifted and the promised land seemed just over the horizon. As they filed out, Jess came over to him.

'Sounds a real big one, buddy. What about a final drink before the fray?'

'Good idea,' said Stephen. 'This time, the drinks are on me.'

They retired early and were woken up at 3 o'clock. The offensive began at 4.20 am and the enemy was indeed taken by surprise. There was no action in the air as there was dense fog and Stephen and his colleagues only took off much later. Two volunteers from 207 squadron did take off to drown the rumble of the Canadian tanks and in this they were a resounding success. When the smaller aeroplanes took off, they inflicted great damage on the German trenches and all but destroyed their means of communication. Thousands of prisoners were taken on the first day and five divisions were overwhelmed.

The mood in the camp that evening was one of elation and continued into the next day. Stephen's luck continued unabated and by 13th August the Allied armies had driven a wedge 12 miles long. Success followed success and on 28th August while they were on standby, somebody read out war correspondent Philip Gibbs' account, which included the words: *the enemy...no longer have a dim hope of victory on the Western Front... On our side, the army seems to be buoyed up...*

It was perhaps the feeling of being buoyed up and the fact that he received another letter from Rachael on the 30th August that caused his luck to run out. He realised later that he had lowered his guard and had inwardly claimed final victory prematurely. He had seen the Black Count and was fascinated by him.

So much so that he did not notice his aeroplane behind him. It was a great piece of luck that he was just turning when bullets smashed through his fuselage and into the cockpit. He turned into the clouds and checked his compass.

Suddenly, a great wave of pain came over him and it was only then that he realised he had been hit in the leg. He weaved around; he dived and then swooped up into the clouds. There was no sign of the Count for which he breathed a sigh of relief. It was short-lived as excruciating pain began to make him feel faint. His discipline and training took over.

Even though the pain was enormous, he looked for landmarks to establish his position. He managed to return to base but overshot and had to go around again. He sent up a flare and managed to land but not without a few bumps. Within two seconds, he was eased out of his straps then carried by stretcher to the ambulance and from thence to the field hospital. He was not much aware of what was happening as morphine had been pumped into him and his consciousness was fitful. He lost all track of time and was a little delirious.

After four days, he was beginning to feel more like himself and eating some rather nice hospital food brought by good-looking nurses. He was there ten days and allowed to get up and walk about with crutches. Fortunately, the bullet had gone through the fleshy part and not done too much damage. Two days later, he returned to the camp and was summoned by the CO.

Stephen thought the worst and expected a reprimand but when he entered the room, he saw a smiling colonel; quite the opposite of the man next to him, the irascible Captain MacHeath who was occasionally holding his jaw being in a certain amount of discomfort with his toothache. Stephen saluted and the colonel asked him to put the crutches down and have a seat.

'You have done well, Robinson. You are out of action for a while and by the way things are going, you won't be needed again. The war looks nearly over. Got a job for you. It's time for a morale boost for the lads. In short, some music. Right up your street, eh? We have arranged for you to go with some of the other musicians to the British base and form a band. The bandmaster there says that by joining forces we can make a hell of a noise. What do you play?'

'French horn in the orchestra, sir, and tenor horn in the band but my instruments are back home in the States.'

'Not a problem. You will find anything you want down there. As you are in that condition take some of your gear with you in case you have to stay overnight.

We are having a concert at the British HQ first and then one here a week or two later. Should be a really good show. Any questions?'

'No sir,' said Stephen feeling quite pleased.

'Good. The liaison officer will make himself known to you at the British camp. His name is on your orders here. That's all. Dismissed.'

After saluting Stephen went out to get the necessary gear and then got a lift to the British camp. He was welcomed and introduced to some of the bandsmen then asked to see the store of instruments. He was picking out a nice-looking tenor horn which must have belonged to a deceased bandsman when he heard somebody practising in a neighbouring room.

He recognised the melody immediately as it was the opening of *Eine Kleine Nacht Musick*. At the appropriate moment, he butted in and answered the next phrase on his horn. There was a pause before the next phrase was played in the adjoining room. The player stopped whereupon Stephen played the next few bars. There followed the sound of hurried footsteps then that of the door opening.

A man with wide and wondering eyes entered and the pair of them looked at each other in utter disbelief. Stephen dropped his crutches and then both were immediately locked in a bear hug. It lasted so long that some of the other bandsmen were not sure whether it was a fight or not. After all, they were wearing different uniforms. Both men had tears in their eyes when they parted. The others waited with a mixture of fascination and amusement then waited for a belated explanation. Stephen turned and said: 'Sorry about all this fuss. This, gentlemen, is my future brother-in-law who we thought was dead and lying at the bottom of the sea.'

The others immediately began to understand. The band coordinator turned and said: 'I expect you two have a lot to catch up on. Even so we have got our orders and that will have to wait otherwise we will have our testicles fried. There will be time for you both to catch up later. Corporal! Have you arranged a billet for Sergeant Robinson for tonight?'

'Yes sir.'

'Good. Let's bloody well get on with it then.'

'Yessir.'

'See you shortly, buddy,' said Stephen wiping his eyes.

'You certainly will, mate.'

The band was made up of players with a wide range of ability. Consequently, the rehearsal, which normally both men would have enjoyed, seemed an interminable length but when it was over Stephen and Bobby went to the canteen to eat. They spent a long time over their meal and the drinks which followed and were about the last to go which peeved some of the catering staff who were keen to get away.

The only place afterwards where they could get some privacy was to go for a walk which was painful for Stephen. Eventually, they both called it a day, feeling quite exhausted. The most disconcerting subject was the inordinate amount of time it had taken for Bobby's family to know he was alive and well. By now any lingering doubts about his father's behaviour had been dispelled. Stephen knew full well who was responsible for this cruel deed.

'For a long time I suspected that he scanned nearly everything that came in like hand-written letters; not magazines and the like. Steamed them open. That's one subject I could never bring myself to tell you as I have been so ashamed and embarrassed.'

'We believed that to be the case but never knew for sure.'

'How often did you write?'

'I sent a cable not long after I was rescued and about six weeks later an envelope with letters to you all inside. Then again at Christmas. Then once more to Emma and Chuck. I'd kept putting off writing because I wondered if my mother and father had disowned me or were too afraid to receive anything but I realise now those thoughts were stupid.'

'We never got them or the cables. Good lord, I never thought he would stoop as low as this. Many are the times I wish I had a different father,' said Stephen.

'Many were the times I wished I had a different boss,' said Bobby then added. 'At least you don't look a bit like him. He's brawny and muscular but I suppose you favour your mother.'

'I guess so. Anyway at least you were the only one who stood up to him. Good for you. When I got the letter from Rachael telling me you were alive, I felt like a new man. I'm getting back to my old self and will be airborne again soon.'

'It's strange. I saw on the paper we were getting a Yank liaison officer named Sergeant Robinson. Never thought for a moment it would be you. Anyway, let's get back. It's getting cold and I expect that you could do with getting rid of those crutches.'

Rehearsals for the concert went well. Stephen had to return to his base to see the MO, who was very pleased with his progress. He said that Stephen could do without the left crutch and that helped. They arranged for a photograph to be taken of the pair of them and had it sent via Emma and Chuck at *Hillington*. It was not long before the concert took place with a few of the top brass attending. General Rawlinson was present and he made a speech just before the interval after which he left for diplomatic discussions.

Gentlemen,

It is a real privilege to be here this afternoon and listen to music instead of guns and bombs. Music played by men of our three allied countries; our French hosts, our British servicemen and American cousins. There are also representatives from Canada, Australia, New Zealand, Ireland and others. Please forgive me if I have left anyone out. I understand that we are to be guests at the American base in a few days on a date to be decided.

It is also my good fortune to tell you the following. The enemy is in disarray. Our intelligence tells us that large numbers of the army are deserting and there are huge problems for them in the matter of supplies. It could well be that it will be soon that you all will be going home.

At this point there was loud applause and even some cheering.

In the meantime, be on your guard all of you. The Hun is a crafty fellow and he will fight to the bitter end even if the situation is hopeless. Just because the war is ending it is no less dangerous. I hope to be with you all for part two of this wonderful offering of music. Thank you and good evening.

Even though the skies were less occupied, there was the regular sound of aircraft taking off and landing. All of them had flares and bangers available should any unwanted visitors decide to do a spot of gate-crashing. However, all was pretty quiet and the second half of the programme was a great success. The American colonel then got up and invited everyone to be their guests in about a fortnight's time for a repeat performance.

That did not mean to say that there was no music in the meantime. There was a pile of sheet music for all combinations of instruments available in the band room. No expense had been spared as the top brass realised the stimulating effect music had on battle weary troops. Twice, the group which included Stephen and

Bobby went several miles from the front and performed in front of a delighted and appreciative French audience. Quite a lot of servicemen who acted as drivers and equipment movers did everything they possibly could to wangle a place in the convoy as it meant a night out, some absolutely divine French cooking and gorgeous French girls as well as the music. The atmosphere seemed to be lightening day by day as more rumours spread about the impending end of the war and a German surrender.

The day for the return concert was fixed but revealed to everyone only twenty-four hours before the actual event, again for security purposes. In the meantime, Stephen had rid himself of his second crutch but was walking only slowly and only when he had no other option. The MO told him that it would be several days before he would be allowed in the air and then only if there were good reasons for him to do so. He accepted that it was right for him to be grounded and threw his weight into the second concert; the war seemed to be slipping away gradually and that suited he and Bobby just fine. If it were so then they would soon be on their way home.

The rehearsal contained some difficult music chosen by the American bandmaster. Bobby went over to see Stephen and waved his sheet music part in front of him.

'Look at this,' he said with an air of disgust. 'Just look at the opening. I will have to do a couple of hours practice on this. At least most of it is in the chalumeau.'

'What is it? Hm. *Molly on the Shore* by Percy Grainger. He's that brilliant Australian pianist, I believe.'

'That's the one. Good thing there are some other clarinets doubling me.'

'You'll do it well. I've heard Grainger has joined the US army as a bandsman.'

'Well then get the bugger across the "pond" to us here and he can play it himself!'

At the American base the marquee had been erected for the band and chairs placed outside for the audience. There was a second marquee near the canteen containing all the food and drink which looked very tempting. An announcement was made at noon to say that the concert would start an hour earlier. No reason was given but everyone assumed it was because the light might not last as there were clouds forming and the forecast was for heavy rain.

However, the concert was just as good an affair as the one at the British base. The late October sun was holding its own as the last notes of the first half were played. Not to be outdone by the British and French the American catering staff had put on an amazing table of goodies and drinks which not many present had seen the like before especially in wartime. The generals and staff did not stay as they had a hastily arranged meeting in Amiens to attend. The war was coming to an end and soon it would be out of the trenches and round the table. Not that the generals had any experience of the trenches. They all had one quick drink and hastened to their transport.

To everyone's surprise, MacHeath was with them. It was announced that the CO had an abscess in his mouth and the doctor on site said a specialist dentist was needed at the hospital. He was whisked away. They were told that Lieutenant Parr would be in charge. All the time this was happening, there were aircraft taking off and landing. Two F2s took off and escorted the general's path as he and his staff returned to HQ.

Whilst all were enjoying themselves, Bobby and Stephen wished for some time alone. The interval had been timed to last at least half an hour in order for the bandsmen to "get their lips back". They walked out into the autumn sunshine chatting; the main subject being what each of them was going to do after the war. Stephen was the first to volunteer information.

'The first thing I am going to do is to marry your sister and you, if you please, will be my best man.'

'You have not even asked my permission to marry yet.'

'Quite true but I did not need to. I asked your parents.'

'Did you now? Well, well. I would be very interested to know their response.'

'I remember what your mother said. She said that it may be that she had lost a son but was glad to be gaining me as a son-in-law. Or words to that effect. Then she gave me a really big hug. She will have gotten both of us.'

'My, oh my,' said Bobby.

The pleasure of this news was written all over his face and he gave a Stephen light punch. They had strolled over to where Jessie was working on the Bristol F2B. He looked hot and harassed and extremely exasperated.

'What's to do, Johnny reb,' said Stephen teasing his ground crew man.

'Couldn't seem to get this working, yankee Steve. I've spent hours on it. It's the air to ground communication equipment. Taken ages for me to find the bug. "Mac the Mouth" has threatened me with death if it's not ready for tomorrow. I can't understand why he is so bothered about the goddamn thing. I guess it's just spite. I contested something with him yesterday and he went berserk. He has threatened to bust me down a rank. This is his way of revenge. He knows I'm in a no-win situation as the trouble is there's nobody to test it. There are a few in the air and 3 on standby. Everyone else is at the concert including plenty that shouldn't be.'

'Mac the Mouth will not be worrying you for a while. He has gone to town.'

'It's no secret he has a floozy girl there. To a place of dubious reputation, I believe.'

'Not this time. He has gone to hospital. Sounds as though he has an abscess. Lieutenant Parr is acting CO. He's a good sort so if we do get caught I am sure he'll turn a blind eye. He's convinced the war's all over for us. So while MacHeath has gone we'll test it for you, Jessie. That will get you off the hook if it's working. Knowing you it will be. We do not have to go more than a mile or two.'

'You are grounded.'

'Nobody will know if we are quick. They are all at the concert. Besides you are the best ground crew man and I owe you one. In fact more than one.'

'What about the concert?'

'There are plenty of clarinets and horns. With any luck we can be back in time. If not we'll say I started bleeding again and Bobby had to take me to the medical hut. Look after our instruments, please.'

'You going to take this Limey gent?'

'Any good reason not to? Say hello to Bobby Williston. He is half-American.' The men shook hands.

'Okay, Stevie, Bobby. But be very quick. There is some spare kit in here to save you going back to your hut. By the way there are two bombs underneath.'

'There's no time to unhook them. They will have to stay.'

In less than five minutes they were ready and two minutes later they were in the air. The kit for Bobby was on the large size but that did not matter. Stephen was uncomfortable as soon as he got the cockpit as his leg seemed to be going anywhere but where he wanted it to. He taxied down to the end of the field.

Literally three minutes later Bobby called up Jessie and his voice came through loud and clear. He sounded elated.

'Brilliant, Bobby. I can't tell you how grateful I am. You are my number one "Limey". Come back as soon as you like.'

They chatted for another half a minute until Jess suddenly interrupted what he was saying. He blurted out: 'Hell's teeth. Stevie, Bobby! Can you hear me? We are under attack. Repeat. We are under attack. There's a dozen of the bastards. They are all around. Merciful Jesus, they are dropping bombs. There's been a direct hit on one of the marquees Some of our boys are attacking them! I am not safe here. Great God! Watch out for yourselves; I am going for cover. Over and out.'

Bobby and Stephen climbed and watched with horror at the carnage below. People were fleeing in all directions. One or two of the aircraft on standby had seen the danger and had taken off. Stephen tapped Bobby on the shoulder and pointed at an aircraft. It was none other than the Black Count. He was doing another turn and about to do more damage. He had seen the main group take off but had reckoned without Bobby and Stephen being already in the air in that sector.

Now Bobby was positive brilliant with engines, machines and with lots of things. However, he was a rotten shot. He caught the tail of the Count who took evasive action. Some damage had been done which affected the manoeuvrability of the aircraft but it was a case of Stephen's flying ability more that worried the Count who just could not shake him off. They were separated from the other action and Stephen followed him doggedly. He forced the Count to go where he did not want to fly and suddenly, out of several hundred shells, by sheer fluke a few bullets found their mark.

One hit the fuel tank which steadily started to leak. The Count was unaware of this especially when Bobby fired the second salvo and out of another hundred one hit him in the thigh. He almost lost consciousness and only realised too late that the engine was spluttering with lack of fuel and would soon be going down. He did not know his position or how far he was from the German lines. There was only one option for him and that was to try and land.

He knew the pain was so bad that he would not be able to remain conscious for much longer and therefore chose a fairly flat field without any inspection run.

There was no time to do that. He came in too quickly with the wind and made a bad landing but there was little chance of a fire as his fuel was spent. However, there was another hazard and that was debris all over the field. He bumped and jolted which prevented him from passing out. His front wheels slid into the edge of a pond and became embedded in mud and he himself slumped forward, seemingly lifeless. Stephen was also in pain but for a different reason. He tapped Bobby on the shoulder and gave thumbs down and then to the latter's amazement realised that he was going to land.

'What the bloody hell are you doing, Stevie?'

Stephen was white. 'My leg. I have opened up the wound and it's agony. I just can't hold on much longer.'

With that he circled the field and landed the plane safely in the field then taxied over to where the Fokker was resting. Bobby helped Stephen out and got out the first aid kit then bound his friend's leg. It started to rain quite heavily.

'Is the Count dead?'

'I'll go and look. Will you manage for a minute?'

'Yes. Get going.'

Bobby ran off quickly and reached the gradually submerging aircraft. After surveying the Count who was slumped over the controls, he ran back to Stephen and said:

'He's alive but his kite is sinking in the mud... Hello, we have company. I hope the natives are friendly.'

They waited with a certain amount of fear. Bobby's hand went into his pocket but his gun was not there. For the moment he had forgotten he was wearing borrowed kit. Three men, obviously French farm workers, came up and greeted them cordially. 'Bonjour monsieur.' They shook hands.

'Bonjour. Aidez mois s'il vous plait.' He took the farm workers to the Count and climbed and cut his harness. They got him out of his Fokker just in time as it slid and became more and more submerged. He was losing blood badly. One of the farmworkers gave him a fairly expensive silk scarf to tie around the wound and stop the bleeding. Bobby marvelled. Here was their mortal enemy yet here in the face of death, they were trying to save a life. They carried him back to the Bristol F2 where Stephen was waiting, having managed to get out unaided.

'Bobby. Ask them where we are.'

Bobby enquired in his best textbook French. He turned excitedly.

'We are only about four miles from base.'

'In that case get him back to the field hospital and then come back for me,' said Stephen. 'Don't delay.'

Bobby was incredulous. 'Are you out of your mind, Stephen? You can't be thinking straight. Why risk it?'

'Quite the reverse. We might not get into quite as much trouble if you get him back. He is quite a capture. It makes sense, Bobby. Be quick about it as it'll be dark soon. Ask these good people if they will get me to some cover over near the bushes and bring some cloth back with you to stop this bleeding. There is a farm hut over there and shelter. You can taxi over there for me when you return.'

'Hell's teeth, Stevie, I have not flown for over three years.'

'You'll be fine. Get them to start her. For God's sake, tell them to stand back from the propeller or we will have more blood and death.'

Bobby thought Stephen was losing his mind. Later he wondered why he had ever given in to him as he had done that time before at *Hillington* and regretted it. They managed to get the bulky count into the F2 but it was not easy. Bobby then explained to the French farm worker what to do with the propeller and to stand immediately back.

The tail was swung around and at once he felt excited to be in the cockpit again. All went according to plan and he took off with no trouble apart from the driving rain smashing into him. He was surprised how easily the controls responded compared with those early machines at *Hillington*. There was no trouble finding the American base but then he realised that the biggest difficulty lay ahead, which was, of course, landing. He felt a surge in his stomach as he came in against the wind and switched off as a precaution. He kept telling himself to keep calm, keep calm. He came in nicely and was slightly bumpy but there was no reason to reproach himself. The relief on his face was in stark contrast to the look of amazement on the faces of the ground crew.

'Get him out,' said Bobby. 'He is hurt in the thigh I think. It's the Count. Is Mac the Mouth back yet?'

'No. Could be any time, though. Where the hell is Sergeant Robinson?'

'In the middle of a field probably in no man's land. I have made note of some landmarks and am going back for him. He has opened up his leg wound badly. Will you get me a first aid kit, please? Swing the tail around then get me started.'

The ground crew did as he had asked but all deep down wondered if there would be lots of trouble ahead for Stephen and they themselves for aiding him. Still, they had been given an order, although from somebody in a different uniform! The first aid kit arrived and Bobby stowed it in the cockpit. He actually felt a thrill but other emotions soon took over. Meticulous as ever, he had taken note of the landmarks and took off. It was a great relief after about three minutes he saw the church he was looking for and then the farmhouse.

He decided to land near the hut so that Stephen did not have to walk far. Unwittingly, it turned out to be an unlucky mistake. The F2 slithered to a stand, nearly tipped and refused to budge as the ground was almost waterlogged. Both of them knew instantly that they would have to await help in the morning and that was if there was any to be had. If Stephen had been fit, Bobby would have risked walking hoping there would be no enemy presence on the way.

There was no sign of the farm workers let alone any infantry which was hardly surprising as the rain contained hailstones. When Bobby looked out during a lull, he noticed there was very little showing of the Count's Fokker in the pond. That was good because it would be harder to spot from the air in the morning. There was only one thing they could do and that was to take shelter in the hut and wait for dawn. They retrieved the first aid tin, bound Stephen's leg properly this time then huddled together and spoke very little for fear of their voices travelling a long way. The painkillers helped Stephen enormously and there were some emergency rations including some chocolate.

The two men spoke little and when they did, it was in whispers. At some point, Stephen broke the silence.

'Well buddy, it looks odds on we have a mole somewhere in the ranks.'

'You think so, mate?'

'Don't you?'

'Yes, I do. The Huns must have known about the concerts AND which of the top brass would be there. It was a carefully planned attack but because of the threat of rain and thus the early start, they got the timing wrong.'

'Lucky for the General we started early because of the rain and he did not stay to the end. Lucky also that the F2s that escorted him back to HQ were on the scene when the attack came. The Huns did not bargain for that. One of the ground crew said the Huns lost half their attack force.'

32. Jules Rameau

It was cold. Although they huddled up to each other, there was no benefit as they were still very wet. They felt worse because of the thought of what would happen to them when they returned to base. That is, if they were ever to get back. If they did, it would only be to exchange the frying pan for the fire. At this moment they both felt the odds were stacked against them as they had no clear plan for when daylight would appear. They remained silent for a long time until their thoughts were suddenly interrupted. It was about 2.00 am when they heard voices and the door was opened sharply. A light shone on them.

'Attention. Se levez. Levez vos mains.'

Bobby knew what to do instantly and Stephen followed suit. They relaxed when they realised they had been discovered by a group of French soldiers even though guns were pointed at them. They were searched and a Webley found in Stephen's jacket was confiscated. Stephen had no idea it was there.

'Venez avec nous.'

They were taken to a nearby house, which was in an appalling mess. Its occupants had fled. A French corporal came across and they were given coffee. Their commander sat at the desk. He spoke to them.

'Vous parlez Francais n'est ce pas?'

Bobby replied,

'Oui monsieur, un peu mais ne pas, mon ami.'

'In that case I will do my best to speak English. I am Captain Jules Rameau. Who are you and what are you doing in these parts?'

They both gave the French captain their names and numbers and said:

'We were testing the air to ground equipment and suddenly, without warning, found ourselves in a dogfight. The Huns did not realise there was a loose plane about. We managed to shoot down the Black Count.'

'Ah, bon. So it was you. Merveilleux. Congratulations. We all saw it. Good shooting. What is your next move?'

'To get back to base before the Boche get here. Our plane is near the hut and is hidden somewhat by the trees. It will not remain for long like that tomorrow. It is stuck in the mud and we need some help, please.'

'We can help there, mon ami. In four hours it will be dawn and, God willing, we will get you on your way.'

'There is one problem, monsieur. It has been raining heavily and I think we shall have difficulty getting airborne from the field.'

'That is certainly a problem. Have you a solution?'

'Yes, we think so. It would mean you and your men pulling the aeroplane to the road and taking off from there. Fortunately the road is straight.'

'We will do what we can. Let us hope "Fritz" does not get here before that time otherwise we will be…how do you say in English?'

'Sitting ducks.'

'Ah yes. Sitting ducks. Anyway you will be celebrities when you return. *Le comte noir*. Tres bien, mes amis.'

'We will probably be in for a court martial for taking the aeroplane without proper permission.'

'We hope not for your sakes, messieurs. It is MacHeath your commanding officer.'

'Unfortunately yes. Do you know him?'

'Oh oui monsieur. We know him. He is well known in town for being a patron of the girls' house. Number 27 Rue de L'ecole. Vous comprendez?'

'Oh you mean the brothel.'

'Oui. That is the word I search. The brothel.' The captain laughed. 'I believe he is also married with 6 children. He sneaks in after dark when he thinks nobody will see him. But we see him and with his parcels. Ha ha! Here is the return of your gun.'

'What do you mean by parcels?'

'Food parcels, mon ami. There is little enough in the town at the moment and the girls are glad of what he gives them.'

Hm, thought Stephen. *Stealing from the kitchen eh. That might be something we would do well to remember.*

They dozed fitfully for a couple of hours. Stephen had to take another couple of painkillers but could not get up. Bobby was asleep so for a moment Stephen was at a loss as to what to do. Fortunately, the French soldier on guard saw his plight. Stephen made the motion of drinking and the guard procured a cup and filled it with water. Somehow it tasted divine. He thanked the soldier and lay back. He dozed and all too soon found himself being shaken awake. The officer then did the same to Bobby.

'Reveillez, monsieur; reveillez.'

Captain Rameau appeared.

'Venez, monsieur. Venez avec moi…Ici…Regardez la carte.'

A bleary eyed Bobby got up and was shown the map. The captain said they were a small force that was protecting a bridge and also a lookout for their main force a few miles down the road.

'We are 'ere, mon ami. This is where we will go to stop the Boche if they come at this road junction. That, 'opefully will give you time to get away. The war is all but over but for some of them it will never end. They will fight to the death or until ordered to stop.'

'Too right,' said Bobby.

'The Count is…how do you say…*Un chef de Guerre.* A celebrity. We believe they will try and find what has 'appened to 'im. One of my men has gone to tell our main force the situation. It is dangerous as nobody is sure where the front line is. We 'ope he gets through. It is all unnecessary as the war is finished and there is no point in further bloodshed.'

'You are very brave, my friend, and I thank you.'

'How many of us will you need to get your aeroplane on to the road? It has stopped raining for the moment.'

'Difficult to say. My friend will not be of any use and I shall have to do the flying. Can you spare 6 men?'

'If that's what it takes then you shall 'ave them. They will rejoin the rest of us as soon as they can. Voila!'

They all had coffee and some sort of tasteless porridge. Then it was a case of all getting kitted out and ready. Stephen found it a bit of a problem moving to start with but then walked quite well albeit with a limp. They inched forward in the dark to where the plane was covered and to their relief found it intact and as it was. An owl hooted and the eerie sound only heightened the tension.

Stephen gave orders as to where the soldiers were to handle the plane and then they pulled her out. For a full minute, she did not seem to want to budge but then she rolled nicely backwards into the shorter grass of the field. There were a few puddles but nothing of any large size. They swung the Bristol F2 around and waited a few moments while Stephen checked the wheels.

The dawn was breaking and it would soon be possible to take off. The gate on to the road was quite a distance away and on the opposite side of the field. They advanced a few yards but Bobby called a halt as there was some water ahead. They then were forced to do a wide detour which was a nuisance but they did not dare take a risk as they had no idea as to the depth of it. However the going got easier when they reached the deserted farmhouse and they reached some sort of a track. Some stray orphaned chickens clucked and ran away when they sensed danger.

From then onwards, they found fewer problems and reached the road just as the sun peeped over the horizon. So far so good they all thought but that feeling did not last for long. In the distance there was a low rumbling sound which could only mean one thing. Tanks! The Huns were out and probably looking for their lost Count. They were using the road as the shorter route over the field was waterlogged and misty.

Stephen tapped Bobby on the shoulder.

'Can you hear them, buddy?'

'Loud and clear, mate.'

'Are you thinking what I am thinking?'

'That we should give them a parting present?'

'Right on, buddy. Let's do it!' The tall poplar trees that lined the road was keeping them camouflaged for a time. The French soldiers looked at each other with worried faces but they were soon able to haul the F2 up a little slope on to the road. Bobby explained that they only needed one person to stay and swing the propeller. The others shook hands and rushed off to join their colleagues at the bridge.

There was no need to stay here now that Bobby and Stephen were in the F2. It only needed to start which it did on the second attempt. They both knew that the sound would be heard for miles so there was no time to lose. Bobby nursed her and pulled back the throttle gently. She responded well and soon raced down the road. The F2 soared into the air with the greatest of ease and Bobby initially took her westwards for less than half a minute. He then turned 360 degrees and flew back straight along the road from which they came.

Stephen knew exactly what to do, a task made infinitely easier because the morning sun was right behind the oncoming tanks. The enemy could not believe a plane was out so early and were completely taken by surprise. Bobby levelled out at 60 feet just above the trees and Stephen opened fire. It was nothing more than a turkey shoot. The enemy scattered and to a man dived for the cover of the trees. One tank tried to take evasive action but only succeeded in slithering into the ditch.

Once clear of the line, Bobby did another 360 degree turn and put the F2 in such a position that made it easy to fire. There were only a few harmless pot shots at them as the tank main guns were facing the opposite way. As well as that the tank commanders were forced to dive below the hatches to prevent being shot to pieces. This second burst by Stephen lasted for only a few second as, unfortunately the ammunition ran out. Bobby did one final circle and delivered the *coup de gras* in the form of the bombs.

There was no need to stay a second longer so they made for base. As they did so, they saw the French soldiers instead of retreating were on the attack in spite of hugely inferior numbers. The German soldiers did not know this and most of a dishevelled and demoralised starving army unit fled eastwards. Many prisoners were taken and the German offensive had hardly fired a shot. It was only four minutes later that the duo landed at base much to the surprise and delight of the ground crew who were already up and about.

First to speak was Jessie. 'Never thought I'd be so glad to see a Blue belly. Are you both OK buddy?'

'Bobby is fine. I'm OK apart from my leg. What happened here?'

'One bomb hit the side of the band marquee. Two of the band dead and Lieutenant Parr. Six others wounded, two seriously. Two dead when a bomb hit the showers. We lost two F2s but the pilots are OK. Could have been a lot worse. The roads are flooded because of all that deluge. It has been chaos as we have been cut off from HQ. There is a rumour that HQ was targeted as well. The telephone wires were down for a time and the lights have only just been repaired. The dispatch rider is waiting for the CO to wake up.'

'Does Mac the Mouth know anything?'

'He was very late back last night from the hospital. Early hours. He and the adjutant Mason had to wade through the last few hundred yards and he collapsed when he got here. He recovered enough to be briefed about the deaths and damage but knows nothing about you two. They gave him a shot of something and he passed out. At least he was not at the floozy house this time, lucky for him. We have just been waiting for daylight to try and clear up and get the telephones working again. Anyway, what happened to you two?'

'We've been hiding. We were looked after in a damp farmhouse with some extremely kind and hospitable Frenchmen.'

By now, the noise of their arrival had alerted many of the other staff who were eager to hear all the news of the heroic action of the duo and all seemed to be talking at once. Stephen put up his hand and shouted at them to stop and listen for a moment.

'Listen, everybody. Get every available man in the air and go and finish them off. Here is the map reference and coordinates. That way there will be no chance of the Frenchmen being outflanked and cut to pieces. Get going. Get going!'

There was no need for a second bidding and everyone dispersed in an instant. Stephen's head began to swim and he clung on to Bobby to prevent collapse.

'It's all over camp about you two and the Count.' said Jessie. 'The CO will have to know sometime. The doc gave him a big shot of something. Said he will be out for quite a while. You two should get some rest while you can.'

'That's exactly what we're going to do. We need get a message to Bobby's camp and his CO.'

'We can see to that for you when the lines are repaired. They will want to know about your shooting down of the Count. Let's hope all turns out well and there is no comeback. Damn fine bit of flying, both of you. Thanks for checking the radio. I will now be able to live at least another day!'

33. Mac the Mouth

Stephen and Bobby walked off and into the billets where they crashed out and into bed. Their valet was given orders not to say anything until the last moment. Fortunately, it did not take long to repair the telephone wires and details of the rescue of the Count and repulse of the tanks were relayed to the British camp. It took longer to re-establish contact with the American HQ and when this occurred, adjutant Mason tried to waken Captain MacHeath without success.

An hour later, when MacHeath eventually awoke, it was natural that he could remember little of the events of the previous 16 hours due to the drug that had been pumped into him. At least his mouth felt easier. He had hardly sat down at his desk when the telephone rang and the CO of the British base congratulated him on a joint allied venture which had showed great initiative and would he send his boy back before too long? A confused MacHeath said yes, not knowing a thing about what he was talking and just having to play along. Red-faced, he bellowed out for the adjutant.

'Right. Let's have it, Mason. Every damn thing. What the f*** has been happening on my patch? What does everyone know that I don't?'

The obsequious adjutant spilled all that he knew and while he spoke, MacHeath got redder and ever more furious.

'Where the f**k are they? I'll throw the book at them. They're dead. They'll wish they had never been born. Where are they?'

'In their billet, sir.'

'Get them. Get them here as if it were yesterday. Hurry it up, Mason, or I will have your arse for dog meat.'

Mason rushed off to get the men who were sleeping soundly. They were not allowed to wash or shave so it was a sorry and dishevelled looking pair that presented themselves to the office. MacHeath drew himself up to his full height and glowered at them menacingly.

'Right, Robinson. I can tell you that I can hardly believe what I am hearing. Grounded yet you take a kite out without permission. You take an unauthorised person with you. You engage the enemy and risk an expensive machine and you then go AWOL. You disgusting insubordinate piece of upper crust shite.

'I never did like you and your sort. Privileged f***ing class. As for your associate here I am sending him back for his own CO to deal with. This afternoon you will face a court martial, Robinson, and I am not just going to throw the goddamn book at you. I am going to throw the f*****g library at you. Do you hear me. No. Don't bother to answer. Guard! Take this man to solitary confinement.'

Before the guard came in, the telegraph operator pushed past him and came in with a message marked urgent. The telegraph had been restored to the American H.Q but as yet not the telephone.

'I'll deal with it in a minute, corporal.'

'It would be best if you read it now, sir.'

'Who the f*** do you think you are talking to? I will have your ba—'

'Please, sir, for your own sake, read it now,' blurted the corporal, being unusually bold.

MacHeath snatched the paper and within a few seconds his eyes nearly popped out of his head. He looked at it, rose from his chair and turned away from them in an apoplectic rage. He could hardly contain his anger and his cheeks went bright red. When he had regained some sort of composure, he cancelled the order to the guard.

'Get out.' The guard hurried away and MacHeath managed to lower his voice.

'You two go and have a wash and shave and make yourselves presentable. Get something to eat and be back in this office in one hour. Do I make myself clear?'

'Yes sir,' came the chorus.

'Now get the hell out of here! Both of you.' They saluted but it was not returned.

Outside, the pair looked at each other and were quite bemused. People kept coming up and congratulating them and there were more than a few back slaps. They did as they were told and with the aid of a borrowed razor made themselves look reasonably presentable. The adjutant came and gave them a brush down which improved their appearance somewhat. That done, they reported back to the CO's office at 13.00 hours sharp. MacHeath looked at them with an almost uncontrollable and ever growing hate.

'I never liked you, Robinson. I don't like your sort. You think you own the f*****g world. As to your friend here, I don't know about him. I suppose all the Limeys can't be bad. It seems that people in high places are pleased with what you have done and any misdemeanours that I have pointed out have been overruled. AND I DON'T LIKE BEING F***ING OVERRULED. You are to receive awards, both of you. You are to report to British HQ at 17.00 hours. and together with Captain Rameau, you will receive Le Croix de Guerre. Marshall Foch will make the presentation. Have you any questions?'

'None, sir,' said the relieved but confused pair in unison. At that moment the reprieve was more important to them than any award.

'You, Wilson, will report to your CO immediately on arrival. Now get the f**k out of my vision.'

They wasted no second leaving and were surrounded by yet more well-wishers. The car was already waiting. Their chauffeur was none other than a smiling Richard Squires to whom Bobby introduced Stephen.

'Glad to meet you Sergeant. Bobby has told me a little about you.'

'Right now, Squiz, we could do with you getting us out of here.'

Without another word, Squires whisked them to British HQ where Bobby was separated from Stephen and led to an office. Three upper crust ranking officers, all with extravagant moustaches, were in the room and all were beaming with pleasure.

'Come in, Williston. Good to see you. Bloody good show and all that. Congratulations. We have brought you here to say well done. A massive coup. Real initiative. There is one thing more and that is you are to receive your wings and be promoted to sergeant. Can't have the Yanks pulling rank and stealing the show, eh what?'

'Thank you, sir. Thank you very much.'

'Now, let me introduce you to these gentlemen and then we want to know all about what happened, if you please. Everything. And then the press will want you. Damn good story for the people at home, you know. They are ready for something like this. This is a real coup. What an interesting life you have had, sergeant, and what a coincidence being reunited with your employer's son. Remarkable. Now sit down here, sergeant. Cup of tea?'

34. Limelight

Just before the ceremony, a smart young woman officer of the WRAF came in to sew on Bobby's stripes. Her left breast kept bumping into him and he had to admit the feeling was rather nice, especially when she gave him a seductive smile on completion. He looked down at his stripes and felt a glow of pleasure. Then again, why shouldn't he feel that way? He was taken to a building where he rejoined Stephen who was pleased for the promotion and shook his hand. There were too many about for a hug so they had to settle for that.

After what seemed an interminable wait they were whisked into Amiens where a fair-sized crowd was waiting. There was cheering and applause, some of which had been rehearsed for the benefit of the cameraman as they got out and then they were met by none other than Marshall Foch's secretary who spoke perfect English. All at once they were reunited with Captain Jules Rameau.

'Eh bien mes amis. Bienvenue. Good to see you again.'

'Et vous aussi, monsieur Jules, if I may call you that.'

'Please do, mon ami, please do.'

It did not take long for proceedings to get under way. The town mayor spoke of the bravery of the men by the side of him and emphasised the fact that each of the senior allies had made a contribution to this remarkable incident. He naturally gave great emphasis to the fact that his compatriots had turned retreat into attack and had captured many German soldiers who had fled.

What most people did not know was that the German division had been living on less than half rations with dwindling ammunition and little medical support. Illness was rife and when Jules and company had attacked, some of the Germans were only too ready to surrender. They were thoroughly demoralised and exhausted. Jules escorted them into town where they were herded into a schoolroom. They were humanely treated and grateful for being fed.

The mayor then went on to talk about the two young allies who had made the whole thing possible. Bobby translated for Stephen who looked embarrassed. Bobby realised that the incident was being pumped up for propaganda and public morale as well as a genuine award for a daring feat. Anyway, they accepted the medals graciously and then listened to Marshal Foch's speech, which was mercifully short. Bobby replied in his best textbook French which was greeted with rapturous applause from the mostly French crowd.

What the two young men were not prepared for was the embrace on both cheeks that the great man administered. They were then rushed back to their respective barracks by car. Stephen was emotionally and physically drained but he entered the mess for a drink and was surrounded by pilot colleagues and nearly all the ground crew.

Eventually, he managed to extricate himself and drag himself to his room. He fell on his bed completely exhausted. Much the same happened to Bobby who, unlike Stephen, received some more information. The Count was recovering nearby in hospital and had sent a message of gratitude to the allied pilots for saving his life. He also expressed a wish to meet the brave men in person who were the first ever to shoot him down.

Little does he realise, thought Bobby, that it was a lucky shot and they only had half a "kill" each to the Count's 57. Even the German newspapers gave grudging praise to the two allied airmen, especially for saving the life of their illustrious compatriot.

Two days later and in a much better frame of mind, Captain MacHeath sent orders for Stephen to change into uniform and await transport. He was too jealous to inform him where he was bound so left it to the adjutant. He was to team up with Bobby at the British hospital and meet the Count.

The lobby held several reporters and at one point they had to push their way through. Bobby in his best French said that they would speak to them when they had seen the Count. They waited patiently to be admitted. Bobby spoke in French to two of the nurses only to find one came from Mansfield and the other from Sunderland.

'Let's make it look good, Stevie. No point in swimming against the tide.'

'No point at all,' said Stephen.

They marched in, stamped, saluted the Count and promptly removed their hats. The Count greeted them cordially and shook hands. He told them in his best English that he was full of appreciation for their skill and daring. He was completely unaware of the true facts and the pair made no attempt to enlighten him. One thing the Count did say did say was that he hoped this wretched war would be over soon and that they could be friends. It was a sentiment that the two young men endorsed readily.

They chatted with him for about half an hour until the ward sister appeared and said that time was up. They left the hospital but not before two very forward French nurses had come up to them in the corridor and kissed them without warning. The two men did not resist although they thought perhaps, they should have done. It was then a case of dealing with reporters whose quick-fire questions made their heads swim. Jules was there by then and helped enormously. He sat beside them on a platform.

'Have you a girlfriend at home or even here, sergeant Robinson?'

'Judging by what's just happened in there, I have got several. Please do not let this information get back home!'

'So there is somebody back home?'

'Several possibilities but with all the activity over here, I haven't managed to pinpoint the one with the best bank balance.' There was laughter. Stephen was giving nothing away.

The reporter of the British Morning Post stood up and spoke with the inevitable two-million-pound home counties cultivated upper crust accent.

'Gentlemen. My paper has received a lot of telegrams which we would like to pass on to you and I believe the same applies to some of my colleagues. There are several offers of nuptials as well for each of you,' he said sardonically. 'What's your reaction to that, Sergeant Williston?'

'Capital. My ambition when I leave the Air Force is to take all of them without exception to a foreign country where bigamy is not only not a crime but actively encouraged.' There was laughter from the other reporters. He was giving them just what they wanted.

'What are your plans when you return home, sergeant Robinson. Will you be working for your father again?'

'It seems to me that he does not need me anymore. He has done quite well without me since I left. Perhaps I might stay in the aircraft business. We will see when I get home.'

The questions went on and on but somehow the two men managed to hold on without leaving themselves wide open. It was made easier when Bobby was asked about his survival from the *Lusitania* and this gave Stephen some respite as his leg had begun to throb mercilessly. Bobby had to go through it all again for the French press who seemed mightily impressed. Eventually they went to the reception for something to eat and drink.

'Sacre bleu. C'est fini,' said Jules Rameau.

'There will be more tomorrow or the next day I bet,' said Bobby.

'Merde,' said Jules.

Eventually, they said adieu to Captain Rameau and with great relief finally got back to their respective barracks. They each received notice of a day's leave but the day after they would be called for at ten o'clock for a briefing. Bobby thought that he would worry about what was in store at nine o'clock and not a moment before. Stephen thought much the same and did his best to relax and unwind although pain in the leg made it difficult. When the adjutant came in, Stephen asked for the MO to call which he did shortly afterwards and provided some much needed painkillers.

35. Paris and London

They were brought separately from their respective barracks and met inside HQ at Amiens. There was a committee of three officers from each of the major allied countries waiting for them. They introduced themselves but their names meant nothing to the trio. They were all very polite and congenial and offered them coffee which tasted really good compared with the stuff made from acorns which they were used to. The officers spoke informally to them for a while to put them at their ease before asking them to be seated.

'Are we lambs for the sacrifice, monsieur Jules?'

'Peut etre. It could be so, mon ami.' The middle man of the trio spoke up.

'Gentlemen, we have brought you here to be of assistance to us. For you, the war is over although it will be over for everyone soon, we believe. You have all been very brave and effective and we want to take advantage of your success. We have been through over four years of absolute hell and it has been tough on all the civilian population here, at home and in the States. People need cheering up. They need to witness a victory and you can help us do that by taking the stage and being put in the limelight. I hope I am making sense.'

They looked at each other. The French officer spoke rapidly to Jules who nodded in agreement.

'Do we have to accept sir or have we the right to refuse?'

'Well it all depends on whether you want to go back to the daily grind or whether you would like some fame and a bit of fortune. Listen. You are not fools and you realise this is a bit of theatre but there are literally millions lying out there dead, wounded or dying. The public need to feel that they have got something out of this damned war and you can give a small piece of success. There have been some real pilot aces on our side but the difference between them and you is that most are dead and you two are alive. There is the added bonus of Sergeant Williston's survival and the pair of you meeting up again as the result of a fluke. Quite a story. My advice is to take this opportunity as you will be unlikely to get anything comparable in your lifetime.'

'When you put it like that, sir, we can hardly refuse,' said Bobby.

'Good. Sergeant Robinson?'

'I feel the same, sir. What do you want us to do?'

'It would mean photocalls in Paris, London and New York plus lots of interviews.'

'Et vous Monsieur, Capitaine Rameau?'

Jules then piped up in French. He said he would be glad to do what they asked but pointed out that he had not had leave or seen his wife and two teenage boys for many months. They were over in Vannes on the west coast. Was there any room for them? The colonel said he thought there would be but the British colonel said that the army would fund Jules' family in the U.K. Bobby suddenly had a brainwave.

'Are you in touch with the British newspapers, sir?'

'All the time, Sergeant Williston.'

'In that case would you tell one, and I don't mind which one that we will give an in depth and possibly exclusive interview if they sponsor my aunt and cousin down from Boston so that we can have some of my family involved? Also, my uncle is in Ruhleben prisoner of war camp and I would appreciate any information about him. If you could deal with those matters then I would be very grateful.'

'That should not be a problem. Sounds like a good idea. Leave it to me.'

'When do we leave, sir?'

'The day after tomorrow.'

'Merde,' said Jules quietly.

Bobby's transport came to pick up Stephen on the way to Amiens station. Captain MacHeath called them into his office just before they left for one last show of pathetic defiance. He glowered at Stephen and Bobby and said some disparaging words of which well over 90% were either outrageous or untrue. Bobby knew this was going to happen so he was prepared. After they had been dismissed, he handed over an envelope to MacHeath who took it with surprise. The adjutant watched with ever growing interest.

'When we have gone, would you deal with this for us please, sir?'

'What the hell is this?' He tore it open and revealed a ten franc note.

'What the f**k is this all about?'

'A parting gift, sir. We would like you to put it towards your next visit to 27 Rue de L'ecole. Instead of food parcels.'

For once, the CO was dumbstruck. They left the embarrassed MacHeath with smart salutes and were out of the door before he could say a word. The adjutant who was in the room whipped out then bit on his handkerchief to suppress his laughter. Inwardly, he felt a sense of deep satisfaction seeing his vindictive superior officer squirm. Needless to say, he lost no time in divulging this incident and thus the news reached one and all on site.

They met Jules' wife and boys on the platform at Amiens and after presentation travelled south to Paris. Madame Rameau spoke fairly good English which meant that Stephen conversed mostly with her. The boys' English was almost non-existent so Bobby spent most of his time with them. They were enthralled at his escapades and bombarded him constantly with questions.

When they reached Gare du Nord, there were scores of people waiting and press everywhere. They were interviewed in detail and were presented to some very eminent people in the government all of whom were anxious to be seen and photographed with *Le Grande Trois*.

Late the following afternoon, they boarded a train for Calais and reached there in the dark. The hotel was somewhat drab which was hardly surprising after more than four years of war but was clean and comfortable. The proprietor was absolutely delighted to have such distinguished guests and kept asking them if there was anything else they needed. Their main needs were peace, rest and solitude. In the morning they took the first available ferry to Dover and were shielded from the somewhat unruly mob of reporters whilst they boarded their first-class carriage and compartment.

This time champagne was laid on which pleased Jules' boys. Madame Rameau, who appeared very strict, would let them have only one glass much to the chagrin of her sons. All the while, they were protected by three bodyguards who were not in uniform. One was in the compartment and the other outside in the corridor. The other one who had a beard and a constant morose face kept coming and going.

'What did I tell you, Jules. It does not always rain in Angleterre,' said Bobby.

'I believe you, mon ami. It just seems to come at inconvenient times.'

'True. There is a reason.'

'Which is?' intervened Stephen.

'It is because we play a game called cricket on this island of ours. It's the last rain making ritual extant in Britain.'

'Sacrebleu,' said Jules.

When they reached the Regent hotel in London, they were astounded to find out that they were to be awarded a medal by Lord Curzon, a member of the war cabinet. It seemed appropriate that he should confer the honour with his Alabama-born wife at his side.

David Lloyd George, the Prime Minister and the King were unavailable at the time as the hairy problem of what to do with the Czar and his family was a thorn in King George V's side and seemed insoluble. Lloyd George was busy on another front; he knew the end of the war was near and was desperately making plans with friends, foes and former enemies to win an election that loomed ominously.

The *Morning Post* had sponsored Bobby's family from Boston and had put them up into a smart London hotel. They were also informed that Edward, the Prince of Wales had expressed profound admiration for *Le Grande Trois* and had ordered an audience with them at Buckingham Palace. When the Prince heard that Bobby's family had travelled down from Boston he invited them as well. Uncle Arthur was back in England having been part of an exchange of prisoners but as yet he was too weak to travel as a result of too little food for too long. Marion's fiancé, the dour Philip Honegger, came in his place. Aunt Ethel was almost overwhelmed. She hugged her nephew and did her best to stem the tears of joy.

'Dear Bobby, we are so proud of you,' she fumbled for her ever elusive handkerchief so Bobby produced his.

'Here you are, auntie. By the way, this is supposed to be a happy occasion.'

'Oh dear, I feel such a fool,' said Aunt Ethel.

'Congratulations, dear cousin,' said Marion. 'You are famous now.'

She hugged him very tightly and he was sorry when she pulled away, especially as there was a very searching look on her face. It was obvious how much she cared for him. Philip Honegger offered a limp handshake and remained constantly po-faced. All the time Bobby felt somewhat of an imposter and to deflect his thoughts from that feeling, he introduced Jules and his family to them followed by Stephen.

'We have heard so much about you,' said Aunt Ethel.

Jules bowed, took her hand and then Marion's. He kissed them in turn.

'Vraiment. Beauty is abundant in this family.'

Marion coloured a little and the starchy Honegger remained aloof during this effusion but by now Stephen and Bobby, used to the affable and lovable Frenchman's manner, just smiled.

They were all excited and apprehensive about their visit to the palace. The Rolls Royce car arrived and the chauffeur guided them skilfully into the limousine with consummate skill and precision. The Rameau family were on the edge of their seats whilst witnessing the sights and sounds of *Londres* previously known to them only in books. Now the experiences were in the flesh and the excitement reached its zenith as Buckingham Palace appeared and the gates opened. The Prince of Wales was waiting for them and put them at ease skilfully. No time was wasted as the first item on the agenda was the medal presentation followed by a photographic session.

The press left and then the Prince lead them into another part of the palace. Queen Mary looked after and talked to the women whilst the Prince took the men to see his collection of photographs taken whilst he was in France in 1915. Knowing the Prince was interested in photography and had been in France in the trenches albeit three years earlier, the three heroes had put together a few of their spare shots in a small album.

Marion and Philip had gone out early in the morning to buy an album and their selection of photographs were hastily mounted. When the whole party was reassembled Bobby and Stephen insisted that Jules, as senior member of the trio should present it to the Prince. Learning of this Jules, for a moment was quite overcome. He recovered and bowed to the Prince, explaining that all of them had contributed one way or another causing the Prince to be absolutely delighted and who said to them:

'Dear people, all. I am a privileged person of which there can be no doubt. If you look around you will see the result of many inanimate gifts that other privileged people have brought or sent here. This in my hand is something different because it is alive and is about living people who have been fighting for our respective countries, for freedom and liberty. Three of those living people are standing before me now and it is me that feels humble at this moment.

'It is true that I have witnessed the terrible conflict at first hand in the trenches but most of the time I was shielded whereas you have risked life and limb so that one day we can enjoy peace and a better world. I shall treasure this album and it will have a special place not only in my library but in my heart as well. Thank you so very much.'

There was a smattering of applause as the Prince bowed. From thence the conversation did not falter for one moment and they were all sorry when they had to go into the hall for a bite to eat. Eventually, it was time to bid the Royal family farewell and take their leave. They returned to the hotel feeling very pleased with themselves. There was somewhat of a scrum at the hotel when reporters jostled for position. Their bodyguard shielded them well but Aunt Ethel was just a little flustered and was glad to get to her room.

There was a mountain of mail to sift through which was dealt with by all except Jules and his family. One on the men assigned for their protection also helped. The only way to thank people was to take out a *thank you* advertisement in the main newspapers and hope that would suffice. That whittled it down to about forty letters some of which were offers of employment or sponsorship in the UK. These were discounted, of course, as Stephen and Bobby knew that it would not be long before they would be returning to the USA.

Each time Stephen thought of home and Rachael, his heart leapt. He managed to send her a brief telegram There was one offer of employment which was sent to both of them and which looked very interesting.

For the moment Bobby put it down and turned to his friend: 'You have not said a definite yea or nay whether you are going back to work for your father after being demobbed.'

'Not unless it is the absolute last resort. Not unless I am faced with starvation and that is most unlikely. I am hoping that Chuck might need me at least for a while. After tasting real freedom, I do not want to be cooped up at *Frankfare*. What about you, mon ami?'

'Well, as you know, I am *persona non grata* at *Frankfare*. I shall have to meet mother and dad somewhere else. And Rachael, of course. I'll have to get a place of my own.'

'I feel sickened and angry every time that subject crops up.'

'Hey matey. Steady on. I don't blame you. Don't ever think that. Not for one second.'

'I know, buddy, but it hurts like hell when my father behaves the way he does. And he gets away with it.'

'Shall we have a look at these offers then and take some advice when we get back. I have a bit of money saved up. I shall have to see auntie about that because I left it all at Boston in case I did not come back. I nearly didn't. That's twice. Isn't there a saying "never two without three"?'

'Stop being superstitious and keep opening those damned envelopes.'

The next day brought three important announcements. The first was that the Rameau family would not be going to New York. No reason was given but Jules did not seem disappointed and neither did his wife. Bobby and Stephen did not ask any questions as they both felt it was beyond their ambit. The second announcement was that Aunt Ethel and family would be returning to Boston that afternoon. Aunt Ethel came to see Bobby in his room but made as if to withdraw when she saw Stephen was with him.

'No. Come in, auntie. I have no secrets from Stephen. I wanted to give you this. It is a wedding present for my cousin and her husband to be. I got it in Amiens. It is to add to the one you bought.'

'I did not buy it because I don't think he has actually asked her yet.'

'Great God in heaven, auntie. What's keeping him? He is a medical man. Surely he is not still reading up about what goes where!'

Stephen, unable to contain himself, was convulsed with laughter and threw his head back on the pillow.

Aunt Ethel was quite shocked. 'Bobby, really…that's very naughty of you. No; I think he was waiting until the war was over.'

'Well, it is, just about. Tell him to get on with it and put the poor girl out of her misery.'

'You should have taken it and given it to them yourself. Never mind, I'll do it. We are packing. I came to give you this. It's your box and money. I never took any because I just couldn't. Anyway, I knew you would come back safely,' she said somewhat triumphantly.

'Of course, you didn't take anything, auntie. I know you well enough by now. Anyway this envelope is for you and Uncle Arthur to get back on your feet. No. No. No protests, NOT A WORD, auntie. Don't open it until you get home, please. Are you going from Liverpool Street?'

'From King's Cross.'

'We can't come with you as we'll be meeting Lord Curzon at the Foreign office.'

'No matter. Let's have a final drink together.'

With that the three of them repaired to the lounge bar to join Marion and Philip. They parted most reluctantly and after some tearful farewells Bobby's relatives left for the station. Shortly afterwards the heroes were taken to the foreign office where a rather pompous Lord Curzon met them. It was brief and clinical, a fact remarked upon by Jules. The Rameau family then packed and came in to say a very wistful goodbye.

'Mon ami, it 'as been my great privilege to know you both,' said Jules.

'Et vous aussi, mon ami. Nous sommes les freres pour toujours.'

'Vous etes les celebrites, mes chers.'

'Even I can translate that,' said Stephen as he hugged Jules and waited for the inevitable embrace on both cheeks.

Jules extricated a solemn promise from the men that one day they would have a holiday with them in Vannes. This was readily given although both wondered if or when that could ever be.

36. Homeward Bound

The next important announcement made to Stephen and Bobby was that they would be returning to New York on November 2nd. The question of demobilisation for Bobby would be worked out later and he was told he would not have to return to Britain if he did not wish to do so. When they were informed of this the two men slipped out of the hotel incognito and went into the West End to buy a few presents. They returned with several parcels and organised some cables to be sent to *Frankfare* and also to Chuck and Emma at the airfield.

In that way they both knew the messages would be certain to get through. Bobby also sent a cable to the *Imperial Hotel*, Cork, and asked Joe Cassidy to do the necessary leg to the farm at Bunmaskiddy and give them the time of their arrival. He instructed Joe to invite of one of the Cork newspaper men and promised an exclusive when the ship, the *Aquitania*, docked at Queenstown.

It was a question of whether Declan and company wanted to do the trip and see him again but he hoped as many as possible from the village would make the effort to be there. He also asked if one of them would bring the dogs. The ship was to carry many of troops back home but as she was to be returned officially to civilian service in December, there were quite a number of paying passengers on board, mainly government officials and a sprinkling of businessmen with their families.

The next morning, Stephen and Bobby thanked those in the hotel that had looked after them so well. They were then escorted to Euston station for the train to Liverpool. Stephen remarked that he had done this journey once before except in the opposite direction. Their very quiet escort remained with them and made sure they were not besieged by the press and autograph hunters. They left London with a little regret but inwardly, they were thankful that all had gone well. Two down, one to go.

Their bags were taken by two hefty porters who took them to their first-class compartment. It was close to the near end of the platform and only the third compartment in the coach. The inspector explained that this had been arranged so they had minimum of prying eyes and autograph hunters. It did not prevent one of the Liverpool MP's gate-crashing into the compartment and introducing himself.

His offer of assistance and a seat at his luncheon table was politely refused, much to his chagrin; they told him would be dining at Liverpool in the London and North Western Hotel. The train pulled out and only stopped once, three hours later at Crewe. Less than an hour later they pulled into Liverpool Lime Street.

After their meal, they managed to avoid the crowds by being taken straight to a waiting cab and taken down to the *Aquitania*. They were surprised to find their quarters were quite comfortable in spite of the fact that the ship for a long period had been used almost exclusively for troop movement. However there were no luxuries and few frills as the ship did not compare with the lovely and much lamented *Lusitania*.

Before the ship left, the captain came down personally to see them. Their bodyguard was next door; the British military had departed and they were now in the hands of the ships' security. A steward came down with a number of letters and cables which they decided to read later except for one. That of course was from Rachael to Stephen and the effect on him was profound. Bobby said nothing but inwardly he shared Stephen's joy.

Twenty minutes before departure, crowds or no crowds they called security and wished to go on deck. The crowd was only a fair size and no sign of a crush. Just about everyone was in a buoyant mood because most were going home and yet more news was filtering through about an imminent German surrender. They went below and only came up about 11.00 pm to see the ship dock in Dublin. They retired and slept long and late.

There was a fairly rudimentary breakfast waiting for them which they found very wholesome if not exotic. In the end most people respected their privacy after the first few hours and from then on it was a case of nudges and whispers from the other passengers. On the second day they docked at Queenstown and whilst post and parcels were transferred and provisions loaded they were whisked away to see Bobby's friends who were waiting on the quay. Ryan and his wife were missing, having been delegated to look after the farm. Declan,

Eilish and Aoifa were all there and so were Father O'Leary and Mavis O'Neill. Joe Cassidy and Annie completed the party. They hugged and kissed and each was presented to Stephen. Mavis O'Neill completely forgot herself and hugged Bobby tightly.

She said: 'Oh glory be, God love you, Bobby. It's so good to see you again. I thought I never would.'

'It's good to see you, Miss O'Neill. I hope you have been good whilst you have been out of my sight.'

'No chance of anything else. Now why don't you fetch your bags and come back to us?'

'I will under one condition, Mavis.'

'And pray what is that?'

'That you agree to marry me.'

'Oh begorrah. That's the best offer I have had this month!'

The photographers had a field day and dredged every piece of information that Bobby thought relevant from him. He was very careful in what he revealed. He did tell the reporters about the incident in the lifeboat when the very irreverent preacher had been the cause of he and Justine being pitched overboard. Bobby asked Declan the obvious question but he shook his head. There had been no reappearance from Justine and no communication from her.

Bobby had not raised his hopes so he was not too upset. His spirits soared when the dogs were brought to him who both literally went berserk. Even though it had been eighteen months since they had been together they knew him instantly. They jumped up (which they did not reckon to do) and so he had to kneel down and fuss them. Any facial area that Bobby might have missed in his morning ablutions was swiftly dealt with. Then Declan whispered in Bobby's ear.

'They have not been the same since you left. I do not know what they will be like when we take them home. I was loathe to bring them for that reason but only did as you asked.' There was a pause. Declan continued: 'By rights they are yours. Do you want to take them? We have looked after them, you know. Would they allow them on board?'

Bobby only briefly paused and said: 'I am sure you have looked after them and yes, I do want to take them. I was hoping you would offer.'

'What will the captain say?'

'Sod the captain. We'll sneak them in and will be away and on the high seas before he knows anything about it.'

Declan grinned and nodded. Just at that moment Father O'Leary came over to him.

'Well, me boy, congratulations. You really are a star. It only leaves me one thing to ask.'

'Which is?'

'Have you chosen the day for when you become a good catholic?'

'Yes, Father.'

'You have? Marvellous. When is it to be?'

'The same day as your wedding night, Father.'

Father O'Leary was convulsed with laughter and said: 'As we say here in Ireland. May you be in heaven for at least half an hour before the devil finds out.'

The party reluctantly broke up. The pair boarded and waved and all too soon the coast of the Emerald Isle disappeared. The dogs were taken to the cabin and flopped after their excitement. The captain was indeed somewhat peeved about the introduction of fierce canine passengers but did not want to risk alienating decorated war heroes and thus put a damper on the voyage. It was not long before he and others had reason to be grateful for the dogs' presence in an odd manner.

The acclaimed duo had spent the evening relaxing by having a walk on deck before retiring. They got up at a reasonable hour and spent time chatting before and after breakfast. Later in the morning there was a huge fracas amongst the troops and a bitter fight between two of their company. The CO managed to restore some order but eventually news filtered through to the captain who appeared. There were some wounds to patch and some evidence to be heard which began early in the afternoon.

It was simply a case of theft. One corporal had accused a private of stealing his wallet and would not back down even though there was little or no evidence that the particular private was the guilty party. When all had been interviewed, a search was made which revealed nothing. The private smirked at the corporal's discomfort and said that he would file a formal complaint on arrival in New York. Bobby was nosy and asked one of the guards the details. The chairman was about to wind up proceedings when Bobby, who had deliberately dressed himself in his British uniform, came into the room and saluted.

'Please accept my apologies for this intrusion sir, but I have come to offer my assistance if you think it might be of use.'

The CO was surprised to say the least but under the circumstances, did not wish to be impolite to someone who had recently assumed celebrity status. Bobby asked for details of the missing wallet and the bag and then asked if the corporal, under guard, would fetch three items of his clothing and return without delay. The troops looked on with an ever growing curiosity. Bobby asked to be excused and disappeared for three or four minutes only to appear with Smasher.

He asked for the corporal's clothing which he presented to the dog. Bobby spoke to Smasher who set off and then paused at one of the cabin doors. He sniffed all around and went to one of the cupboards and scratched. Bobby ordered him to heel and then pulled away some wood. It was an old trick. The private had shaped the wood he had procured to create a false hollow and make it look as if it were the end of the cupboard. The hiding place was behind it with the wallet.

'There is your evidence, captain.'

The private shrugged his shoulders and accepted the handcuffs before being taken away to confinement. Bobby turned to the assembled company who were looking on in admiration.

'Well, gentlemen. I think this exceptionally fine animal deserves a pat on the head.'

At this point nobody wanted to miss out and several photographs were demanded, which took quite a time. Bobby stopped and turned to Smasher:

'The corporal wants to thank you and shake your paw, Smasher.' Smasher, tongue out, duly obliged and the onlookers and troops applauded. Later the grateful corporal came down to thank them ask them if he could buy Bobby and Steve a drink. Bobby replied that they were receiving free drinks regularly and that they would take him for one. He was told to get a couple of his buddies to come along and in this he was very happy to oblige. The ship's captain joined them as well as a very relieved CO of the platoon who could now claim a *coup* on reaching New York.

The following evening to entertain the troops Bobby asked the ship's Captain to choose somebody in the company or passengers unknown to he and Stephen and to ask him or her to begin a tour of the ship for at least twenty minutes. He then said that he and Stephen would come into the main hall and tell them the route that was taken and the person that did it. Some of the troops raised their eyebrows in disbelief and others openly scoffed. To be fair, some of them had not heard about the incident the day before.

The only things that Bobby wanted to know was the cabin or place they set off and if the chosen person would at the end pass a couple of small items they were wearing to the captain who would give them to Bobby at the starting point. Bobby told Stephen that he wanted him to bring Grabber with him as to take out Smasher on his own would cause Grabber an upset. They were like Bobby and Stephen, inseparable. As the dogs were sleeping in their cabin and getting to know and like Stephen, this was no problem.

In any case, Stephen was taking Grabber down to the kitchen twice a day for his meals. The starting point was revealed and the pair set off, pausing every now and again to write down where they had been so as to leave no doubt when they faced their audience later.

They did a meandering trail around the ship and at last they reached the hall where there was an expectant audience. This was the most difficult part as the floor had been occupied and trodden on by many pairs of feet during the last few hours. Smasher took his time; he took two minutes and then wagged his tail in front of a thirteen-year-old girl passenger. The applause was tremendous. They then revealed accurately the route that the young girl had taken.

'Is there no end to your ability?' said the captain. 'You are full of surprises.'

The captain had an onerous task. Five times in two days, he had to perform burial at sea which was done at first light so as not to be in sight of the passengers and thus cause potential distress, especially to the younger ones. There were no facilities to cope with that number of deaths aboard ship. It caused a gloom with some of the troops and morale on the deserted Atlantic Ocean sank even further.

Accordingly, the captain asked Stephen and Bobby if they would go and talk to some of the wounded and try to revive their spirits. This they did but it was a tiring business and neither of them was qualified to know what was best to say. With the less serious cases it was much easier as there was less pain and the men were eager to hear about the escapades of the two heroes. They invariably got back to their cabin, very tired which was exacerbated when the dogs immediately expected to be taken out.

Still, the fresh air had a magical effect; now and then they stopped to talk to passengers who had wrapped up warm and braved the elements. In the evening they rued the fact that there were not enough players to form a band let alone locate any sheet music. Stephen wearily got on his bunk and put his hands behind his head.

'What time is it, buddy?'

'Nine o'clock, mate.'

'What time will it be at home?'

'Round about five or six o'clock, at a guess.'

'If that is the case, they might be getting ready for Guy Fawkes Night, rockets, bangers, the lot.'

'They might wait until we return and combine the two,' said Bobby.

'I suppose they might but I doubt it. It has become quite a fixture.'

'All because a small group of recusant Catholics decided to blow up our Houses of Parliament. Did you know that it was only a small group who plotted it? I believe they were cornered underneath the parliament building in the nick of time.'

'Talking of Catholicism, did the priest in the village, Father O'Leary, wasn't it? Did he try to convert you?'

'Not really. He is a nice peaceful sort of man. Live and let live I think was his motto. There ought to be more of him. Not like that bastard on the lifeboat who had us tipped out.'

'I hope he gets his just reward. You told some of the reporters about him. I heard you talking to them.'

'Yes, I did. Nobody seemed to put forward a name but enquiries are ongoing I believe. They'll find him and hopefully publicise his infamous behaviour. One thing is certain that my God is not the same one as his.'

'So do you believe in God, buddy?'

'Listen, mate, when we were in the water I prayed as I had never done before. I said I would do anything for the "big fellah" up there whether it is a Him or Her or it if only I could have another chance. Strangely enough that is exactly what Justine said she did while we were recovering. She wanted to do something useful and special for someone whilst she was on this earth and promised as much in her prayers. It was she who made it all possible on the farm possible and not just by her money.'

'You did a lot for them yourself, buddy. Don't sell yourself short.'

'Thanks, mate. You know it is strange but we were just about to talk about the existence of God when the torpedo hit. After then I don't think she mentioned the subject. Except she did say something cryptic in her last note to me.'

'Tell me what she said, please. Unless it hurts then don't bother.'

'I don't mind telling you. It's in that little box that she left me.' Bobby stretched and opened the lid. He took out Justine's note and read aloud:

'*You will find your treasure in the cross.* Why did she say this? Do I fall short of following the teachings of Jesus?'

'No, I don't for a minute believe you do. Not for a second. Show me the cross, please.'

'Put it back when you have had a look and the note when you have read it. It's all I have of her,' said Bobby, leaning back on his pillow and yawning.

He handed him the box then put his head back on the pillow and closed his eyes as he was quite weary. Stephen gave an exclamation of delight when he saw the cross.

'Well, well, well. I have seen one of these before. They are quite expensive, I believe. Old granny Robinson had one. She gave it to Emma and I had her ring. I gave the ring to Rachael before I left to wear and pray that I would come back home safely. You see this little device at the top. It is like a secret entrance. You press carefully, pull this little clip and then it opens. Look.'

Bobby reluctantly eased himself forward and was quite unprepared for the shock that followed. Stephen performed the action and the spring was released and the cross opened. A second later, the two men gasped in utter amazement. Neither spoke for a full minute. Then they stared intently at each other and then reverted their gaze at the interior of the cross.

'I don't believe this. Tell me I'm dreaming or the Count shot me down and I'm dead.'

'Neither do I believe it.' There was another long pause. It was finally broken by Stephen who said: 'You're a wealthy man, buddy. Rich and rich again. Just look at them. I've not seen anything like them yet alone so close.'

Inside the tiny compartment were six shiny objects that glistened even in the poor light of the cabin. Six exquisitely cut diamonds. Bobby stared around hoping for divine guidance. His jaw was unwilling to open but did so eventually.

'But why? Stevie,' he almost whispered. 'Why did she do this? Why the hell me?'

Stephen waited a minute before replying softly: 'Because she loved you, Bobby. She most likely still does love you but thinks herself unworthy or unsuitable. I am only guessing because I do not fully understand love. I know I love your sister and can only compare it with that. Beyond that I'm also like you at a loss.

'My guess is that we only really understand the meaning of love when we get to the end of our lives or at least near to it. We learn more and more about it on the way. Anyway, the facts are that she wanted you to have it. Doubtless you told her what it was like at home and so perhaps she wanted to set you free and this is her way of doing it. Take it, brother, take it. It's what she wanted for you. At last you are having some luck in this world and you damn well deserve it.'

'I can't argue with that. My goodness, what a strange life it is. At least it is for us.'

'Once the shock has abated then make your plans on how you are going to use the wealth they will give you.'

'I am sure I can think of something. A whole lot of worries have gone in an instance. I can buy a home of my own now. I'm banned from *Frankfare*. My mother and father can visit me there instead of some café in the city. Hells bells! I'll send a cable to Joanne and ask her to have a list of property available in our locality when we reach home. Their shop is next to a real estate agent.'

They talked in fits and starts for the next couple of hours and then reluctantly turned in as fatigue was winning. Two and a half more days and they would be back in New York and then home.

When they awoke next morning, there was an envelope that had been pushed under the door containing a cable. Stephen picked it up and read the contents out. It consisted of an invitation from a Mr Vernon Bond of *Silver Film Studios* offering employment and a substantial salary for both of them. It emphasised that it was not just a temporary job but one that would need their flying experience. If they agreed to a meeting then he would come to their hotel address in New York if they would kindly tell him which one it was.

'Well, I don't want to go back to *Frankfare* on a permanent basis if at all and you can't so shall we accept the invitation and see what it is all about? I am sceptical but seeing the man can't do us any harm. I would like to stay in the aircraft business if I can.'

'Indeed, we might as well,' said Bobby. 'I feel the same about aircraft so perhaps we could still be together. That really would be a bonus. I will draft a cable of acceptance and get it sent off.'

'By the way, buddy. In all the excitement, I have forgotten something.'

'What have you forgotten, mate?'

'Do you know what tomorrow is?'

'6 November 1918. Oh blimey old Reilly. I am very remiss. In all this activity I think I have forgotten something.'

'Yes. It's my birthday tomorrow and I am 21.'

'I won't forget to wish you happy birthday tomorrow.'

'Can we put anything else about it on ice, buddy, whilst we are on the ship. I have had enough excitement and well-wishers to last me until my middle age. I don't want people turning up at the door using it as an excuse.'

'Your secret is safe with me, mate. I'll make it up with a present now I am well off!'

'You are certainly that and a whole lot more!'

The following morning Bobby had a small brainwave. He approached on of the ranking US officers and politely enquired if there was anyone in their company who had been jewellers in civvy street. To his delight there were two to whom he was separately introduced. They both gave invaluable advice whist Stephen hurriedly took down notes.

They got back to their cabin and Bobby said: 'I'd like to hold on to them for a while and learn more but it's a case of needs must. I can buy my own place now. I don't want to have them in my pocket or in view on the mantle-piece. That would be silly.'

The rest of the journey passed pleasantly enough but both men were weary and longing for home. Finally, the sight of land appeared. The *Aquitania* coasted in and the last few miles seemed to take an age. Stephen looked out over Bridgeport where, some ten years earlier he had seen Whitehead gliding and thus causing him to get the flying bug.

'You know something, buddy. Here I am with you. We are celebrities; and all we have under our belt is half a kill each. We are only here because we are being used as propaganda fodder. We are in the acting profession.'

'I know, mate. Perhaps we should say that together we are 28 and a half kills each like they do in conkers.'

'That's that crazy game you British play with horse chestnuts in the fall. How do you arrive at 28 and a half?'

'You tell your opponent what your score is beforehand and the winner adds it to his score afterwards. So that is half the Count's tally plus our half each. That would make us 28 and a half each.'

'Forget it. Things are getting complicated enough as it is. Look. That girl in the boat is flaunting her assets at you.'

'Why just me? What about you?' said Bobby.

'She knows I love someone else and I just can't wait to be with her and hold her tight.'

37. New York

Compared to the other two capitals, the welcome was much the same and lavish but without top members of the government. The military were there and they presented the medals. However, to Stephen and Bobby it did not feel quite the same. What they did not appreciate was that members of the government were all meeting and debating what should happen after the Armistice was signed. As the ship coasted in, they had looked for familiar faces on the quayside. For the first time the attention was not on them because people were looking for family and loved ones.

They made out not a single soul until they reached the reception area. Martha and an unsmiling George were there but nobody else. No Rachael, or anyone from Bobby's family. The press allowed them to greet their son and then they were set upon. George made no real effort to acknowledge Bobby's presence or status but Bobby was prepared for his snub and lack of recognition as a human being. He made the first move as it was the only way of gaining information.

'If you please, where are my parents, Mr Robinson?'

'Back at *Frankfare* where they should be,' said George in a voice of granite.

'Couldn't they be allowed to come on a day like this?' said Bobby. George ignored him and turned to Stephen and tried to speak to him but Stephen thought he might get more accurate information out of his mother.

'Where is Rachael, mother? Why was she not allowed to come?'

Martha looked at him furtively and said: 'I'm not quite sure but she's back in Boston, somewhere.'

'Why somewhere? Is she not home at *Frankfare*?'

His words were drowned as the press lost patience and used weight of numbers to surge forward. There was a barrage of questions. The liaison officer swept them to a reception room so that they could have some order. The questions followed in staccato fashion which left both men in a slight daze before they recovered.

'Mr Williston, do you think that you are lucky to be alive.'

'Very lucky and a bit of skill thrown in as well. I was either very lucky or simply a cat in a previous existence.' There was laughter whilst pens and pencils worked furiously.

'Where did you learn to shoot like that, Sergeant Williston?'

'I just pointed, pulled the trigger and hoped for the best.'

'Mr Robinson. What are you going to do now? Presumably you have left the air force?'

'Yes, I am no longer fit for active duty. I am awaiting my discharge and am considering a few offers.'

George who was on the front row then got in on the act and interjected.

'He is coming back with me to run the business like any good son and heir should.'

'Is that correct, Mr Stephen?'

Stephen hesitated momentarily.

'Who am I to argue with the boss,' he said thinking quickly and diplomatically. There was some polite laughter.

It went on and on until they were all swept away for the medal ceremony and yet more speeches, interviews and photographs. The liaison officer had booked them in the same hotel as George and Martha but there was a pressing problem and that was what to do with Smasher and Grabber. For once they were not themselves and were quite subdued due to all the toing and froing plus the bustle crowds and noise.

Occasionally, each would let out a rather plaintive whine. Fortunately one of the stewards at the hotel offered to look after them at his home and Bobby went with him secretly to see they were pacified and reassure them. Whilst he was away Stephen knocked on the door of his parents room to get information on Rachael but there was no reply. In desperation, he telephoned *Frankfare* in the hope that Marcus or Sarah would be able to come to the telephone. An unfamiliar voice was on duty at home and said this wasn't possible which made Stephen think more and more that something was badly amiss.

He began to believe there was a conspiracy going on but in the end he was so tired that he had to give in and succumb to sleep. There was no sign of his parents in the morning and they did not appear before Mr Vernon Bond's arrival at 10.00 am Bobby and Stephen had no idea what to expect but settled down to hear the distinguished looking Mr Bond's proposals. He said nothing about the employment for a long time but merely asked a lot about their individual history. They did not have a break until 11 o'clock when they went to the bar for a drink.

A steward handed Stephen a letter the envelope of which showed it was from George. In it he expressed his dissatisfaction that he, Stephen, had not thrown his weight and enthusiasm about resuming at *Frankfare* and that he and his mother were going back to Boston alone. George wrote that he had made some arrangements for a photograph call for he and Stephen immediately on his return when it would be announced that Stephen was resuming his position at the firm as deputy director. He required the time of Stephen's arrival at Boston. As for Bobby, he could have one hour to see his parents and remove all his property from his room at *Frankfare*; George stated that he considered he was doing him a real favour by granting him this.

When Stephen saw it, he felt sick, angry and even humiliated.

'Do you know he did not even wish me a belated happy 21st birthday. What are you going to do, Bobby?'

'The only thing I can do which is to turn a couple of these diamonds into dollars while we are here. Normally, I would like to look and learn about them but it goes without saying that I am in a hurry and need a place of my own and can't rely on Chuck to provide a billet for me forever. The gems have given me an unexpected lifeline. I have an idea when we get back to Boston and will need your help. No time to tell you now because Mr Bond is back again.'

The imperious Bond smiled at them confidently and sat down this time to discuss the actual plans in mind. He took out several sheets of paper from his briefcase but did not distribute them at once. He cleared his throat and began to explain his proposals lucidly and succinctly. The whole meeting was not a complicated or protracted affair, which inwardly pleased the duo greatly, as a large part of their minds and emotions were occupied by other issues.

Bond more or less spoke in the same genre as the Colonel had in France only a few days ago; the people wanted heroes. The people needed heroes. They, Bobby and Stephen were just that and here was an opportunity for them to give the country something back for all it had suffered and for losing so many brave men. The idea was to show the population that it had been necessary, been worthwhile and victory, albeit gained at an enormous price, was to be shared with those still living who had witnessed the sacrifice. At the same time, they would receive a very generous remuneration.

Bond cleared his throat and prepared to elucidate further: 'The situation is like this, gentlemen. We have made an investment of some Jenny biplanes that are surplus from the war. They cost about $5,000 dollars to build and we paid about $350 for each of ours. Some people got away with $200 dollars but I should not complain.'

At this point he sniffed ruefully as any business man would who had paid more than necessary. However, he soon regained his air of optimism.

'We are not looking for you to be barnstormers, gentlemen. There has to be a little bit of that but that will be done by volunteers, not you. Your part in the proceedings would be to reproduce those daring minutes you did in France, this time with somewhat slightly less danger to yourselves, I might add.' He smiled at his euphemism. 'There will be other attractions during the day's proceedings, of course, but yours would be, hopefully, the big draw. As well as that, we would need you to do talks and demonstrations and autograph signings for the lottery winners.'

It was to be nothing but pure *al fresco* theatre. They would literally re-enact, with suitable embellishments, the day that the Black Count met his fate and how the Allies, in the form of Stephen and Bobby had come out triumphant by saving a whole French unit. It was to be well advertised and a subsidiary of his firm would be responsible for all the filming rights. They would get a fee for every performance and royalties for every showing in cinemas across the USA. It was deceptively simple. They had already assembled all the equipment and transport ready to make a start.

'What if we refused, Mr Bond,' said Stephen.

'Well then, we would simply go ahead without out you.' He hastily added, 'But we don't want it to come to that. You could sue us for plagiarism or something of the sort. Then that might be awkward for us and costly. Best to have the genuine article involved.'

Mr Bond's proposals seemed irresistible and the answer to their immediate future. He waited and then jumped in again:

'Look at it this way, gentlemen. It is not going to do any harm. And you both can earn a lot of money out of this, more that you ever thought of possible. The whole thing will not last for ever as such a thing as this is finite. I estimate somewhere in the region of eighteen months or two years. In that time you would earn more money than you would in twenty years at least. You both have not told me if you have any plans.'

'The only thing I had planned was NOT to go back and work for my father if I could possibly help it. Beyond that…well…the airfield with my brother-in-law…your guess is as good as mine.'

'What about you, Mr Williston?'

'I terminated my employment with Stephen's father over three years ago and as a result of merely resigning, am unwelcome and banned from his complex. I have recently come up with an idea of moving the Williston family into a place of our own and finding us fresh employment but it would require the complicity of my parents. Either way, it would not prevent me from working for you. However, we have a close relationship, Stephen and I, and I expect he, like me, would like a little bit of time to mull over your proposals.'

'Naturally. Are we talking about minutes, hours or days?'

'Half an hour will be all we need.'

'Capital! That means we should reconvene at…12 o'clock. Excuse me. I will be back here then.'

Bond looked happy and got up whilst the other two went off to find a quiet corner to be alone. Bobby looked at Stephen squarely in the eye.

'Well,' he said. 'All things considered, I am for it.'

'So am I. It would be foolish to say no and it is only for a comparatively short time. Then we can do what we want in life. And no more *Frankfare*. Hooray! No more being in modern day slavery. I shall be free; free as a bird. Now I must try and get through on the telephone to Rachael before my father gets back home.'

He turned to go but Bobby stopped him and held his arm fast much to Stephen's surprise.

'Hold on just a tad.'

'Something wrong?'

'Very likely. Listen Stevie. Like you, I sensed something was amiss yesterday at the welcoming so while you were dressing, I telephoned the airfield and spoke to Emma and then Chuck. I held fire telling you this until after we had spoken to Mr Bond because, well…forgive me but you might have flipped. It seems as though there has been trouble involving Rachael and Jason Lyon, and Rachael was arrested.

'It all happened on bonfire night. Jason Lyon was in hospital for a time with a deep scar down his cheek and maybe maimed. That's all I know. I'm certain he tried to force himself on her. Again.' Stephen went white and for a moment had to be steadied.

'How soon can we leave?'

'We have an appointment with a government official at 6 o'clock and a reception tonight at 8.00 pm. This afternoon I will change some of my pounds sterling into dollars and see a jeweller about one or two of these diamonds. I will lose a bit on their true value but we need some money. NOW, Stevie.'

'OK. So we can leave first thing tomorrow?'

'Yes. Let's keep calm. Remember, Rachael is my sister and I love her too.'

Stephen felt sick and it took all his resolve to appear calm and collected. They rejoined Mr Bond and said they were prepared to accept but there were still a few more questions. There was the question of salary and on that subject he banded figures that made both the young men's eyes boggle. That was real money that was being offered. He also said there would be a small advance as soon as they signed. He could see about it that afternoon if they so wished.

'Where would the events take place?'

'In several places, starting in Texas. We would then work our way Eastwards which would coincide with the coming of spring. The shows would be twice on Saturday and once on Sunday afternoon and on holiday dates. The people in charge of the props would leave on Monday morning and travel to the next venue, rather like a circus. In fact that is what we are. Your action would be one item in amongst several but, as I say the longest and most important and then the signings and questions thrown in. You will be busy but, hopefully, you will be able to enjoy it very much.'

'We are happy about that but would like our own airfield at *Hillington* to be added to the list if that were possible.'

'Hm…that might be arranged but it would only be at a time when the weather was more agreeable. A decision like that would need the agreement of our committee.'

'That sounds fair. When do you envisage a start to the show.'

'In late January. You see that when the euphoria of the announcement of peace dies down it will soon be Christmas and people will be concentrating on that and rightly so. Afterwards people will come down off a high and then will be ready for some escapism. That is where you two come in.'

'You seem to have it well planned.'

'We are experienced and try to consider all the facts and possibilities.'

Bond was about to order some drinks to seal the deal but Bobby stopped him.

'In a moment, sir. Firstly I have to tell you something and come clean with you. I am sorry to throw a spanner in the works so soon but you should know this. We have a family problem which was not of our making. I assure you that neither of us is guilty of any misdemeanours with the law and not involved in any activities that would cause you or your worthy company to be embarrassed or compromised. However I can see that we might need a first class lawyer and I wonder if you can provide one for us, please? It would be in your interest to help us sort these matters out before our employment with you begins and then we can put our minds fully and without any possible further interruption to the job in hand. Perhaps you have a permanent attorney?'

'It is possible but I would need to know the subject matter before committing ourselves and yes, we have a permanent attorney.'

'Very well, sir. I believe a rape or an attempted rape has been committed on my sister by the wayward son of an eminent but very controversial Massachusetts state senator. Moreover, she has been made out to be the guilty party in spite of professing self-defence. This situation has to be our number one priority.'

'I see.' Mr Bond looked grave. 'That is a very serious matter.'

'What's more, the young man made an attempt a couple of years ago but the whole thing was hushed up by some people who wielded a lot of power and still do for that matter. This time to cover themselves it has been made to look as if it is my sister's fault and that she encouraged him.'

Vernon Bond tapped his pencil. He was silent for some time and then asked a series of leading questions after which he appeared satisfied. He suddenly perked up and then said: 'How does this affect you, Mr Robinson?'

'The young lady in question is my intended but it is imperative that fact remains confidential, if you please.'

'Of course, you have my word.'

Bobby interjected.

'There is no more a gentle person on this earth than my sister, sir. This accusation is a travesty and unless we have somebody to advise us and defend her AND somebody not in any way connected with Boston we are bound to be losers. This is the last thing we expected on our return home.'

'What is the name of the senator and his son?'

'Senator Lyon. The son's name is Jason.'

Bond stiffened. He looked at them both in turn and very intently. He turned his head and looked out the window before speaking.

'Really…is that so? In that case I will arrange an attorney for you. Now let's have that drink.'

'You speak as though you know him, sir.'

'I know of him and that is enough.'

38. Worrying Times

Very early next morning, having packed the night before, they checked out of the hotel, not forgetting to thank the manager and staff. The journey to the new and magnificent Penn station was uneventful but there were a few anxious moments before the early train left as the carer for the dogs did not arrive until almost the last moment. Bobby stood on the platform completely oblivious to the new and sumptuous surroundings of Penn station as he was in no state of mind to appreciate them.

Needless to say, Smasher and Grabber were overjoyed to see them; they enjoyed the journey and kept looking out the window. Bobby retrieved the bowls from his rucksack and a friendly steward brought them some water. It was on the train that Bobby revealed to Stephen that he had been to the bank after Bond had left in order to set up an account and ask for a possible overdraft. He told Stephen that he had shown one of the diamonds to three back street jewellers in Manhattan who had offered cash there and then.

At the third shop when Bobby had said he was going to return to the first, the proprietor immediately offered an extra $200 to which Bobby accepted, although he realised the diamonds were worth a bit more. No questions were asked and none given.

'We are now solvent, mate, and can breathe easier. I do not have any worries on that front for quite a while. Let me know if you need any dough.'

'I would have come with you, buddy.'

'Listen, mate, you needed to catch up with some rest and in any case I was less conspicuous on my own. There are reporters outside watching our every move. Do you know what one of them said to our steward?'

'Tell me.'

'He gave him ten dollars to let him know if we invited any women to our rooms.'

'No kidding.'

'None at all. That's why I thought I would go alone.'

'That sounds fair enough. I'll not be happy until we get back to Boston and have seen what they have done to her,' said Stephen. 'I want to know what swine has caused this.'

'Me too on both counts. Several times we just seem to have gone from great delight only to great dismay in quick succession.'

Neither of them remembered anything about the journey except for one thing which appeared just before their terminus and which was impossible to overlook and ignore. It was the end of that time when the trees of New England put on the most glorious mantle that only the hardest of hearts could fail to appreciate. For an all too brief moment the duo were pleased to see evidence of home before reality took over. The train pulled into Boston station at 1.00 pm where the mayor was there to greet them with the council and the host of reporters. The applause echoed around the train shed and was multiplied.

Bobby did most of the talking and expressed his gratitude to the mayor and his staff for the wonderful welcome and how good it was to be back in their home town and not to be dodging bullets and bayonets. He praised the mayor for what he had done for Boston and reminded the listeners that they should be grateful as their city was not like the state some of the places in Europe they had visited on their travels.

Naturally, the Mayor beamed with delight at this personal endorsement. The whole proceedings went very well. They were delighted to see brother Charlie and Joanne who had come for them in the car and with much clapping and the band playing Handel's *See the conquering hero comes*, they left for home.

On the way, Stephen turned to Bobby and said: 'You know something, buddy. I don't feel anything like a conquering hero at the moment. Certainly not Judas Maccabeus.'

'Right on, mate. Personally, I feel more like Judas Iscariot.'

Bobby took George at his word that he had one hour but did not discount that there might be the possibility of confrontation. For that reason he left the dogs at the gate house, an action for which they felt most displeased. To their surprise Emma and Chuck were there but not so George and Martha. They had been missing at the mayor's reception as well which, although extremely surprising, suited Stephen well as there would be no photo-call and no need to prevaricate about working again at *Frankland*.

He could imagine his father's reaction to that. Finally, they reached the bakery to be greeted by at least half of Lexbridge outside and all the staff inside. After greeting Emma and Chuck, Bobby went alone into the servant quarters to see his parents for the first time in over three years. For at least three minutes nobody could speak whilst they were in a threesome embrace.

'We're so proud of you, son,' said Marcus, struggling to keep his composure. Charlie demurred.

'And I am proud to be your son. Come here, mother.'

Sarah had been weeping that was for sure. Bobby sat her down and said: 'I'd hoped for a different homecoming than this. You'd better tell me what happened.'

'Fetch the others', said Marcus.

Chuck and Emma were greeting Stephen separately before coming into Sarah and Marcus' parlour to hear the saga of Rachael's arrest. Stephen then blurted out: 'Where is she?'

'At the police holding centre.'

'Merciful God. I want to know what bastards are responsible for this.'

There normally would have been a stern rebuke for this sort of language but today there was a silence until he added: 'Since when?'

'Two nights ago. She's being kept there because the jail is sealed off. It's because of the flu epidemic and they are not taking anyone as a precaution.'

'How did it happen? Let's have the whole story right from the beginning.'

Marcus spoke: 'We were all enjoying the fireworks and eating baked potatoes. Sarah, Rachael, Charlie and I were serving when suddenly a young man came up to Rachael and spoke to her. She rushed off with him.'

'Do you know why?'

'We learnt later the young man had said that Joanna had hurt herself badly and asked for Rachael to come at once. After a while Charlie got suspicious and went to look for her. He looked in our house then the empty one. He found Rachael sobbing on one of the beds with blood everywhere. There was a trail of it. She said that Jason Lyon had forced himself on her but she fended him off and scratched him down his face.

'Apparently, he has a terrible wound. Charlie helped Rachael back to the house and helped her clean herself and change. Lyon and his minions had gone out the back way. It was a while before we could get back to the house as we were serving. Sarah went first and I got some others to help me.'

'Do we know what happened to Jason Lyon?'

'His friends were forced to take him to the hospital and seeing the wound, the sister on duty called the police. He was kept in overnight and the police interviewed him the next day. He said Rachael invited him to the bedroom and they were kissing when she suddenly knifed him. Rachael said that it was the ring you gave her that caused the wound, Stephen. When Mr Robinson came back and heard all about it, he accused Rachael of enticing Jason Lyon and stealing the ring. You know that is not true, Mr Stephen.'

'Indeed I do. What happened to the ring?'

'Mr Robinson confiscated it. He called the police who came and took Rachael away. We have only seen her once and have been at our wits end. We knew you were on your way and hoped you would get here quickly.'

'Right,' said Stephen. 'No time to waste. Time to enlist the help of our mentor, Bobby. Give me that number Mr Bond gave us.'

Although it was late afternoon, Stephen went to the telephone and asked for the number Mr Bond had given them. He turned to Bobby.

'I'll do the talking. You get up to the office switchboard. Stay and make sure Richards isn't listening in.'

Stephen called Bond's lawyer and explained what he wanted done about Rachael's bail. He thanked his lucky stars that his parents were still not home and something had delayed them. The reason became clear as the telephone rang about an hour later which he, Stephen, answered. It was his mother on the other end.

Martha explained that she and George had set off for Penn station to catch the midday train. On the way George had felt ill and had gone to the toilets in the first class lounge and had been sick. They missed the train and whilst they waited for the next one, he had experienced terrible pain in his abdomen. A doctor was called who suspected appendicitis and thus George was taken to hospital. He stayed there overnight and the pain seemed to decrease.

However, they felt justified in keeping him in just a while longer to make sure nothing was amiss. Martha indicated that if all was well they would be back later in a day or two at the most. With that she signed off with little ceremony. Stephen came back feeling pleased that there would be breathing space and opportunity to take control unhindered.

What a bit of divine intervention, he thought.

It took several hours and a few more calls before the legal process was complete. Then Bond's lawyer telephoned to say that Rachael could be bailed, the money guaranteed and she could be released first thing in the morning. Stephen found out later that Vernon Bond had set the ball rolling some hours before and the paperwork was almost all ready. By now everyone was quite exhausted and needed sleep. Stephen then excused himself and went across to his old room and collapsed onto his bed. It was a while before he had the energy to undress. His room seemed to him to be unwelcoming and alien, part of a world of which he now felt an intruder.

In the morning he went across to Sarah's kitchen to find everyone pecking at their respective breakfasts.

'Right. At last. Let's commandeer the car and go and get her, Bobby.'

In his haste Stephen grated the gears and the tyres squealed in protest as the pair of them set off. It was only a short journey but it seemed interminable to the young men in their single minded pursuit. When they got to the police holding centre there was a long wait. Stephen paced up and down. However, the warders were very congenial being in the midst of feted and somewhat illustrious company.

The formalities completed, they waited patiently for Rachael to be brought out. Eventually she came, slowly and stiffly. Her eyes were wide when she saw them both as if she were unable to comprehend the reality. Once released, she fell into Stephen's arms and her head hit his chest with some force. Stephen gasped but held on. It was some time before she was able to speak.

'Oh Stevie. Thank God. At last you're home. What a nightmare and so unfair.'

Although not wanting to pull away from him, she transferred her affection to her brother for a brief hug. Stephen said: 'We're taking you home. Get your belongings and sign for them,' he said with a massive sense of relief.

'I wanted your homecoming to be happy, not like this,' she said as a few tears began to emerge.

'Never mind. We are together again and somebody is going to pay for this debacle,' said Stephen.

Bobby drove and Rachael clung on to Stephen like a limpet mine. When she asked where they were going, her eyes filled with alarm.

'Your father does not want me back ever again. And I did not do anything. It was Jason Lyon. Again.'

'We know. Anyway, your big brother has some plans. As to coming home, my father is in hospital until tomorrow so you have no worries there.'

Although all the staff had been told that Bobby was *persona non grata*, when the gate man saw Stephen he was not prepared to argue the toss so they passed through without hindrance and went into the servant's quarters where Rachael's parents hugged her in turn. Bobby waited for them to finish but was obviously impatient.

'Right, all of you,' said Bobby. 'There is urgent work to do and I will be back as soon as I can. No, mother. No questions. I'm going to get us out of here. Dad, never mind what you are doing. I want you to come with me, please.'

Marcus looked completely puzzled as he had never experienced before the authoritative tone of voice in his boy but obeyed immediately. He looked at Bobby and realised how much he had grown up and matured in over three years. They walked to the car and father looked intently at son.

'Can you tell me where we are going, Robert?'

'Into the village. Now then, dad. Would you like to get out of this place and into one of our own? Somewhere where we can be together as a family.'

'Well, the way things are, of course, I would. Without so much as a thought. And your mother too. But where would we go and what work would we do? We can't live on fresh air, son. We're trapped. We've always been trapped and will remain so.'

'Not if I can help it. Let's get going and I'll show you what I have in mind. Heck, I've forgotten about Smasher and Grabber.'

'*Smash and Grab*? Who are they? What's this all about? I am going mad with all that's happening.'

'Two new members of the family. Come on. I'll introduce you. Then get in the car.'

The dogs were very glad to be released and immediately noticed a new face. Then they were then fed. It was obvious they were very hungry. Afterwards, they scrutinised Marcus intently to see whether they liked him and when he in his delight tickled them both under the chin it was not long before they decided that they did. They prodded him now and then to remind him to stroke them and were most insistent in their demands.

They drove into Lexbridge and parked at the *Red Lion* guest house and walked in having left the dogs in charge of the car. Thelma Gilbert, the co-owner with her husband of the hotel, was in the foyer and being her usual busy and bustling self. She was surprised and absolutely delighted to see them.

'Well, well, well, how nice. What an honour, Bobby. Many, many congratulations. Do come in. What can we do for you? May I call Graham?'

'Yes please. I want to speak to both of you.' On hearing that Mrs Gilbert took them to their lounge.

Graham Gilbert was summoned and after an inordinate period of time he lumbered in wheezing like a cumbersome ox. He spread his big smile all over his face when he saw who had arrived. He shook hands with both Marcus and Bobby.

'Well, well. To what do we owe this pleasure? This is a turn up for the books. I know; don't tell me; you want to stay here a while; no, not that. You have come to buy the hotel. Yes, that's it. I don't know what has taken you so long apart from wandering around half of Europe.' He laughed at his own joke.

'Is it still for sale? We saw Joanne Radstock at the reception in Boston and she said you have been trying to retire.'

'Yes, but no takers and no interest for quite some time now.'

'Why hasn't it been snapped up?'

'Perhaps to start with, we asked for too much. We dropped the price but to no avail. Not easy for people to find money during war and little prospect of visitors. There's another reason. You have probably only recently heard that while you were away there has been an awful influenza epidemic. Between 3 and 4 thousand dead in the city and surrounds. It has been nothing short of terrible on top of losing so many in the war.

'It is only last month that most restrictions were lifted and schools reopened. Theatres and the like too. As a result, we have had just a handful of guests. Things are so bad that we have just had to dip into our savings to stay afloat. We can't afford the same number of staff and what is more, we can't go on like this for too much longer.'

'How much do you want?'

Graham Gilbert told him.

'Well, Mr Gilbert; it will surprise you but yes. You are quite correct on both counts. First and foremost, there are four of us that want to stay at the hotel tonight and secondly, we have come to buy it off you. Cash.'

The others gasped and looked wide-eyed. Marcus was equally astonished and his head swam a little. Eventually, as the shock subsided, everyone awaited Gilbert's response.

'You are not serious. You are kidding,' said Graham Gilbert looking absolutely astounded. For a moment inside, he felt indignant at what he believed to be a fatuous remark but held back knowing Bobby's reputation and the look of absolute sincerity on his face.

'No kidding. This is exactly why we're here. Believe you me, Mr Gilbert, I've never been more serious. I think we can meet your price or something near it.' Bobby continued,

'There's two or three provisos. One: it must be decided today. Two, we need to have somewhere in your outbuildings to store mother and father's belongings, furniture and the like and three, we would need you to stay on for at least a month or two to show them the ropes. That would give you time to look around for somewhere where you would like to spend your retirement. I emphasise we must know today. Is all of that possible?'

'Well, I am sure we are interested. But what is the rush?'

'Mr Gilbert. My former boss George Robinson is a mean and difficult man to say the very least. You do not need me to tell you that. For private reasons, which can be explained later, I need to get our family out of *Frankfare* at once. Today and in the next few hours. You are well aware of what has happened to Rachael recently.

'My sister's honour has been impugned and I want her to have somewhere safe to live while we prepare her defence. Mr Robinson would not put up her bail and she endured three nights and days in police cells. And then as to my parents,

337

the effect on my mother's health has been awful. There is also the fact that I was missing for over three years and all that has compounded her problems. Robinson has banned Rachael and I from the firm and the complex and so we have to find somewhere to stay and live. If you are unable to come to a decision today then I will have to buy a house in the village; there are one or two for sale in the next street and doubtless there are more than those two.'

The Gilberts were silent for nearly a minute and stared at each other in utter bewilderment. Finally, Mrs Gilbert shook herself out of her stupor and spoke.

'Can we have a few moments, please, Bobby? I understand perfectly your position but I am sure you will understand ours. This is a big shock but hopefully a pleasant one and can be resolved,' said Mrs Gilbert. 'Help yourselves to a drink in the bar while Graham and I talk privately. We may well be able to sort this out with the minimum of fuss.'

'Thank you. We will,' said Bobby as both Thelma and Graham Gilbert left the room.

When they were out of earshot, Marcus looked at his son completely perplexed. He found it difficult to speak. When he did, he said: 'Where is the money coming from, son? Your mother and I have none to speak of.'

'Dad. Believe you me, that's the very least of our worries. I've the money for the hotel and more and it's all been earned legally, without injury to anyone else and is all above board. I can reveal the reasons for my affluence later. A lot has happened to me these last three years which is impossible to reveal now. So I'll just say this. Do you have faith in me? Faith in the son that loves you and my mother as dearly as any son could do?'

'I do, dear Robert. Implicitly and therefore will question you no more,' said Marcus sincerely but inwardly still reeling from the shock.

'All that remains is for you to decide whether you want this or not. I know you have said ideally you always wanted something like this. It is all in a terrible rush but at the moment, thanks to George Robinson and others, we are in danger of being crushed. What would happen if somebody else came along and offered to do your job?

'After dismissing Rachael and me, he might cast you off without a care whether you had worked for him for years or not. You and mother have no security at *Frankfare* but here you would have and you would be your own boss and we could be a complete family again. There is still time for you to say no but if you do, it will not be very pleasant at *Frankfare* as well as Rachael and I not being able to visit you apart from having nowhere to live. It is an adventure and it surely is much the best option in the circumstances.'

'Yes, it is,' said Marcus. 'We might kick ourselves later if we did not give it a go. Yes, please, son. Let's do it and thank you from the bottom of my heart.' He hugged his son.

It was not too long before they were called in and a beaming pair of Gilberts agreed to everything without reservation. Thelma Gilbert was the one who spoke up: 'We agree to your proposal, Bobby. We would be extremely foolish to spurn your offer. Talk about miracles; I have prayed for one and here you are in person.'

'We'll be back later, Graham, and hope you can cope with the invasion of at least four of us.'

'Three bedrooms?'

'Yes, please. May I use your telephone please? I want Charlie to be in on this.'

After telephoning *Hillington*, they shook hands on the deal and the pair of them returned to *Frankfare* at a very fast pace, which had Marcus feeling somewhat queasy. It was quite the opposite for the dogs who took advantage of the slipstream whilst assuming a regal air of canine importance. Bobby turned to his father as they were about to enter their quarters:

'Right, pater. It's your turn now. You can have the privilege of announcing to the others that all of them have spent their last night at *Frankfare* and will be moving to pastures anew.'

'Me? Why me? You are the one responsible for setting this up.'

'Because you are the head of the family and any announcement should come from you and you alone. It is only right and proper.' They entered the kitchen to find Charlie already there as well as Chuck who had brought him and who was worried about the possibility of any further problems to his friends.

Sarah was completely bamboozled when Marcus finished talking and when all was explained could only say: 'What about poor Mrs Robinson? How will she cope without me?'

'That, dear mother,' said Bobby, 'is up to whom they appoint in your place. You owe her nothing. She'll be glad for us and will tell you later that we have done the right thing.'

Sarah, although feeling she was in a whirlwind, realised that any further hesitation and obstacles she might put in the way were futile. All that had been said made sense and soon she was swept up in a tide of feverish activity. Everyone without exception experienced a feeling of liberation as they gradually got all of their property and personal belongings together. Stephen helped but could not do much in the way of lifting because of his gammy leg. He went over to the factory and asked three of the male workers to come and help transfer everything to the front of the house.

'How are we going to get things down to the *Red Lion*?' said Sarah, still in a state of shock and bewilderment.

'As soon as the trucks get back from their deliveries, we will load everything up.'

It took until about 11 o'clock in the evening for most things to be put in place or store. The drivers who were well disposed to Stephen were given a handsome tip and sworn to secrecy, at least for the next few days. By the time they got to bed, it was well after midnight and there was still plenty to do in the morning.

Stephen took the car and went back home to experience yet another fitful night of tossing and turning. It was eerie being on his own in *Frankland* and quite unnatural. The telephone rang but he decided not to answer it. In the morning he was up and about early and making preparations for his own exit. Before he ate any breakfast, he decided to get into George's office and have a good look round. There was something he badly needed to find. He went into George's bedroom and searched the place to see if there were any spare keys. He drew a blank so he went down to where the night watchman was preparing to leave.

'Eric!'

'Yes sir,' said Eric smartly.

'I need you.'

'Yes, sir. Coming.'

'Come with me. Any of your keys possibly open the bosses office?'

Eric hesitated. 'Hey sir, I am not happy about this. You will get me into deep trouble. You know I'm lucky to have got this job as I have a record. I got done for no good reason. This could get me fired.'

'Eric, here's five dollars. There are five more for you if you can get me in. I'll not say a word and assure you nobody will know anything about this. Except for the ones out of sight in the bakery there is only you and I on the complex at the moment. Besides which, getting me in might save somebody going to jail.'

'Who?'

'Rachael.'

'Sarah's girl?'

'Yes. There's evidence of her innocence in there that I need. Now will you do it?'

Eric brightened. 'If that's the case then I'm your man.'

Five minutes later, the aged lock yielded and they were in. Stephen knew exactly where to look for the ring that he had given Rachael as he knew George's habits all too well; it was in a drawer in the bureau, not even locked. George had not hidden it as he believed nobody would want to or even be able to venture into his office. Besides the ring, there were other things there that nauseated him beyond measure. For there in the cabinet were letters which had either been opened and kept or a few not opened at all. The cable and letters from abroad were all there seemingly kept as trophies.

There was no wonder Bobby's location had remained a mystery for so long. George Robinson was nothing but a narcissist. Stephen stuffed a select few of them in his pocket and then left everything else as near to when he came in as possible. Eric was getting nervous while waiting and so Stephen decided that, as much as he would like to explore more it was time to go. With a bit of difficulty Eric managed to relock the old-fashioned door which was made many years ago when the building was the official rectory. Stephen paid him and both of them left pleased but for very different reasons.

He had telephoned Chuck and asked to stay up there thus having the opportunity of expounding Mr Bond's proposals. Chuck said that he should know that he was always welcome and never needed to ask. Stephen knew that his parents would not be back until the afternoon at the earliest but even so he got most of his property down to the hall before 8 o'clock. It was then a case of getting two of the staff to load it up on one of the lorries.

It meant that particular delivery round would be late but Stephen did not care. He telephoned Chuck to ask him and to be ready and then, with the truck driver, drove off. They were soon there and unloaded. They were back only twenty-five minutes after the roundsman was due to go out.

'I'll do my best to make it up, Mr Stephen.'

'Don't rush, Tony. I'll take any blame. Let me know if you have trouble. Take this for your trouble. I'm leaving here; I have had enough.'

'Thanks for the tip and good luck to you, Stevie. We could all do with following your example the way things are here. The trouble for most of us is that we have no alternative.'

It was only a few hours later that a rather sore and somewhat disorientated George together with Martha got out of the car and went into the house. The scene that greeted them was one of quiet unearthly emptiness. They looked around in bewilderment. Everything was bare in the kitchen and instead of any activity, there was total silence. There was nobody on hand to attend to their wants and needs.

George shouted and Martha called in vain. At Bobby's orders no note of any sort had been left. Sarah had written one but when Bobby saw it, he grabbed it and confiscated it. George raged and went around making enquiries but nobody was either willing or able to divulge anything. He came back, slumped in his chair and poured a whisky. He drank it and poured another.

'Where are they? Why have they done this to me? Why, why, why?'

'They've gone. Can you blame them the way you have treated them? Somebody has offered them a better life than they have here. They will be able to be a family again.'

'What have I done to deserve this?'

'Everything, George Robinson. You've turned into a monster. You've treated Bobby and Rachael like horse shit and others too. They can abide you no longer and for that matter, neither can I.' Martha turned on her heel leaving him stewing on his own gastric juice.

At *Hillington* Stephen explained to an excited Chuck what the plans were for the Bond flying circus and that he, Chuck could have a slice of the action and the profits if he so wanted to be in on it. He pointed out the redundant aeroplanes that were for sale at a knock down price which set Chuck's heart beating fast.

'Hey, favourite brother-in-law. You are a real ace. This sounds great fun as well as a money spinner.'

'You mean I am an unprincipled fraud and going to learn to be a good actor.'

'Don't look at it that way, Stevie,' said Emma. 'It is a piece of good fortune. Let's make the best of it. We will be set up for life and will be without dependency on father.'

'If you say so, big sis. I expect most of the action will be down in Texas to start with. We would only be here once and it would have to be at the end of the season. That will be enough though to give you a real shot in the arm, Chuck.

Hopefully the fall will not be early and no ice. Right. I have some calls to make. Mother and father will be back by now. Expect some more trouble from father. Lots of it.'

39. Summons

Two days later George was feeling much better health-wise and because he had been able to recruit some replacement staff in the kitchens. He ordered Stephen to his presence and who, despite his anger at the treatment his father had meted out to Rachael, knew that he had no option but to appear in front of him. By now, there was no thought in Stephen's mind that he would ever work for his father again in any shape or form.

It was showdown time and Stephen knew he had to go and get it over with. His great regret was that he could not buttonhole George about the confiscated letters and cables. It would mean only one thing; that somebody had made a forced entry and this would prompt George to check on the ring. When he got there, deliberately early, he found his mother alone which gave them the chance of a rare private conversation.

'I am sorry about Rachael but your father is in Senator Lyon's pocket at the moment and is beholden to him. He has lost thousands at poker and will not give in. And the cost of that damned aeroplane. He thinks that I do not know but I do—' Her voice broke off as George entered. There was no greeting.

'Well. Are you involved in any way with the disappearance of my staff?'

'Good morning, pater.'

'I said, are you in any way responsible?' he said not looking up and shuffling some papers on his desk.

'I heard you, father. First things first. Good morning, father. I know we discarded pop or pa a long time ago.'

George quickly began to get angry. He changed tack.

'What I want to know is when you are coming back to do the job that you deserted earlier this year. As heir to the Robinson empire, you should be here ready and able to help run the business and take over when I am old. I want you to have some sons and for them to take over from you. It is a matter of family honour.'

'It ought to be my responsibility now, father, as you don't seem to be a very effective leader and certainly not a respected one anymore.'

'Why, you insolent little brat. How dare you speak to me like that? What gives you the right to say that?'

Stephen ignored that remark.

'What are the hours and what is the rate of pay?'

'Well… Same as when you left I suppose… We can work something out.'

'Then I want to know a specific figure now, father. Not in a week or month, now; this minute; before I leave this room. Can't you get that into your head.'

'I…I don't know offhand. I shall have to think about it. And there is no need to be rude; remember who you are talking to,' said George.

'To be quite truthful, I only asked knowing full well what your answer would be. If I was a native American Indian, there's a phrase which would be very apt for you.'

'And what the devil is that?'

'You speak with the forked tongue. You have hornswoggled me long enough.'

'That's enough!'

Stephen ignored that and continued unabated:

'I only asked out of interest. I've already had firm offers in writing. Not like you. Jam tomorrow George, that's your nickname amongst the staff.'

'What! If I hear anybody saying that, they can start walking to the gate.'

'Hopefully to a more salubrious and lucrative form of employment, which is exactly what I am about to do.'

'Pooh. What nonsense. What else can you do? You've no special skills.'

'I have experience, father. I have a pilot's licence. As well as that Bobby and I had plenty of offers even before we left England.'

'That scoundrel. He is never to set foot here again. I forbade his name to be mentioned and that includes you. I'll skin him alive if I have half a chance.'

'Oh I see. Caligula George has spoken, is that it?'

'I don't know what you are talking about. I did not have the benefit of your education. Just do not mention his name and better still do not associate with him. I forbid it.'

'To hell with that idea, father. You can whistle into the wind. He and I are as brothers and I will continue to say his name everywhere I go including here in front of you and mother and whosoever I please. He's no scoundrel, father, in fact he is, like me, a decorated war hero. What we achieved, we did it together. Got the better of you did Bobby Williston. Escaped from your clutches and stranglehold and cut off his iron bit and made it good, entirely by his own effort.

'You don't like losing but you took a real beating on that occasion to be witnessed by all our staff and the community. It has given people here hope. Hope that the once omnipotent George Francis Robinson is vulnerable and can be defeated. You have lost just about all respect from many people hereabouts and it serves you damn well right.

'There is another reason why I shall be refusing any offer you make. As well as Bobby, there is the question of Rachael whom you have treated like horse shit. You know that she's completely innocent of the charges laid against her and incapable of hurting anybody.'

'Well, she cut the boy and that's enough for me. She can stay in gaol and rot for evermore for all I care.'

'What a wicked thing to say. Self-defence was what it was. Anyway, it might interest you to know that she has been released on bail.'

'What? I gave orders... Who the hell put up the bail money?'

'You've been doing dirty business by the back door, it sounds like to me. A gentleman named Mr Bond put up the bail money if you must know. Now father, seeing as you seem to be losing your grip on this firm and the world in general, I fear I must bid you and mother good day as I am very busy. There is nothing more for me to hear from you except plans for your own misguided and selfish interests. You have nothing to put in the pot.

'The only way I would ever come back to this prison is to be director and for you to be no more than a sleeping partner. I could say that I will return when you have something sensible to say and offer but there seems to be little or no chance of that. You're living in a fantasy world and have become irresponsible. You are welcome to visit me sometime in my new place when I am settled, wherever that may be. I will send you my new address when I know it.'

'You insolent and ungrateful brat. Your address is this one here. *Frankland*, Boston, United States of America. Get it into your head.'

'For the last time, father, that cannot be so. I am a free man with a free choice. Heaven's above, that's what our ancestors came here for—to escape your sort of tyranny. You are behaving like King Charles of England and look what happened to him.'

George laughed contemptuously. 'Oh I see; you think that somehow I'm going to lose my head.'

'It's very possible, father. You seem to have already lost your soul.'

Those last words really found bull's eye. George flinched and was unable to reply. This moment of respite gave Stephen the opportunity to turn his attention to Martha.

'Goodbye mother. I will be in touch and will see you soon.'

'Goodbye, son.' Martha kissed him whilst George searched vainly for means to have the last word. It was Stephen who had them.

'Good morning, father. I will see myself out.'

Stephen left smartly and before George could say anything more. There was a pause before a red-faced and angry George spoke. He was almost apoplectic as he picked up his whip, smashed it on the desk and said: 'Damn him. Damn him. How dare he speak to me like that. He'll be back, you see. He's got no trade. He will have to come back and I will make him crawl. Just you see, Martha.' He smashed the whip across his desk again.

'One of these days, you will come down to earth with a crash, George Robinson,' said his increasingly sorrowful and despairing wife.

40. A Time of Activity

Bobby and Stephen were much in demand for all sorts of people and functions. Their locations meant that they now had almost immediate access to a telephone and could do any business quicker and more efficiently. Stephen was very glad of the money but to Bobby this was just a bonus as he was already a rich man. The downside was that, as more and more people knew where they were staying the telephone rang regularly.

Rachael came into her own and not just as a receptionist. She began to wade through the mountain of letters and cards every day that came from all parts of the country. It seemed as though everyone wanted a slice of Stephen George Robinson and Robert Marcus Williston. One letter they were waiting for with trepidation was the summons to be at court for Rachael's trial. One morning Stephen telephoned the hotel and found Rachael at the other end.

'Oh, it's you.'

'Were you expecting another fine upstanding young man?'

'Well. It might be nice to have a few comparisons before I burn my boats.'

'It is my earnest hope that point in time has long gone, Miss Williston.'

'I see. Sounds fair. What can I do for you, sir?' Rachael emphasised the word sir.

'Get yourself ready and we will drive downtown.'

'What for? Anything special?'

'Yes. Two things. First we are going to see an attorney about the trial and then we'll go down Washington Street to buy you a thing that sparkles. And if you decide you want to be with me for the rest of your life then we have an appointment with Rev Joseph Wilkes tonight at 8 o'clock when it is dark and there are no snoopers about.'

'Sounds wonderful. There were times when I thought this would never happen. I will get ready at once.'

They met Mr Lilley the attorney in a nondescript café in the city centre to avoid recognition but this possibility was receding by every day as the initial euphoria of Stephen and Bobby's success had begun to die down.

'In the words of William Kemp, Bobby and I are a nine-day wonder, my darling,' said Stephen.

'Not to me,' said his fiancé whose eyes had begun to shine again. She was rapidly beginning to recover and feel more like her true self, trial or no trial.

Mr Lilley told them that Mr Bond's company were funding all costs. In the event of Rachael being found guilty, Stephen would pay her costs at the rate to be decided and deducted from his salary. They had set a date for the first show on 25th January near Houston, rehearsals beginning a fortnight before. Stephen was asked if they would be coming down together to which he replied that it was their hope. There were some simple forms to sign. This completed, they then took their leave from Lilley.

They then made a beeline to the jewellers in Washington street and spent nearly an hour choosing Rachael's ring. Stephen was adamant that she took her time. In the end she chose and Stephen was thankful that it was only minutely over the budget he had planned. He had taken cash as he was afraid his name might be recognised on a cheque and therefore give the game away with regard to their engagement.

He had to explain to Rachael why he was wearing dark glasses, a hat and was sporting four days' growth of a beard. Bobby had offered him money but Stephen had his pride and did not want to borrow except as a last resort. Rachael put on the ring and they walked happily out of the shop and looked for a café.

They then lost no time in getting back to the hotel where Marcus, Sarah and Mrs Gilbert looked on with delight and indulged in the happy moment. Needless to say, they were all reminded that secrecy was absolutely essential for a while longer. In the late evening when most of them were together and relaxing someone broached the subject of flowers for the happy event. Stephen was quick to quell any talk on that matter.

'Not now. There's plenty of time for that later. Listen. When Bobby and I were in Amiens, a poster was put up to encourage us to keep our mouths firmly shut.'

'No war talk,' said Bobby.

'Exactly,' said Stephen. 'Except this time, it's WEDDING and not WAR. So no more wedding talk for now. Not for the moment.'

'One last word,' said Bobby. 'A toast. Here's to the happy couple.'

Even the dogs seemed to sense something nice was happening and wagged their tails. Stephen and Bobby left for private words so that the latter could be briefed with the news and dates for his diary. Bobby had relied on Stephen to collect all the information of their employment from Mr Lilley and bring back what was necessary for his personal signature. He had no intention of playing gooseberry whilst the happy couple chose the ring so he busied himself by attacking a mountain of paperwork, answering letters from well-wishers and most of all the telephone.

In the evening Rev Wilkes welcomed them and did his best to put them at their ease.

'Now then, you two. Have you a date in mind for your wedding?'

'Bobby and I have to be in Texas by 9th January or 10th at the latest. We would like to be wed before then so that we can all go down together and for we two to have our honeymoon there. There will be no time for us to go away after the reception. We have a long journey and then some training to do. Our first show is on January 25th.'

'You realise that in time, it will be hard to keep this secret but we'll do our best to keep it so as long as possible.'

'Yes. If we can keep it under wraps until after the trial. Also, we intend it to be a simple affair, if at all possible.'

'Very wise. When does your trial take place, Miss Williston?'

'We expect it to start around the week beginning 30th December.'

'Good. Then if justice is done, you can be free in all ways for your marriage. January 4th is a Saturday. I suggest we aim for that.'

All was agreed and after talking to the affable and kindly minister for nearly an hour, the meeting broke up and Stephen took Rachael to the *Red Lion Hotel*. He kissed her goodnight and she said: 'You have not even mentioned about my wearing the ring on Bonfire Night let alone given me a rebuke.'

'Damn good thing you did have it on you otherwise that slob Lyon would have succeeded with his dirty work. I am sure you have an explanation.'

'That's why I love you so much. You are so trusting.'

'Tell me all.'

'On the evening before, that is 4 November, I was last to bed. I put the ring on, said a prayer for us both, settled down only to realise I had left something in the oven. In my haste, I burnt my fingers. Nothing too bad but in the morning my hand had swollen and I could not get the ring off. I managed to cover it up during the day and in the darkness in the evening, it wasn't noticed.'

'A blessing in disguise, then?'

'No doubt about it.' She leant over and kissed him and disappeared into the hotel. Stephen then returned to his airfield quarters.

The next day, a buff official letter arrived to say that the trial would indeed be on Monday 30th December at 10.00 am It contained all to do and do not plus all the official jargon associated with it. It cast a cloud for a few minutes until it was pointed out how much needed doing to be ready for Christmas and beyond. Thereafter all parties busied themselves with their respective tasks and tried to put the trial out of their minds. Stephen and Bobby were regularly at the airfield, training for the *circus*, as they now referred to it while studying the form laid out by Bond's company.

Another thing the efficient Mr Bond had arranged was payment to Chuck for the use of his aircraft and the cost of the fuel. It was a lot cheaper than the expense of Bobby and Stephen rehearsing in Texas, staying in Houston hotels then rushing back for the trial. Bobby took the dogs with him each morning and exercised them which was to Mrs Gilbert's liking as she was not fully at ease with them when they were cooped up.

The days went by quickly and Christmas was soon upon them. The hotel was full and provision had to be made to open an old servant's room for Rachael and also to furnish the attic for Bobby. There was just enough room for Smasher and Grabber to sleep there. Even at that height the dogs sensed an intruder in the grounds one night and the three of them crept down carefully. Out in the back Bobby let them go but whoever it was had fled leaving behind a nice rather warm and woolly scarf. Further on there was a shoe. He bent down and looked closely at the two dogs.

'Well done, both of you. Now listen. We will say nothing of this to the others.'

All he got in reply was several slurps across his face.

Another day passed and still George thankfully had no inkling of the engagement of his son and his former servant girl. Nothing had filtered through as everyone was trying to be water-tight lipped. Although all were inwardly worried they were unaware that there was a great advantage on their side which was, of course, George's blinkered vision.

He was not without ability but this had largely remained dormant and undeveloped while he pursued his three goals which were profit, more profit and pleasure. His mind was set on the present; he could only deal with cure and not prevention and left it to others to venture into uncharted territory. People around him had gradually become pawns to be exploited rather than allowed to progress through their own natural path. It is not surprising therefore that many things such as the needs of his family, the welfare of his staff and certainly matters of the heart went increasingly unnoticed right under George Robinson's selfish nose.

Stephen would have liked to have taken Martha into his confidence but decided to err on the side of caution. It was too risky even though she and George had become more and more estranged since the hero's return. A few days before Christmas, Stephen received an invitation from her to a 26th December lunch at *Frankfare* which contained an RSVP.

At first he was determined to refuse but all the others felt he should go as it would look badly on him and make matters worse. Stephen said he would not go without Rachael but still the others were adamant that this position was completely wrong. Rachael was still *persona non grata* and to take her would not only pour oil on troubled waters but would almost certainly give the game away with regard to their relationship and give an advantage in court to the prosecution.

Apart from that, Rachael had suffered enough at George's hand and to go back together to *Frankfare* would be nothing short of madness. It was be best to go alone if only for his mother's sake. He realised this made sense and it was not long before he had curbed his youthful impetuosity. He further realised that to defeat his father, he would have to proceed with the utmost patience and subtlety.

The post brought another letter which was from Mr Lilley who asked for the paperwork including description, photograph, bill of sale and insurance details of grandmother Robinson's ring and legacy to Stephen. He explained that he did not want a situation to occur which involved *voir dire*. Stephen and Rachael had to consult a law book to understand what that meant.

Each day and every other hour, most of them wondered why George had not discovered that the ring was missing and prayed that this state of affairs would continue until the time of the trial. In fact George had hardly given it a thought; after all, who would want to or even have the temerity to break into his office?

Christmas Day was a happy one for all at the hotel. It was busy but less so than previous years for the Gilberts as this time, they had four extra pairs of hands. There were a few guests who had families locally but had nowhere to put them up and who therefore stayed at the *Red Lion*. They enjoyed themselves greatly, especially in the music making. There was room for Emma and Chuck to stay overnight and they and Stephen on the next day which was a Thursday left for lunch at *Frankfare*.

They departed in separate transport because, as Stephen pointed out, if there was any undue friction with his father he would leave, an action which would cause Emma and Chuck to be marooned. They took their time driving to the bakery in order to keep calm and maintain their equilibrium and composure. It was no surprise the find senator Lyon and his wife were there as well as a few dignitaries from the town.

Also there were his widowed aunt and his two cousins, William and Gordon, with whom he had only briefly met since his return from Europe. They were pleased to see him and congratulated him yet again. Even so, Stephen felt very isolated and uncomfortable because George had turned from Jekyll to Hyde and was in a jovial and very benevolent mood, which was infectious on all of the guests except he, Chuck and Emma.

The three of them smiled and tried to enter the spirit of the occasion but inside, they were not at ease as they felt the whole scenario contrived and insincere. Three hours later there were some games organised and done so in such a way that gave George time an opportunity to buttonhole Stephen and get him on his own. He wasted no time in getting to the point.

'Look, my boy. I feel we got off on the wrong foot last time you came. I don't mind telling you that you are needed here. We've lost a lot of good staff due to the war and I need somebody to whip some of the new ones into shape.'

'Do you know something, father? I can go along with the fact that you need me. There are two things I want you to know. Firstly, you do not know how to take no for an answer. I am earning more than you paid me just by giving talks each week. You still have no idea that I will soon be earning fifty times what you would pay me, if not more, and I will enjoy it in the bargain.

'That's not counting the royalties I am going to receive in due course. I can't convince you because you have lost track of the new world. You shut your eyes to things you don't want to believe and sometimes invent a story then finish up believing it. That applies to your treatment of Rachael who is innocent and deep down you must know it. Her parents received a pittance from you. Many have been the times when they would have liked to get away from here but had no opportunity to do so until now.'

'They will never make a go of that hotel with all the overheads and a mortgage,' said George haughtily.

'You have it wrong, father. The hotel is bought and paid for. There IS no mortgage. No mortgage.'

'Never. Never. That's impossible. They've never had that kind of money.'

'But a certain member of their family has. You can easily find if it's the truth because you have connections with the bank. After Christmas, give them a call. If they say I am lying I'll come and work for you for nothing.

'As to Rachael then what we are talking about is rape. Jason Lyon tried it two years ago and it was brushed under the carpet. You helped because it put you in favour with the senator. What about a young girl's feelings? What's more, you have now helped cover up Jason's latest wicked crime. Senator Lyon's son is nothing but a reprobate and now, in the next room, you butter up his dubious father to whom you owe a lot because of your gambling with those New York heavies and are quite happy to see an innocent young girl go to gaol for a crime she did not commit. All she was doing was to defend herself and her honour. Even a servant has the right to do that.'

'She had a knife,' said a defiant George.

'Knife, my ass. You know that is a load of crap. Just a fairy tale to get the Lyon scumbag off the hook. The only knife she's had in her hand is to cut your bread. The fact is that you and the senator for different reasons want a wayward and thoroughly obnoxious son off the hook. Therefore, Rachael is expendable, just as we were only a few weeks ago and three thousand miles away killing people. The only difference is that our opponents were anonymous and probably nicer people than you. All I could think of then was coming home and having a life of my own. Instead, I have gone from the frying pan into the fire.'

At that moment George actually felt he was beginning to lose ground. There was only one thing for it and that was to change the subject.

'Look, never mind that for the moment; we can still work something out. We ought to rejoin the others. The senator's daughter is in there. She's different from Jason and is a nice girl, just right for you. By the way. Whilst you were in France…have you done it…yet…?' He broke off, laughing.

That was the one subject that was enough to throw Stephen and for him to lose his composure for a minute. George immediately saw an area where Stephen was vulnerable and lost no time regaining the initiative and in pressing home his advantage. He smiled wickedly and said: 'Come on. You can tell your old pa.'

Stephen paused only momentarily, even though he had been taken off guard.

'If you must know, I hope to be seeing a girl at the end of next week, not that it is any of your business.'

'Oh don't be like that. Pity you won't be able to give me a full report.'

'Why? Not that I would tell you anyway. There was a time when you would never behave like this.'

George conveniently ignored that remark. He added: 'The reason is because I am going all the way to Florida for some rest and warmth for a couple of weeks.'

'Who is in charge while you are away and when do you go?'

'Your cousins will take the reins in the wake of your desertion and as for me, I am leaving the day after tomorrow.'

Bloody good, thought Stephen. Then he added: 'You said I. What about mother?'

'She's decided to stay at home.'

'I see. Talking of home then that is where I am going, father. All in all, you have offered me next to nothing and certainly nothing new.'

With that he turned on his heel before George could say anything more and retrieved his coat himself. One thing heartened him as he realised that it was very convenient that his father would be away at the time of the wedding. He didn't want him there anyway. George would soon be leaving and would have no chance of picking up any whisper about the marriage.

Martha would be able to be attend although as yet she did not even know about the engagement. Any invitation to her would have to be held on ice until the last possible moment. He went to find Emma and Chuck who were getting increasingly worried for him as the clock ticked round. They were relieved to hear that although there was still an impasse there had been no major altercation between father and son.

'Listen, you two. Will you leave Saturday 4th January free, please? And not a word to anybody.'

'What's afoot?'

'A very important and big day, hopefully. Details later, big sis. What you don't know in full then you won't have to lie if anyone asks. Got to win in court first. Softly, softly for a few more days then all will be revealed.'

Emma understood and squeezed his arm in her deep happiness for him.

'Very good, little brother. Wonderful news. Pity it had to be during all this turmoil.'

'That's painfully true,' said Chuck. 'You have had and are still having more than your fair share of problems. From what you say George must be very confident of Lyon winning if he is going off to Florida. And that is a man with money problems.' At that point they said goodbye and left for their respective homes.

There was still a fair amount of activity at the hotel as the British contingent were celebrating the day after Christmas as Boxing Day. It lasted until midnight and although everyone buckled down to doing a lot of clearing up before bedtime there was still plenty to do on the next day which was Friday 27th. During the morning they were all in the middle of their respective chores when a visitor in the form of the church choirmaster arrived and who sought out Rachael. She looked at him with an air of surprise.

'This is unexpected, Mr Gossage. To what do we owe this honour?'

'It is about Sunday, Rachael. Carol service. What about your solo?'

'I'd forgotten all about it. Do you still want me? There are a few people who are convinced I'm a bad lot and can't wait to see me put away.'

'You're nothing like that and almost everyone I talk to is rooting for you on Monday.'

'Nice of you to say so. When is choir practice?'

'Tonight as usual. 6.30 pm You won't need a lift from here, you get out your chair and you are nearly there,' he said, chuckling at his own joke.

Stephen arrived and came upon them. He looked grave while the situation was explained to him.

'It would be nice if you could do it, baby. Keep your mind off the trial and show 'em you are not afraid of any of them.'

'Very good, I'll do it,' said a determined Rachael. 'Is the solo the first verse of *In the Bleak Midwinter*?'

'Correct. You might be interested to know that our famous Senator actually turned up to a church committee meeting and demanded no German music on the Carol Service programme. I had to give in although I am still seething about it even now. We aren't even allowed to have *Stille Nacht*.'

'That's sad. I always thought music like that didn't have any boundaries,' said Rachael.

'Never mind, Rachael. There is some good stuff on the programme. You'll sing your bit beautifully.'

'Mr Gossage, sir,' said Stephen. 'Are you available next Saturday morning, that is a week tomorrow? I would like you to play a few things over for me with the band. We will need you for two hours. Say between 11 o'clock and 1 o'clock?'

'I am available in the week, sir, if that suits you better.'

'No, it has to be then as that is the only time all the band will be available. I will give you your usual fee for your time plus an extra hour.'

'Fine. In that case, I will see you then. See you tonight, Rachael.' With that Gossage left, humming a tune.

'That was cannily done, Mr Robinson.'

'Just so, Mrs Robinson to be. By the way, when we're out can you keep your ring covered just for a day or two.'

'Will do,' said Rachael. Although she felt uneasy attending to the practice the choir welcomed her warmly and inwardly she felt glad that she had accepted and conquered her initial misgivings. Stephen was at the back of the church keeping a watchful eye on the proceedings. Joanne came up to them afterwards and had a chat. Rachael took the plunge:

'Jo. Are you free a week tomorrow?'

'Can be. What's cooking?'

'Tell you next Wednesday, hopefully. Come to the hotel after work. Not a word to anybody and I mean anybody, Jo. And no speculation.'

'OK, I think I get the drift. Say no more.'

'You are an ace, dear friend.'

Saturday fell a bit flat and nerves began to jangle until about mid-afternoon when Mr Lilley arrived having booked into the hotel a couple of days before. He was tired and only spoke briefly about the trial and said that anything else could wait until the next day. There was only one thing he asked for and that was to have the ring that had cut Lyon put in his possession. He examined it carefully under a magnifying glass.

On Sunday morning after breakfast he declared that he was coming to the Carol Service and was looking forward to it immensely. He then disappeared to work in his room.

The church was packed in the evening with standing room four deep at the back. It was somewhat of a squash in the pews; Lilley sat next to Stephen whose immediate right contained all the Williston family bar Rachael. Bobby nudged Stephen and nodded his head in the direction of the upstairs and Stephen noticed the Lyon contingent all laughing and joking and appearing very happy and contented with life. All of them exuded an air of confidence and superiority. Stephen looked away and studied his programme.

The first half went well and then followed the community carols which were sung lustily by the tightly packed congregation. At the end many people stretched their legs until the warning bell sounded for the recommencement. As people were filing back there were loud and angry voices raised in the gallery. Senator Lyon, who was a music committee member, although he rarely attended meetings, was involved as was Wilkes and Gossage.

Senator Lyon was waving his service sheet and then started wagging his finger at Wilkes who could be heard to say No! No! No! Wilkes hurried downstairs and buttonholed Gossage about some matter. He nodded curtly just as the congregation began to be aware something was wrong. Conversation in the congregation subsided and all turned their eyes to where the noise had emanated then all awaited an explanation. It all seemed very unseemly especially during a church festival. The second half was to have begun with *In the Bleak Midwinter*, but Rev Wilkes asked and waited patiently for silence. He looked pained, angry and had a face which resembled an overripe tomato.

'Ladies, gentlemen and children. I am sorry to interrupt proceedings but there has been an objection to the next item by one of our committee members. As you know every year we try to put on two or three new items into our programme and this year is no exception. Because of this terrible war the committee decided, er…rather were forced to concentrate on living American and British composers and their music rather than that of our enemies.

'That is why, unfortunately in my opinion, *Stille Nacht* is not on the programme this year. Our committee member who objected is under the misconception that the composer of the next item, Mr Gustav Holst, is German. HE IS NOT. In fact, he hails from England. I understand his father and grandfather were also born and raised in England. I'm further informed by Mr Gossage that Mr Holst is in the army somewhere in Europe organising music with British, American and allied troops. In the light of this information, I hope there will be no further disruption and therefore request that without further ado we get on with the programme as printed in your service sheet.'

Stephen could not help smiling at Bobby. Senator Lyon had made a fool of himself although it was a pity Rev Wilkes did not name him specifically. The senator had obviously not wanted Rachael to perform and thought, erroneously, that he had good reason to order the next item to be deleted. The *coup de gras* came a few minutes later when Rachael stood to sing. The choir joined in at the second verse. The applause at the end was rapturous while Senator Lyon looked a little blue as did the rest of his entourage.

Lilley turned to Stephen and said: 'If that's not a hit in a few years, I'll eat my hat. That was brave of your rector to say what he did and the same can be said about your girl for appearing. Bravo.'

Before the end of the concert it was encored and the congregation were allowed to join in. Afterwards as they walked the short distance to the hotel Lilley said: 'At the moment, thanks to tonight's performance, we are just a little ahead, Stephen. Let's see if we can maintain the trend.'

'Pity some of the jury weren't at the show to hear her sing.'

Lilley stopped him in his tracks. His eyes twinkled.
'They might well have been. A few of them were sent free tickets.'

Stephen's eyes widened and he marvelled:
'Why, you wily old fox. How did you manage that?' Lilley grabbed his arm.
'Listen Stevie. The Lyon dynasty believe they should win and rule by divine right. They have been painting a nasty picture of Rachael but her performance tonight will have given undecided people a push in our direction. The Lyon

family is ruthless and consists of dirty fighters who are not concerned about justice. The trial to them is an unnecessary irritation. They are so, so confident. Tomorrow they are going to have a shock and I am going to give it to them, right up their supercilious upper-class rectums.'

Stephen smiled at that remark and took heart. They reached the hotel and warmed themselves by the fire. The evening of Sunday 29th December was spent in going over all the final details for the trial which wearied them. They were all very thankful when, with a deft flick of his fingers, Lilley shut his file and placed it into an expensive looking case. There was then a mass exodus for their respective beds with the exception of Lilley who asked for a brandy and soda. He spent a long time over it whilst mulling over his plan of attack for the next day.

On this occasion, Stephen did not return to *Hillington* but stayed in one of the spare hotel rooms, albeit in the attic and one designated for servants. For a while he propped up his pillow and remained in deep thought. Realising he was going around in circles, he gave in and replaced the pillow. He hoped Rachael would be able to sleep and be fit for the ordeal, which was now only a few hours away.

41. In Court

On Monday morning all the people in the hotel breakfasted at different times and said little. They then congregated at the appointed time leaving the Gilberts in full charge. Half an hour later, they filed into the courtroom in State House Boston. The courthouse itself was thronged with the press and photographers who were all milling about and vying for position. The Boston morning paper, known locally as the *"Lyon's mouth"*, gave the trial as headlines and another, sympathetic to the senator's politics, gave the following:

Senator Expects Justice for Maimed Son

'That is an ambiguous headline and cleverly worded,' said Stephen.

Lilley merely nodded and, cool as a cucumber, went through the final briefing with them in a small office as if he were on a Sunday afternoon picnic. They all filed into court and awaited the arrival of the judge. They were pleased that it was Judge Michael Watson who was presiding as he was well known for his impartiality. Good so far. That meant the Senator had not gotten the man of his choice and would not have been able to grease his palm.

Rachael sat next to Mr Lilley and was immediately asked to stand. She pleaded not guilty in a firm but nervous voice. Prosecutor Finch then outlined their case and with consummate ease made Rachael look like a street corner whore. He said that there would be no doubt that the jury would find her guilty and would demand the stiffest sentence for the wholly unwarranted attack on his client whose intentions were pure and honourable. Stephen's fists automatically clenched but he kept calm under enormous pressure.

A smiling Lilley then faced the jury. He informed them that Rachael was nothing of the sort of person that had just been portrayed but was the victim of an attempted rape by a person of low morals and diabolical intentions. The defence would call witnesses who would be able to corroborate these statements. He then sat whilst Finch glared at him for what he termed as impudence. Who was this man and where had the Williston peasants managed to dredge him up? No matter. There would be no problem with this case. Finch then called the Detective Sergeant in charge of the case to give his evidence.

Finch stood and began thus:

'Detective Sergeant Crawford, will you tell the court how and when you became involved with this case.'

Crawford cleared his throat.

'On the morning of 6th November of this year, I received two telephone calls, firstly from the hospital to say there was a patient there who had suffered grievous bodily harm then, shortly afterwards from Senator Lyon to say that his son had been attacked and injured. At about 10.15 am, I visited the Senator's home and spoke with him. Then I went to the hospital and took down a statement from Mr Jason Lyon. I left there approximately one hour later.'

'I see. When did you visit the accused?'

'Later that afternoon. I took down a statement from her.'

'As a result of the evidence you had taken, what was your next movement.'

'On the morning of 7th November, I visited the *Frankfare* complex and charged the accused with grievous bodily harm and arrested her. She appeared in court the following morning and was detained, bail being unable to be met.'

'Thank you Detective sergeant.' Finch turned to Lilley, 'Your witness.' He then sat down and smiled confidently at Jason Lyon. Lilley strolled over to the policeman.

'Detective Sergeant. Why did you visit the senator first and not the hospital?'

The Detective Sergeant was thrown of his guard for a moment and had to think.

'Er...I believe the senator said he had an important meeting so I went there first.'

'Interesting. Why was there such a long delay before Miss Williston's arrest?'

Crawford hesitated. 'It was a question of examining the evidence and speaking with others, sir.'

'Who, for instance.'

'Mr Walter Beston.'

'I see… Interesting… Is that the only reason? Did you receive any calls from anyone else with regard to the incident?'

'Only the press.'

'Are you sure? Did you hesitate just a moment ago because you were subject to external pressure?'

'I am not sure what you mean, sir.' At this point Finch looked across and glared at Lilley who remained impassive.

'What I mean, sergeant, is this. Did you or did you not receive a call from Senator Lyon or Mr George Robinson or both saying that they expected you to do your duty and arrest my client?'

Finch arose in anger.

'Your honour, this is intolerable; there is no evidence that such a conversation should or did take place. And thus, this is irrelevant.'

Judge Watson then intervened. 'Mr Lilley. Have you any hard evidence of such a conversation?'

'No, sir. I withdraw the question.'

'Please continue, Mr Lilley.' Finch sat down with a smirk. 'This is going to be easy,' he remarked to his junior.

'Did you receive a telephone call from Mr George Robinson, then? If so what was the substance of the conversation.'

'Yes, sir. He told me that the accused was not to set foot on *Frankfare* soil again.'

'Very strange why he should say that. Did he expect you to put a guard on the gate?'

'No, sir. I have no idea why he mentioned that.'

'Did he tell you he had confiscated a ring my client was wearing.'

'No sir. He said nothing about a ring.'

'When you interviewed my client, did she tell you that she thought a ring had been responsible for Mr Lyon's injury.'

'I can't recall anything of that nature.'

'Really. What happened then?'

'When there was nobody to provide the necessary bail, I took her to the police holding cells. I then awaited developments.'

'Thank you, detective sergeant. Just one more thing. Did the accused deny assault and tell you that there had been an attack on her and attempted rape.'

'Yes, she did.'

'In that case why was she arrested and not Mr Jason Lyon?'

The detective looked somewhat nonplussed. 'Well, there was the nasty wound…'

'Did you in your questioning of Mr Jason Lyon ask him whether he had attempted to force himself on my client.'

Crawford was uncomfortable. 'No, sir, as the hospital refused to allow him to be questioned.'

'But there must have been a time later when he was well enough to help you with your enquiries. Was this question put to him.'

'I don't think so.'

'Why not?'

'Well, in the light of all the evidence—'

Lilley interrupted. 'Can you categorically say that you had no external pressure to do your best to make my client look as though she was the guilty party?'

Finch rose furiously. 'Your honour; we have been down this road and it is already a dead end. There is no evidence of outside influences. This is out of order.'

Judge Watson considered. 'Objection is sustained.' Finch looked across in triumph. Lilley was impassive as the detective was allowed to leave the witness box. He was followed by Jason Lyon's minion, Walter Beston.

'State your name.'

'Walter James Beston.'

'What is your relationship with my client.'

'Mostly at the polo club. We are both on the verge of the National Team.'

This statement was spoken with the utmost pride and confidence and with an elevated nasal protuberance.

'Ah yes. We all have great hopes of you both, Mr Beston. How would you describe my client? You know him pretty well, of course.'

'Oh he's a great guy. Much liked. Wouldn't hurt a fly.'

'Tell us about the night in question when my client was attacked and injured.'

'Williston came up to me and asked if I could arrange a private meeting with Jason. I asked her if there was a problem. She said there was for any girl in her condition.'

'What did you assume she meant by that.'

'That she was with child.'

'What happened next?'

'I asked her if where she wanted to see Jason and she said that the spare house was empty and there was no chance of being disturbed. We went up there and a few minutes later, she knifed him.'

'Thank you, Mr Beston. Your witness.'

Lilley scrutinised the man first of all. He then rose and walked over to the witness.

'Mr Beston. Were Lyon and Miss Williston alone in the bedroom?'

'Yes.'

'Was it dark.'

'Well, yes, it was November, wasn't it?'

'Indeed it was, Mr Beston. Thank you for reminding us of that. Therefore all light that was being used was flashlight?'

'Yes.'

'So you did not witness the injury to Mr Lyon.'

'No, but I saw the aft—'

'Just answer the question, Mr Beston, nothing more, nothing less. You did not see the injury to Lyon.'

'Well, no. I suppose not but I saw—'

'Never mind what else you saw, Mr Beston. I will ask you again. Did you see the actual injury to Mr Lyon?'

'Well no. I suppose not but—'

'No buts, Mr Beston. We have been told that a knife was used. What did the knife look like? What happened to it afterwards?'

'I...I don't remember what it looked like. I expect she disposed of it afterwards.'

'You mean you and anybody else for that matter did not deign to pick it up so that it could be shown to the police?'

'Well, it all happened so quickly.'

'In fact, it never happened at all, Mr Beston, did it? What we are talking about is assault and attempted rape which you duly aided and abetted. That is the truth of the matter, isn't it, Mr Beston?'

'No. No. It is as I said.'

'Tell me, Mr Beston. You say that you and your friend are on the verge of the polo national squad.'

'Yes, and we are proud to represent our country.' He said this puffing out his chest.

'First, though, you have an enquiry to go through.'

'I don't know what you mean.'

Finch rose.

'Your honour, what is the purpose of this line of enquiry?'

'Shall we wait and see, Mr Finch?' said Judge Watson. 'Continue, Mr Lilley.'

'You and Jason Lyon are suspended at the moment for the mistreatment of an animal which happened after you lost your last but one club match. So much for Mr Lyon not ever being capable of hurting a fly.'

'Nothing has been proved yet, nothing,' said an increasingly angry Walter Beston.

'Of course. You may stand down.'

Finch glared wondering how Lilley had dug up that information. Finch stood as the steward boomed out.

'Rachael Williston to take the stand.'

Rachael gingerly crossed the floor and sat. Finch came across and smiled condescendingly.

'Miss Williston, how old are you?'

'Twenty two.'

'How many lovers have you had?'

'None.'

'None?' Finch laughed contemptuously. 'I have been led to believe on good report that you have been quite promiscuous in the past.'

'Then your informants, whoever they are, have told you a pack lies.'

'Have they indeed... How many boyfriends have you had?'

'One.'

'Only one. Really and yet you say you are already 22 years old.' Finch smirked disbelievingly and turned to make a face at the jury. 'And when did that finish?'

'It hasn't, sir.'

'So you deny…how shall I put it…being a woman of…shall we say experience?'

'I am a woman of experience, sir. Making all kinds of cakes, cookies and delights for the local population. Doing accounts. Possibly you yourself have indulged in some of them. I have no qualifications in any other subject except music.'

'What did you do with the knife after you attacked my client.'

'I have never had a knife other than a fairly blunt one for kitchen usage and I did not attack your client. He forced himself on me.'

Finch turned belligerent at this point having failed to make any early inroads. He could see already that Rachael was certainly no pushover. He then made some very nasty aspersions on her character. She stood it well but both family and Stephen wondered if at some point she would crack. It was obviously that it was beginning to be more and more an ordeal for her especially as she had not got over her time in the cells but fortunately there occurred a timely recess.

When Lilley took to the floor he was smiling and totally in control. He painted a completely different picture of Rachael and at one point asked if she had ever been in a sexual relationship with a male. She said she had not and stated quite categorically she was a virgin. There were murmurs from the onlookers and some eyebrows raised.

'Take your time and tell the court what happened to you just a few weeks ago on the evening of November 5th.'

'It was on Guy Fawkes Night that my parents and I were serving on the food stall. A young man, unknown to me came up and said my friend Joanne Radstock was hurt and needed me urgently in the house. I went up there with him but thought it strange. Suddenly I was grabbed from behind, a bag put over my head and a handkerchief or cloth was stuffed in my mouth. I tried to scream but was prevented from doing so. They took me to the empty house and threw me on a spare bed and then took off the bag.'

'What were your feelings at this time?'

'I was absolutely terrified.'

'Were you in darkness at this time of was the electric light on?'

'The electric light was off but two of them at least had those new Flashlights.'

'Then what happened?'

'Jason Lyon was there and said we had some unfinished business of two years previously.'

'What happened two years ago?'

'It was a previous occasion that we had a Guy Fawkes night. Lyon attacked me by the lake until somebody stopped him.'

'Please continue with this more recent attack on you,' said Lilley. Finch glared at this remark but declined to object.

'They tore off my blouse and some of my underwear. They held my mouth so that I could not scream.'

'And then?'

'Luckily my right arm came free and I swung out in panic. The ring on my finger caught him on the cheek. The next moment Lyon screamed out and let go. The other men let go. They put on the Flashlights. There was blood all over the bed and pillow.'

'Did anyone say anything?'

'Yes. Someone said, *The bitch has caught your vein, Jason. We'll have to get you to hospital.*'

'What was Lyon's response?'

'He started yelling and saying *Jesus Christ, Jesus Christ* all the time and occasionally screaming. Somebody went to the telephone in the house. Then the others carried him out.'

'What did you do?'

'Nothing. I was just paralysed and could not move an inch. I was like that until my parents and brother Charles turned up a short while later.'

Lilley then produced the diamond ring and took it across to her.

'Is this the ring that you were wearing?'

Rachael looked at it carefully and said: 'Yes, sir. That is it.'

'How came this into your possession?'

'Mr Stephen Robinson gave it to me.' There were murmurs at this statement which swelled, causing the judge to use his gavel again.

'Miss Williston. The prosecution say that you attacked Lyon with a knife.'

'There was no knife involved and I have never had a knife in my possession except a fairly blunt one in the kitchen as part of my duties.'

'Mr Lyon has said he was in love with you and believed you to be in love with him. Is this true?'

'I have never felt anything for Jason Lyon except one of fear and revulsion.'

'When Mr George Robinson confronted you later that evening what happened?'

'I told him that the ring had done the damage and when he inspected it recognised it and pulled it roughly off my swollen finger. I told him how I had come by it but he did not believe me and took it away.'

'One last thing, Rachael. When Detective Crawford interviewed you did you tell him that you thought your ring had caused the injury?'

'Most definitely.'

'Thank you. That is all for now,' said Lilley.

'You may step down,' said Judge Watson. 'Call the next witness.'

'Call Jason Lyon.'

Jason Lyon entered with an air of injured innocence. His head was slightly in the air and his posture had been rehearsed well. Finch, the prosecution attorney went over to him after he had been sworn in. His voice was soothing and condescending.

'Now Mr Lyon. Will you tell us in your own words about this terrible attack on you.'

'I thought she cared for me. Now look at me. Will another girl ever look at me?' Lyon buried his face in his hands and pretended to sob. Finch theatrically turned and looked at the jury with an air of inviting their sympathy.

'You have had a terrible ordeal Mr Lyon but we need to know why you were treated like this.'

'I am sorry,' said Lyon, pretending to recover. 'I do not know myself. I fell in love with her and I made her what I thought was a good offer. She was a different person to what I had been led to believe. Still, you can never be sure with the servant class. My mother did warn me, though.'

Stephen clenched his fists again. He was not a violent person in any shape or form but with a statement like this he realised that even he could be roused to fury. He remembered the words of Mr Lilley and tried to keep calm. There was still a lot of water to run under the bridge and he had to be patient.

'Why did you go to the empty house and not stay in the kitchen or lounge, say?'

'It was her idea. She said it was the only place that we could have some privacy as it was likely that other members of the family might appear.' He raised his nose in the air.

'Is it true that some of your friends were with you. What is your response to Miss Williston's accusation about rape.'

'The escorts, that is my close friends, were only there in case we were in danger of being disturbed. It was vital we talked in private. They were outside all the time only to prevent anyone else interrupting us. If she was raped then somebody else came in later and was responsible for it. There were a lot of people there that night and it was very dark. I am extremely hurt and dismayed that anybody could think I was capable of such an action. I come from a very distinguished and well-established Boston family and we resent these aspersions and refute them in the strongest possible terms.'

There were murmurs of approval from a certain section of the gallery. One tap with his gavel and judge Watson truncated any possible disturbance.

Hm, thought Stephen. *Jason Lyon has had the benefit of a skilled tutor and he delivered it convincingly. What an utterly contemptible liar he is.*

'How did your discourse end with the accused?'

'She didn't want listen to my offer as she said there were more important things to consider first. Firstly, she was unsure as to whether she was already pregnant by somebody else and wanted money to go to a private house for an abortion where there would be discretion about her condition. I was so shocked at that news. I said there was no way I could afford it even if I wanted to. When I told her that I was astonished and had believed she was a different sort of girl and was inclined to call it off, she went for me like a wildcat.'

'And then your friends took you to hospital?'

'Yes.'

'And you had eighteen stitches.'

'Yes.'

'Thank you, Mr Lyon.'

The prosecution attorney turned with a look of superiority on his face and said: 'Your witness.'

Stephen's stomach turned and seemed to have a separate life of its own. He looked over at Lilley and prayed that the man had something in his locker that would turn the tide and counter Jason Lyon's vile assertions. Lilley arose and went over to him and for a brief moment looked him closely in the eye.

'Mr Lyon. From your statement, it appears that you set great store on morals and personal behaviour.'

'Absolutely. A subject that's very dear to my heart,' he said with unabashed mendacity.

'And you say you had no knowledge of Rachael Williston's supposed lifestyle before that evening of November 5th?'

'Not at all. None whatsoever. It was a great shock and I still haven't recovered from it.'

'Mr Lyon. You said that you did not think Miss Williston was *that kind of girl*. Do I take it that you disapprove of her alleged, and I emphasise alleged kind of behaviour before marriage and would not act like that yourself?'

'Of course. I still can't understand how she pulled the wool over my eyes.'

'Really... Would you be so good as to tell the court your whereabouts on October 31st last?'

'Oh, goodness. I don't remember,' said Lyon contemptuously. 'I have not got my diary with me and I have a poor memory for dates. How can you expect me to remember that at the drop of a hat?'

'Are you sure you don't remember, Mr Lyon? It is not quite two months ago.'

'Not at all. I have said so, haven't I?'

'Indeed you have, Mr Lyon. However, if you think clearly you will realise it was Hallowe'en. Surely a young man like you would have been enjoying yourself at a function of some sort. Your family had a party on that evening.'

'Oh yes. That's correct. Silly me. We all went into Boston to my father's function. Yes, that's it.' He smiled with satisfaction but it was obvious he was beginning to get irked.

'I beg to differ. I believe you were not at all with your father. My information is that you were somewhere else and nowhere near where you say you were.'

'If you know so much then why are you asking?' smirked a confident Lyon, who, deep down, was still convinced of his impregnability.

'I require confirmation.'

Judge Watson intervened, 'The witness will answer truthfully and without prevarication. Continue please, Mr Lilley.'

'Where were you on the late evening of October 31st?'

'I'm sorry, I really can't recall. I must have been on the way home from somewhere.'

Lilley tried again. 'I have it on good authority that you were with friends at a Halloween party at Salem.'

Lyon realised he had no option but to answer.

'If you say so then I suppose I was,' said Lyon. 'What's the big deal about that?'

'No big deal at all. I want you to tell me what you did after the party? It is that of which I am really interested.'

'Like I said. I went home.'

'Did you indeed? I rather think not. I beg to differ. I think that you and a certain young lady booked into a Salem hotel and spent the night together. The name you used was…Mr and Mrs Lynx. Rather a good name, I must admit.' He smiled condescendingly.

Lilley's smile was more of a smirk and he held it for several seconds until Finch was forced to act. Finch realised they were going into potentially very awkward territory so an intervention yet again was necessary.

'Objection. your honour, why is this line of enquiry important? We are wasting time. No crime has been committed and there is no relevance to this case.'

Lilley actually sported a laugh. It was not really a laugh but rather a cross between a giggle and a guffaw. He was not in the least troubled by this intervention and countered.

'Your honour, I beg to differ. The prosecution has levelled some sordid and quite untrue accusations about my client and at the same time purported their own to be squeaky clean and as pure and white as snow. I intend to show Mr Lyon is not the man he and the prosecution make him out to be and is in fact guilty of a vicious and unprovoked attack on my client.'

'Objection is overruled. Pray continue, Mr Lilley.'

Finch sat down, looking decidedly miffed. How on earth had Lilley managed to dig up information like that? This was unexpected and could be serious. More than serious in fact. He had sailed through most of his cases during the last 11 years and now, somehow he felt more than a little anxious.'

'Did you offer her money or did she come of her own accord? An answer, if you please, Mr Lyon.'

Finch realised that Lilley had set a neat trap and there was anger etched all over his face. He was about to object again but Lilley was quickly in again.

'An answer, sir. The court demands an answer from you this minute.' Judge Watson motioned Finch to sit down.

Jason Lyon was trying to think. How the hell had they found out that, particularly as he had been so careful to cover his tracks? Somebody had blabbed, for sure. He opened his mouth without being able to speak. Lilley waited for a few moments and then pounced.

'Mr Lyon. Allow me to help you. We showed the desk clerk of the hotel in question, who was on duty during that time, several photographs and he picked out you and the lady in question without a moment's hesitation. He says that you both shared a room together. He is waiting outside in the hall to be called if necessary. We also have the name of your young lady whose identity as yet we have not revealed in order that her name might not be besmirched and dragged through the mud that seems to follow you wherever you go. Now will you stop prevaricating and tell us about the night of 31st October last?'

There was a long pause during which Jason Lyon visibly gulped.

'Yes, it is true. It was me with someone.' Jason Lyon dropped his head, a thing he was told not to do at his rehearsal. His mother looked on with horror in the gallery.

After a pause that allowed the hubbub in the courtroom to subside, Lilley continued: 'Did your parents approve of your supposed friendship with a girl not of your social standing? I refer to Miss Williston, of course.'

'Not to start with; later they came around,' Jason Lyon lied yet again.

'I suggest to you that there was no such friendship, Mr Lyon, and you are an unprincipled liar and an attempted rapist.'

There was a noisy reaction from the audience to these accusations for a time, which drowned Jason Lyon's reply. Finch's fury new no bounds. Eventually, order was restored and the trial proceeded. Lilley then asked a few technical questions as to how Rachael had managed to strike a blow in the way that Lyon had described. Lyon started to fumble badly and Finch had to keep interrupting as each time Lyon tried to explain, he kept contradicting himself. In the end Lilley caused a stir when he first asked the usher to bring in two parcels. They were unwrapped to show busts of two heads. For the first time in many a long year, Finch did not feel in full control. He was on his feet again.

'Your honour, do we have to have this theatrical farce imposed on us?' he said. 'What is the purpose of all this.'

'Until Mr Lilley tells us what he has in mind, I have no idea, Mr Finch. At the moment and in the interests of justice, I am eager to see his demonstration,' said Judge Watson. 'Then, and then alone I will decide whether it has any bearing on this case. Please continue, Mr Lilley.'

Finch sat down with an air of abject reluctance. Lilley then rose and demonstrated that expert opinion believed it would be almost impossible for a blow from a knife to inflict such a wound as was found on Lyon. He also asked photographs of the injury to be distributed amongst the jury.

'Your honour and members of the jury. These casts are made of a special kind of plaster and have the same density and texture as human flesh. I will demonstrate the effect of this sharp diamond on it, that is the one Miss Williston was wearing at the time.'

Mr Lilley, having had several practices during the last week, brought the diamond ring down the cheek of the bust. He then asked the bust to be passed down all the members of the jury to compare that and the photographs taken of Jason Lyon in the hospital. He then took a knife to the other bust and demonstrated the different result to them.

'Members of the jury will see that the wound the diamond produced is entirely compatible with the photographs whereas the wound with a knife gives a completely different result.' He then turned to Jason Lyon.

'This is what really happened, isn't it, Mr Lyon. You and your other contemptible hooligan associates lured an innocent and defenceless young woman to a dark and frightening location where you attempted to force your will on her—'

'No, no,' said Lyon.

'You frightened her almost out of her wits and in her panic and self-defence, she struck out and accidentally caught you with this ring—'

'No, no, it's not true, she did it on purpose—'

'And what is more, you are a liar, a cheat, a rapist and have been proven to be before this court.'

'No, no.' Jason Lyon began to flounder. 'I loved her and she did this to me. She did it. Look at me...' He half sobbed the last sentence.

Lilley calmly turned his back and enlisted the help of the steward. He asked for the busts to be removed and gave way to the prosecutor. Finch tried to attack once more and he jumped up with a look of even more anger on his face. His neck was red.

'Mr Lyon. Will you state unequivocally and clearly that it was a knife that Williston attacked you with.'

Jason Lyon gulped. 'Yes sir. Absolutely. No question about it.'

Finch sat down but only felt a miniscule amount better. He had been quite unprepared for a fight of this nature and was not even sure if his head was above water. He looked hard at Lilley, who returned his look with an engaging smile.

After lunch, Lilley called an expert witness to the stand, one of the coroner's doctors.

'Dr Redlich, you have examined the wound of the plaintiff. Tell me. Have you seen a wound like this before?'

'Never. It was a unique experience for me,' he said with a strong mid-European accent.

'Have you any theories of what might have caused it?'

'Something very sharp and a small head that would have caused such a thin laceration.'

'In your opinion, doctor, is a knife the most likely to have caused this?'

'I can't discount it but very much doubt it,' said the doctor. 'In all my years with recovered weapons, this was singular.'

'Could a diamond have done such a wound?'

Finch was on his feet instantly. 'Objection. Counsel is leading the witness.'

'It seems a fair question to me, Mr Finch. Objection overruled.' Lilley looked over his spectacles condescendingly at Finch and then resumed.

'Yes. A diamond would be a prime candidate. One with a sharp edge and thin point.'

'Can you tell us what direction the blow would have taken?'

'It would have come from above and finished just under the jaw.'

'What reason do you give for this conclusion?'

'Well sir, the damage was done it seems to me to be by a downward movement.'

'Are there any other reasons why you think a knife was not involved?'

'Just one. Knife wounds are usually aimed at the stomach. This incident suggests to me a somewhat involuntary action, rather like self-defence.'

There were a few murmurs and shuffling at this statement.

'Dr Redlich, I would like you to examine this diamond ring. Could this have caused the wound?' Redlich used his magnifying glass.

'Yes sir, it could, easily. It has the type of sharp point I mentioned and would produce a thin but very damaging result.'

There were no further questions from Lilley. The prosecutor then did his best to enquire as to the doctor's knowledge of knives. In the end, he said: 'Let's be clear, doctor. You say you can't discount the possibility that the wound was caused by a knife.'

'I cannot discount the use of a knife.'

Dr Redlich was allowed to stand down. The prosecutor felt a little happier as did the Senator. Both did not anticipate this situation as they thought the whole thing would be a pushover. Finch called no other witnesses so he handed over to Lilley who asked for the next witness to appear.

'Call Mr Stephen Robinson.'

Stephen entered to applause which caused Judge Watson to bang the gavel and issue warnings to the perpetrators that any repeat would bring about their ejection.

'Mr Robinson. Will you tell us how you know the accused?' said Lilley.

'We went to school together and go to band together. She was a valuable employee in our family along with her parents.'

'She says that just before you left for France, you gave her a ring.'

'That is correct.'

'Is this it?' Lilley brought the ring over to Stephen.

'Yes.'

'Your honour, I would like this to be entered as the next exhibit. How came you by this rather expensive item?'

'It belonged to my grandmother. She gave it to me a few years ago.'

'Why did you give it to Miss Williston.'

'I asked Miss Williston to keep it as a reminder of me whilst I was overseas and facing the enemy in France.'

'Was there any particular reason for this act?'

'Yes. I hoped her thoughts and prayers would be enough to help keep me alive. If I failed to return then she was to dispose of it in any way she saw fit. If she decided to sell, she was to buy something for herself and her family by which to remember me.' There were murmurs of both surprise and approval at this point.

'Mr Robinson. You have been in court to witness that there have been some rather nasty aspersions on the character of the accused. As a respected war hero and distinguished member of this community, what is your reaction to those remarks?'

'Outrageous, sir. An absolute disgrace. Nothing could be further that the truth, sir. On the contrary, the accused bears no resemblance to the picture painted by the prosecution. That is the view of my mother and cousins who are in charge of *Frankfare* in my father's absence.'

'Thank you, Mr Robinson.' Lilley gave way to Finch.

'Mr Robinson. Your father, when he was on the scene after the accused attacked my client—'

Lilley immediately interrupted, 'Objection, your honour.'

'Sustained. Mr Finch, please rephrase your question. I think a man of your experience would know better than to say that. Members of the jury will ignore that last comment.'

'I beg your honour's pardon. Mr Robinson, your father confiscated the ring because he said she had stolen it and then dismissed her. What have you to say to that?'

'Understandable. He did not know that I had given it to her. He was probably unaware at the time that the ring would have been the cause of Lyon's injury. When I returned home, I was able to convince him that no theft had taken place.'

'How has it come back in your possession only now. The police made no reference to it in their report.?'

'As I just said, sir, he was unaware that it might have caused the injury. My father has been somewhat absent-minded recently; he obviously mislaid it and it was found just a short time ago, thus enabling me to bring it to court. As to it not being mentioned in the police report, I have to say I find that fact very disturbing.'

'Mr Robinson, are you seriously telling us that you gave an extremely expensive ring, a 21-carat sapphire ring, willy-nilly to one of your servants on what can only be described as a whim. Why is it that you are covering for this woman?'

'No whim whatsoever, sir. It was an action done after serious thought and I'm covering for nobody, Mr Finch. I also resent your accusation. The first fact is, sir, that I can give what is mine to whom I want, servant or slave, prince or pauper and without reference to you or anybody. Miss Williston and I grew up together and I have never regarded her as a servant. Furthermore, I gave an expensive gold tie pin and cufflinks to her brother and a silver pocket watch to my brother-in-law.'

'And what, pray is the second,' said Finch superciliously.

'The second is simply this, sir, that I knew before leaving for France that every pilot had a very short life expectancy, a fact that was concealed to most of our great country's population. The most we could expect was six to eight weeks, sir. It meant that the chances were overwhelming that I was not going to return and thus not be here today. Even so, I was wounded twice and am still not fully recovered.

'If you have the opportunity to see some of the footage taken in France then, you will be aware that Bobby Williston and I are very fortunate to be alive. As to the ring, I gave it to Miss Williston whose family has served us well over many years and told her that if I did not return she could use it for their good. That included her parents and brother Charles.'

'Of course, this is all your invention. For some reason, you are protecting a thief and violent person.'

'I resent that remark and say this, sir. The ring was mine and mine to give and I do not have to ask anybody's permission before I do so. It was my prerogative to bestow a bounty on anyone I chose and in this case it was Miss Williston. It saved making a will. As to violence, she was protecting herself against somebody who wished to force himself on her as he once did before.

'I know this because on the previous occasion I was there at the time and due to the fact that his family have some extremely powerful friends the incident went relatively unpunished. History is now in danger of repeating itself. My father, for reasons best known to himself ordered a gag on it and at the time we were a lot younger and did not dare not disobey.'

At that statement, there was noise in the court. Judge Watson banged his gavel and tried to restore order. When the noise subsided, an irate Finch came over to Stephen and eyeballed him angrily and said:

'That is a serious accusation, Mr Robinson. You cannot substantiate those remarks.'

He turned to the Judge Watson.

'Your honour,' said Finch, 'I demand these remarks to be expunged from the record and the jury disregard those statement made by the witness.' Judge Watson agreed and as a result, Finch sat down feeling happier after Stephen's outburst. Mr Lilley was a little disquieted at those particular comments by Stephen but did not show it.

The senator upstairs was the man feeling blue. He had, over the years, managed to have the District Attorney almost in his pocket and as a result gotten an assurance that the most formidable prosecutor in Boston would lead the fray. Yet the easy victory that they expected as a matter of course was at this moment in the trial by no means assured. It had been made harder for them when a judge had been appointed who could not be bought. He tried to comfort himself. The mighty Finch had not lost a case in eleven years. Nobody in the court have even dreamt what happened next as Lilley prepared his *coup de grace*.

The steward went out and boomed: 'Call Mrs Frances Richards.'

At this point Stephen experienced a sudden jolt in the head and the chest. He at once felt worried to the point of being petrified and he was not the only one in court to feel so, particularly the other members of the Williston family. To say this was unexpected would be the understatement of the century. He could not comprehend Lilley's motives who looked at Frances Richards and smiled broadly.

'Will you state your name, please?'

'Frances Shirley Richards.'

'Mrs Richards. You are employed by the *Frankfare* company bakery as a telephone operator. Where were you at the time of the incident on November 5th of this year?'

'On duty on the telephone switchboard, sir.'

'At that time of the evening?'

'It was my late turn of duty,' said Fanny Richards.

'Was anyone with you?'

'Nobody. Just me on that occasion.'

'Were there any calls on that evening?'

'Only three inward. Just asking for Mr Robinson who was otherwise engaged.'

'What about outgoing calls?'

'Just one from in the house as that is the only one connected at night time.'

'Did you hear anything that was said and did you know the caller's name?'

'Yes sir, the caller only identified himself as Walter. He called a number in the village.'

'Tell us what was said.'

'I have to tell you, sir, that there was some awful swearing and I do not have any use for such language.'

'That's quite alright, Mrs Richards. All you are doing is quoting someone else's remarks. You may read it from your paper.'

'In that case, he said, *Fred. It's me, Walter. Get off your arse and into your car and come in the back way of Frankfare quickly, like yesterday. Jason's been hurt badly.* The person at the other end said, *If it was that bad, why not call an ambulance?* The caller, Walter, said: *Jason has tried to screw the Williston bitch but she's cut his face and there's blood everywhere.* He said, *We don't want to let this get out or we will have hell to pay.*'

At this point there was in that particular courtroom an unprecedented eruption of noise. Judge Watson had to have several violent strikes with the gavel before he could get it to subside. Stephen could hardly believe what had just taken place. He shut his eyes and gave up a prayer and inwardly promised never to think badly of Frances Richards again.

After this revelation and the restoration of order in the courtroom, the judge asked the two counsellors and foreman of the jury to approach the bench. The three men nodded their heads in agreement. It was all over. There was no need for the jury to retire as judgement was immediately found in favour of the defendant. The judge found it difficult to restore order in the courtroom for nearly two minutes. He then asked Rachael to stand.

'Miss Williston. I have directed the jury to find you not guilty. Moreover, you have been through not one terrible ordeal but three; first the assault, the second having been kept in the cells and thirdly attendance in this court. You have also have had aspersions on your character that have proven to be entirely unjustified. You will leave this court free and your integrity unblemished. Costs will be met by the plaintiff and in time I expect there will be a considerable amount in damages forthcoming.'

'Thank you, your honour,' said Rachael. For a moment she stood bemused. Judge Watson then turned his attention to Jason Lyon and ordered him to stand. He was told that he would face a trial in the new year for perjury and attempted rape and would face a substantial custodial sentence. The law would also fall on some of his irresponsible and lying associates. Senator Lyon held his head in his hands while Mrs Lyon erupted with her mammoth wail. Several of her grim-faced super-rich friends tried to comfort her.

'All rise.'

The appropriate people bowed and judge Watson left the court. Lilley looked around at the bench of the prosecution team. Finch's face was like a concrete grave. Lilley, being a refined and accomplished man, waited for Finch to come over but his subordinate came first who was a young lady aged about 28.

'Congratulations, sir. It will take him quite a while to get over this, Mr Lilley. He has not lost a case in many a year. I was still at high school when that last happened. Anyway, very well done. You really are a man of wisdom and resourcefulness. I hope I do not come against you again, or at least for a long, long while.'

'Thank you, dear lady, and the very best for your future career.'

'Thank you, sir.'

Seeing that there was no way out for him and that the floor was reluctant to open and swallow him up, Finch came up to Lilley and offered his hand. He was shaking.

'Congratulations.' With that he gathered up the rest of his papers. Senator Lyon came over and spoke to him. He was flushed with anger. Lilley could not hear much of Lyon's conversation but he heard the words *you have failed me miserably.* He then heard Finch say something about being unable to wave a magic wand followed by shrugging his shoulders, an action that caused the senator to appear more incensed than ever. Senator Lyon then saw Stephen and walked over to him and pulled him away from the others. Rather than cause a ruckus, Stephen allowed this to happen albeit reluctantly.

'Well now, Mr Robinson junior, I hope this makes you feel good and proud betraying your own people and your own class.'

'I am not sure about being proud but yes, I feel good. Very good.'

'You don't care a damn that a promising young man on the verge of representing his country at polo is now never going to get a chance and his career wrecked.'

'I look at it from a different perspective, Senator. An innocent girl, a talented human being for that matter, has been spared jail and a guilty one will be put away and rightly so.'

'Not if I can do anything about it. Anyway, she is only a two-bit servant.'

'A beautiful living creature made by God, Senator, with feelings and emotions like you and me. She is a lot more skilled than your fun-loving son and at the same time is totally honest. She is not going to be your sacrificial lamb. You have some power, Senator, but not that much that will keep your boy out of jail. You are going to lose a lot of votes over this. It must have been pretty galling for you when someone of Mr Lilley's calibre turned up to oppose you instead of a local rookie who you could box into a corner. He really exposed your rat of a son.'

'How you got the wherewithal for somebody like him really beats me. Your father did not pay. What he is going to say about his bill when he returns will not be good for you, especially as he owes a lot of money around and about, which includes me.'

'For your information, not that it is any of your business, I bankrolled this myself. As to my father's reaction, I can tell you that it bothers me not one jot. At the moment he does nothing to earn my admiration and as a result of this trial belongs in the same gutter as you and your family. Be sure to tell him that when he returns. I shall be far away and will be unlikely to return here until the fall.

'One thing more, senator; I am not of your class and never will be. The America that I want to see should not be ruled by people like you and I shall strain every nerve to tell people what a hypocrite and dangerous man you are. Now please excuse me while I go to celebrate our great and fully deserved victory.'

Stephen left to join the others while Senator Lyon's distorted face betrayed his anger and hate. He turned and crashed through the chairs as he left.

Mr Lilley found himself surrounded by all of the Williston family. He shook everyone by the hand except Rachael who hugged him, much to his surprise and a minor amount of embarrassment. As they left, Stephen could not resist putting a question to him.

'How on earth did you manage to dig Mrs Richards up?'

'Ah, Mr Robinson. We have our ways and our trade secrets. Put it this way. In the course of our deliberations you told me of Mrs Richards' penchant for listening in. If she can listen to conversations about you or Rachael or anybody for that matter, she can also be privy to those of Mr Robinson although I will not elaborate on that for the moment. If he kicks up about her giving evidence, she could quite easily report some revelations about her boss, particularly his romantic liaisons. I was on tenterhooks right until the last moment that she would give evidence, and that's why I had to make more of the head busts.'

Stephen could have kicked himself. 'Why on earth did I not think at all of Richards?'

'No matter. You had me and I must say I have already had a lot of satisfaction on the outcome of this case.'

'I have to say, Mr Lilley, that apart from the prosecution's opening, it wasn't quite as bad as I thought it would be. Bad enough on top of a terrible homecoming. But how did they expect to get away with it?'

'Just consider,' said Lilley. 'We have been dealing with people who wield and exercise a lot of power in this district and even believe they own it. They have a lot of status and money to use as sweeteners and know how to manipulate. They also think they are invincible which in fact is their Achilles Heel.'

'True. There's bound to be times when overconfidence causes someone's undoing.'

'Absolutely correct. There is another reason which may not be clear to you and that is that you had me.'

Stephen smiled. 'We are very gra—'

His words were cut short as Lilley interrupted,

'Not in the way you think I mean it, Stephen. Consider. Finch is the most formidable prosecutor in these parts and there is no doubt in my mind he was selected as a result of some underhand means. He has not lost a case in eleven years, I believe. Nobody would want to represent Rachael unless it was a two-bit greenhorn lawyer who needed the work and nobody would believe she had any money to fight the case.

'At a guess, such an attorney would have gone through the motions, taken a small fee, and Rachael would have gotten anything between 6 months and 2 years. Thus the Lyon family would have strutted around Boston celebrating their completely undeserved and dirty hollow victory. Jason Lyon's behaviour was of no consequence to them as they rule with divine right. His father would give him a rap on the knuckles and tell him to be more careful in future or if not certainly he must not get caught.

'As to me, I've come from a different part of the country; nobody here knows me and that I have money, resources and staff to go out to delve and if necessary buy information. It may be that as a result you might not get as much of the costs and damages as otherwise you might have received but I am damned sure you don't care a jot about that. I used money in the case of information from one of those young men with Lyon with the promise I would not reveal his name. The opposition completely underestimated our firepower. You yourself made a great difference.'

'How come?'

'By standing by the one you love and giving her confidence. It must have been a real ordeal for her. Also the fact that you managed to find that ring. That in itself was a huge bonus. When I examined it, I thought we could win and would win and win handsomely. We have done just that. Vernon Bond is going to be very pleased about this. There should now be nothing in the way for our project which will entail you and your friend flying again and entertaining the crowds. Well, we hope crowds.'

'We hope so too and we will be ready. I am so grateful to you.'

'And I am so glad for you all. You are all a nice family. Let's hope the tide has turned for you all.'

'We are sorry to see you go,' said Rachael who had joined them.

'You will see me again and quite soon. I will be on hand for the "flying circus" in case I am needed for legal matters and at times will be travelling with you. A show like this needs somebody who knows all or most of the things we can and cannot do. You'll not be getting rid of me that easily.'

'That's really done my heart good. Perhaps you will allow my wife-to-be and me to take you out for dinner when there is a favourable occasion.'

'I accept readily,' said Lilley and after a gracious bow and kissing Rachael's hand turned and left.

His departure was not easy due to the army of reporters. Stephen and Rachael managed to dodge most of the melee as they quit by the back door mostly unnoticed. On this occasion the focus of attention was more on the Lyon family of which the senator, who was unprepared for this result, was having a very rough time as was his utterly disconsolate and inconsolable spouse.

The senator was perspiring profusely as he fumbled with his words and could only managed sentences which broke up half way. In the end, he threw in the towel and pulled his wife through the scrum whilst the reporters tried to prevent his progress with further penetrating queries. Matters were made much worse when a reporter fell and brought down several others in an unseemly tangle. Eventually, the police got the Lyons away but not without the utmost difficulty.

42. Aftermath

At the time of Rachael's acquittal, George and his recent concubine were enjoying the sun and sea on the beach. They were cut off from the world and were happy to be in that situation. George was not in the least worried about the trial as he was sure that the senator had bribed enough to secure Rachael's conviction and he himself had made a few telephone calls and in one instance issued a series of threats.

If he, George and his friends did not rule most of Boston by divine right they ruled with divine might achieved through their wealth, influence and sometimes intimidation. Now it was over, he could look forward to the senator's financial support as he needed to be tied over as a result of his addictive gambling. It was only a day later on New Year's Eve that he and his mistress returned to the hotel and read the newspaper.

Senator's Son to be Tried for Attempted Rape

Sensation At Trial of Servant Girl

Perjury of several witnesses revealed

For a while, George did not register but then he suddenly came to his senses, grabbed the newspaper and read the article. The shock took a while to subside. What on earth had happened? This situation was unthinkable. It was late afternoon but when he tried to get connected to *Frankfare* on the telephone, there was no reply. Several times he tried but the result was the same on each occasion. He slammed the telephone down in utter frustration. It was hardly surprising there was no answer because there was in fact nobody at the bakery except the night watchman.

He tried the senator's number but was told that Mr Lyon was not taking any calls. William and Gordon, George's two nephews who had been left in charge of *Frankfare* had decided enough was enough and whilst the cat was away the mice would play. Everyone at the bakery was allowed to leave at midday on 31st December and told not to come back to work until 3rd January, except for a small group of volunteers, mostly single and unattached employees who were responsible for bread.

The staff was ecstatic and promised to work overtime at the appropriate times to fulfil all orders. George stamped his feet when for the fifth time he drew a blank and so in desperation telephoned Emma at *Hillington*. George fumed at the amount of delay in getting connected. Emma knew very well what her cousins had instigated but was well aware what her father's reaction would be if she admitted knowledge of their unprecedented generosity.

She thus feigned ignorance and pretended not to have any inkling of the status quo at *Frankfare*. She told her father that, as far as she knew, the switchboard staff had been given some extra time off. George raged at her even at that snippet of information and almost had a seizure but realised that for the moment, he could do absolutely nothing about it. Emma politely reminded her father that she was not on the spot or the payroll and therefore warranted no criticism. George mumbled a half-hearted apology and hung up.

The New Year celebrations for the Willistons, the Ellis duo and the solitary Robinson representative were like as never before. Everyone felt as if a new era was about to begin let alone a new year and nobody could blame them after the events of the last few days and the previous year. There was something that was impossible to keep under wraps and that was the date and time of the wedding. Preparations were put on hold until after trial but everyone knew that New Year's Day was not one for recovery but for action.

The concert hall was to be used for the reception. Soon the cat was out of the bag; gifts and cards kept arriving in large numbers and so did the press. One potent question kept being asked. How had they managed to keep their relationship secret for so long? It was a question two days later that an irate Senator Lyon asked people, especially the hapless Finch who he accused of being incompetent and complacent.

At the hotel, Bobby had the dogs on hand and warned a few people that if they overstepped the mark, the dogs would leave their very unpleasant and long-lasting calling card. It was a very effective deterrent as most reporters were aware of the result of a single bite from a German shepherd dog. Those who were most inconvenienced were the guests in the hotel but surprisingly all but one got caught up in the whirlwind of happiness and expectation.

Stephen had to go back to *Hillington* in the evening and was thankful to get away. The press followed but Chuck had organised a new gate at the airfield and by it was a guard who shut and locked the gate immediately he was safely inside. Gradually the hours ticked away and the time drew near for the happy event. Joanne came to see Rachael and they hastily decided on her bridesmaid dress. Joanne was the one and only attendee as all the other potential bridesmaids were needed in the choir.

Stephen felt it was time to talk to his mother. He telephoned her and asked for her forgiveness for concealing everything from her but Martha respected his reasons and reassured him on that front. She said she would go out at a convenient moment and buy a new hat. This time there could not be any possible opposition for such an action. Later the next day, Eric arrived with a large package from her, which contained a plethora of legal papers. He was stunned when he read her letter, which contained the following:

...my husband has been pressing me to sell the Retreat as he wants money to pay off his creditors. I have reminded him time and again that the Retreat is mine and the deeds bear my name alone. I have seen my lawyer and completed the necessary forms for it to be yours and Rachael's with immediate effect. The deeds are hereby enclosed. It is my wedding present to you both and also your 21st birthday present, which my husband either forgot or deliberately ignored. I am proud of you, my son, and not just what you have achieved recently and wish you every joy and many years to enjoy the gardens, lake, house and all its contents. They now belong to you and your wife who I welcome most heartily as my daughter-in-law.

How wonderful. Strange that she referred to my father as "my husband", thought Stephen with a shake of his head. He showed it all to Bobby who beamed spontaneously and automatically punched Stephen's shoulder. Stephen was pleased that he and Rachael could now have until Monday morning on their own instead of being amongst others at the hotel.

Saturday dawned and the final preparations were put into place. The band was ready and so was the choir, organist and Rev Wilkes. Stephen arrived from Hillington at 11.30 am to loud cheers. He remembered Chuck's discomfort of his collar a few years earlier and wished he'd been more sympathetic. His mother, cousins and aunt arrived and a few hand-picked members of staff. On the Williston side to begin with there was only Sarah, Charlie and Marcus's cousin Mark as all their other family were in England. Most of the invited staff from *Frankfare* sat on the bride's side to even things up. These included Francis Richards and Eric, who looked completely uncomfortable in a hired suit.

Rachael entered just after the clock had struck 12 o'clock noon. She looked stunningly beautiful on Marcus's arm. Sarah and Charlie were on the front seats looking on with great pride and joy. Bobby checked his pocket for the 15th time for the location of the ring. The ceremony began with a hymn and Stephen felt as if he were dreaming. *It is actually happening*, he thought. He listened to the words and concentrated. There was a very intense moment when Rev Wilkes said: *If any man can show any just cause why they may not lawfully be joined together, let him now speak or else hereafter forever hold his peace.*

There was a silence for three or four seconds, which seemed like an eternity. Stephen prayed his luck would hold. The ceremony continued without interruption and the only hitch occurred as the choir left for the vestry when the head boy chorister's cassock got caught up in a stand of flowers and the vase hit the deck. The bells rang out and Rachael remembered her A. E. Houseman poem, *On Bredon Hill* where *still the steeples hum.* Except, unlike the Houseman poem, her occasion was a happy ending.

The band played, the people cheered and the reception was a success. The cake had been designed by William, Stephen's cousin, who made a speech in place of the absent George. He also managed to pull the wool over a few people's eyes by saying George had gone to Florida because of his health problems and was very sorry not to be present.

As the evening came, Stephen and Rachael changed and prepared to leave. Only a handful of people knew where they were going. The media were absolutely enraged when, after Stephen drove away, many of the bandsmen and women blocked the road to prevent the happy couple being followed. Less than three quarters of an hour later, they were at the Retreat by the lake and on their own. They looked at each other.

'Hello, Mr Robinson. And now you are all mine.'

'Hello yourself, Mrs Robinson. At last you are mine too.'

'What a lovely place this is; you realise this is the first time I have been inside. Pity we only have two nights.'

'We will come back here next Fall when showbiz time is over.'

'Your father will put a stop to that idea.'

'He can't do anything about it because it does not belong to him.'

'Who does it belong to? Your mother?'

'It did but it now belongs to you and me. It is now our home. It is our wedding present from my mother and belongs to both of us.'

Rachael was stunned into silence. When she did manage to speak, she said: 'There can't be many girls who go from prison to palace in just a few days. It will take quite a while for all of this to sink in.'

They revived themselves by the warm fire that had been prepared by one of the servants and drank tea. The servants who had been employed by Martha then left for the pair to be on their own. Then it was time to consummate their love and their marriage. They spent the whole of Sunday there and actually went through the motions of trying to fish. They caught nothing but did not care.

Early on Monday morning after the briefest of honeymoons, it was time to pack. They called in at *Hillington* where Bobby was waiting. He was adamant that he did not want to make the journey with them as a threesome but they protested. In the end they had a compartment each and Bobby had the dogs with him for company. They took the morning train, which was scheduled to arrive in Houston 64 hours later. It was not long before *Frankfare* had been left behind with its memories being more bitter than sweet.

43. The Way Out to the West

George Robinson arrived back on the day after their departure; his face was as black as thunder when he was briefed with the latest events but Martha only smiled. He went into the house to telephone to try and wheedle some concessions out of the senator. Senator Lyon, his mind distorted by a mixture of twisted anger and lack of logic, was having none of it. In his book George had failed and he, the senator, had been let down badly and he did not tolerate failure. Together with the hapless Finch he, George F Robinson, was a convenient whipping post.

The faces of the three on the train were in complete contrast and the dogs were enjoying being with Bobby constantly. The journey was long and only arduous towards the end when they all felt that they had had too much of a good thing. Just after midnight on Thursday, they drew into Houston to be met by Bond's staff. They looked at the dogs with consternation but Bobby only glared at them and they averted their gaze.

Their lodgings were comfortable and they did not realise they had longer time in bed because each of them had forgotten to adjust their timepieces. After breakfast Mr Bond joined them and after the briefest of courtesies outlined what was in store. There would be a rehearsal for everyone that afternoon. Bobby and Stephen would go to the airfield and check the equipment and test the machines. The ground crew had been hand-picked and they would be part of the "circus" and travel with them constantly. Afterwards, they would study the routine and familiarise it which should be easy. All this took an hour and a half which left Bobby time to give Smasher and Grabber a run around the field.

In the afternoon, the rehearsal began. Stephen and Bobby were in their F2 whilst a veteran flier called Bill Rodgers took the place of the Count. His plane had been converted as much as possible to look like a German Fokker but without being overzealous. They would do several circuits and then Bill would be shot down with fake smoke set off by the tail. The ammunition would be blanks as there was absolutely no need for live rounds being fired. There would be enough noise anyway.

Bond had taken every precaution. There would be some sounds of gunfire coming out of loudspeakers when this was needed. Then, behind some covered canvas the German tanks would appear with extras from the local population taking the parts of the soldiers. Apart from one tank which had been acquired and shipped across the Atlantic the rest were mostly made of rubber and were mounted on simple rollers.

At the final assault by Stephen and Bobby, the tanks would topple and the extras fall down as if dead. There were various flashes and liberal amounts of bangs. Then Stephen and Bobby would circle around in triumph, the whole episode taking just under 30 minutes. When Bobby told Bond that for the moment he would be pilot due to Stephen's foot wound which was still healing, he pointed out nobody would recognise them in their kit.

The rehearsal went smoothly and efficiently. Bond informed them that they would perform two weekends in Houston and then move on. During the second week the film company would be arriving and they would spend two or three days acting under their orders. The coming Saturday was for an invited audience in the morning and paying public in the afternoon. It all augured well.

Mr Bond showed them the itinerary for the next forty weeks. They would visit twenty or twenty-one different places with airfields and complete their tour by the end of October. They would have a holiday between November and the end January and then resume in the western part of the US for 1920.

They were contracted for two years with an option on both sides for another year. Mr Bond said it would be unlikely for that to happen if his estimations were correct. On the first Saturday morning, VIPs and their staff poured in to be greeted, wined and dined. It all went splendidly and effectively with all participants breathing a sigh of relief when it was over. In the afternoon they felt more confident; the crowds cheered and threw their hats in the air and there were many of them. Sunday afternoon was just as effective and very enjoyable for all concerned as there was no pressure whatsoever on them.

During Monday, the film crews arrived and set up. There was time for the participants to have some sightseeing and the dogs to be walked. Tuesday started with a vengeance and there was a lot of arguing with the film director. It took more than two dozen attempts before he was satisfied and this left them all weary and irritable. Consequently they were all glad when the second weekend was over and they moved on to their next venue, which was Austin.

Mr Bond went through the drill with the "extras" but there was little for the others to do. However, they were by no means bored, especially Rachael for whom the world had been opened. Coupled with that, she was snuggled up at night to the man she loved and in a blissful state that at one time, she had thought would never happen. Bobby and Stephen were happy and enjoying their time in the air as it was just like the early days at *Hillington*. What was more important was that now there was nobody shooting at them as had been the case only three or four months previously.

The spring passed all too quickly and the summer was upon them. Rachael was drafted into office duties because one of the other travelling office girls found she was pregnant and returned home. Rachael could not believe the salary that she was receiving. One of the girls in the office took her into the city and induced her to buy a couple of new dresses. She appeared in a new stunning summer dress at dinner in the mess room shortly afterwards and went to choose her meal.

There was an involuntary drop in sound and conversation was halted whilst as least twenty pairs of eyes followed her progress. She was quite oblivious to this fact, of course, and continued carefully sifting through the tray of vegetables in order to find specimens that had not been murdered by the semi competent canteen staff. Vernon Bond brought his meal tray and sat by Bill Rodgers and nudged him when she appeared.

Bill's eyes were already fixed on Rachael and so were those of Jessie Keaton who had recently joined them. Jessie had found difficulty getting work when returning home after the war and in desperation had written to Stephen enquiring whether there was an opening for him. He had been snapped up straight away and within days had joined the company. Rachael went to fetch some cutlery and looked around to see if there were any familiar faces.

Vernon Bond was the first to speak: 'Look at that, Bill. Isn't that really something. Wow and wow again. Stephen Robinson sure is the luckiest guy.'

'True, but look what he had to go through to get there,' said Bill Rodgers.

'She's worth it. Really good-looking, film star figure and such a lovely nature. She does not even have to wear make-up. What I would go through or give to have someone like that.'

'If you wish it, I will be on the lookout for you, Mr Bond. My agency fees are very reasonable.'

'Bill, I am beginning to appreciate you more and more. I just wish I could find the right word to describe her.'

There was a pause.

'Delectable,' said Jessie.

'Just so!' said Bond bringing his fist down on the table. 'Absolutely spot on. It's the word to describe the fairer sex without a male appearing lecherous. Spot on, Jessie!'

By now Rachael had seen them and they arose when she arrived.

'Please do not get up. May I join you?'

'Of course.' The reply of the unison trio was immediate. Rachael began the conversation.

'You all seemed deep in thought as I came across. What was the subject?'

The others felt guilty seeing she had been the subject. Bill had to think quickly.

'The Shepherds of the Delectable Mountains.'

'My goodness. Deep stuff for this time of day. Well, there's four of us here and there were four shepherds. Who's who?'

There was a silence as the men were caught out. Bill managed to recover.

'That's easy,' he said. 'Jessie is the one with Knowledge; Mr Bond is the man with Experience; I am ever Watchful up in the skies; and you, dear Rachael, are Sincere.'

'That's quite a compliment, Bill.'

The subject immediately changed, much to the relief of Jessie who had never even heard of *Pilgrim's Progress*. He was left alone with her soon afterwards as the other two had duties.

'Thank you for looking after my husband when you were in France. He is very fond of you. You must tell me all about yourself sometime.'

'Rather ordinary except for the time in France. Wish I was educated better. Now the others have gone tell me who or what is *Pilgrim's Progress*.'

'A book by an English writer named John Bunyan. Spent a lot of time in jail as a result of being a Nonconformist.'

'I did not have much schooling and I have nothing much to tell you. I'm no shepherd with knowledge. I feel a bit of a dummy beside Mr Bond and Bill. I know all about you, though. I remember visiting Stevie in hospital and bringing your letter. Best tonic he could have had at that time. You should have seen the effect on him. He soon got better.'

Rachael smiled happily. They talked for another few minutes before Jessie had to leave. Rachael felt an inward contentment that she had never experienced before. She wondered if it would last and suddenly thought of her old life at *Frankfare* and of her parents. She shrugged off any negative thoughts and went back to her office yet during the next few months there were on odd occasions feelings of foreboding. Unrequited feelings which arrived inexplicably and made her shiver whatever the temperature.

Memphis, Nashville and Connecticut all passed and Charleston beckoned. On one Friday evening when they were free many of the "circus" attended the local cinema and found themselves looking at their own exploits. It was very gratifying when all of the cinema audience clapped little knowing that the protagonists were all sitting in the audience.

During that week, some adjustments were made to the choreography but it did not cause any major incursion on their free time. Washington and Philadelphia all went well and at last they prepared to go to the final venue for that year which was their own airfield at *Hillington*. Any doubts Mr Bond had about numbers were dispelled when he saw the advance bookings and tickets sold. Like two or three of the other places, *Hillington* was over-subscribed.

Charleston had the most visitors as Independence Day had fallen on a Friday so that the *circus* had been added to the weekends activities. Another addition to the coffers had been the selling of lottery tickets and the prize for the winners had been a tour with Bobby and Stephen and a photo-call. That had been a real money spinner. They all tried not to feel too guilty or complacent about their newly acquired affluence.

Gradually, familiar sights and sounds emerged as they got nearer home. Rachael and Bobby were looking forward to seeing their parents and brother Charlie as well as friends from the band. Rachael had kept in touch with friends whilst on the circuit and described in detail where they were especially to her bridesmaid Joanne Radstock who had made it possible for she and Stephen to come together.

It was a delight and surprise when they all learned that Charlie and Joanne had been hitting it off and seeing a lot of each other. Joanne was quite explicit in her letter and confessed she had done all the running with the shy and quiet Charlie. What amused them more than anything was the postscript Joanne had written on the bottom of the letter.

She said she was not worried if Charlie did not pop the question within the next couple of months because 1920 was a leap year and she would do it on February 29th as permitted by St Patrick! Finally, they all reached the airfield and were greeted with big hugs from Chuck and Emma and handshakes from the staff. Stephen managed to get Emma on her own.

'How's it going, big sis?'

'Fine, little brother. How's married life?'

'Fine. Just fine. There is something I must tell you though.'

'Which is?'

He went up and whispered so the others would not hear: 'I think my wife's wobblers are just a mite bigger than yours.'

There was no verbal response but this time the slap on his arm was much harder than on previous occasions and may even have had a slight edge!

Some of the staff stayed at the airfield but Mr Bond and others were billeted with Marcus and Sarah at the hotel. One thing Sarah mentioned to her family was Vernon Bond's cavalier attitude to his bills. He only took a cursory look at his cheques and signed without a moment's hesitation. On one occasion, Sarah asked him if he was satisfied with the price of some article to which Bond replied that he knew when he was dealing with honest people.

'Waste of time when dealing with beautiful people like you,' he said.

Sarah felt warm inside and looked a different woman now that she was no longer a modern day slave.

After Rachael was reunited with her parents and Charlie for a short while, it was all systems go to look after the influx so she and Stephen repaired to the Retreat for some privacy and, more important, to recharge their human batteries. Whilst this was happening Stephen made some mental plans.

Hopefully, he would see his mother on Sunday at church and then cope with any fresh verbal assault by George later which was bound to come. He was not ready to go to *Frankfare* as he was sure that George would never give up with his demands on him and knew there would be shouting and disagreement.

No; he wanted to be in the right frame of mind for his performance on the airfield. Monday would be concerned with rehearsals for Tuesday 11th was to be a commemoration of the Armistice so he hopefully, he could defer seeing his father until after the parades and unveiling of the memorial. From the 12th onwards, it was the holiday season for all the group and, although they all were enjoying their work, they were looking forward to a break immensely.

On the Saturday morning, the crowds were there in abundance and all were enthralled with the spectacular show that ensued. One advantage of the *Hillington* airfield was that it had trees on one side plus the lake on the other and thus no opportunity for gaining a free viewing space or gate-crashers to gain access.

Saturday afternoon also went well and in the evening when all the crowds had dispersed they all had a well-earned drink and indulged in a period of back slapping and self-congratulation. It was, however, well deserved. Stephen and Rachael left the lakeside Retreat the next morning and as there was no show at that time of the day went and joined the others at church. Rev Wilkes was delighted to see them as were all the congregation to such an extent that well-wishers caused delay and the service started five minutes late. Stephen barely had time to greet his mother and kiss her. She handed him a note which was from George and demanded a meeting immediately after morning service. There was now no chance of leaving it until Tuesday as he had hoped.

'Where's father?' said Stephen, opening the letter and reading it.

'Not coming. Hasn't done so for many, many weeks. His faith has gone.'

'So I have got to go home. He wants to try and make me crawl.'

'I am afraid so. I hardly see him. We are virtually living separate lives.'

That perturbed him as he loved his mother dearly and her well-being was very important to him. He realised at that moment all vestiges of feeling for his father had vanished. *What a place to have such a revelation*, he thought. He looked at the acerbic and abrasive contents of the letter and realised he could indeed not now wait until after Armistice Day as it would be on his mind while he was in the air. He was afraid that his concentration would suffer and that would be potentially harmful to others. He would go to *Frankfare* at once and get it over with.

'It will have to be quick as we have the show. I will go and get my kit on and be ready. I take it you are going back to *Frankfare* and will be there, mom?'

'Yes. I will be there; hopefully to support you. Try not to provoke him too much, please, my darling.'

'Mother dear, that will be impossible. What has sent him over the edge?'

'One thing was giving you the Retreat for a wedding present. It was mine to give, though. But the biggest trouble is his insane jealousy, my darling.'

'Of whom?'

'You, dear, you.'

'Me? How come? I can't believe he has reason to be jealous of me.' Stephen was incredulous.

'Your achievements and fame, against all the odds. You have the limelight and not him. Oh yes, he is one of the old-fashioned brigade who feels that sons should follow in father's footsteps without question. That's not the whole picture. If he is boss over you, he can get some of the reflected glory as well as showing the locals that he is the real kingpin by having you as his subordinate.

'And then there is Bobby turning out a hero as well; a man who stood up to him, defeated him and for all to see. Everybody is glad about it which makes him more and more angry. And there was Bobby's parents for what can only be described as great release for them. It has given the bakery workers hope and there is much more union activity, much to your father's disgust.'

'It is hard to understand. He is rich and still has some power.'

'Don't you believe it, dearest. He has gambled away a lot and spent things on luxuries. Look at the cost of the share in the aeroplane that he bought for no good reason and behaves in it like a reckless teenager. He does not come to my bedroom any more. All I have now is the comfort of knowing my children are happily married and are doing very well at what they do. Tell Rachael I am looking forward to seeing her.'

'She is looking forward to seeing you but without father being there. I still can't understand about the jealousy bit.'

'Do you remember years ago when we were playing some piece by Mendelssohn and somebody quoted the composer's father?'

'Not offhand. What did he say? Remind me.'

'Abraham Mendelssohn said, *Firstly, I was known as the son of my father. Now I am known as the father of my son.* That is an exact replica of George Robinson's status.'

'I am beginning to understand…I will slip back to the hotel, change and then see him. It grieves me to say this, mother, but I shall tell him that from that point on I shall ignore any communication from him and make a complete break. Just as grandfather did to his sister. I am not bothered in the least about my inheritance; my cousins can have it. From now on, it will be as if I have no father.'

44. Animando

After changing into his kit, Stephen quickly snatched a leftover mince pie off one of the breakfast room tables. He was surprised when Bobby, already kitted out, arrived with Smasher and Grabber who greeted Stephen excitedly. He fussed them and looked for an explanation from his friend.

'Hello, mate,' said Bobby.

'Hello yourself, buddy. What are you doing here? You lost or something?'

'Not at all. Just saw your mother and she told me what is afoot so I am taking you in. You're not going to be on your own AND by the way, that is the wish of Emma and Chuck. I'll wait by the car but my furry friends and I are going to be on hand if you need us.'

'Surely you don't think it is going to be as bad as that. He is not going to kill me.'

'Hopefully not, but I am not taking any chances. We've come through a lot, you and I. More than ten people have in two lifetimes and I don't want to see it all go up in smoke thanks to George C. Robinson. He is capable of just about anything. I see you are ready in your gear. That will save going back to the hotel. Come on, let's go and get it over.'

The drive was pleasant for early November and within thirty minutes they were at the entrance to *Frankfare*. The gate man looked at them suspiciously and flinched when Smasher took a dislike to him and growled.

'I am sorry, Mr Stephen. I have orders not to let any of the Williston family in under threat of being fired.'

'Open the gates, Eric, or I will fire you when I get in charge of this place.'

Smasher growled again.

'Just tell Mr Robinson that I threatened you with the dogs. It's payment for that extra piece of wedding cake you stole.'

Eric opened the gates but it was obvious he was worried. There was an atmosphere of foreboding which seemed to permeate the whole complex. There was plenty of activity as George had asked for staff to do overtime to prepare for the Armistice commemoration.

'You're not really going to give in to him, are you?' said Bobby. 'You're going to see this next year with the "circus" through? Then come back to it, perhaps?'

'Of course not. What a silly question. I am going to tell him that he and I will only meet again by accident. The subject of my return is closed. I will simply ignore all communication with him. I'll be back shortly. Don't worry about a thing.' With that statement, he disappeared into the house.

Bobby was anxious though and on his guard. The dogs were restive and seemed to sense there was something afoot as they were not let off the lead for a frolic on the grassed area. It was Martha that greeted Stephen. She took him by the arm to the office then had a hug. She looked at him.

'You were a boy this time last year. Now you really are a man.'

'That's what war does to you. Rachael sends her love. Now I hope this is not going to take long as we have a show this afternoon and people are arriving already. I don't want to get into a queue and be delayed, otherwise the redoubtable Chuck will separate my essentials from my necessaries.'

Martha sported a smile and they chatted about happy things, especially the wedding and the fact that Martha had the sort of daughter-in-law she always wanted. She was quite intrigued and full of admiration how they had kept their association and intentions from she and George for such a long time. It was not long before an unsmiling George came into the room and went straight behind his desk. There was no greeting, no handshake and when he eventually looked up, there was a heavy scowl on his face.

'I won't mince words. I am well informed that today is the last day of this obscene circus of yours. When do you intend coming back and taking your responsibilities seriously? That's what I want to know. You should be at your desk this week.'

'By responsibilities, I presume you mean those I owe to you and *Frankfare.*'

George bashed his fist on the desk and said: 'Of course I damn well do. And don't be a smart ass with me. You have been given leave long enough.'

'Leave is not the word, father. It's called conscription. That is over and done with. At this moment, I have a choice as to my movements.'

'Don't quibble with me. Your duty is here as heir to this empire and you will be back on Wednesday to carry out that duty.'

'On Wednesday, my wife and I are taking a holiday somewhere. Then next year at the end of January, I will be resuming my role with our company and fulfilling my contract.'

'What contract? Cancel it. It can't be legal. You were underage.'

'Not when I signed it. I was twenty-one years old, a fact you have never acknowledged. In fact I was twenty-two last week, in case you have forgotten.'

'What if I did. You have had plenty out of me and dipped into my purse during your short lifetime and I get nothing in return.'

'It is possible that I have had more material things than most kids, father, but the fact is you have conveniently forgotten a citizen's right in this country of ours. I do not have to work for you if I do not wish to do so and I do not wish it. I am not a slave. I am earning more in a month that you are prepared to give me in 5 years and I'm enjoying it immensely. And there is the prospect of more to come. Also, I am not stuck behind a desk here and listening to you ranting at mother and me and others.'

'I see. It's like that, is it? You have seemed to have forgotten that the bible says—*Honour thy father and thy mother*.'

'Honour you, father? The way you behave? It also says somewhere. "A man shall leave his father and mother and hold fast to his wife and the two shall be as one." Genesis, I believe, and again in Matthew.'

'My, my. Who is the biblical genius, then?'

'Don't be sarcastic, father. It doesn't become you. You can't have it both ways. What does become you is the fact you have not even acknowledged Rachael as my wife or asked to see her or congratulated us.'

'Nor will I after giving her family refuge and then they walk out on us. What do you say to that?'

'If that is your attitude, I say this to you, father. You have become a loathsome and deceitful man. I am ashamed of you and wish you were not my father. You knew Rachael was innocent but you kept quiet because you are in debt to Senator Lyon, thanks to his loans and baling you out of your gambling debts. You and Detective Crawford between you concealed the existence of grandmother's ring and yet I found it in your desk.

'And that Sopwith plane that you bought a large share in. What was the purpose of the expense of that? Want to try and outfly me, father? You are not in the same class. I would not trust you with a kite in the park. The only way I'd ever come back here is not even as your partner. You would have to retire and take a pension. And that's more than you deserve.'

'Why, you little rat. How dare you say that.'

'Easily,' said Stephen, 'there is more I can and will say about you.'

'You have said all you are going to say, you little skunk.'

George picked up his whip and aimed at Stephen who ducked and hit George in the solar plexus. It was only a temporary victory as George was broad and muscular, quite unlike his son. Stephen turned to walk away but George grabbed him. The two grappled and fought, overturning the lamps, some figurines and other objects. Stephen was no match for George and a punch drove him into a glass cabinet containing whisky and other drinks.

The noise of smashing glass could be heard through the open windows and workers stopped in alarm. Martha screamed and tried to pull George off her son without success. She tried a second time but George's flailing arm caught her face and caused her nose to bleed. She fell on the floor holding her nose whilst blood ran down on to her white collar and blouse. George had his hands around Stephen neck and was choking him. His contorted face showed at that moment he was capable of anything.

'Damn you, I will kill you whether you are my son or not,' he said, tightening his grip.

Martha got up off the floor and picked up a paperweight off the desk and hit George over the head. It only stunned him but was enough for Stephen to roll clear. She screamed and shouted at her husband: 'He is not your son! He is not your son. Do you hear me, George? Do you hear? Damn you. HE IS NOT YOUR SON.'

George was about to do a fresh assault on Stephen but the door burst open to reveal Bobby and Smasher. He had taken the dogs for a walk and had heard the noise of the fight through the window and had charged around. The dog barked noisily and strained at the leash. George ignored Bobby for the moment as he sought clarification of his wife's statement. He had to shout above the din the dog was making.

'What do you mean he is not my son? What do you mean by that? Tell me what you mean, you lousy stinking bitch.'

'I mean what I say, George Robinson. I have known for some time although for an age I dared not admit it even to myself. You are not his father. His father is someone else. A human being, unlike you. And I am glad he is someone else's son as it means that there is no way he can be like you. Do you hear me, George? He is not your son. HE IS NOT YOUR SON.'

'Tell me, damn you, woman. Tell me whose he is.'

'No way will I tell you. You will have to torture me before I reveal his name. I will only tell you this, George. It happened when we went to New York that time back in '97 and you left me to continue your damn gambling. I was at my wits' end when you deserted me and luckily I met someone who I knew. Of course, it was wrong and I have lived with the guilt for a few years now after I saw the resemblance. I went with somebody kind and gentle for two days. Two lovely blissful days. Now I know. I can see his true father in him and it is not you.'

George for once was lost for words Stephen went over to his mother and said: 'Mother. Come with us to the airfield. You are not safe here.'

George recovered and said menacingly at Martha: 'Whose son is he, you treacherous little whore. Tell me now, I want to know.'

'Wouldn't you like to know, you philandering swine? Go to hell. I shall never tell you. I can tell you that his father is worth more than a hundred of you. A thousand of you. I am sorry about this, my son.' She turned to Stephen and sobbed. She was still bleeding.

'Don't worry, mother. Do not worry one little bit. That is the best news I could possibly have that this grotesque slob in front of me is not my father.'

George made to get up and whip Stephen again but Smasher snarled and Bobby had to hold him back.

George suddenly became aware of Bobby's presence.

'What the f*****g hell are you doing here? I told you never to come back. Get out. Get out before I send you into the next world.'

'You are welcome to try, Mr Robinson, but you would get more than you bargained for from this fine animal. I'm here just to make sure you do not cause any more grief and injury which seems to follow you around with the greatest of ease.'

'Get out! Get out, all of you. I never want to see any of you again.'

'Gladly, Mr Robinson. Gladly. We don't need you and we can all live happily without any help from you. Thank you for opening our letters and cables in the past but from now on, we can manage without any assistance from you.'

George had no answer to this but merely flung his whip on the debris as the others left. Many of the staff stared sympathetically as they made their way to the car. Stephen bundled his mother into the back seat unceremoniously. Grabber was rather irate in being tied up whilst Smasher was taken in alone. However, he was much fussed by Stephen and soon forgot his displeasure.

They drove flat out to the airfield and towards the end were held up by crowds. In the end Bobby had to overtake the stationary cars to get to the gate and received some jeers and nasty comments. The gate men let them through and they arrived at reception. Chuck appeared angry but immediately softened when he saw the state of his mother-in-law.

'What the hell has happened? Who is responsible for this?'

'George Robinson has flipped. We'll explain after the show. Get Emma to take mother out of the view of the public and news people while we get fully changed. We are late.'

'You certainly are,' said Chuck who was far from being pacified. However, Martha revealed all the salient details of what had just happened and soon put him right in between sips of water and smelling salts. Fortunately, there was only one reporter who had seen Martha's condition and queried it.

'Nosebleed,' said Stephen truthfully and that seemed to satisfy the man.

Meanwhile, back at *Frankfare* George cursing and fuming went to the bathroom to clean himself up and bind up a cut that had been caused when the cabinet overturned. He went to his drawer and put his pistol in his pocket. It took him a minute or two to get his car started and then he went off full pelt for the airfield, cursing anyone in the way. Some pedestrians had to dodge the car for fear of their lives and shook their fists. He was oblivious to all around him so great was his rage and madness. All the time he was travelling, he kept cursing and repeating the same words.

'I'll kill him. I'll kill him. If he's not my son, I'll kill him. I'll kill him anyway.'

Although the opening gambits were a little late starting, nobody seemed to mind. There were other features to start with and these took a while. There was great applause for all the pilots as they returned. During these manoeuvres

Bobby, Stephen and Bill walked towards their machines which were at the far end of the field. They duly checked all that needed to be done and then awaited the flare that gave them permission to taxi out.

Bill went first as he was in lieu of the Black Count. His aeroplane was decorated with the appropriate German logos and signs. He and circled round to a few misguided cheers and then loud boos a hissing noises as he came in lying low. Then Stephen and Bobby taxied out. Both of them said later that they saw movement at the end of one of the hangers and that it was the modified Sopwith "Pup". They saw Charlie remonstrating with somebody in the cockpit but then they flashed past and were unable to make anything of it. At that point it was a case of concentrating on the job in hand.

Bobby and Stephen were quite correct in what they saw but had more important things on which to focus their attention. Inside the "Pup" was none other than George. He had reached the airfield and none of the staff had paid any attention to this as he was a regular visitor, a shareholder and a pilot in his own rite. All eyes were now on what was happening above and nobody was paying attention to George Robinson. The "Pup" was on standby and on ground crew duty was none other than Charlie who was more than a little surprised to see George fully kitted out.

'Get her ready,' said George. 'Is it loaded?'

'Yes, but…'

'Get her started.'

'What's to do, Mr Robinson? This kite is on standby—'

'Just get her ready, Charlie, or it will be the worst for you.'

Charlie hesitated and that was enough for George to bring out his pistol.

'Do it, Charlie Williston, or by God I swear I will be forced to use this. I'll show him who is the best pilot.'

Charlie had no option but to swing the propeller and allow George to taxi out. Charlie had to almost dive out of the way to avoid being mangled. Nobody took any notice of the "Pup" until George got to the end of the runway and took off. Most people thought it was part of the act but further down near the office, Chuck and Emma soon realised something was badly wrong and watched with an ever-increasing alarm. Charlie ran to them and told them what had happened. Chuck left to seek out and inform Vernon Bond.

When Stephen had made the disparaging remark about George and the kite in the park, he could not have been more wrong. After only a couple of minutes in the air, Bobby and Stephen were taken totally by surprise when another aircraft appeared. At first they were unaware of it as they were pursuing Bill.

All at once, they heard the rat-a-tat-tat of machine gun fire behind them. Immediately, their training instinctively took over and they both forgot about Bill and took evasive action. It was as if they were suddenly back in France and the adrenalin was flowing in ever increasing quantities. George stuck to them like glue and fired again but still nothing hit the duo.

Suddenly, they had the refuge of some cloud. They flew miles out of their way and eventually decided to turn back and try to land and then make some sense out of this utterly insane situation. By now they both knew who was in the "Pup". George, in frustration and in the faster machine, pulled alongside so Bobby, who was at the controls, immediately pulled back and made for the clouds in a steep climb.

So did George who by this time was in an utter and completely demonic rage. Bobby turned and came out of the cloud in the hope of making a safe descent but at that moment both he and Stephen had no idea where they were, let alone the location of the airfield. It was bitterly cold. The duo continued to circle and sometimes gain and sometimes lose height exactly as was impressed on them months before by their instructors. All the time, Stephen felt completely impotent. The tension was made more unbearable as for a considerable time, there was no sign of George.

Suddenly, he appeared out of nowhere as the cloud dispersed just for a few seconds and came straight for them which made Bobby take the easiest escape route and, this time, dive. It was only seconds later that the canny George was on their tail and he opened fire. There was a lot of noise but no effect on Bobby and Stephen. It was then and only then that the men in both aircraft realised that George had been firing blanks.

In desperation, George drew alongside and fired his pistol. It was a pathetic gesture as Bobby immediately climbed and then circled and looked for landmarks. Soon they had reached the limit of their height and gingerly tried to plot a roundabout course for *Hillington* and, hopefully, safety. Both men now realised why George had managed to miss them when he had them firmly in his sights and knew that there should be no danger to them barring a collision.

They also knew that Bill had wisely left the scene and would make his way home. The thing now was what explanations would be given for this fiasco when they were finally back at the airfield. For a while, there was no sign of the 'Pup' and then they saw what was happening. It was plunging downwards in an uncontrollable spin and it was instantly obvious to both of them what had taken place. It was just as if they were back over French fields and German trenches.

George, not being familiar with such height and knowledge of G force, had pushed himself and his machine too hard. The forces of nature had taken over and in a reckless manoeuvre, he had found himself pinned to the side of his cockpit and unable to move. He had then either experienced a stroke or blacked out as he was, at that moment, completely impotent. For what seemed an interminable age, the other two watched helplessly and with increasing horror knowing full well what was inevitable.

The next few seconds were agony as George spun round and round and inevitably hit the edge of the lake with bits of the plane being scattered. Most of the spectators at the airfield were unaware of the tragedy but fifty or so people and some fishermen by the lake were horrified. A few knowledgeable spectators at the airfield only started to guess that something was amiss when Chuck from a distance had seen part of the spin and dashed off in his car followed by the emergency ambulance whose people had been jolted out of their lethargy as they had been expecting an easy and uneventful afternoon.

Bobby, after flying over the lake three times and realising the enormity of the situation, decided to return to base and landed safely. Bill had put some distance between the other two planes and only returned when he felt it was safe to do so. He arrived on the runway just as the announcer said there had been a technical hitch and calmed any fears. The timetable would have no further interruptions and stated that the winners of the ticket lottery would be able to meet the pilots as promised and there would be a repeat of the show. When the duo had reached the hangar, Bond was driven up in a car.

'I know it looks bad, gentlemen, but the show must go on. We will investigate thoroughly when everyone has gone home. Chuck, Charlie and the ambulance are down at the lake and will report when they know anything.'

Stephen and Bobby both felt numb in two different ways. The show did indeed go on but when it was over, the crowd dispersed with one topic of conversation on everybody's lips and that was that they had experienced a great afternoon. It would not register about the tragedy until they read the next available morning newspaper.

It was late on a gloomy afternoon and before long, it started to get dark. There were lots and lots of questions asked but as yet nobody could be absolutely certain that it was George in the plane as only Charlie had seen him take off and at that moment he was busy elsewhere. The press were told that they would be informed when the full facts emerged but this did not in any way satisfy them. It was left to the police to restore some sort of order, which was easier when it began to get dark.

They escorted everyone off the premises and prevented anyone following Stephen, Rachael and Martha who all went to the Retreat. Bobby and Charlie stayed at the airfield as did Emma and Chuck as they had made a permanent and very comfortable home there. Emma asked her mother if she wanted her with her but Martha said she would be fine with Rachael. At both locations in the evening, there was a lack of conversation and, more to the point, there was a lack of any visible grief.

45. 'When the Birdman Falls'

Early on Monday morning, the police telephoned to say that if all stayed put, they would visit both locations; there was no reason why they had to be altogether. The interviews were fairly short as it seemed a cut and dried case. George had simply had an unfortunate accident and that was that. The airfield remained closed and the three in the Retreat stayed put and tried to relax.

It was a special time for Martha as it was the first occasion she had been able to be with and talk to her daughter-in-law. The two women warmed to each other, which pleased Stephen very much. He left them from time to time to do some jobs around the house and at one point stifled any belligerent thoughts he might have by chopping a huge amount of logs.

An occasion did not arrive when he could speak to his mother alone about the events of the last occasion when he, his mother and George had been together. He admitted to himself later that at the time in the Retreat, he would never have had the courage to ask her about paternal matters. During the course of the day, a salvage team had reached the lake and begun the grisly job of finding George. It was fortunate that he had crashed near the side of the lake and not in the deeper middle.

The wreckage had pinpointed his location so it was not too hard for the diver to locate the body and what was left of the submerged part of the "Pup". Due to the location, it was impossible to keep the media away until further officers were drafted in and the area cordoned off.

In the evening, Stephen spoke to his wife and mother,

'What would the two most important women in my life say if we were to be up at the crack of dawn and go in early to the hotel?'

'I would like to stay here,' said his mother. 'It will be a shame to miss the service but I cannot face everyone just yet.'

'In that case, I will stay with you, mother,' said Rachael.

Thus in the morning Stephen went out at first light and avoided all but one insomniac reporter who followed him to the hotel back door. Fortunately, Marcus was already at work and sneaked him in quickly. It was not too long before crowds formed as well as a multitude of restive men from the press. It was not easy getting down to the church for the service; Stephen had to keep saying, 'All in good time gentlemen, all in good time.'

At the Armistice service on Tuesday morning, Rev Wilkes felt it appropriate to include George in his sermon and spoke of his contribution to the locality and its wellbeing at his hand. He said there would be opportunity to pay proper tribute at the appropriate time. Emma shed a few tears at that moment but nobody else except Frances Richards seemed to be deeply affected by the unexpected and untimely demise of George C. Robinson.

Vernon Bond and his escorts, who had stayed to help, shielded them from the press as they left church. The reporters were determined to get a statement and the narrow path was thronged with them as they attempted to block the way. They reckoned without Bond's men who were provoked too far and in the scrum punched two of the reporters who fell and brought down two more. Still the melee continued in a very undignified manner. At the church door, Rev Wilkes for a few moments hid his eyes with his hands and said that the first Armistice Day should never have ended like this. Stephen and Bobby were spirited off to the hotel and the reporters camped outside and refused to budge.

'Thanks for being here and on hand,' said Stephen to Vernon Bond.

'Think nothing of it,' said Bond. 'I am protecting my investment.'

'Is that all?'

'Of course not,' said Bond, becoming unusually irate. 'We have become friends. Or at least I damn well hope we have. As such I suggest that you have a press conference at the concert hall and get it over with and thus it will be out of our hair. If you agree, I will go outside and make a formal announcement. Two o'clock seems a good time.'

The others nodded in total agreement as it made a lot of sense.

'Sounds good to us,' said Charlie and proceeded to tell the family of his brush with death at George's hand. 'His face was absolutely bright red and contorted. I have never seen such a grisly sight,' said an unusually diffident Charlie.

411

The others realised Charlie must have been frightened and sympathised with him. After lunch Stephen, Bobby and Bond slipped out the back way of the hotel to the hall before anyone realised what was happening.

While the chairs were still being put in place by the hall stewards, Stephen looked at Bobby and said: 'Do you remember a few years ago one Christmas we were looking at our family trees? There was that confession of my ancestor, who of course, in all probability will not be my ancestor now.'

'Yes,' said Bobby. 'Vividly. The curse would end when the bird man would fall from the sky and into the mire.'

'Except that instead of the mire, it was the lake.'

Bond heard them and interjected, 'You two don't believe in that sort of stuff, I'm sure.'

'No, not really. It just seems a very strange coincidence, that's all.'

'That's all it is,' said Bond. 'Stay out of sight while they are all let in. When they are seated I will call order and make an announcement. Then come in.' He left them in deep thought.

'One thing is certain that if what my mother said is true, and I'm sure it is, then George is the last of the line. Perhaps that will be the end of it if there is such a thing as a curse. Perhaps we can live normal lives if Elizabeth Robinson's soul is satisfied.'

'Has your mother told you who your real father is?'

'Not yet. I'm still taking it all in. I meant what I said that it is a great relief to know George Robinson is not my father. At that point I felt a huge weight came off my shoulders. I only hope that my real father is somebody kind and one I can look up to and admire. And alive, of course.'

'Have you any idea? She might refuse to tell you.'

'Not at the moment. There's been no chance with all that has been happening. Quite honestly, it would be nice to let the dust settle before going down that road. My brain seems to be completely befuddled. If she does refuse then we'll have to do some digging. At the moment there are other matters that are more important but I shall want to know in time.'

When everyone was in the hall and settled Bond in his immaculate style prepared the way beautifully. He pointed out to the assembled company that this was a traumatic time for all the Robinson family and they should remember that and act sensitively. There would be orderly questioners picked by he, Bond. Anyone who overstepped the mark would be ejected if necessary by force. He pointed out the stewards by the walls strategically positioned who would do this. Bond beckoned Bobby, Stephen and Bill Rodgers to enter and then picked someone at random to start proceedings.

'Mr Robinson. We're all puzzled as to why your father joined the proceedings in the manner he did. Have you any theories?'

'He has been under a lot of pressure and has not been himself for some time. Things had been getting on top of him to such an extent that he was behaving very strangely.'

'Such as?'

'The business and the war.'

'Surely the business is in good shape? There have been no rumours of problems.'

'That did not stop him having bouts of depression. A few years ago he fell and hit his head. Occasionally, he had bouts of pain and was unpredictable in his behaviour and this might well account for what happened on Sunday.'

'But why did he suddenly decide to intrude into the proceedings in that fashion?'

Bond jumped in. 'He was angry with me. He desperately wanted to be in on the action and show he was a good pilot. After all, he was responsible for some of the funding for *Hillington* especially in the early days and he felt left out. We said he could have a fly around and show his skill at the end of the day but it appears that was not good enough for him. He took matters into his own hands and you all know the result.'

Here, Bond lied about allowing George to fly but he hoped in that way it would be a plausible answer take away some of the doubts and leading questions.

'Mr Williston. When was it that you knew something was wrong and what did you do at that point?'

'The same as any pilot would do in the same circumstances. Take evasive action. I did not know who was in the plane that suddenly appeared behind us. There was the sound of machine gun fire and at once I felt back in France and reacted accordingly. I think Mr Robinson was trying to surprise us; nothing more. Just his sense of humour.'

'Gentlemen,' said the smooth-talking reporter from the *Boston Herald*. 'There is a rumour that Mr Robinson had been using live ammunition in his practices recently. Was he of the belief that the "Pup" was loaded with live rounds and that he was actually trying to shoot you both down?'

There was a gasp at this point and a lot of murmuring but Bond put up his hands and waited for it to subside. He took the mettle again and said: 'All the aircraft were fitted with blanks on my orders and everyone informed of the situation. This has been our policy all along, in every location and was to prevent any risk of participants and spectators getting hurt. The aeroplane in which the airfield has a share was on standby at Mr Ellis's request and also contained no live ammunition.

'Mr Charles Williston took the live ammunition out last week on my instructions. There was plenty of noise from the blanks but no danger to a living soul. It has been like that all the time and all the places we have visited. No, gentlemen; there might have a bit of rivalry between father and son involved but that is all. I understand Mrs Robinson suggested that but Stephen assures me that there was no feelings of that sort where he was concerned.'

There were a few murmurs but although some remained sceptical, there was no doubt Bond had managed the situation admirably and contained possible awkward inquiries.

'Mr Rodgers. Were you alarmed while this was going on?'

'Very much so as I could hear shooting,' said Bill. 'I was surprised rather than alarmed to start with but when the script seemed to have been abandoned, I thought the best thing I could do was watch things at a distance. There was no help I could offer nor should I have intervened so eventually, I returned to base.'

'Mr Stephen. Now that you have lost your father, will you be taking up the reins of *Frankfare* and directing operations from now on.'

'Those will have to be in somebody else's hands as I am contracted to Mr Bond's company for at least one more year. That applies to Bobby and Bill and we will, of course, be honouring that contract.'

'Who will run the business at *Frankfare*? And all the other parts of the Robinson empire, for that matter?'

'I expect my mother will return to take a front seat in conjunction with my cousins, William and Gordon.'

'And then will you return?'

'Oh I expect they'll be so successful at running it their way that there'll be no room for me. I will decide on a career only when Mr Bond has no more use for me.'

There were smiles at this remark. There were a few more questions and then people prepared to leave. At last it was all over and the panel on the stage looked at each other with relieved expressions. Bobby and Stephen went out via the wings into the back room as they had done many times before with the orchestra and when they were out of earshot and prying eyes Bond met up with them they indulged in a period of self-congratulation.

'Well, you guys. I don't know how you see it but think that went off rather well seeing as we were in the middle of a very dangerous minefield.'

The others agreed and with no inhibitions sighed with relief again and slumped in their wooden chairs. Bond sensed their weariness and decided to put his foot down.

'Off you two go to the hotel and get some rest. No protests.'

That thought was least in the young men's minds and they trudged off to more comfortable surroundings. Sarah and Marcus welcomed them back with obvious relief on their faces.

The day before the funeral of George C Robinson, it began to rain. And rain it did so that the description of deluge in this case was completely accurate. However, early the next day, it abated a little but not for long. It was a typically dank, dark and dismal November day. As the coffin was taken into church, the mourners had to have the cover from their umbrellas before they filed into the porch. They sat down and waited for the minister to begin.

Rev Wilkes spoke of George's contribution to the prosperity of the community and this statement was justified. He also spoke of George's contribution to the artistic life of North West Boston, a fact that also could not be denied. There was music and some hymns sung but the only instrument that played on the day was the organ. The band members that were present were in the congregation. Rev Wilkes said there would be a memorial service and concert in due course. However, the overriding memory for Fanny Richards, for the minister and the staff that were there that all were dry-eyed. There were no tears to speak of for George C. Robinson; *Jekyll and Hyde* George who had started life so well and ended in the sight of those he sought to impress so ingloriously.

Outside the rain resumed and poured down as the close family stood by the grave side. The pall bearers lowered their burden in to a grave that was rapidly filling with water. The coffin was immediately submerged in a murky brown liquid and disappeared long before it reached the bottom; lumps of mud fell in at the same time.

Stephen whispered to Bobby and said: 'Now tell me there's no such thing as the Robinson curse. If you remember she said: *It will end when the bird man falls from the sky and into the mire.* Makes no difference that the mire is on a different day.'

'I'll go along with that,' said Bobby, albeit reluctantly. He shivered involuntarily and hoped in vain that the sun would appear and the obsequies would be soon completed.

It was a merciful release for all of them when it was all over. They lost no time in getting into the transport which efficiently took them away to the wake. They reached the concert hall where they greeted all who had attended. Martha shook hands with everyone as they entered; Stephen was at her side followed by Emma and Chuck. After the last persons to arrive, which were Wilkes and Gossage, all were bidden to partake of the buffet. They were having a drink when to their surprise, Senator Lyon appeared. After a few minutes, he saw Stephen was on his own and made a beeline for him. There was no chance of avoidance so Stephen waited to hear what he had to say. Lyon put his totally false and insincere smile coupled with his million-dollar dulcet accent.

'Ah, Mr Robinson junior. Stephen. I wanted a word with you, if you have a moment, please.'

Stephen kept calm and cool and decided to play him at his own game.

'Of course, Senator. Always happy to assist our local politicians whatever their colour.'

The senator was aware by now that Stephen was not a pushover but even so he did not waste time and got straight to the point.

'I wonder when it will be that you will get around to settling your father's affairs including his obligations to us.'

'Obligations? I have no knowledge of his financial affairs whatsoever. He never mentioned anything to me. In any case, this is no concern of mine.'

'O come now. We do not want any unpleasantness over this. We have your father's notes and have every intention of securing their redemption. The banks were most reluctant to give him further credit so he came to me.'

'You took a big risk doing that.'

'Not really. He put up your very lovely Retreat as collateral for part of them.'

'Then you are in for a big disappointment, Senator, and are unaware of the true situation. As I understand it, Father's borrowings were private arrangements between him and yourself and unsecured loans. Let me assure you I have no reason to pay you anything. As to the Retreat, then I have to say Mr Robinson deceived you. It's always been the property of my mother until recently.'

Senator Lyon was visibly shocked at that revelation. He recovered and said: 'Surely your father must have had at least a half share?'

'Not even one per cent.'

'Was he aware of this fact?'

'I don't know and I really do not care. Mother always kept the deeds locked up at the bank together with some other valuable possessions just in case we had a fire. As far as I know, he never bothered about them. No point. Just left it to mother.'

'You said it was the property of your mother until recently. What do you mean by that?'

'I mean, senator, that she has disposed of it.'

The senator looked white. He recovered and said: 'I beg to differ that it is no concern of yours. There is the law. By the way, have you not heard of such a thing as family honour?'

'Of course I have. First, I would like to ask you a question. Have you ever heard of a man called Michel de Montaine?'

'I can't say that I have. What is that to do with your father's debts.'

Stephen was unperturbed and continued very confidently whilst enjoying the senator's increasing discomfort.

'He was a French philosopher and one of his famous sayings was *death, they say, acquits us of all obligations.* So, sir, don't think that you can swing my father's debts on to me. If I may say so somewhat euphemistically, Senator, you have backed the wrong horse, and the wrong polo player on top of that. You are going the same way as the *Red Sox* are at the moment. An irrevocable decline.'

The senator stiffened at that remark. 'You realise I can make life difficult for you. I have a lot of influence.'

'I doubt that, senator.'

'I can't expect you, especially at your young age, to understand the working of politics and business. I have lots of clout in both and can call in a few favours if you are stubborn over this.'

'Senator, let me enlighten you with a few facts even if it appears that I am being somewhat immodest. Bobby Williston and I have come back home as heroes. We have been wined, dined and feted enormously. There have been dozens of people in high exalted positions who wanted a slice out of each of us, many, mostly for their own ends.

'The photo calls have been endless but a by-product has been that we have been offered many favours from people including those who don't like your politics or some that even despise you. I have powerful friends of my own now even in the unlikely event of your being re-elected. Realistically, you are history. There's an important factor in this equation of which you are unaware.

'It is simply this: Mr George Robinson disinherited me not long before his tragic accident. You can ask my mother for confirmation of that fact as she was present when he informed me of his decision. I have no connection any more with *Frankfare.'*

The senator looked even more perturbed at this and made as if to say something else but Stephen cut in.

'Talking of honour, Senator, if anything, you owe me and plenty. In fact you owe me several times over. Twice your wayward and disreputable son attempted to rape my wife. She in turn had to spend time in jail for something she did not do and you well knew this fact. How you could live with yourself after that I do not know. Mr Robinson must have told you that my wife said it was the ring that did the damage, which was something you both concealed. It was lucky that I knew exactly where to go to find it but I had to spend a lot of money on my attorney just to get an innocent person acquitted.'

'We paid your costs.'

'You had no choice and you may have to pay out a lot more to my wife very soon. It will not done with any remorse on your part. It doesn't alter the fact that for a time, I went through hell as did my family and the Willistons. The culpability for that belongs to you and your degenerate and totally immoral son. There is an open secret that he will never make his way in the polo world. He is too much of a liability.

'After being close to death several times in France and escaping by the skin of my teeth, I come back home with high expectations only for you to spoil the run up to my wedding and all with the complicity of my father. What price do you put on that? My cousins and mother are running *Frankfare* so you must deal with them but don't raise your hopes one iota. That's all I have to say.'

'Very well. But you have not heard the last of this.' Senator Lyon swung on his heel and walked off angrily.

Stephen watched him go and smiled. Senator Lyon was a beaten man but still refused to admit it. The thought of defeat was an anathema, an invasion of his divine right. A familiar voice behind him interrupted his thoughts.

'What was that all about?' said Bobby who had been keeping an eye on proceedings from a discreet distance.

'Demands for money with menaces. The debts of Mr George C Robinson which the senator won't now recoup.'

'I hope you told him where to get off.'

'He can take a very long walk off a very short pier!'

Bobby's laugh caused people to frown disapprovingly, believing the occasion demanded more respect. Bobby noted their faces, bowed and smiled condescendingly.

46. Finale

The days of November were punctuated by dealing with George Robinson's estate. Although Stephen had told Senator Lyon that he had been disinherited, this had not been put into writing and when the will was read, all the family were surprised that Emma, Stephen and Martha received a quarter share, the other quarter shared between William and Gordon.

Stephen saw his cousins and came to a business arrangement with them that pleased them greatly. Soon preparations were in hand for Christmas and all the musicians in the family were drafted in to take part. After Christmas, there was a New Year Concert which had a packed audience and children. The first item was the overture to *William Tell*. They were in the queue to go on stage when Rachael spoke to her brother and husband.

'It will be soon that we'll be off and back to work. No more the idle rich for us.'

'I can't believe that any of us would want to be like that forever,' said Stephen.

'It says in my programme that Rossini was like that and said so openly.'

'How come?'

'Well, after *William Tell*, he did next to nothing and a friend asked him about writing a new opera. He replied: *I have a passion for idleness as you have a passion for work.*'

The others laughed.

'Well, I am looking forward to work but I wonder for how long this will last,' said Bobby. 'We must enjoy it while we are able.'

Bobby's reservations were well founded. During the summer, Mr Bond's prediction that the *flying circus* as it became to be known would last only two years at the most proved to be completely accurate. They all had earned a great deal of money added to which the cheques rolled in for the film rights. They received many offers to speak at functions and this only added to their wealth.

At times Rachael felt quite overwhelmed. She used some of her money to help equip her parents' hotel with some new furniture. It was given a new coat of paint and, after some renovations, the place looked very smart.

By June 1920, Mr Bond brought them all together to announce that the end would come in the first week of September and the whole operation wound up. There was a feeling of sadness but everyone had been under no illusion that such an enterprise could last. They enjoyed the last few weeks but the crowds were only about half the size of the previous year.

In the first week of September, a huge farewell party was organised in Houston where proceedings began and lasted the whole day and half the night. There were speeches, speeches and more speeches, toasts and more toasts. Vernon Bond at one point got quite emotional. He praised everyone for working so well together; there had been very few instances of friction and as a result of this and all their efforts they had achieved all that they set out to do.

It had been successful enterprise and their efforts had inspired a lot of people in the country and even abroad. Every individual and their contribution was named personally and the group as a whole dubbed by Vernon Bond as *an esprit de corps*. He had organised a very fitting finale and at the end put his plan into action by clicking his fingers to the performers.

He picked up the loudspeaker.

'Ladies, gentlemen and friends,' he began. 'We are not going to end on just that; I think you will agree that some music is required. You have all heard and some of you have been singing the latest hit, that is George Gershwin's *Swanee* and that's what we are going to have now. At the pianoforte is the lovely Mrs Rachael Robinson and to lead the singing, her husband Mr Stephen Robinson and his brother-in-law Mr Robert Williston. Take it away, boys and girls.'

There followed two fortissimo renderings of Gershwin's new song followed by applause and cheers. When it had died down, Rachael struck up with *Auld Lang Syne*, which brought proceedings to a close but not the tears from many of the assembly, most of whom were grown men. Jessie was inconsolable.

Present at this occasion was none other than Mr Lilley who had been summoned to tie up any legal leftovers and make sure everything was concluded in apple-pie order. He sat there impassively without giving any indication of his innermost feelings. Bobby and Stephen went over to say *au revoir* and use the opportunity to thank him deeply for that which he had achieved for them several months before. When Lilley saw them coming, his face was wreathed in smiles and he literally jumped up to pump their hands.

'Good to see you, Mr Lilley,' said Stephen. 'We could not let this occasion go without thanking you for what you did for us and for giving the opposition the best bloody nose of their lives.'

'That goes for me too, sir, for seeing to the legal side of the hotel,' said Bobby.

'Believe you me, it was a great pleasure to be of service to you. There was one other reason that probably escaped your notice both of you not being in the legal profession.'

'Can you explain, sir, in layman's terms.'

'Easily,' said Lilley. 'There was another winner on that day and that was the law. It is no use having law in this relatively new country of ours if rich and influential people can manipulate it to their own advantage. Your case sent out shock waves in Boston and around and caused some changes. For that fact, I am really happy and truly thankful.'

'I think we both understand your sentiments on that, sir, but there's one thing at the time that puzzled me and still does.'

'Well, get it off your chest now, dear boy as it may be a very long time before we have the pleasure of each other's company again.'

'Quite so. It's this. How did you manage to get Frances Richards to testify for the benefit of my wife? She always appeared to be in Mr Robinson's pocket.'

'Still on your mind after all this time, eh? Well, you yourself told me that she was notorious for listening in. That made me put two and two together. She may have had some information, something that somebody had let slip. I had to devise a way to get her to talk without arousing suspicion.'

'How did you manage that?'

'Luckily, she has a telephone at home. This was in case she was needed at short notice. I asked her to come into town one morning when she was off duty and that we would send a car for her. We did not inform her that we were the opposition and she did not ask. I knew Mr Robinson was elsewhere and she would be unable to reach him for advice even if she wanted to.

'We used the personal touch and got your minister, Rev Wilkes, to come with me to remind her that as a devout and professing Christian withholding the sort of information she possessed in court as she had given us was a mortal sin,

Mr Robinson notwithstanding. I put emphasis on the busts and the wound as I was on tenterhooks until the last moment, wondering if she would shirk and run away. It was to our good fortune that she did not.'

'Well done again, Mr Lilley. I still haven't received the bill for those extras after all this time,' said Stephen.

'All paid for, dear boy.'

'By whom?'

'Ah. That would be telling. I can't reveal that sort of information without permission. Shouldn't be hard to find out.'

Stephen suddenly felt like Lot's wife on Mount Sodom. He wanted to say something but Lilley chipped in again.

'Just a postscript, my dear friends. You may think I am an idealist but look at it this way. Two generations only ago the mail was being delivered by Pony Express. Sixty years later, we have trains, planes and telephones which were once thought as impossible. It may have escaped your notice but we have come out of a horrendous war victorious and will soon be the most powerful and influential country in the world, if we aren't that already. You have your lives in front of you and you will see it. Mark my words and when they come true, we need to be a just and honourable country as well.'

Without further ado, he smiled, shook hands again and took his leave.

Stephen still felt rooted to the spot and had to suddenly grab Bobby's sleeve to prevent him from leaving.

'Hey, mate, what's up. I need the place you call the rest room.'

Stephen hung on tighter but was still unable to speak. Finally, he did so.

'So it was you.'

'It was me, what?'

'Come on, buddy. You paid the bills; don't deny it.'

Bobby paused but realised further prevarication was useless.

'Yes, mate, what of it?'

'You never said a word. There must have been a reason.'

'You were not well off then. In any case, we are family.'

'We did not know that then.'

423

'You are more to me than Charlie and he means a great deal to me. They say that blood is thicker than water but not in your case. Listen, mate. When we were on the *Mauritania* coming home, you reminded me that it was your 21st the next day. You asked not to make it known. Remember?'

'Yes, I do.'

'I never got you a birthday present, a Christmas present or a decent wedding present as for a time we were tear-arseing about like headless chickens as there were a host of other pressing priorities. I was the one who returned a rich man, not you. I could have bought you a silver pot or expensive figurine for the Retreat which would be a prime target for the cat to knock off the mantle-piece but thought that a waste of time as, if I remember rightly, there is enough of that sort of thing around the house already. The best present and best way to serve you was by doing what I did. Here's hoping that you approve.'

Bobby drained the last of his glass and accidentally burped. He laughed but there was no mirth on Stephen's face.

It was that last comment about serving that proved to be Stephen's undoing. After a period of a few seconds and without warning, he burst into tears, something that had not happened since he was a child. It was as if several years of pent up emotions had reached their climax and the dam had burst.

Bobby had to help him into one of the hall chairs and try and comfort him while the intensity of his feeling subsided. He put himself in between Stephen and the others to try and conceal matters whilst holding his head. Several friends and acquaintances moved as if to see if help was needed but Bobby waved his hand to indicate nothing was seriously amiss. It was impossible to do this when Rachael became aware of the situation and she hurried over to ask her brother for an explanation.

'Nothing serious, sister. Just hit a raw nerve. The past has just caught up with us a little. We will explain later. No worries.' Rachael put her arm in his and led him to privacy outside in the fresh air; it did not take long for her to work her magic.

Within two days, the whole company had left in all directions, leaving just a memory on the airfield. The only visible reminder of human presence was a large amount of litter blown into the grass and tree foliage due to a couple of dustbins overturning in the wind. Bobby, Stephen and Rachael prepared for the sixty-hour or so rail journey back to Boston.

Bill Rogers was with them for part of the way; he shared the compartment that Bobby had with Smasher and Grabber. As the journey progressed, the four of them all felt a little deflated and by the third morning were looking forward more and more to being home as the journey became more tedious. Rachael had gone to get some refreshment which left the two men on their own.

'Have you decided where are you staying, buddy?'

'At the hotel, mate. See my folks first and then we will see. You two will be going up to the Retreat.'

'Correct,' said Stephen. 'I must say that I am looking forward to it very much. Peace and solitude for us both.'

'Have you any plans after that you have not yet told me?'

'Not really. I am not going to sit on my ass all day, that's for certain. I will see if Chuck needs me and if not, I am going to scour the ads in the newspapers. Now it is time for you to tell me about you yourself.'

'I might do the same as you and start looking in the *Herald.*'

'Forgive me, buddy, but I have got to say this. You are OK and happy when you are busy but sometimes in situations like this when you have time on your hands, you go into your shell somewhat. It was never like that when we were growing up and beyond. Don't punch me on the nose but are you still hankering after HER?'

'I suppose so… Yes. It's not nearly as bad as it was, though but I can't deny it.'

'It was not hard to guess,' said Stephen. 'I wish there was something I could say or do for you.'

There was a pause before Stephen continued: 'I have to say this to you and hope you won't take offence. We have been through a great deal together and survived but at this point I don't want to tread on a raw nerve as you are more to me than just flesh and blood. But you need and deserve somebody in your life. Somebody for you to care for as well. It's five years since she took off. Justine was not right for you and she knew it. That's why she…what's that word you British use?'

'Scarpered.'

'That's it. Scarpered. I like that word,' he smiled, doing his best to lighten the gloom.

'Deep down, mate, I know you are right. If I only knew where she was and what she was doing; if she were dead, I could accept the situation much easier. To scarper like that makes me feel as if I am still in limbo somehow.'

'Look, buddy. If she had stayed and explained her feelings to you then you would have resisted. You would have tried to stop her then followed her and that was what she did not want as she didn't think it right for both of you in the long term. You have to respect her feelings on that score.'

There was a pause during which Stephen wondered if he had said the right thing and encroached too far.

'You know, mate, I have to say that you are right. Give me a miniscule bit more time to let that sink in and I think I will be back to my old self all the time and not some of it. I am sorry if I have been a pain in the arse.'

'You have been anything but that. It has been great these last two years now that we have survived. Tell me something. Has there ever been another girl you fancied who you could have lived with?'

'Nobody in Boston. I would have told you. You would have seen anyway. What chance did we have there?'

'None at all thanks to the man who I thought was my father. Nobody else? There were chances in France.'

'I did not want it to be like that. Of course, there were no end of girls available and willing in Ireland but it would have meant a lifetime there.'

'That sums it up then.'

'The only other girl I've ever really liked was Uncle Arthur's girl.' He sighed.

'She is your cousin.'

'Nothing wrong in that on the kindred and affinity chart. Technically, she is not my cousin. She is Uncle Arthur's child by his first marriage. His first wife died not long after Marion was born. Pleurisy, I think it was. Uncle Arthur married Auntie Ethel a couple of years later. That's my mother's sister, of course.'

'She is a long way away at this moment,' said Stephen.

'Not only that, she was on the brink with a doctor at the Pilgrim hospital and it looked like turning into something permanent. Probably is by now; I've sent her cards and details of our exploits but most likely will never see her again. You'll remember them from London.'

'Yes. I liked her too. She seemed lovely. Anyway, it's time for me to get back to Rachael,' said Stephen.

They both stood up. They instinctively had a hug but it lasted for a mere second as the dogs butted and pushed in and would not allow any affection to happen unless they themselves were involved. At that moment Rachael opened the door and looked at them.

'Well. Have you put the world to right since I left you?'

'No, honey,' said Stephen. 'We have just been putting ourselves to right.'

'I like you both just as you are,' was her reply.

The last few hours on the train were interminable but on arrival this time at Boston, there were no crowds with which to contend. A smiling Charlie met them and took them to the hotel. First thing they did was to ask how it was between him and Joanne to which he told them to mind their own business. Martha was already at the hotel so it meant that there was no need for a special journey to *Frankfare*.

As there was a spare room vacant for the night, Sarah begged them to stay instead of going to the Retreat and this offer was accepted. In the morning Stephen and Rachael went off to the home which they could now regard as permanent and to be alone and have some time to themselves. On the following day, their laughter could be heard a long way off. Yet again, they had failed to catch any fish.

47. Coda

Bobby did find plenty of work to do for Chuck and Emma at the airstrip and time went by pleasantly as it also did for Stephen who was in big demand as a speaker. He only charged a modest fee and expenses but even by evening talks and the odd daytime one thrown in, he was earning more than he had at *Frankfare* which was rapidly becoming a memory. Before anyone realised it, almost a year went by and with no major incidents. It was a happy time as the *Red Lion Hotel* was making a small profit and maintaining its good reputation.

The terrible influenza epidemic which had wiped out a lot of people had abated and thus the population began to move more freely. The hotel began to have many more patrons and the management had no problem keeping their heads above water financially wise. Marcus and Sarah were able to enjoy life so much more now they were no longer kept as virtual menials and were masters of their own destiny.

They even had a week's holiday during which the Gilberts were only too glad to act as locums. It was left to Bobby to disturb the equilibrium of the place on a day Stephen appeared at the *Red Lion* and they sat chatting.

'How's things, buddy?'

'Very steady, mate. Business here is good. How's the missus?'

'Lovely as ever. Your parents did a great job. Not forgetting you and Charles.'

'Very kind words. How much money do you want to borrow?'

'Hey, with all your wealth, I'd expect a gift, not a loan at an exorbitant interest rate.'

Bobby chuckled at Stephen's humour. It was a fact that they were both wealthy.

'Anyway, you gave me plenty once before if you remember.'

'No, mate, I don't,' said Bobby deciding to tell a white lie and thus obviate the necessity of further discussion on that subject.

Stephen decided to be quite forward. 'Are you settled? What is the situation with regard to the memory of a certain person?'

'I am getting there. I am 95% percent over it, thank goodness. I just need something to give me a final push.'

'Good. You've kept quiet about that. Since we returned, has there been nobody here take your fancy? No, there can't be. You would have told me by now.'

'No, and I know why. When I was working for your father or should I say very quietly, George Robinson, I was the one taking around the boss and thus people presumed that he and I were close so I was never fully trusted. The car wasn't mine and I spent most of my money learning to fly in a place where there were no girls. There was nothing I could offer a girl and most of the ones I know at present still hold the belief that I was in George Robinson's pocket and are uncomfortable with me, money or no money.

'I discount the females in the city who like the idea of my money more than they do me. In a sense I feel a bit tainted as a result of being chauffeur to the boss. I may be wrong but that's how I feel, mate. A lot of the band girls I knew at school are married and some of the single ones are a lot younger than me. I am rapidly becoming the male equivalent of an old maid.'

Stephen laughed. 'I know you don't really mean that,' he said.

'Being absolutely frank, mate, I do not know if I really belong here. There is only one thing I would really miss if I left here, mate, and that is you and your family to a lesser extent. But your life should revolve around Rachael now and your kids, which we hope you will have. I have money, lots of it, and like you have invested it in secure things. I've bought some gold, by the way. I would like to do a little bit of travelling and go back to England and see some more of the sights and sounds of the old country.'

'In that case if you decide to go then Rachael and I want to come too,' said Stephen. 'We have been thinking about doing something spectacular like that for quite some time. Perhaps we could go across to Paris and show her where we visited and some of the sights. Maybe even get Jules up from Vannes.'

'I wondered about mother too. See Aunt Ethel again. Dad would probably have to stay but he wouldn't mind.'

'In that case, I would have to ask my mother as well.'

Bobby thought carefully before speaking and then decided to take the plunge. 'Has she told you who your father is?' he whispered.

'No. But I have a very good idea.'

'I won't ask even though you are as a brother to me.'

'What about a cousin?'

'How do you mean?'

'I have a feeling that his name is the same as yours.'

'What? Who?…You don't mean… Of course…Mark!'

'Shush… Yes.'

Bobby paused. He thought for a moment and held Stephen's arm.

'If that is so…but that makes us second cousins.'

'Yes.'

'Bloody hell fire. Have you told my sister?'

'No. I have not had the courage.'

'Are you going to?'

'One day perhaps. Not a word to anyone for the moment. I shall have to choose the right moment.'

'I won't let you down, mate.'

'I am quite sure about that, buddy. Now then, you have really set my juices running about England. Let us send off for some information about the sailings.'

The idea of the trip across the Atlantic came as a small shock to the others but it did not take long for them to warm to the idea. Soon they all began to talk about the prospect excitedly and shortly afterwards laid some plans. Within eight weeks of their holiday's gestation they were travelling to New York to pick up the ship. They were determined to travel in style and had waited for the next sailing of the *Mauritania* which was now back in service. The party consisted of Stephen and Rachael, Bobby, Sarah, Mark Williston and Martha. Much to everybody's surprise and not a little dismay, the dogs came too as Bobby could not bear to leave them behind.

Everyone had got used to Mark Williston being around during the last few months so there were no eyebrows raised when Martha said she wanted him to come too. Mark had said that he just could not afford it but when he was told that he would not be paying he jumped at the chance. He obtained a little bit of extended leave but knew he and Martha would have to return on an earlier crossing to that of the others.

The crossing was pleasant and uneventful. It was quite dull and windy when they docked at Cobh which was the new name for Queenstown. Bobby had written to all the close friends of Bunmaskiddy to tell them of their passage on the *Mauritania* but did not really expect anybody this time to be there to spend an hour with them. It was cold and a few scuds of rain that caused him to return to his cabin. The dogs approved of this as they were not enjoying the unseasonal temperature.

They had left Cobh and had been sailing for about half an hour when suddenly Smasher and Grabber heard sounds outside the door. They did not bark and pricked up their ears in excitement as they recognised one of the voices. Both gave out a somewhat plaintiff whine. A knock came on the door and Bobby got up to answer expecting to see the steward. He was totally surprised to see the two beaming faces in front of him, none other than Joe Cassidy and Annie. Bobby whooped with delight and was enveloped in a bear hug with his friend. Annie, of course was treated more gently and respectfully.

'What are you doing here? How did you manage to work this one? Come in, both of you, come in.'

'It's like this, Bobby. When you wrote and said you would be on this tub, Mrs Cassidy spoke to me and proposed a visit to England.'

Annie interjected: 'My father is English, Bobby, and we have never met our grandparents and it is they who we are going to see and stay with.'

'And we hoped that we would be able to see you on the way and here we are.'

'Well, well, life is full of surprises. It's good to see you both.' He hugged them both again and even suppressed a tear.

'It took a while to decide and then there was no time to answer your letter, Bobby so we parked our gear then came to your cabin straight away.'

'Not content with saving souls in Ireland you do mighty deeds in France and then back in your own country to do even more spectacular ones. You and Stephen Robinson are real celebrities,' said Annie.

'It's not something we wear easily, Annie. And as for *my* country, I don't know which one really does belong to me.'

'Well, you will just have to split the difference and settle for the dear old Emerald Isle. Mind you, there are places where it is not very safe at the moment. There's no doubt in my mind that there will be an independent Ireland in months rather than years. Justine said that too,' said Joe.

'When did she say that?' blurted out Bobby.

'Oh about six months ago. They visited Declan and Aoifa and company and then we looked after them because they stayed a couple of nights at the Imperial.'

'You said they.'

'She and her husband.'

'Husband?'

'Yes. Did you not know? Some rich Canadian diplomat. Can't remember his name. I thought that after all we went through, she and you would be in touch.'

'I've not heard a word.'

'She said she saw you at some presentation in London after you returned from France.'

'She did not speak.'

'Odd,' said Joe. 'But that's women for you.'

'That's enough from you, Mr Cassidy.'

'If you say so, Mrs Cassidy.'

'What's her husband like? How old is he?'

'About fifty and somewhat porky. Very rich. Always seemed to have a cigar in his mouth,' said Annie.

'I am surprised she has lost touch with you,' said Joe.

Bobby had all sorts of feelings bumping around him so much that he could not see the wood for trees. Moreover, he had two special and loyal friends in front of him that deserved his attention. He tried to force his mind to focus on them and put off other thoughts and questions until later.

'Are you alright, Bobby? I hope I have not said anything out of turn.'

Bobby recovered. 'I am fine. Of course, you haven't said anything wrong. It's just that there has been a lot to take in from what you have just said. No, no, I'm fine and it is good to see you. More than good. If it was not for you two I would be pushing up daisies or even something worse. You two must have dinner with us all tonight and tell us the rest of your news. It will not be long before meal time so we will have to get ready and organised.'

Joe and Annie both smiled and had obviously appreciated the compliments Bobby had showered on them. Bobby meant them and told them he would introduce them to the other members of the party that evening. A huge round table was specially organised and in a way all could speak to each other. It was difficult for a while after they had finished eating to ward off autograph hunters as word had got about as to their identity. Stephen beckoned to the steward and asked him to put the charity box on the table.

'Anybody who wants an autograph can give a little something,' he said.

Soon there was, for a time, a queue of well-wishers. After a lull in proceedings, a prosperous businessman approached. Without a word he stuffed some notes into the charity box and, rather than hand his autograph book or speak to Bobby, half dropped it in front of him.

'What is this for, sir?'

'Well. An autograph book for your signature and a few words.'

'That all?'

'That and Robinson's all I want,' said the man with an air of arrogance that Bobby found irritating.

'If that is the case then I am afraid that I will have to politely refuse.'

'How so?' said the man with a voice manicured by years of barking orders.

'Because one way or another, just about all of these people around the table are just as important as me.'

The man looked confused and the others around the table felt a little tension. Bobby continued to look at the man with a firm gaze.

'Why do you want my autograph?'

'Well, you two are celebs and famous persons and I would to have your autograph to show the folks in Texas.'

'I see. Do you see this gentleman here? He is a very modest Irishman.' Bobby pointed at Joe whose eyes began to widen by the second at that remark.

'I'll take your word for that. What's your point?'

'My point is this. You know, sir, you say I am a celebrity but if it were not for him I would not be here talking to you today. I would not have even got on the boat to France if it were not for his bravery. He saved my life and several others at very great risk to his own person. He still bears the scars and yet you only want my autograph and Mr Robinson's.'

The man was slightly taken aback.'

'I am sorry, sir, I had no idea. If that is what you say, I would be proud to have his autograph. Would you tell me how it came about, if you please?'

'Certainly. This gentleman without a thought of his own safety got us out of a shed where we had been captured with literally three seconds to spare before a huge bomb, planted by some very nasty people went off and would have blown us to smithereens. You may shake his hand if you wish. His name is Joseph Cassidy.'

The man did just that while Annie's chest swelled with pride. Joe looked a little awkward as he stood up but he too felt proud inasmuch as he realised for only the second time in his life that his actions had indeed been thoroughly appreciated. The man put something extra in the charity box and left contented.

In between time, Sarah looked proudly on her son and said: 'You have never said a thing about this.'

'Mother, dear. When we returned from France, I had no home and it was much the same for Stevie. Rachael was in the holding cells about to go to gaol. We had to find somewhere to live for you and father for your sanity and well-being. There was no time to tell you things such as that as your health came first. The present was much more important than the past.'

'What else have you not told us?' Mark suddenly blurted out.

'Lots,' said Stephen.

'Lots,' said Bobby. 'When you have got three hours to spare with nothing else to do, we will tell you all. And you can all put something in the charity box.'

There was laughter at this remark. More autograph hunters arrived and the box swelled. The captain appeared and greeted them all and asked if all was well. He joined them for a drink which was handy really as that action seemed somehow to stem the flow of well-wishers and to keep folk at bay.

'Pass over the box to the captain, Joe,' said Martha.

The captain was delighted and kissed the hand of all the ladies before leaving.

'I would like to know more about this bomb,' said Mark.

'Later, uncle, when we are not so tired. It may cause nightmares. Let's talk about happier things,' said Bobby.

Even so, it was midnight before the party broke up. Sarah, Martha and Mark had retired but Stephen and Rachael stayed to keep pumping Joe and Annie for more information about the events at the Bunmaskiddy farm. They were certain that Bobby had left out lots of exciting information and in this they were quite correct. Several times, Joe reminded Bobby of various incidents which caused Bobby to explode with laughter.

Stephen looked across at him and thought that for some inexplicable reason it was almost certain that somehow the old Bobby had fully returned. He had no idea how or why but he felt so very glad. Inwardly he felt as though the last remnant of a certain lady had been fully put to rest. How this had happened was an enigma to him but he knew that at some point Bobby would elucidate. The party broke up and went to their respective cabins. Stephen felt very happy and contented inside. He got into bed before Rachael and as soon as she was beside him, he grabbed her. His amorous intentions were clear but Rachael was quite taken aback with the hunger he possessed.

'Mr Robinson. Such goings on. Have you any idea what time it is?'

'The time that you prove what a sensational temptress you were put on earth for.'

'If you say so. Mind you, one thing.'

'And, pray, what is that Mrs Robinson?'

'Did you not know that a preposition is a weak word to end a sentence with?'

'Ha ha. Very funny. Come here!'

It was a happy and contented party that docked at Liverpool and piled into the transport waiting for them. They stayed the night in the city and then caught the same express that Bobby had travelled on four years earlier. They changed at Nottingham where Joe and Annie parted company with them vowing that the next year they would travel to Massachusetts to have a holiday with them. When there was a quiet moment on Nottingham Victoria station and the ladies had gone to powder their noses Bobby and Stephen found themselves on their own for a short while. The latter remarked that since Joe and Annie had joined them Bobby seemed unusually buoyant and cheerful.

'I am, mate. I feel truly free and liberated.'

'Is there a reason or do I have to keep my trap shut.'

'There is a reason and you will know all in due course.'

Shortly afterwards a smart green locomotive rolled into the station bearing the letters G.N.R. They all piled into their compartment and settled back to await departure. Soon they were out into the countryside which looked lovely that day in the late afternoon. After they had stopped at Sleaford, it was obvious that Sarah was getting very excited about being home again after many years. The party reached Boston almost on time to be met by the Wesley and Williston families monopolising the station platform. Some of the locals found it difficult to find a gangway out of the station.

'What's your name, then?' said an irate old passenger. 'Lord Muck?'

'Bobby Williston. What's yours?'

'Then I am the King of Egypt,' said the man, still very peeved.

At that moment, somebody called out Bobby's name which caused the old man to turn and take a closer look at him. He paused for a moment but was too proud to say anything and merely shuffled away. Everyone was introduced but it was a special moment for Sarah and Ethel who could not bear to be parted.

Smasher and Grabber were a nuisance and did not behave very orderly. They were the most obedient and loyal animals in all instances, bar this one. That, of course, was when there were occasions which expressed affection and then they expected to be of equal importance and part of the scene as well. When people did turn their attention to them, they held up their paws to be shaken. The party had to be split up, some to the hotel but Sarah went with her sister and so did Bobby and the dogs.

Mark and Martha went to his relatives to begin with but later patronised the hotel. Only Marion, who he learned was still living at home and still not married, was missing from the group as she was staying overnight at the hospital due to staff shortage. The next few days were hectic with the whole group meeting people, sightseeing and being subject to an absolute barrage of questions. They all occupied two large stalls at the Stump the following Sunday morning much to the rector's great pleasure and that of his congregation.

Uncle Arthur was not very mobile so Bobby took it upon himself to spend more time talking to him and taking him out in a wheelchair as there were occasions when he was in danger of being left out. The dogs were always with them. Then Bobby hired a car and took him out to see Tim Whythorne, who was absolutely overjoyed to see him again and pumped his arm until he thought it was going to drop off.

'We have read about your exploits, young Bobby. I am proud to know you. Is it good to be back?'

'Very much so. I have said nowt to the others yet but I don't know how I am going to be able to go back to the States. I somehow don't know if I can wrench myself away.'

'There's only one answer. Stay and live here. Have you thought about it? Is that why you brought your dogs?'

'Subconsciously, I think that is the case. Like keeping my options open. They and I just can't be separated. Anyway, if you are not doing anything how about a drink?'

'Best offer I've had all day,' said the kindly coalman. 'Give me a few minutes to make myself look a bit tidier and more presentable.'

It was not until the evening of the third full day that an exhausted Marion came home to find only Bobby alone in the house except for the dogs. Uncle Arthur had managed to sum up all his energy for a trip with the others. Bobby had said he wanted a day with the dogs.

It was not that, of course, he just felt that he was the odd one out and playing gooseberry. All the others existed as couples of one sort or the other. Marion was overjoyed to see Bobby but a little peeved to find nothing had been left for her to eat due to Aunt Ethel's excitement over her sister's return. She appeared to be hungry and quite worn out. Bobby then told a little white lie.

'Oh it's all been arranged. I am taking you out as your mum would have had to come back from the trip to get something for you. I am looking after you tonight. Go and make yourself beautiful for me so I can swank you off. I hope you are happy about this.'

Marion needed no second bidding.

'More than happy. Delighted, in fact.'

She instantly forgot about being worn out and gave him one of her engaging smiles as she swept out of the room to go to change. Bobby turned to the dogs and said: 'Now listen, you two boys. This is one time that I'll have to leave you on your own. You'll stay and guard the house, that's your task this evening. You both can't be with me on an occasion like this. When you're a bit older, I'll tell you about this sort of thing.'

Smasher cocked his head and Grabber gave a slight squeak. Bobby was sure they understood the situation well enough.

Bobby mused. 'Lucky sod that Philip Honegger. But why still no marriage?'

Marion appeared and presented herself for his approval. Bobby's asked her to do a twirl which she willingly did. They went to the hotel and both remarked how very much improved the place looked since the war. Some paint had been applied for a start and the interior and fittings had been altered.

'Well, this is a bonus, Bobby. Knew you were coming but I did not expect this tonight.'

'Ah, a nice surprise then?'

437

'Yes, it is.' She looked at him intently. 'Can't think of anything else I'd enjoy more.'

'By the way,' he said. 'We had a problem for a while with sleeping arrangements. I had to use the bed last night that belongs to the young woman of the house.'

'That should have been no problem.'

'The problem was something else.'

'Which was?'

'When I got in, she wasn't there.'

'Bobby! Really. Don't let mother hear you say things like that. What about all those French girls that must have been falling over each other to gain your charms?'

'Not my style, Marion. Not what I am looking for.'

'What ARE you looking for?'

He was about to reply but was prevented from doing so as the waiter appeared. They were ushered to their table and Bobby helped Marion to her chair. Once seated, he took a long look at her closely. Marion was about to say something but he jumped in first.

'So good to see you, my delightful and favourite cousin.'

Marion looked at him intently and said: 'I don't believe you have another one.' She pretended to be stern.

'It wouldn't matter. Better to have one very special one rather than half a dozen ordinary ones.'

Marion enjoyed his compliments but had to look at the flowers on the table for a moment in order to avert his scrutiny. It was the first time ever that she had been paid such flattery and as yet was unable to know how to react in such circumstances. On impulse she decided to open up a front of her own.

'It was such fun when you were here all that time with us. I felt bereft after you had gone. We never thought we would ever see you again but here you are in the flesh.'

'There were times in France when I didn't believe I would see out the war. Yet here I am indeed. Turning up like the old bad penny, as the saying goes.' He surveyed her again.

She is not pretty, he thought. *She is beautiful.*

'You have earned a great deal of fame with your exploits. You, Stephen and others. Thank you for your letters from your travelling circus, by the way. It sounds as though it wasn't really dangerous. Just great fun and I expect quite spectacular.'

'It was and well paid too. Anyway, never mind that. Three years since we met. Why are you still not married?'

'You have to have a man first to embark upon that most worthy of institutions.'

'Where the hell then is Dr Honegger?' said Bobby with a rising voice and causing a few heads to turn. 'Auntie Ethel has said nothing about him. Nobody has mentioned his name and I was surprised to find you still living at home after all this time.'

'I expect with all the excitement of the arrival of you all that he has been forgotten. It has been a while since it all came to an end and the subject is taboo. Mother was very upset, and still is, when it fell through, particularly as I'm nearer thirty than twenty. Perhaps she thinks I am destined to be an old maid. It was over with him some time ago anyway and as to where he is, I've no idea. He arrived one day and said it was off and he was very sorry. He had an interview in London for a post and an important one at that but he never revealed its actual location and nobody is sure at the hospital.'

'Callous brute leading you on for so long. I've met a few people like that in my time. Did he give any reason for his abrupt jilting?'

'Not really. Just said that he couldn't go through with it and that we weren't suited.'

'Must have cut you up,' said Bobby.

'Do you know something, Bobby? It didn't at all. Not one bit. I shed no tears and in some ways felt it a release. There was a feeling of liberation but I can't explain fully because I don't properly understand myself. Perhaps I fell in with him because I never really liked any of the other men who took me out. Perhaps I agreed to the relationship with him as the best of a bad job and to prevent being lonely.'

'That must have been the reason you felt liberated.'

'Yes and there was more. There was nothing about him except work and more work. No fun or music in him. No concerts; I'm sure he's tone deaf.'

439

Bobby stared at the tablecloth for a few seconds. He was trying to work over a few options in his mind when suddenly an idea came to him.

'What are your work patterns for the next few days? Have you any leave?'

'I have at least five days holiday to take if I want. I could really do with them at the moment. We have been so short-staffed and still many casualties to coming in to deal with. They are loaning us two or three more nurses from the city hospital in Nottingham and they are due to arrive tomorrow.'

'How much notice do you have to give for leave? Could you take it soon?'

'I can ask. They can hardly refuse unless there is an epidemic. You haven't brought the plague with you or that terrible Boston flu?'

'Don't think so. I am asking about your leave in the hope you will allow me to make a fuss of you from whenever the hospital will let you take a break.'

'What about the others?'

'They have each other. Your mum and mine; Stephen and Rachael; Mark and Martha. Me on my own.'

'What about your fearsome dogs? I can't believe you have brought them all this way. It must have cost a lot.'

'I can afford it. Never mind them. How about a trip to Lincoln or even London?'

Marion gasped. 'Oh, Bobby. That would be absolutely wonderful. I have only ever been to London once. That was to see you last time. Do you really mean it?'

'I wouldn't have said it otherwise,' he said with emphasis in his speech.

After the meal he helped her on with her coat and then she turned. He leaned forward and kissed her on the cheek. She was quite surprised but having got over the initial shock allowed herself to enjoy the moment. She looked at him intently for a moment, realising full well that though she was conversant with the human body, she had no real experience or understanding of human emotions. They held hands on the way back got back to the house.

Marion then said she was tired and needed an early night. Bobby said he was going to give the dogs an extra walk. Just before she retired, she thanked him and returned his kiss; it was just a peck on the cheek but enough to make him wonder just a little more than a little.

They did go to Lincoln then to London and stayed overnight. They visited several of the main attractions some of which had been shut during the war. The highlight for both of them was their attendance at St Paul's cathedral for Evensong. Marion was shocked at the price of the hotel.

On one occasion, they were on the way back to Kings Cross on the underground and were standing and being crushed in the London rush hour. They were closer than ever before and were very aware of each other. Neither of them was able to say anything as it was a new situation for them. He gave her a little peck and she held him around his waist.

On the way home, they changed at Peterborough and then took the Grimsby train. It was sparsely patronised and at one point they were on their own in the compartment. Conversation was at a premium; suddenly Bobby put his arm around her and pulled her close. She melted into him and closed her eyes when he kissed her.

'You are going home soon,' she croaked.

'I sometimes wonder where is home,' he replied.

During the next fortnight, there were a lot of visits for the party and talks to people once their presence had been made known in the town. The rector had been responsible for praising the great duo from the pulpit which did a lot to advertise their presence. It was a bit embarrassing for Bobby and Stephen who already had been more in the limelight than either of them had wanted and now history was repeating itself.

At the end of that fortnight, Martha and Mark left first for London and then for Fishguard and back home to Boston and the US. Stephen and Rachael also went to London and from there to Paris to meet Jules. They had asked Bobby to join them but he had surprised them by declining their invitation.

His thoughts and mind were elsewhere. He rued the fact that most of the day he was on his own as Marion was working. However, there was an occasion when she had an afternoon off with Bobby, enabling them to have a walk by the river. Whilst all this was happening, Sarah and Ethel, who were rarely apart for any length of time, spent their days shopping, visiting and looking after Arthur.

They came back one day and made some tea. Ethel looked around and said: 'Where are Marion and Bobby, Arthur?'

'Out walking. They seem to be hitting it off. That's good.'

'Oh they are both just a bit lonely, Arthur, that's all.'

Arthur grunted as if to say he was somewhat unconvinced by this remark.

48. Perfect Cadence

To his deep chagrin, Bobby saw little of Marion during the next few days as she was even more busy at the hospital. They only had one more full day together and a few evening dinners and most of the rest of the time were surrounded by others. She was with him when he gave a talk to the newly formed Women's Institute and they had a late walk by the river on the way home. Almost a fortnight elapsed and the date for return to USA drew ominously nearer.

The next day, Stephen and Rachael were due back from Paris and two days later was the day scheduled for departure. Arthur was upstairs resting, Sarah and Ethel were talking at the gate with a neighbour and Bobby was in the kitchen making tea. Marion appeared with a box in her hand and placed it on the kitchen table in front of him.

'Here, dear cousin. This is rightfully yours.'

Bobby at once guessed what it was but pretended not to know.

'Now then, dear cousin. What is it?'

'The present mother bought with the money you left for me for my wedding that never was, dear cousin.'

'Keep it, dear cousin.'

'It would not be right. It is very expensive.'

'You are more than worth it. You deserve it.'

'Nice of you but it would not be right.'

'What situation would there have to be for it to be right and for you to accept this?'

'I don't know… You are confusing me, Bobby. What are you getting at? You're an enigma, you know.'

'I don't mean to be. What I am trying to say is that it still can be a wedding present if you wish it.'

'Who for?'

'For you from me.'

'But there is nobody. Are you making fun of me? If so, I didn't think you were that sort of person.' For the first time, he noticed a slight tang of reproach in her voice.

'Yes, there is somebody. And I am deadly serious and not joking.'

He got up abruptly and stared at her intently until the dawn began to break and she began to understand what he meant. After a few moments, he drew her to him then kissed her but very gently. She was quite unable to respond and was completely dumbfounded. Suddenly, Marion's legs went to jelly and Bobby had to grab her and hold on. She opened her mouth to speak but nothing came out. When it finally did, she said. 'You can't mean it,' she croaked. 'You are going back in two days' time.'

'Not necessarily. I do not *have* to go back and at the moment that is the last thing I want to do whether you say yea or nay. If you will consider what I've said, please...I will stay longer and perhaps only go back later if you decide to say a definite no. At the moment, I like the idea of buying a house here. You wouldn't lack for anything, you know.'

'I am sure, Bobby, but wealth is not important to me...I...I can't believe this is happening. Do you realise what this means, Bobby?'

'Perfectly. I am very serious and have given it a lot of thought for quite some time.'

'But...but we have only known each other for a month.' Marion's voice rose but she did not mean it do so.

'There was last time. I decided I liked you then and wanted to stay. The trouble was that I was forced away to war in another country. There was another factor and that there was another man on the scene even though he was a supercilious robot.'

'That is true but it is quite a while ago since you were over here,' said Marion. 'I thought you had just about forgotten all of us let alone me.'

'O come off it, Marion. In that case why did I bother to send you all those cards and letters while we were on our flying circus? And another thing you might as well know. When we were on the ship coming over Stevie asked me if there was anybody I had loved or could really love. There was somebody once on the *Lusitania* but she wasn't for me. I told him that the only other person I've ever felt deeply about was you.

'I couldn't believe it when you told me that Honegger had done a bunk. Gradually, the scales came off my eyes and then I knew deep down that at some point, I had to pluck up enough courage to ask you. All you have to do is say yes or no or perhaps in time. If it is NO then maybe I'll go back with the others as I couldn't bear to see anyone else holding your hand or to live here knowing that somebody else was sharing your bed.'

For a moment, Marion flushed when he said that but recovered quickly and said: 'Oh Bobby. Do you mean it? NO. I am dreaming. I am just not awake. Somebody pinch me.'

'Of course I mean it. Absolutely and you are wide awake. No more obstacles, please.'

'No, I am in a deep trance and am going to wake up soon. Slap me.'

'What! On your bottom? You could get me arrested. Would you come here please?'

She came willingly and they kissed, this time passionately and as never before.

'Was that superior to Philip Honegger's efforts?'

'Much superior... No comparison... Not in the same league. When you left last time, I was forever thinking of you.'

'I am really glad about that.' He paused for a while. 'You realise that if you say yes at some point, we will have to tell the others and very soon for that matter. Deadline for departure is the day after tomorrow.'

'I have heard of whirlwind romances but this beggars belief.'

'Not really a whirlwind, dear love. The thought of asking you has been going on inside me for a while, in fact as soon as I knew Honegger had done his disappearing act. Come on! Let's have a walk in the fresh air. After all of that, I need some open space and I guess you might feel the same.'

She required no persuading. They walked for a long time often with arms around each other. Nobody took any notice as down by the river there were many others doing exactly the same and to greater or lesser degrees of intensity. When there appeared to be nobody looking he pulled her closely to him and kissed her gently. Her eyes still held some bewilderment but even so on the third occasion he performed this action, she returned his embrace and immediately and inwardly surprised herself.

She never for a moment doubted his sincerity and thus, being a sensible and practical young woman, she realised that it would be foolish to turn him down. In any case, his declaration had acted as a catalyst and she knew she loved him deeply. They began to make their way home and prepared to face the family elders whilst experiencing a tingle inside the pit of their stomachs.

At home and after Bobby and Marion had gone for their walk, the sisters burst into the kitchen chatting nineteen to the dozen and noticed the wedding present on the table. Aunt Ethel then looked at it and explained to her sister what it was.

'I'll lay a bet that Marion has put it there as she must think she should return it.'

'Of course,' said Sarah. They resumed their endless chatting until Bobby and Marion returned and interrupted them. They were only too pleased for the younger ones to join in. Eventually, a rueful Aunt Ethel referred to the gift.

'Are you taking it with you, Bobby?'

'No, auntie. For the moment, it is staying here. And so am I for that matter and for keeps, I hope.'

'How do you mean? Do you mean staying here in Boston?' She was quite taken aback.

'Yes, and if all goes well, I hope it will be a wedding present for my wife.'

'But you are booked to go back in three days' time… What do you mean by your wife?'

'Yes, auntie, but I'm staying until a certain young lady says yea or nay to my proposal.'

The older women looked astounded and seemed unable to understand. Bobby let them flounder in their bemused state for a little while longer until he realised he should come clean. He continued confidently even though the tingle was still there.

'I have asked Marion to marry me and I am staying here until she tells me her final thoughts on that subject. It is a case of yea, nay or perhaps, so if you—'

Marion interrupted, 'I have decided to accept and am so, so happy.' She hugged his arm and a few involuntary tears of happiness appeared.

There was a long and protracted silence from the older women who stared at each other for a while. Eventually, it was broken by Bobby's mother.

'Well, you do know how to take people by surprise, Bobby,' said Sarah. 'You have kept this quiet from us. How long has this been going on?'

'Long enough, mother. Never mind about formal niceties and conventions. It's just that I have not gotten around to asking Marion until tonight as I had to be fairly sure of her feelings. Besides this, you may be my mother but I do have some secrets even from you.'

'I suppose that's fair,' said Aunt Ethel. 'Just tell me you want this, Marion.'

'Honestly, mother, it was what I wanted after only a few weeks when Bobby was with us last time. I could not bear to hurt Philip. It was a relief when he pulled the plug but I never expected this.'

Bobby then chipped in. 'Mother, it means then that I will not be coming back with you. If all works out well for us then I will only ever be coming back for a holiday. I can't explain it but somehow I believe I belong here and this is my real home. It will be a wrench not seeing you, dad and Charlie just about every other day and to say I will miss Stevie would be the understatement of the year.

'On the other hand, he and Rachael have each other and hopefully there will be little ones soon. That's how it is. Tomorrow I will find myself a place in town either to buy or rent as, under the circumstances, I should not be in this house at night for a while. Is that acceptable to you, auntie?'

'Yes of course. Of course it is, dear boy. I am almost at a loss for words. Come here and give your auntie a hug. Arthur! Arthur! Where are you?'

'Are you happy about all of this, mother? I would like your blessing.'

'Yes, I am, my son. Of course I am; you have my blessing; it is just that I may not see you again for a while. But if it is what you both want...is it, Marion?'

'Yes. He has taken me by surprise, auntie, but I can cope with that. It was subconsciously what I was hoping for inside. It's the dogs that I worry about.'

They all burst out laughing followed by tears of joy from all the three females.

'Just make sure that there are plenty of little Willistons,' said Sarah, which sounded unusually bold for her. Marion coloured slightly.

Bobby thought for a moment and said: 'We won't waste any time, if that's what you are thinking, mother.'

This time Marion blushed.